D0502040

SPECTACLE

SPECTACLE

Jodie Lynn Zdrok

TOR TEEN

A TOM DOHERTY ASSOCIATES BOOK

New York

SPECTACLE

Copyright © 2019 by Jodie Lynn Zdrok

A Tor Teen Book
Published by Tom Doherty Associates
175 Fifth Avenue
New York, NY 10010

www.tor-forge.com

Tor® is a registered trademark of Macmillan Publishing Group, LLC.

The Library of Congress Cataloging-in-Publication Data is available upon request.

ISBN 978-0-7653-9968-7 (hardcover)
ISBN 978-0-7653-9967-0 (ebook)

Our books may be purchased in bulk for promotional, educational, or business use. Please contact your local bookseller or the Macmillan Corporate and Premium Sales Department at 1-800-221-7945, extension 5442, or by email at MacmillanSpecialMarkets@macmillan.com.

First Edition: February 2019

Printed in the United States of America

0 9 8 7 6 5 4 3 2 1

To my parents, for reminding me to never, never, never give up.
To Steve, for reminding me to soar and roar.

SPECTACLE

Nathalie used to think that if she wrote of death, she'd only need two words.

"She died."

Or, "he died."

What else was there to say? That should be enough. Why embellish death? It's the story of someone's life, come to an end, with that person's thoughts, prayers, and feelings all culminating in the same final reality. Everyone knew what it meant, or should mean, if they thought about it.

The past two weeks had taught her that most people didn't really think about it. Not in that way. "She died" wasn't the end of the story. Sometimes it was only the beginning.

All of this went through Nathalie's mind as she surveyed the trail of straw bonnets, pipes, and walking sticks behind her. Death brought them all here, piquing their curiosity, to show them what would become of them. But not yet. Today it was someone else's turn to be dead.

A crow perched itself over the entrance and cawed. A warning or a lament?

Eight people left to go until she'd be allowed inside.

She'd expected a longer wait than usual, given how quickly the news had spread this morning, but she hadn't anticipated a line *this* long. Even people watching, always a favorite pastime, had become tiresome. The mother entertaining her toddler with the story of *La Belle et la Bête* (the little girl squealed with delight when the beast became a man again), the old gentleman with the wheezy cough (he was most likely to die next, she supposed). The American couple who discussed something called a Florida, which was not a term she'd ever heard in English class. The portly man wearing white gloves (in this heat!), the woman who twirled her parasol incessantly as she hummed. The British drunkard in a shabby top hat who stumbled by, ranting about both the price of absinthe and Queen Victoria, and who was shooed away by a guard . . . well, there was only so much curiosity you could muster about the people in line after an hour. Even the beggars had moved on.

The sun, which hadn't made an appearance in days, came out just after Nathalie arrived. As it grew more intense, the people in line began to sweat, and before long the stench of Paris invaded her nostrils.

She'd used a washcloth this last night but, guessing by the waft of perfume that mingled with the stink, she supposed the people around her hadn't in days. True, she was getting over a cold and her sense of smell and taste were still impaired. Yet nasal congestion didn't mute the raw notes of that distinct scent.

Nathalie pulled out the journal from her bag and jotted some notes about the sun, the perspiration, and the crowd. Monsieur Patenaude had told her to pay attention to details whether they seemed important or not, because sometimes the asides in an article were "like giving coffee to a tired story."

Someone touched her arm. "Flowers, Mademoiselle?" It was the old woman who shuffled up and down the pavement selling bouquets, one of many merchants who sought to entice the ever-present crowd. She had to have been born during the Napoleonic Era, Nathalie thought. Her skin was weathered with time and memories, and her eyes betrayed resignation. Or boredom. Maybe both.

The woman held up yellow blooms for Nathalie's inspection. Bold. Vibrant. The epitome of summer.

"My mother would love this bouquet," Nathalie said. Papa always brought Maman flowers on the day of his return. Unfortunately that was months away—he'd been at sea since April and wouldn't be back until September. Her mother could use a burst of color these days. Her recovery was bleak and painful and anything but yellow blooms and sunshine.

Nathalie tucked the journal and pencil away in her satchel. She searched her dress pockets until her fingers found several centimes. *Liberté, Egalité, Fraternité*, the République Française motto fiercely proclaimed everywhere the state could stamp it, glistened as she counted. "Is this enough?"

The elderly woman plucked some coins from Nathalie's hand and left the rest. "This will do," she said, her voice hoarse. "Take them."

She handed Nathalie the flowers and slipped away. Nathalie counted the remaining coins before returning them to her pocket. Good. She'd still have enough for the café afterward.

"Pretty flowers," said a young voice behind her.

Nathalie turned. She didn't understand why people brought children here, although she'd seen it many times before. The brown-eyed little girl, a three-year-old reflection of her petite mother, grinned from beneath her red-ribboned hat.

"Well, then," said Nathalie, plucking a bloom from the bouquet. "You should have one."

The girl beamed as Nathalie gave it to her. "See, Maman?" She raised the flower to her mother, whose bright blue frock made the bloom appear even more radiant. "For me!"

Nathalie smiled and faced front again. Only four people separating her from the entrance. The little girl spoke to the flower as if it were a new friend. Her voice faded into the background as Nathalie's anticipation grew.

Her parents had forbidden her to come here until she turned fifteen, and she'd mostly obeyed, except for that one time when she was thirteen. A man shot himself and hadn't been found for days; the newspapers offered such provocative descriptions that she and Simone, an adventurous ally who was a year older and whose parents were less strict, couldn't resist going after school one day. The man's face, or what used to be his face, was nothing more than one eye and half a nose. Simone reported having lost her appetite for a day, and for a week Nathalie dreamed the corpse was in her bed.

And yet, as with many people, the experience intrigued her as much as it repulsed her.

The old man in front of her spat blood before going inside. Sidestepping the foamy mess, Nathalie began to follow him.

"One moment." The guard held up his hand.

She peered over his shoulder but couldn't see anything. After a minute that seemed like twenty, the guard waved Nathalie into the public morgue.

A dozen bodies were on display, but only one captivated the crowd. Murder victims always did. The morgue was—officially, anyway—a means to identify bodies found in the public domain. Parisians came here because it was something to see, like the great Notre-Dame Cathedral that stood in front of it.

To go to the morgue was to poke the grim reaper in the ribs, to tell him he was riveting. Because if he was riveting, he wasn't scary. Death was for other people.

Nathalie still couldn't see the bodies. People clustered on the left side of the viewing pane, an X on a macabre treasure map. The fetching young morgue worker stood, as he did almost daily, beside a black velvet curtain on the other side of the glass. With an alert, steadfast expression, he watched the crowd. She always watched him in return but looked away whenever it seemed he was about to catch her. Including today.

A few people shuffled away and she stepped up behind the gathering. Despite her considerable height, she was unable to see much other than the poor victim's matted, sand-colored curls and the bloodstained pink dress hanging behind her. Nathalie's eyes leapt to the other eleven waxen corpses resting on slabs. One additional man from yesterday, sunburned and nondescript, making it nine men and two women. In the old days a stream of slab-cooling water dripped from overhead, a constant baptism of indignity. Now the corpses were refrigerated for hours, then displayed in a chilled room.

Behind the bodies hung the clothes they were found in, as with the victim and her dress. The only thing clothing them now was fabric over the groin. Most of the dead would be here several days, until the display room couldn't preserve them any longer. Unless someone claimed them—that is, knew them to be a person with a name instead of a corpse on a slab—they'd be taken away. Buried alongside the forever unknown.

The group shifted as several onlookers left the room. When she saw, truly saw, the air in Nathalie's lungs went along with them.

Angry gashes screamed from the young woman's flesh, mocking her state of eternal silence. More girl than woman, she had full lips and plump cheeks. One side of her face was bruised, a ghastly palette of purples, blues, and reds.

The other side of her face was sliced like a slaughtered pig belly. Deep knife wounds ran from the right corner of her mouth down through the center of her neck and traveled to her collarbone.

Nathalie found herself clasping the collar of her dress and let go. She shifted her weight, unable to pull her eyes off the victim. Never had she seen a corpse so viciously slain.

Whoever did this would get sent to the guillotine. Nathalie wanted to see it, just as she wanted to be there for the execution of that horrendous murderer Pranzini. Anyone who slashed two women and a girl—in their beds!—deserved to go, she thought, and so did the monster who killed this girl.

The elderly man beside her let out a raspy sigh. Softly, tenderly, he spoke. "*Requiem Aeternam dona ei, Domine. Et lux perpetua luceat ei.*"

Nathalie recognized this funeral prayer. *Eternal rest grant unto her, O Lord. And may perpetual light shine upon her.* Indeed.

She leaned toward the glass, swallowing away the lump in her throat. The anonymity added to the callousness of it. The girl with the bloodstained dress, the victim; that's all she was to everyone right now.

She couldn't have been more than seventeen or eighteen. Her freckled skin was yellowed and even more bloated than the other corpses because she'd been pulled from the Seine. In life she must have been pretty.

What's your name, you unfortunate soul?

The little girl, quiet since coming inside, now whimpered behind her. "It's too dark," she said. "I don't like it here."

Nathalie had never been afraid of the dark, even as a child.

If anything, she wanted to know what was in it.

She heard the little girl moan, followed by whispers and a rustle of material. Nathalie peeked back. The toddler buried herself in her mother's bustle.

Nathalie held the bouquet in her left hand and drew it closer. The flowers, en route to decay since the moment they'd been cut, were still more fragrant with life than death. She brought her head closer to the glass, all but touching it.

"Home, Maman. Home." The little girl's faint, muffled voice dissolved into tears.

"MAMAN!" The toddler's shriek echoed tenfold. Nathalie jumped like a skittish colt, catching herself on the viewing pane.

Instantly she was in another place, as if whisked by train from the morgue and shoved off it at the next stop. She was kneeling inside a room. A study, maybe, or a living room.

Beside her was the morgue victim.

The girl's dead eyes were open and blood streamed backward, drawn *into* the cuts. Everything happened in reverse: The wounds healed, from ripped flesh to smooth skin, as a knife plunged in and out of her face and neck, undoing its damage. Her eyelids closed like a pair of shutters. Life rolled across the victim's face; she struggled from side to side, bawling yet not making a sound. The poor girl was so near Nathalie could touch her.

But she didn't, she couldn't, because Nathalie was back in the morgue once again. With a gasp she pulled her trembling hand off the glass.

Her eyes stayed on the victim. Nathalie had seen street brawls between men. Once she saw a man grab a woman roughly by the arm, and it bothered her the rest of the night. She'd never, ever seen a man strike a woman. Never mind . . . this.

Which was what, exactly?

She lifted a shaky hand and touched the glass again. Nothing.

The morgue worker behind the glass clenched the black velvet curtain, ready to draw it the way they did when swapping out the bodies. He exchanged looks with the guard.

Nathalie felt like she'd just been woken from a deep slumber, aware but distant. As if the horror she'd witnessed were both real and not real. Only one of those could be true.

She looked down at her hand. *Why am I holding flowers?*

As she studied the bouquet, the guard approached her. "Mademoiselle," he whispered, "would you mind going through that door to the left?"

He pointed to a wooden door beside the viewing pane. What choice did she have but to obey? With a reluctant nod, Nathalie shuffled over to it and waited. She half wondered if the carving of the ugly, snake-haired Medusa in the center of the door would turn her to stone.

"Could you understand what she said?" The words traveled as a whisper. Apprehensive, uneasy. Fear just barely in check.

"No, I wasn't close enough," said a hushed voice. "I've never seen anything that . . . eerie. Almost like something from a séance."

Nathalie, feeling slightly sharper now, turned around to see most everyone in the viewing room gawking at her. The crowd was too thick and the room too dark for her to observe the faces in the back. But she had no doubt they were staring, too.

What did I do? What did they *see?* The question withered on her tongue as she saw one glance after another dart away. The mother and child behind her in line were gone. Her eyes swept the room. She noticed a trampled yellow flower by the exit, the same kind of bloom that comprised her mystery bouquet.

Nathalie gazed at the crushed flower on the floor as she revisited the last few minutes. She remembered entering the morgue and how the little girl screamed; she recalled being startled and touching the glass. And of course the hallucination, the conscious nightmare, whatever it should be called.

All of that she recalled well. Too well.

Facing the door again, she stroked the flower petals with a quivering thumb. *Then why can't I remember how I got these flowers?*

Nathalie stared at the door, just above Medusa's tangle of snakes.

And then one of them hissed at her.

She jumped. *Impossible.*

Was it? Take what had just happened with the viewing pane. Or hadn't happened. She didn't know what to believe. Nathalie reached up to trace a snake and then quickly yanked her hand back. What if touching the door threw her into that—that place again?

She backed up a step, just as someone opened the door.

"Did I startle you? I'm afraid this door sticks in hot weather." The young morgue worker gestured for her to enter. Up close she could see that he was in his early twenties, stood two or three centimeters shorter than she, and had the most perfect nose she'd ever seen. His light brown hair fell just the right way. He also had a crooked eye tooth, charming in its imperfection. "I see you bought some flowers from Madame Valois?"

She crossed over the threshold, shuddering as she passed Medusa. "I . . . don't know . . ."

He closed the door. "The old woman who sells flowers outside the morgue."

"I suppose," said Nathalie. She put her hands in her dress pocket and realized she had fewer coins than before. That must have been it. "I mean, yes."

"Sorry," he said. He relaxed into a smile. "How would you know her name? I forget that not everyone nearly lives at this place."

"Except for the dead," said Nathalie, finally remembering to smile.

He raised a well-groomed brow. "Rather clever. And speaking of names, you are Mademoiselle . . . ?"

"Baudin. Nathalie Baudin."

"A pleasure," he said, extending his hand. He smelled of something fragrant—woodsy with orange blossom, perhaps? "I'm Christophe Gagnon. As a liaison between the morgue and the *Préfecture de police*, I'd like to ask you a few questions. Follow me, *s'il vous plaît*." His demeanor became more serious with each word.

She shook his hand, silently apologizing for her sweaty palm. "Monsieur Gagnon, I'm—I'm only here to see the displays like everyone else. What would you like to know?"

His only response was to lead her down a winding hall.

She inhaled, relieved the air didn't smell like rotten meat. The scent was sharp yet not overwhelming, a mixture of faint decomposition and chemicals.

They passed an open door. She glimpsed a young man washing down a bony male corpse and gasped; the worker spotted her and promptly shut the door. As they rounded the corner, she saw a door to the outside propped open. Two men carrying a stretcher checked the angles to their left and right. "Found him on a hotel stoop," one of the men said as they passed by with a plump, sheet-covered body and entered a room marked "Autopsy."

Nathalie felt like her stomach was ripped out and pushed back in again.

"Mademoiselle?"

She looked from M. Gagnon to the Autopsy room and back to M. Gagnon again. "It's nothing. *Ça va bien*."

He nodded and went into a drab, windowless room with a desk, two uncomfortable-looking chairs, and an overstuffed bookcase with everything from Paris travel guides to tattered novels. The top row had a series of large, burgundy volumes marked "Photographs" arranged by year.

"So . . . the murder victim. You'll take her photograph, too? Or only if no one identifies her?" Nathalie pointed to the books.

"We photograph all of them," he said matter-of-factly as he crossed over to the desk. As if it weren't fascinating to catalog bodies. As if every corpse that ever came through the morgue didn't have a story to tell.

Opposite the bookcase was the only wall adornment, a crude reproduction of a painting depicting an autopsy. A group of men stood around the body, as one man prepared to cut it and another rolled a cigarette.

M. Gagnon invited her to sit and, if she wanted, to lay down the flowers on the edge of the desk. She did both. He settled into the desk chair opposite, gathering some papers and shuffling them more than they probably needed shuffling. He had a slight awkwardness he attempted to hide; he was trying, she concluded, to act older. His large blue eyes had a quickness that appeared to take in everything at once, like a bird.

"An autopsy painting?" she said, gesturing toward it.

"Ghastly, isn't it?" M. Gagnon said, stroking his chin. "It was a gift from one of the street artists who sells his paintings around here. It's a reproduction of something else, I think. In any event, we're not here to discuss art, Mademoiselle Baudin."

Ah, he was one of *those* men. The sort who put on "official airs," as Nathalie thought of them. Like the formal, irritable department store clerk on the second floor of Le Bon Marché who shooed her away for petting the fur coats. "What *are* we here to talk about?" Nathalie sat back, pressing against the chair.

"We're here to talk about the murder victim." He pulled an inkwell closer. "It's my duty to take down identification statements."

She swallowed, even though her mouth was dry. "I can't identify her."

"You appeared to recognize her," he said, holding her gaze. He clasped his hands and leaned forward slightly.

Nathalie's breath caught. She felt so exposed she might as well be sitting here with her dress gathered up to her knees.

She couldn't tell him what had happened, obviously. And until she figured it out herself, the best option was to pretend nothing out of the ordinary had taken place. She needed to get out of here before he asked too many questions.

"I don't know her and never saw her before today. May I go? I have work to do." Nathalie knew he'd assume housework or the laundry or something other girls her age did. Not "write a column for the most popular newspaper in Paris." Never would he think that, as of two weeks ago, a sixteen-year-old girl wrote the daily morgue report. No other woman, of any age, had ever written for *Le Petit Journal*. M. Patenaude, the editor-in-chief and a longtime friend of Papa's, gave her the job because Maman wasn't able to work after the fire and wouldn't for some time. If ever.

He took the pen out of the inkwell and began writing. "I have work to do, too. In fact, I'm doing it right now. Shall we?"

"Yes, sorry. I have to do something by a certain time, and I have—" *I have more questions than answers right now.* "Let's continue."

"Your affect was . . . bizarre." He glanced at the print on the wall and then back at her. "You went from observing to having an expression that was distant yet somehow astonished. Almost as if the ill-fated girl got up from the slab and walked toward you."

"The girl did no such thing," Nathalie said, struggling to keep her voice steady. "Or you'd have seen it, too."

M. Gagnon clenched his jaw. He stared at her the way her teachers did when she'd spoken out of turn.

"That was discourteous. My apologies." She shifted her weight in the chair. "I'm not myself today, and I'm in a rush." *To get out of here. To think. To calm myself down from whatever it is that happened in there.*

"We're almost done here," he said, tapping the sheet of paper.

"You also said something. I couldn't hear it from behind the glass, but the people around you did, judging by their reactions."

The reversed vision filtered through her mind once again. The muted cries, the victim struggling, the blood dripping into the cuts.

How could she explain what she didn't understand herself?

She noticed her hands trembling and tucked them under her legs. M. Gagnon waited, pen hovering over the paper. She had to give him some kind of answer.

"I thought I recognized her." Perspiration tickled her brows. "I—I realize now I was mistaken."

M. Gagnon wrote something down, and it was more than what she'd just said. He scratched his chin with the pen and looked up at her. "Are you sure?"

"I am," she said, making an effort to sound confident. *Give the right answers so you can go.* "It bothered me to see her. She is— was—close in age to me. I'm sure I reacted to that."

M. Gagnon's features softened. "I understand," he said.

"Yet you still don't believe me." Nathalie tilted her head. "Do you?"

The softness dissipated like morning mist. M. Gagnon dropped the pen. Leaning back with arms folded, he took in what seemed like four lungs' worth of air before letting it out through his nose, eyes boring into her the whole time.

Nathalie sat up straighter and stared back at him. If she didn't convince him, then what? She could be here for hours. That's all she needed, to submit her article late. As it was she didn't know how she was going to focus on writing and—

"You aren't a very good liar, Mademoiselle. There's something you're not telling me."

Nathalie had no response for this, because if she were in his position, she'd be just as skeptical.

"I'll ask one more time." His voice was careful and controlled, yet not unkind. "Can you identify the victim?"

Why did he have to be both handsome and aggravating? "No, and it doesn't matter how you phrase the question or how many times you ask. I've never seen her before today."

He cocked his head, bemused. "Mademoiselle Baudin, I must say . . . you are very—"

A loud rap on the door interrupted him. He excused himself and crossed the room. Before he could open the door, a second knock followed. Then, a man's voice: "Christophe?"

He opened the door and went into the hall, leaving the door open a crack. Just enough for Nathalie to pick up on the urgency in their whispers.

"My God, Laurent." M. Gagnon's voice stepped above the murmur. "Already?"

Shortly thereafter he poked his head back into the room. "Thank you for your time, Mademoiselle Baudin." He held the door open with a shrug. "I'm sorry to end our meeting so soon. A critical matter demands my attention."

"Certainly," she said, standing up. She picked up her satchel and bouquet. As she approached M. Gagnon, she couldn't help but observe that his woodsy-orange cologne, in the midst of all this death, was full of life and freshness.

"Oh, and you can go out the back door," he said, pointing to the door the men had carried the body through. When they reached the door, he pushed it open for her. She tried too quickly to adjust her satchel strap and dropped the bouquet.

"My goodness." She stooped down to gather the flowers. "So clumsy. I'm sorry."

He knelt down to help her. "We begin and end with Madame Valois's flowers," he said, handing her the bouquet. He might have been smiling, but she was too embarrassed to look.

"And so we do," she said as they both stood up. She glanced at the blooms, still unable to recall the moment she bought them. Perhaps it would come back to her later.

Nathalie stepped onto the street and slid past a vendor.

M. Gagnon called out after her. "Be safe, Mademoiselle Baudin." His tone was far less formal now, tinged with a measure of concern. "Paris is no place for a young woman to be wandering alone right now."

3

Nathalie brushed some crumbs off the table with her pencil again. She'd been brushing incessantly, crumbs or no crumbs, after every few words of her morgue article. The words swam across her journal like confused fish.

She thought she saw blood.

And it was only ink.

Again and again.

Finally she finished writing. She closed her journal, deciding to let the article sit before reading it through one more time.

Although she'd finished nibbling her *pain au chocolat* a while ago, she hadn't yet been ushered along. Jean, her favorite waiter, saw that she was working and let her be.

A sparrow hopped over to the crumbs, pecked away at them until they were gone, and tilted its head.

"I think you ate more of it than I did today. A waste of my favorite sweet." Those chocolate-filled croissants flirted with her sweet tooth whenever she came to Café Maxime. Her friend Agnès loved them, too.

That reminded her. She had a postcard to write out to Agnès, who'd already sent a postcard *and* a letter. Maybe tomorrow. She was in no condition for that today.

She picked up the journal to put it in her bag. As if on cue, the postcard she'd received four days ago fell out. She read it once more.

Greetings from Bayeux!

The water wheel is prettier in person. You'll see for yourself—next year, I hope!

Weather still glorious. Grandmother still baking daily. Roger still a pest.

Me, I still wish you could have come.

Bisous,
Agnès

Nathalie flipped the postcard over and traced the water wheel illustration. Next year. Maybe.

She rubbed her temples and closed her eyes for a moment. *The blood. The knife. The silent screams. The cuts.*

The sparrow chirped at her ankle, bringing her back to the present with a start.

Don't go there. Stay in the present. Observe what's around you.

She swiped the last of the crumbs onto the ground and looked around. She'd been so lost in thought she hadn't noticed the people around her until now.

The café, which had a magnificent view of Notre-Dame, was bustling in spite of the heat. Nathalie caught pieces of conversation all around her. Two spirited, younger girls she recognized from school discussed the shopping they planned to do after lunch. A group of refined older men behind her puffed away on cigarettes, reminiscing about the Paris of their youth. One went on and on about how the renovation-minded Prefect of the Seine, Hausmann, "ruined the city" in the 1850s and '60s to make boulevards. That, the man sniffed, "did nothing but turn Paris into one big, daily traveling circus." Another complained about the foundations being laid for the "outlandish eyesore" that Eiffel had designed. Some people had made a fuss about the structure, saying it was going to be hideous, but Nathalie thought the tower project sounded thrilling. Although it was little more than pillars so far, in a couple of years it would be the grand gate to the Exposition Universelle.

Nathalie slipped Agnès's postcard into her journal and was about to call Jean over when a pang of guilt struck her. Agnès was one of her dearest friends, and already Nathalie was falling behind in their correspondence for the summer. She pictured Agnès waiting for the mail, disappointed yet another day.

She reached into her bag and took out a Seine River postcard. It already had the stamp affixed, a sign of her good intentions two days ago. She stared at it for what seemed like an hour but certainly could not have been. Could it? Time was oily and ungraspable this afternoon.

Putting her pencil to the card, she spilled the thoughts out as they came into her mind, not pausing once.

> *Greetings from our favorite café!*
>
> *I just finished eating a you-know-what and am settling in to write my article. Jean says hello.*
>
> *My day, what I recall of it, has been the strangest imaginable. I have something to tell you and will do so in a letter. I'm still shaking, so apologies for the penmanship.*
>
> *Much more soon,*
Nata

As soon as she finished writing, she got up from the table, squeezed between a pair of sprawling potted plants, and dropped the card into a post office box.

By the time she sat down, she regretted what she'd written. Too mysterious and vague. But she couldn't very well *say* what had happened in that tiny space. Nor could she pretend it was just another summer day in Paris.

I probably should have. Agnès is going to think I've gone mad.

Nathalie studied the post office box, trying to calculate if there was any way her lengthy arm could fit into it, when she heard the word "morgue" from the table beside her. She glanced at the well-dressed young couple on her left and shifted position to hear them better.

"A streetwalker, probably," said the woman.

"Not necessarily." The man loosened his ascot tie. "She could be a foreigner."

"Or maybe the killer is a foreigner."

He paused. "It does seem rather German in its execution."

"Or Russian," she said, sipping her wine. "They're savages anyway."

"Those cuts were precise, not savage. He could be a surgeon of some sort."

Just then Jean came over to them, and they asked his opinion as to who the victim and killer might be. Lovers' quarrel, he guessed. That turned into Jean sharing some of the talk he'd overheard at the café today, and the three of them gossiped so long another waiter had to "ahem" a reminder that another table needed more wine.

People want to make sense of things, M. Patenaude had explained when he hired her. What they don't know, they invent.

What should I invent? I'll say it was my imagination.

Some kind of vision? No, a hallucination from the heat. It *must* have been that. The uncertainty jabbed at her. Over.

And over.

And over again.

Her eyes fell on the yellow blossoms wilting by the minute. No matter how many times she revisited the morning, she simply couldn't recall buying them.

"Anything else, Mademoiselle Baudin?" Jean appeared over her shoulder with a smile.

Yes, can you bring my memory back? Oh, and I saw a murder scene take place. Backward. Let me tell you about it.

That sounded like something Aunt Brigitte would say.

"Just the check, Jean. Thank you."

Aunt Brigitte, who was in an asylum.

Nathalie darted across Quai Saint-Michel, breathless after a close call with a horse-drawn carriage, and crossed the bridge leading to the Île de la Cité. She made her way toward Notre-Dame, which stood directly in front of the morgue, and took in its grandeur against the cloudless blue sky. She'd seen the medieval cathedral hundreds of times yet remained in awe of those majestic towers. When she was young she'd named some of the gargoyles on the very top, above the band of statues, and still greeted them whenever she passed by. Out of habit she looked up at Abelard, Tristan, and Bruno. Abelard leaned forward and shook his head at her disapprovingly.

No. It's not real. You're still seeing things.

She turned her attention to her article, reviewing it as she walked. She paused beside the bronze statue of Charlemagne on horseback.

She'd had to remove herself from the dream, or vision, or whatever it was, in order to clear her thoughts well enough to write the piece. Words typically danced from her pencil; today they'd tiptoed across the paper.

End each article big, M. Patenaude advised on her first day. *So big they can't wait to buy the paper the following day to read your next column.*

After listing the corpses that remained from the previous day and the addition of the body of the sunburned man, Nathalie hesitated. She wasn't accustomed to providing such gruesome details, but she knew M. Patenaude would want an elaborate description.

> The most noteworthy corpse of all was that of a young woman pulled from the Seine, a murder victim. Her youth-

ful features, sliced into horrible distortion, betrayed no sign
of the terror she suffered before her untimely death at the
hands of what can only have been a cold, disturbed soul.

That was it. Two summary sentences. Leaving so much unsaid.
Presenting it as if she hadn't somehow witnessed the murder taking place. Reporting it in a detached voice, as if it didn't unsettle
her down to her bones. Someone else wrote that column.

Or so it felt. Or so everything felt since she'd touched that glass.
In her body but not. In her head but not.

She read the final sentence one more time and started walking again.

"*Attention!*"

Nathalie's eyes jumped from the journal to a haggard man leaning against the statue base; she hadn't noticed him and almost
stepped on his foot. "*Pardonnez-moi.*"

"Don't worry, little girl." His voice was gentler than his face
suggested.

Little girl? No one had called her that for years.

Odd.

Nathalie ignored him and continued walking.

"A little girl," he called after her. His voice was lower now and
had a mechanical cadence. "One who carries dead flowers and has
gaunt, ugly legs. I can see them through your dress."

Nathalie stopped but didn't turn around. Her orange dress was
linen, layered, and ankle-length, not at all see-through.

A chill tickled her neck.

"I can see everything. You might as well be wearing nothing
at all."

He's insane.

"Look at me, I'm St. Francis of Assisi! I have no clothes!"

Don't look.

The man cackled.

Half a dozen pigeons took off from the ground behind her,

making her jump. She continued on her way as the man rambled. After she'd taken a few more steps, he shrieked like the child who'd startled her in the morgue. Nathalie peeked over her shoulder to see him undressing, one garment at a time.

It was like her first time visiting Saint-Mathurin Asylum all over again.

Her parents had gone to visit Aunt Brigitte without Nathalie, as usual. The asylum was no place for a girl, they said (yet again) when she asked (yet again) if she could go. Just the *day* before, during a visit to Aunt Irene and Uncle Thomas outside Versailles, her cousin Luc had called her a baby (she was eleven, so that had been very insulting). She was thus particularly indignant that day about being "too young." So Nathalie claimed she'd spend the afternoon with Simone, which she did whenever her parents went to Saint-Mathurin. Instead she followed her parents, staying just far enough behind to watch where they went.

"Saint-Mathurin Asylum for the Insane" stood in relief over the entrance, gray stone letters outlined with black grime. She'd passed by it before but had never walked below those horrifying words. The intimidating arched doors led to a dungeon (or so she'd always imagined).

Immediately the reception nurse questioned her. Nathalie stammered her way through a story claiming that she was with her parents visiting Brigitte Baudin but had gotten separated from them. It took some pleading, but eventually the nurse told her which floor her aunt was on. She ran up the imposing staircase two steps at a time.

Moans, pierced by a scream she feared was otherworldly, led her up the last few steps to the landing. The door to the ward, a smaller version of the one at the entrance, creaked open a few centimeters as if it had been waiting for her. A smell like sour milk drifted through. Nathalie peered through the crack and saw a pale woman kneeling in a hallway barely wide enough for two people. A high rectangular window cast a sliver of light onto the woman's face. She appeared to be in a trance, arms swaying at her sides, eyes rolled back.

The woman jumped up and took off her hospital gown. Nathalie gawked at the misshapen, sagging body before her. She'd never seen another naked woman, not even Maman. "The sun! I'm burning!" the woman screamed as she began clawing at her doughy skin, raking her nails over her neck and breasts until she drew blood.

Nathalie cried out. The woman turned toward the door and met her eyes. *Save me,* she mouthed, and not a sound came out.

A jolt passed through Nathalie's body. She took a step back, almost tripping as she turned around. She dashed down the stairs and out of the building, making it home long before her parents did.

Papa *knew.* She couldn't prove it, and she never asked, but something about the way he later inquired about her afternoon with Simone told her so.

She could see that episode at the asylum in her mind's eye as if it were yesterday, not five years ago.

Nathalie trotted toward the tram stop, then broke into a run. Almost as soon as she got there, the steam tram arrived. She and a group of young boys squeezed on together, packing an already packed tram.

The tram chugged along, and almost right away she glimpsed the back door of the morgue where she'd parted ways with M. Gagnon.

He was standing there now, holding the door open and shaking his head. Two men opened the rear of a carriage and pulled out a sheet-covered body on a stretcher.

The tram turned a corner, and a building slowly eclipsed her view of the morgue.

Her heart thumped so intensely she was afraid one of the boys pressed up against her back would feel it.

My God, Laurent. Already?

Then M. Gagnon ended their meeting abruptly.

A critical matter.

The concern in his voice when she left.

Be safe.

Now she understood. What else could it be?

Another victim.

4

Throughout the steam tram ride, as she caught elbows from the boys in breeches who surrounded her, Nathalie clutched her talisman for quelling nerves and instilling luck: a glass vial filled with dirt from Les Catacombes, the cavernous tomb beneath Paris.

In fact, it was forbidden dirt, because you weren't supposed to remove any. But she had, that time Papa brought her to the Catacombs when she was eight. She took some, both because it was forbidden and because she figured there had to be at least a little bit of dead person in there (which would be almost like carrying around a ghost). Days later she showed it off to her schoolmates, all of whom admired her bravery. Long after anyone cared, however, she kept the tube close. It held a strange, sentimental value she couldn't quite explain.

When she disembarked at Place de la République, almost tripping over the rails in her haste, she put the tube back into her satchel. Her article was due in a little over an hour. After she dropped it off, she'd go right back to the morgue to see the second victim.

As she walked home, Nathalie pondered what, if anything, to tell Maman. Her mother was a good listener and offered advice from the heart. Yet that was also one of the reasons Nathalie didn't feel comfortable telling her about the episode at the morgue. Maman had a way of making other people's worries her own, and her moods had been especially erratic since the fire. Not to mention, Maman was repulsed by the public morgue to begin with and rarely went. She couldn't confide this to her mother.

Nathalie's building was tucked away on a quiet avenue lined with gray sandstone apartment buildings. She walked with an even quicker pace than usual. The neighbor's black-and-white cats spooked her by leaping onto a wall, one after the other. Embarrassed by her jumpiness, she glanced around. The street itself was empty, but a hundred glass rectangles watched her from behind grime-hewn balconies and decorative wrought-iron grates.

As she approached the steps to her building, she noticed a familiar blonde with painted pink lips and a bright, pea-green pleated dress coming down the stairs.

No one better to lift her spirits or talk her through this.

"Just the person I wanted to see!" Nathalie said, hoping she sounded more cheerful than desperate. She wanted to ease into this conversation, because she wasn't even sure how to have it.

"*Excusez-moi?*" Simone turned to her with a grin. "Aren't I *always* that person?"

Nathalie folded her arms and pretended to think about it. "Eh, sometimes."

"You watch that sense of humor of yours. Or I'll steal those flowers," Simone said, wagging her finger. "I just stopped by your place. Your mother said you hadn't even come home to change yet."

"Believe me, I'll explain why. It's going to take a while." She trotted up the stairs and kissed Simone on both cheeks. Simone smelled of rose water, as always. "First, you and why you're here."

"Are you sure?"

"Yes, I'm sure," said Nathalie. "Now let me guess: You're moving back in with your parents because you miss me so."

"I love you dearly, my friend," said Simone, taking her hands. "Just not enough to give up Le Chat Noir. Too much fun and too many boys." She struck a theatrical hands-on-hips pose and giggled.

Simone's parents were more lenient than Nathalie's, but they drew the line at cabaret performing. It had been almost four months since M. and Mme. Marchand gave Simone a choice: leave Le Chat Noir and work at the family market or live elsewhere. Within a week she'd moved into a small apartment near the club, several tram stops away.

"Besides," Simone added, "I know you enjoy visiting me."

"Only because you have grapes," Nathalie teased. As the only two children in the apartment building for many years, they'd been playmates growing up. Between Nathalie's imagination and Simone's boldness, they were never bored—a trait that was as true for neighborhood adventures in childhood as it was for conversations now about dreams, worries, and all else life left on the doorstep. Visiting Simone across town rather than downstairs had been, to say the least, an adjustment. "So if it isn't moving back home on my account, what brings you here today?"

"Céleste isn't feeling well. Again," said Simone with a frown. Her sister was seven and had been ill on and off all summer. "I came by to look after her so my mother could work at the store for a few hours."

"I'm sorry to hear it, Simone. Happy to see you, but sorry to hear it."

Simone thanked her. "Enough about my day. What is it you wanted to explain?"

The question, natural and straightforward, pressed a hundred thoughts into Nathalie's head at once. So much to share, so much to say. She bit her lip as all the possible ways to begin competed for her voice. "Did you hear about the murder victim?"

"Heard and saw. I stopped at the morgue on my way over." Simone stroked her throat. "Terrifying."

"It was. Is. And—something happened to me in the viewing room this morning. It's going to sound stranger than anything you've ever heard. Promise me you'll believe me," Nathalie said, sitting on a step. She cradled the flowers in the lap of her dress.

Simone sat beside her. "Believe you? Why wouldn't I?"

Nathalie sighed the sigh of someone who didn't know where to begin, who could scarcely mount the incredulity of what she was about to say. And then she told Simone everything she could, and couldn't, remember about the day so far.

Simone asked question after question, even though Nathalie didn't have many answers.

"Silent and in reverse." Simone tucked a curl behind her ear. "That makes it even more peculiar. And you're sure it happened *because* you touched the glass?"

"Either that or it's some coincidence."

"I wonder," said Simone, "if you have . . . I don't know. Some connection to the killer?"

Nathalie interlaced her fingers. "I never thought of that, but then again, who do I know that would do something like that?"

"Who said you have to *know* him? Maybe you were the last person to walk by him on the sidewalk before he picked someone to kill."

"That's like something out of a penny dreadful." Nathalie fought off a shiver. "It was probably an illusion. From the heat, like a fever dream." She said it hoping Simone would agree.

"Maybe. Maybe not. It could be a vision . . . and a gift. Perhaps you're meant to do something, to help."

"I don't know whether anything I experienced is to be trusted as *real*. And speaking in tongues and causing a minor scene doesn't make it feel like much of a gift," Nathalie said. The pit of her stomach moved like a sleeping dog as another thought occurred to her. "What if it's the opposite? Some sort of . . . curse?"

She searched her mind, wondering if she'd upset somebody enough to invite a curse. She didn't think so, but people did get aggravated with her sometimes when she hurried to slide into a steam tram seat. And there was that woman at the market who'd muttered something in a foreign language and glared at her a few weeks ago. For no apparent reason other than a dispute over who got in line first.

"*Non*," said Simone with a definitive shake of the head. "Not a curse. You don't have evil spirits nearby. I would feel it."

Simone considered herself attuned to the spirit world. Well, she'd believed it ever since becoming smitten with Louis, the "worldly and compassionate" poet who frequented Le Chat Noir. Nathalie had yet to meet Louis, but hardly a conversation had taken place in the last month in which Simone didn't mention him. He believed in tarot cards. And hypnosis. And ghosts. A week or so ago he'd brought her to a séance, where she claimed to have communicated with her grandfather's ghost. (Although Nathalie thought séances were nonsense, she still envied Simone a little for attending one.)

Nathalie twirled a button at the top of her bodice. "Whatever it is, I want—as baffling as it sounds, I want to see if it happens again."

"I would, too."

"That *had* to be another murder victim they were bringing into the morgue," said Nathalie. "I'll ask Monsieur Patenaude. He knows everything."

"I'll bet he doesn't know how to read tarot cards like your good friend Simone. When you come over, we're doing that."

Nathalie smiled, grazing her finger along the flower stems. "Will they tell me about this mystery bouquet?"

"Ah, you don't need cards for that. I think your mind is just foggy because of the vision," Simone said, rising to her feet. "You bought them, like the police liaison said. I bet you'll remember when you've had a chance to settle down."

"I suppose," said Nathalie as she stood up. It certainly didn't feel like her recollection of the flowers would come back. She'd tried to pull it from memory too many times already. "Anyway, I've got to go change and run my article over to Monsieur Patenaude. And you must have rehearsal soon?"

Simone nodded and, before turning to go, blew her a kiss. "Until tomorrow evening, Nathanael."

With a playfully annoyed over-the-shoulder glare, Nathalie stepped inside the apartment building. Simone had taken to calling her Nathanael because of the clothes she had to wear to *Le Petit Journal*.

Given that no women wrote for the newspaper, M. Patenaude had come up with an idea to which she'd reluctantly agreed. He thought it best if her fellow journalists didn't know a young girl was behind the anonymous morgue report. The reporter who had the column before her, Maurice Kirouac, received a promotion; part of the arrangement was for him to keep up the ruse as if he were still writing it. As for Nathalie, M. Patenaude asked her to write her articles and submit them to his clerk, Arianne.

He also suggested that she dress as a young man when coming to the newsroom. And pretend to be an errand boy.

A *boy*.

At first she loathed the idea. She wanted to be Nathalie and no one else. Besides, trousers looked hot and uncomfortable, and who would want fabric around their legs like that? She didn't even like wearing pantaloons.

Simone had told Nathalie to imagine she was on stage performing a role, because in a way, she was: Women who wore pants for employment had to get "official permission," and M. Patenaude had obtained it in writing from the Prefect of Police.

So Nathalie tailored some of Papa's old clothes under Maman's careful guidance, and they came out well enough. Wearing trousers was an unusual sensation, and she felt exposed because of the way the material hugged her scrawny legs. The buttons were big and bulky. Yet when she pinned her waves up, put on a cap, and slipped into the heavy leather shoes, the disguise felt almost natural.

Almost.

But she had to do what she had to do. Miss out on a summer in Normandy with Agnès. Work at the newspaper a year sooner than intended and in a bigger role than expected. Wear boy clothes.

This was certainly the summer of unpredictable compromises and newfound responsibilities.

Nathalie bounded up the winding staircase to the third floor. She felt better after talking to Simone, but she knew it was only temporary. The vision was still there, a shadow behind a door, waiting to knock when the time was right.

For now, she embraced her improved mood. It would help her put on a brave front for Maman.

After pausing a moment to rearrange the flowers, she opened the apartment door and greeted her white cat, Stanley. (So named because he had a very British demeanor, and she considered Stanley to be a very British name. Both Simone and Agnès had agreed that it suited him well.)

A plate clanged. Stanley led her to the kitchen, as if she didn't know from where the sound came. Maman was cleaning up after lunch. "Please don't, Maman. I'll do it."

Nathalie took a plate out of her mother's hands and placed the flowers in them instead, clasping her fingers over Maman's scars. "Pretty flowers for my pretty Maman," she said. "The sun was too much for them, as you can see."

"Water will wake them up. They're lovely! Thank you." Maman inhaled the scent, smiling. She reached behind a stack of plates for a vase. "From where?"

"A—a woman selling them outside the morgue." Nathalie felt guilty passing off a logical guess as a certainty. It felt like a lie.

Maman poured water from a pitcher into the vase and set the flowers on the table. "And please eat. Lentil salad and some vegetables. You're too skinny, *ma bichette*."

Although Nathalie was now quite a bit taller than her mother, she had been and always would be Maman's "little doe." She kissed her mother's ruddy cheeks. "Only if you let me finish clearing the table."

Nathalie helped herself to the food and, despite her mother's protests, cleaned up the kitchen afterward. Most every household task was a challenge for Maman since the fire in May. She was healing well enough but still getting used to this new, slower pace. She was restless now, not sure what to do with herself and especially her hands, which weren't accustomed to stillness. Maman had been an apprentice at the House of Worth when she was Nathalie's age and a seamstress ever since. She worked at the tailor shop, creating everything from everyday frocks to magnificent costumes for the Opéra Comique. Nathalie was proud of her mother's talent and felt fortunate to have an abundance of skirts and dresses. Maman bought fabric at a significant discount from the shop's supplier, and Nathalie was often clothed in silks, cottons, muslins, and velvets that her family would never otherwise be able to afford.

Maman had been helping out with costumes backstage at the Opéra Comique when it happened. One of the wings of the Salle Favart caught fire from a gas jet during a show, and life as her mother knew it was forever changed. Dozens of people died and many suffered burns; some people told Maman she was lucky to escape with burns only on her hands and arms. Maman always thanked them politely, as if she hadn't heard it many times before. Nathalie, however, knew her mother was devastated by those very scarred, painful hands and the memory of how nimble they once had been.

As much as Maman claimed she could still sew, her inefficiency frustrated her, and it was clear she wasn't ready to return to the tailor shop. Even arranging her chignon, the color of nutmeg and always so tidy, was a struggle some days. She rejected the doctor's assessment that she might never regain sufficient movement in her hands and fingers, and she made sure she kept her hands as active as possible.

And so half-finished dresses with luscious fabrics and practical cottons and ornamental beads and sensible buttons hung throughout the apartment. Ghosts on dress forms, reminding Maman of loss and happier days. More than once Nathalie had suggested taking them down, but her mother refused.

Nathalie tore her article from the back of the journal and put it on the table as Maman talked about her morning errands at the marketplace, telling a story about a woman who'd tried to steal mushrooms by stuffing them in her cleavage. "May I read your article? Even I'm curious about this one. The whole market was talking about it."

"Please do. It was . . . an especially difficult one to write," said Nathalie, glad to be able to disappear into her room.

She rested her vial of catacomb dirt on the shelf where she kept unusual things. A doll with clothes that Maman had sewn, a jade dragon Papa had brought back from China. A partial bird skeleton (Stanley was responsible for that; the remains of the poor creature were on the edge of the roof, and when the wind carried it to a spot under her window, she kept part of it). Silvain, her stuffed rabbit from childhood, worn out from so much cuddling. A mourning brooch with a braided lock of her grandmother's hair in the center. Some of Nathalie's baby teeth and claws Stanley had shed, together in a porcelain cup Aunt Brigitte gave her for imaginary tea parties as a child. Tangible little chapters of the book that was her, thus far.

Nathalie took off her dress and put on a shirt and stockings. She was just stepping into her trousers when Maman called from the kitchen.

"*Ma bichette*. The victim, my goodness. But tell me, what did you truly see?"

5

See.

How could Maman know?

Nathalie stumbled, one foot in and one foot out of her trousers, and sat on the bed to catch her balance. She finished dressing, put her catacomb dirt tube into her pocket, and stepped out of the bedroom. "What—what did I *see?*"

"The cuts, the bruising. Are you exaggerating?" Maman lifted her soft hazel eyes from the journal. Her own visits to the morgue were few and far between after seeing the mangled corpse of a train track victim several years ago. Yet she devoured the morgue report each day.

Nathalie exhaled. Of course that was what *see* meant.

Perhaps she should tell Maman everything. What the victim looked like in the display room, the murder scene in the fever dream or vision or whatever name it warranted. Her conversation with M. Gagnon and her impulsive words to Agnès and the possibility of a second victim.

"Not at all. What I saw was . . ." She wasn't sure how to finish the sentence. Could she tell Maman? "Much worse."

"I don't like it," Maman said, shaking her head. "Your exposure to this every day. I'm not sure this column is a good idea. Writing for the newspaper, yes. Writing the morgue report, no." She closed her eyes, then opened them. "Monsieur Patenaude is a prince for giving you this job, and I don't want to sound ungrateful or worse, demanding, but . . ."

"You'd like him to assign me another column."

"Frankly, yes."

That settled it. She couldn't tell Maman what happened. Her original instinct had been right, but somehow that wasn't very comforting.

Her mother's world was one of simplicity; she only required sewing and domestic life and all that it entailed. She didn't have a strong desire to experience the world—or even all of Paris, for that matter. Except when it came to fashion. And, Nathalie supposed, her mother would much rather she write about ball gowns than bodies.

She couldn't expect Maman to understand the appeal. "I know you don't like it, Maman, but I find it . . . enthralling. I don't want him to reassign me. I want to do what it takes to be a good journalist. Although I hope someday I can do it without wearing this," she said, presenting her new attire. "I'd rather walk in wearing your dress."

Maman stood up, smoothing out the bustle in her dress, a beautiful multicolored silk brocade she'd made from scraps at the tailor shop. She was often overdressed for errands, and she knew it, but it was a source of pride. "While I appreciate that," she said, trying to hide a smile, "I'm going to worry anyway. You know that."

"I do. Otherwise you wouldn't be Maman," Nathalie teased, picking up the article and folding it. "Don't worry. Such things don't scare me."

Is that true, even after today? The question inserted itself into her mind as if wedged by force.

Maman straightened out a velvet pillow on the sofa. "Too brave for your own good sometimes."

"Says who?" Nathalie kissed Maman on the cheek as she put the article into her bag. "Time for Monsieur Patenaude to put his glasses at the end of his nose and nod in approval."

* * *

Nathalie took the two-level omnibus, full of sweating people and drawn by sweating horses. She preferred the steam tram, which was modern, smoother, and quicker. However, the omnibus was cheaper and, since it was slower, allowed for better people watching. More often than not, it depended on what was closest and available, because Nathalie wasn't keen on waiting at a depot. Or waiting in general.

She stepped off the omnibus. The building *Le Petit Journal* called home was a grand structure, a fitting presence for all the stories it held and shared.

Although she'd only been there two weeks, Nathalie had already gotten used to the hurried pace of the newsroom. The printing press roared almost constantly, men shuffled papers and bounced from desk to desk, and the smell of paper and ink filled every room. She found the hum of frenzied activity intoxicating. As much as she wanted to be a journalist, she'd initially resented having to give up her summer in northern France with Agnès in order to take this position. The plan had been to try to get a job at *Le Petit Journal* next summer and then again after she finished school in two years. Maman's accident changed that, and despite wishing she was with Agnès right now, Nathalie adored being a reporter. Her next two years at school were optional, and given that the purpose of school at this stage was to teach girls how to be a good and proper wife (instead of teaching them Latin and Greek, like the boys), she contemplated not going back. It would depend on her experience at the newspaper, the heartbeat of communication that pulsed through Paris.

M. Patenaude's office was on the top floor. She nodded a curt hello to anyone who passed by, relieved that most people didn't seem to notice her and that the clothing ploy worked. After all, everyone was too busy to pay attention to a newsboy who ran errands for the editor-in-chief.

She knocked on M. Patenaude's glass door, her knuckles striking the *R* in *Rédacteur en Chef*. "It's . . . your errand boy."

"Come in."

She opened the door to see M. Patenaude reading at his desk with a pen in his hand. A half-finished cigarette lay on an ash-tray next to his inkwell. Nathalie hated smoking, but the rest of Paris seemed to love it, right down to the stub pickers who strolled the boulevards spearing discarded cigarettes. With all the paper around M. Patenaude's office, Nathalie didn't know how the place didn't go up in flames.

M. Patenaude beckoned her without looking up and continued reading. He was a fidgety man whose glasses gave the illusion of being thicker on some days than others, depending where on his nose they rested. He also talked more rapidly than anyone she'd ever met, as if the words were in a foot race to get out of his mouth.

She waited as he made a few notes, letting her eyes wander around the office. His degree from the University of France was on the wall, along with *Le Petit Journal* clippings about the start of the Franco-Prussian War, something about the Henard experiments, the death of Victor Hugo, and the capture of the murderer Pranzini.

He took a drag of his cigarette and finally glanced up, smiling politely. "Ah, what do the bodies tell us today? That murder victim would shout it from a Notre-Dame tower if she could, I'm sure."

If you only knew. Nathalie laughed uneasily and handed him the draft. As his eyes scurried across the text, she watched him for a reaction. His practiced passivity divulged nothing.

"This is good," M. Patenaude said, taking another puff of his cigarette. His fingers were stained with tobacco and ink. "Except for one thing. Sit."

He laid the article on his desk and smoothed it out.

"Yes?" She took a seat opposite and sat on her hands. Had she made a mistake? Written something poorly? She was shaken up when she wrote it, so it was possible that she—

"You mention the terror she suffered," he said, interrupting her thoughts. His voice was even. "'Her youthful features, sliced into horrible distortion, betrayed no sign of the terror she suffered before her untimely death.'"

"Indeed."

"You don't know that for certain," he said. He took one quick drag of the cigarette and extinguished it, spending a bit more time crushing it than Nathalie thought necessary. "Do you?"

"I—" Nathalie stopped. She *did* know that for certain, if what she had seen was real. The girl's cries still echoed in her memory. "I assume she did."

"No doubt," he said, gazing at her. Through her.

A fly landed on her arm. She flicked it off and stood up, breaking eye contact. "What does this have to do with the article?"

M. Patenaude rose from his chair, still staring. "No doubt." He blinked as if just waking up, then gave her a friendly wink. "Add those two words to the article. Unless you were present for the autopsy or committed the murder yourself, you can't know if she suffered in terror. He could have poisoned her. Put her to sleep and cut her later."

"Explain my assumption. That's all?" Nathalie said, annoyed. The newspaper was well-known for exaggeration, yet he'd made her nervous for nothing. For two words.

"That's all." He handed back the article. "Make the note, then give it to Arianne."

Arianne, about a decade older than Nathalie, was the only other woman who worked at the paper. Among other clerical tasks, she collected articles and arranged them for the compositors.

"*Merci.*" She stood up straighter. Being the morgue reporter *was* a privilege. Before Nathalie started the job, Maman had warned her not to be too proud. Nevertheless, it was hard not to feel, well, special. And proud.

"I heard the queue was especially long—Kirouac!" M. Patenaude looked over her shoulder into the newsroom. "You've been talking to Theriot for a quarter of an hour. Do you think your chair even remembers who you are?" He turned to Nathalie again. "I swear, ever since I've promoted him he's become ten times more sociable. Anyway, this victim will get plenty of attention, and so will the other one they pulled out of the river today." He dropped his voice. "We don't know for sure yet, but it looks like a second victim."

"I knew it!"

"What?"

"I mean, I—I had a feeling." She blushed, sorry she'd spoken up. She couldn't very well tell him about the interrogation with M. Gagnon. "Just over an hour ago I saw a lot of activity near the door where they bring in the bodies and . . . I don't know. Something made me think it could be another body."

He pushed his glasses up the bridge of his nose. "Excellent journalistic instinct! I knew that curiosity would pay off when I hired you."

She thanked him and smiled graciously.

"Between the autopsy and time required for it to chill adequately, the corpse won't go out until tomorrow, I'm sure. Did you know the morgue often keeps murder victims on display longer than the rest? Sometimes they'll even hold off on announcing an identification if the mobs are big enough." He adjusted his glasses again. "The more dramatic the corpse, the greater the attraction, the longer they keep them on the slabs."

"Don't they start to . . . ?" She finished the thought silently.

A smirk rolled across M. Patenaude's lips. He paused, seemingly lost in thought. "No one in Europe relishes the morgue like Paris, flocking to see the daily dead."

Something nipped at the edges of Nathalie's mind. A vague, unformed discomfort. For two weeks she'd been meeting with M. Patenaude. Today was different. *He* was different.

She thanked him, excused herself, and left. As she descended the stairs, Nathalie thought about their conversation and realized what it was that bothered her.

It was that stare when he discussed the girl's terror.

And the smirk when he discussed the morgue.

Despite what M. Patenaude said, she had to return to the morgue. She couldn't simply go home without checking. Maybe he was wrong and the body would be out. Maybe they'd put it out so the public could see, then chill it overnight.

If the victim's body was out, would she touch the viewing pane again?

She hadn't decided yet.

Although the crowd outside the morgue was much smaller than it had been hours before, the wait was longer. That's what the nervous energy traveling through Nathalie's body insisted, unless it was lying. Which it might have been, because what could she trust in herself right now? Already everything that had happened this morning seemed remote and unreal, more dream than experience. Nathalie put her hands in her trouser pockets and clutched her vial of catacomb dirt.

As she got closer to the entrance, she noticed the elderly woman selling flowers. What was it M. Gagnon had called her? Vallette? Vallery? Valois? Mme. Valois. Nathalie had seen her yesterday and the day before. But not today. Until now. Regardless of the story told by the coins missing from her pocket and the wilted blossoms at home.

The old woman held a bouquet in each hand—one composed of small white flowers, and the other of deep pink blossoms. Everyone in the queue thus far had dismissed her. Nathalie studied the woman as she got closer.

No. She hadn't seen her today.

Nathalie was certain.

When the old woman approached, her stare was like a poke.

She glanced at the trousers and then back at Nathalie's face. "More blooms, Mademoiselle?"

More. Proof that the woman recognized her. Proof that the woman had sold her the flowers this morning.

Nathalie met the old woman's unblinking gaze and shook her head. Mme. Valois regarded the brown trousers, narrowed her eyes, and looked up at Nathalie again before proceeding down the line.

She thought she'd experience relief, even a small amount, if the flower question was undeniably solved. She should have.

But she didn't.

Minutes later she entered the morgue. The man who stood guard inside the viewing room this morning, the one who'd sent her to talk to M. Gagnon in the back office, had been replaced by another.

M. Patenaude was right. No new corpse. Nothing had changed with the display since this morning.

Nathalie's stomach sank when her eyes fell upon the victim. The nameless girl with the bloodstained dress. It didn't matter that Nathalie had seen her several hours ago. The horror and pity hadn't dissipated.

Not so long ago the victim had been a girl. She probably loved Paris much like Nathalie did. She had a family, maybe some brothers and sisters, and friends like Simone and Agnès. She had favorite books and dresses and foods and went to sleep at night on a pillow and wrapped in blankets. She laughed and dreamed and had memories that vanished forever when she took her last painful breath.

And then Nathalie knew.

She had to touch the viewing pane again.

What if she saw something that could help this poor girl? Or could find out her name?

Nathalie looked at the Medusa door, so foreboding earlier today. It was just a door with a decorative carving. She felt foolish for having been unnerved by it, for thinking she'd heard one of the snakes hiss.

Whatever had happened earlier, she was prepared to encounter it again.

Discreetly.

M. Gagnon stood in the display room, again next to the curtain on the left. Nathalie was on the far right, glad to have so many people obscuring her. She didn't want to get pulled into the interrogation room again if something happened.

He crossed over to Nathalie's side and bent over to pick something off the ground; she retreated into the shadows before he stood up again. When he did, he casually eyed the onlookers.

Nathalie turned her face away, hoping he didn't catch a glimpse of her. After a pause she took a peek; M. Gagnon was back at his post.

She positioned herself slightly toward the outer wall. The more she could hide, the less likely she'd be to give herself away. If it happened again.

If if if.

Her body tingled like the kiss of a breeze on sun-soaked skin. With a slow inhale, she reached forward and pressed her fingertips on the glass.

Nothing at all.

She took one step closer to the glass and tried again.

Nothing.

Then something occurred to her. Her fingers trembled on the glass as the realization emerged.

Simone had said maybe Nathalie knew the killer. That could explain why she couldn't repeat what had happened earlier.

Perhaps her vision wasn't really a vision, or a moment of delirium, or her imagination. Until now she hadn't considered that it might be a memory.

6

Sleep, fickle and unsympathetic, abandoned Nathalie that night.

She lay in the darkness, petting Stanley to remind herself that she was in the here and now. Her imagination, showing off how wicked and shrewd it could be, was devoted to convincing her otherwise. She pictured the killer—faceless, hidden, more like a spirit than a man—whispering in her ear. Telling her she was insane. Teasing her about what she saw, asking if she enjoyed watching the murder.

Nathalie couldn't stand it anymore; she needed to get up, to move, to do something else. Tossing off her sweat-dampened sheets, she lit her kerosene lamp and slid out of bed. She grabbed her journal, a pencil, and a small box off her desk. Stanley jumped down from the bed, tail curled into a question mark, ready to follow.

"Only if you promise to be quiet," she said. "And not swat at my pencil when I'm writing."

She put on her shoes and picked up her kerosene lamp. With careful steps, she made her way to the apartment door and slipped into the hallway, shutting the door delicately after Stanley came through. She shuffled down the oak floor of the hall and up three flights on the winding staircase. The door stood before her, proud and menacing, such that she could almost picture it with arms folded.

Thank goodness she was tall, or she'd never reach the key over the door. Simone wasn't tall enough to reach it, and it was a happy day when Nathalie finally could. From then onward, the Rooftop Salon, as they called it, became a favorite new retreat.

She pushed open the heavy door. Stanley pranced forward onto the moonlit roof and leapt onto the ledge. Nathalie took light steps along the perimeter—people lived in the apartment immediately below—and sat against the wall. Voices from Josephine's, the tavern on the next street, danced along the summer air.

She opened the small box and took out the letter from Agnès that had arrived a few days before the postcard.

> Dear Nata,
>
> We've been here five days and Grandmother has baked on four of them—bread, croissants, a tart, and bread again. "We Jalberts put ovens to good use," she likes to say. Starting tomorrow I'll be her apprentice. If I should come home in August resembling a hot air balloon, you'll know why.
>
> Roger is already driving me <u>mad</u>. He talks constantly, and none of it is terribly interesting. He's also been mischievous (he put a frog in my shoe yesterday) and clumsy (he spilled tea on my journal this morning). We are celebrating his tenth birthday next week, and I quite think I'll give him leaves or rocks or some such as a prank. My real gift to him will be a tart, if my apprenticeship goes well.
>
> Incidentally, the journal survived the tea. Alas, the page with my latest short story on it did not. I suppose it's just as well, because it wasn't a very good story.
>
> On the topic of writing: Tell me about yours. I want to know everything about the newspaper, the morgue report, and what it's been like to wear trousers. Save for that, I envy your marvelous opportunity.
>
> Must go. Papa is calling me to help Maman weed the garden. He thinks it's a good "experience with the earth." Bending over in the hot sun and getting covered in dirt is an

experience with the earth, but I would not classify it as good.
A few days ago there was a snake in there, and I screamed.
I have made excuses ever since to avoid working the garden,
but unfortunately I think my luck has slithered away like
that awful snake.

I'll send a postcard soon. Write to me, my friend.

Bisous,
Agnès

If Simone was a rose—bright, feminine, and alluring—then Agnès was a lily. Sweet, elegant, and pure. Whereas Nathalie had known Simone her whole life, she'd only known Agnès since the start of this past school year when Agnès changed schools; they'd taken to each other right away. As someone who'd traveled all over France, and even to England and Germany, Agnès had an explorer's spirit, always eager to find something new or special or different, even in the everyday. Simone and Agnès didn't cross paths with each other often, but when they did, they got on well enough. Nathalie loved the way each of them viewed the world.

She put the letter back in the envelope and took out some blank stationery from the box. Leaning back, she let her gaze drift to the shimmering night sky. What was she going to say to Agnès now? Writing that postcard at the café had been a mistake. She didn't want to tell Agnès what had happened at the morgue, not until she made sense of it. Or maybe not at all. Agnès was on holiday, after all, and that vision was too much to put into a letter. But she had to explain away what she'd written.

Stanley hopped off the ledge and came over to her, pawing at her pencil.

"Is this encouragement or a warning that you're about to break the no-pencil promise?" She scratched his chin, picked up the pencil, and began to write.

Dear Agnès,

I have always wanted to ride in a hot air balloon, and they are rather pretty, so there are worse resemblances. I shall look for you in the sky upon your return.

Baking . . . well now. You must teach me everything you know. If you show me how to make a tart, I'll show you a few things I've learned about sewing. Even trousers. Maybe for next year's birthday gift for bothersome Roger, whose antics make me glad I don't have a younger brother.

Is it hot there like it is in Paris during the summer? Have you gone to the beach yet? I want to hear all about the ocean. I long to see it someday. And smell it, and hear it. (I could do without the tasting.) I should think standing in the waves and feeling that powerful water pulling away is amazing.

Writing for the newspaper is an adventure, what with the obligation of a daily column, the constant buzz of the activity in the newsroom, and my wish to impress M. Patenaude. I've grown accustomed to wearing trousers but cannot say I like them.

I suppose word has made its way to northern France about the murder victim, yes? The queue to get into the morgue was long and my goodness, Agnès. You can't imagine how ripped up she was, this ill-fated girl so very close in age to us. What I saw I will continue to see for days. I sent you the postcard shortly after the viewing; that's why I was so very shaken.

What's it like to stroll the streets of Bayeux? Tell me in great detail, my good friend, so that I feel like I'm there with you.

Bisous,
Nata

As she was writing out the envelope, the chatter from the tavern grew louder and more forceful, pulling her out of her thoughts. Two men started yelling at each other, and the sounds of a brawl erupted. Nathalie tucked the letter into the envelope and crept to the edge of the roof. A gap between buildings framed one of the men as a fist struck him and he fell. The puncher came into view but was soon pinned by the barkeep. The first man struggled to his feet while stroking his jaw, yelled something in a drunken voice, and ambled away. She wondered if he'd remember any of it in the morning.

And then she had an idea.

She revisited the thought she'd had earlier, that perhaps the morgue incident stemmed from a memory. Needless to say, she didn't remember seeing anyone slash a girl to death. Then again, she also didn't remember buying flowers. Who could say what the mind did and didn't suppress? Maman had told her about a tailor whose visit to a hypnotist unlocked long-forgotten details of the day his childhood friend drowned. And Nathalie had once read a story about a woman who, during a fever, recalled pushing her baby brother out a window when she was three.

If touching the morgue glass had indeed untied a memory knot, it should be easy enough to prove or disprove.

Nathalie crawled back to her spot and picked up her journal. She began writing as hurriedly as her hand would move, as if pouring out recent memories might unearth a buried one.

But it didn't.

Other than the memory gap involving the flowers, she could re-create every hour of the day for the past week.

She had no reason, not one, to think that the experience was a memory. That theory could be discarded.

Leaving her with nothing that made sense.

Maybe, as she'd suggested to Simone, it was something like a heat-induced fever dream. Heat did strange things to people sometimes. Or maybe, as Simone thought, it was a vision.

Or maybe she was going mad and instead of paying visits to Aunt Brigitte, she'd be her roommate before too long.

Nathalie picked up her things and went with Stanley back to the apartment, feeling no better, and possibly worse, than when she'd left it.

The next morning, Nathalie was at the morgue before it opened. Even the vendors hadn't arrived yet, and there wasn't a beggar in sight. The only other people in front of her were a handful of factory workers in overalls complaining about their boss, a pair of American brothers who apparently found something to be very funny, an older couple with a small dog, and a boy several years younger than herself.

When the doors opened, she glanced at M. Gagnon's post, which was instead occupied by a droopy older gentleman. She went to the left side of the viewing pane anyway.

"Mon Dieu."

Nathalie heard the words before grasping that she was the one who'd spoken them.

It didn't matter that she'd seen the victim twice yesterday and relived the vision in her mind all night. It didn't matter that she knew there was a second victim and had tried to picture her.

None of it prepared her for the reality of seeing two victims side by side.

She tried blinking it away, as if that could make this sad spectacle of bloodied young women disappear.

The new victim was pale, with a pinkish skin tone, and older than the first. She had very long hair, the color of late-day sun and knotted like a sailor's rope. Her dress hung behind her, blue and green and damp. Rain on a summer picnic.

The young woman's face was ripped open; she was the mirror

image of her sister in death. Together they were a pair of grisly candlesticks on a gray stone table.

Would it happen again?

Nathalie had to know.

Be courageous. Be brave. Be too brave for your own good, as Maman says.

She moved farther away from the others and put her hand forward. Straightening her posture, Nathalie stretched her fingertips toward the glass.

The touch brought her there quick as a bullet.

Three slashes unfolded in reverse. The blade sank in deep, held by an unseen hand; Nathalie was too close to the girl's face to see anything else. The knife ripped from collarbone to throat, then lifted and pierced from the top of the throat to the bottom of the jaw. One more time the knife lifted, plunging from the girl's jaw to the corner of her mouth. Blade and flesh, flesh and blade.

Then the victim stood up and a set of hands pulled back from her. *Pushing.* Nathalie got farther apart from her, as if she was being pushed away. *Running.* The girl moved backward, too, both of them running backward down a long hallway with a dark blue and gold rug down the center. *Chasing.*

The girl's run slowed to a walk and she turned around, a look of excruciating terror on her face that softened into concern, then a flirtatious grin.

Then it was over.

Chasing. Running. Pushing. Killing. The victim's realization that she was about to die.

Someone beside Nathalie coughed. She faced them just long enough to see the couple, the brothers, and one of the factory workers staring at her.

The factory worker turned to his companions, glancing over his shoulder at Nathalie as he wiggled between them, as if to get away from her. One of the brothers whispered to the other, and the two muffled a chuckle. The couple continued to gawk; the man put his arm around his wife and guided her away. Then they gazed at the corpses, or pretended to, once again.

Nathalie took a step in their direction. "*Excusez-moi*—what . . . what did I say?"

They ignored her. The woman pointed to one of the bodies and whispered something to which the man replied with a vigorous shake of the head. Then they began talking to the factory workers and the young boy about the murder victims.

She pulled her bag to her chest, digging her nails into the leather to steady her fingers.

The guard. Did he notice? Nathalie looked over her shoulder. No, he was examining his knuckles, whereas M. Gagnon's replacement was in the midst of a yawn.

No second interrogation, at least. And no suppressed memory, she concluded, because to see and forget *two* murders taking place was very unlikely. She'd already ruled it out, but this confirmed it.

Now what?

Although it wasn't hot this morning, she could still be hallucinating. Especially if she was crazy, a possibility she gave more credence to by the moment.

She had no answers. Only questions.

One of her teachers had said he'd never met a student who enjoyed asking questions quite like Nathalie. "Distinctly inquisitive," he'd called her. It was true, or used to be. Right now questions were just vexing worms that burrowed through her mind.

She didn't want to look at the bodies. Any of them. Obviously she had to, for the sake of her column. Not just look at them but study them.

Nathalie walked to the back of the display room, clutched the catacomb vial in her pocket, and approached the viewing pane again. She stood tall and observed the other corpses, eyes skipping over the victim. The other new bodies on display were an overweight man, probably the other body they'd carried past her in the hall yesterday, and an elderly woman. Their deaths were undignified—no one wants to die anonymously in a public place—yet ordinary. Compared to the two girls, all the other souls appeared to be sleeping.

When Nathalie left the morgue, she headed to the *bureau de poste* to mail her letter to Agnès. She caught herself clenching her fists, nearly crushing the letter, twice on the way there.

She didn't want to sit in the noisy steam tram or on the omnibus as horses plodded along. Nor was she in the mood to be pressed against strangers. A long walk home was inconvenient but preferable. The reaction of the crowd in the morgue both today and yesterday made Nathalie feel like an outcast. Worse yet, she agreed with them.

Taking the route near the Seine, she paused at the water's edge to stare into the river. The river that served as pall bearer for two young women not much older than herself. Before their identities became Victim #1 and Victim #2, who had they been? Perhaps one had been a shop girl who loved the thrill of a new perfume and the other, a studious girl who read Latin and had just enjoyed her first kiss.

How did the killer dispose of them without being seen?

Finding the bodies must have been horrendous. She couldn't imagine how the unwitting discoverers had felt upon realizing that the object floating in the water was human and that the human was a young girl and that the young girl was dead.

And the victims. What went through their minds that harrowing moment, when they knew they were going to die? She'd seen it on the second victim's face, that instant of realization. What did it feel like, that brief intersection of horror between the realms of life and death?

A few blocks from home, she passed a newsboy selling *Le Petit Journal*. The ink shouted at her from the stack of papers, begging her to come closer.

When she did, the headline overtook her like a thief in the alley.

Girl's Killer Sends Letter to the Newspaper

While the boy engaged with a talkative customer, Nathalie paused to read more. The letter was quoted in large print beneath the headline:

> *To Paris,*
>   *I'd like to express my gratitude to you for coming to see my work on display. It was a pleasure to see so many, especially the woman in blue and her young girl—who, I must say, carried in the most delightful yellow bloom. The little one's screams upon seeing my Sleeping Beauty were indeed a welcome surprise.*
>   *Until the next one, I remain,*
>
>

Ever yours,
Me
>

And there, under a lamppost beside the newsboy and the talkative customer, Nathalie threw up the raspberries and cheese she'd had for breakfast.

8

Throughout dinner that evening, Maman eyed her with suspicion. Not eating pistou soup, one of Nathalie's favorite summer meals, gave her away. She tried forcing herself to have some but was afraid she'd throw up again.

"What do you think of the soup?" asked Maman, sinking her spoon into it. "You're not having much. Too much basil?"

"No, it's delicious." Nathalie soaked a piece of bread in it. "I'm just . . . I have an upset stomach."

"Because it's empty. All the more reason to eat." Maman's skepticism was palpable.

"When I get back from Simone's," Nathalie said, eating the soup-soaked bread. "I told her I'd be there at six."

Nathalie cleared the plates and washed them. Her life was ruled by the hour hand these days. Last summer she'd spent a few hours a day reading or writing in the city's gardens or people watching at a café with Simone, and her biggest worry had been getting chores done before Maman got home from work.

Now it was corpses. And unexplainable visions. And a murderer.

She *should* be in northern France with Agnès in a little town where time stood still. A summer where her greatest concern would be how big a slice of tart to take or snakes in the garden or Roger being a nuisance.

With a sigh, she tossed the dishrag on the counter. Maman asked yet again what was the matter.

"Nothing," said Nathalie. She picked up the dishrag, folded it neatly, and placed it on the counter. "I hope I feel better soon, that's all."

Maman folded her hands together, wincing from the effort. Nathalie took her satchel and kissed Maman on the forehead, promising to be home by nine.

Nathalie got off the steam tram in Pigalle a block from Simone's place and bought a newspaper at a nearby tobacco store. Dance halls, bawdy can-can shows, and café-concerts spilled into one another in this part of the city, and Simone lived in the center of it all. (Maman considered this section "a heap of decadence," so Nathalie "moved" Simone's address to a building in a more respectable area several blocks away.)

Because of her schedule at Le Chat Noir, Simone kept strange hours—"vampire hours," as she called them. Some nights she performed in a show, and although she only had minor chorus roles, she was overjoyed just to be on stage. Other nights she waited tables at the club. She often spent her nights off there, too, listening to poetry readings or musicians trying out new compositions.

Sometimes it was hard to remember how Simone had passed the time before Le Chat Noir. Was it really just a few months ago that their evenings had been spent at the Rooftop Salon, watching passersby below and making up stories about them?

Nathalie slid past a beggar in the doorway of Simone's building, noise reaching her ears as she stepped into the dim foyer. Someone was always shouting or playing the piano or having a party; if not, there still remained an underlying hum of voices. The place smelled of cigars and alcohol so thoroughly that it seemed to have been painted onto the walls. The wooden stairs, bearers of countless weary feet, groaned as she made her way up to the apartment.

Simone had her independence, but her new life was far from lavish.

"You won't believe it. Read for yourself," said Nathalie as soon as Simone opened the door. She pulled *Le Petit Journal* from her bag and shoved it into Simone's hands while crossing the threshold.

"I overslept. I didn't even splash on rose water yet." Simone yawned and closed the door. "And my mind isn't ready to read anything."

Nathalie took the paper back from her, rolling her eyes. "I'll read it to you, then."

They sat on the sofa, Simone stretched out like Stanley after a nap and Nathalie bunched up, legs folded under. A tiger ready to pounce.

Nathalie read the article aloud, and by the end of it, Simone was off the sofa and pacing the room.

"I can't believe that monster was there while *you* were there," said Simone. Her wide-set eyes seemed to grow even wider. "I wish you didn't have to go alone."

Nathalie ran her fingers through her hair. "Me, too. Unfortunately there's no other way, practically speaking."

Simone stopped pacing. "I know, it's just . . ."

She didn't have to finish. Nathalie understood. Her stomach gurgled again just thinking about it. Did the killer witness her having that first vision? Did he notice when she was summoned by M. Gagnon? He must have been there, staring at her like everyone else, because her vision happened as soon as the little girl's cry startled her. When did he leave? Did he follow her after M. Gagnon sent her off with a warning about the streets of Paris? She hugged herself tighter with each question.

"I hope they catch him," Simone said, "because I want to be there when he meets Madame la Guillotine."

"Front of the crowd," Nathalie added. She imagined herself first watching the blade fall on the killer's neck, then rushing up to the platform. She'd grab the head afterward and slap his cheek, like that man had done to the assassin Charlotte Corday, then . . .

Simone tapped her. "Did you hear what I said?"

Nathalie shook her head.

"I *said*," Simone began in an exasperated tone, "the letter was sent when only one victim was in the morgue. By the time it was published, the second victim was on display. 'Until the next one, I remain.' Who's the 'next one' . . . the second victim?"

"Could be. I'm sure it's ambiguous on purpose." Nathalie tucked in her elbows. "He's probably sitting in his armchair right now, laughing to himself because he knows all of Paris is talking about it over dinner tonight."

Simone flopped down on the sofa, kicking up a small amount of dust as she did so. Her eyes filled with excitement. "If he does kill a third time, maybe you can help the police."

"But how? I don't have any clues. It's not like that."

Simone squeezed Nathalie's elbow. "Just tell them what you see."

Nathalie thought about M. Gagnon, sitting tall in his liaison office chair, and what he would say if she went to him. In the course of a few seconds, she pictured scenes ranging from him scratching his jaw and jotting down notes to polite-but-firm instructions to place her arms in the straitjacket if she wouldn't mind.

"Do you really think anyone would believe me?" Nathalie asked.

Simone relaxed her grip.

"And what am I seeing, anyway?" Nathalie's shoulders dropped. "A murder scene in reverse . . . but we don't know if it's real or if it exists outside of my own mind."

"Assume it's real. Why not? It's real to you."

"You're the one who told me, ever since I made old Madame Mercier think Stanley was a ghost cat haunting the stairwell, what a good imagination I have." Nathalie smiled at the memory, even if it was a little bit mean, because Mme. Mercier had been, too. And Stanley, being white, *did* make a good ghost cat.

"Stranger things have happened," said Simone. "Remember those stories about the fraud doctor—what was his name? Henard?—and the blood transfusions that gave people temporary magical powers?"

"That was just some craze. And required a medical procedure."

Simone spread her arms out wide. "Yes, but what I'm saying is . . . you wouldn't be the first person to have some kind of extraordinary ability. If he could make it in a laboratory, who's to say you don't just have it?" She leaned forward. "Maybe you stop rejecting the idea that this isn't real and embrace the possibility that it might be. Stop fighting it."

"The police would think I'm unhinged. Wouldn't they?"

Simone dropped her voice to a whisper. "They don't have to know it's you."

"How would—" Nathalie stopped, interrupting her own question. How would that be possible? Of course. Follow the killer's own cues. "A letter to the paper."

"Or to the police directly."

Nathalie chewed her lip. How involved did she want to get? Perhaps she was too quick to consider it "exciting." Writing factual observations for *Le Petit Journal* was one thing; sending anonymous letters about what she saw was another. This would move her from on-the-scene interpreter to actor, a background figure on the stage. It was the difference between reviewing a theater piece and belonging to the show. Was she prepared to be part of the performance?

Then she asked herself if she was willing merely to stand on the other side of the viewing pane, like every other morgue visitor, despite having seen so much more.

So much to consider. So many unknowns.

"Even if what I'm seeing is real, that doesn't mean it's accurate," Nathalie said, twisting her fingers around one another. "What if my mind is stepping in with a paintbrush and changing the scene around?"

"Or maybe your mind is a canvas for truth. Have you thought of that? Visions. Not hallucinations or fever dreams." Simone tugged her braid. "The police will sort it out. I'll bet they hear plenty of nonsense. You can't be any more wrong than the people who purposely make up stories."

"True," said Nathalie. She still wished she had proof, and she didn't have many details to offer. However, it was unlikely she could make anything *worse* by telling the police what she saw. Right?

"Oh, I almost forgot," said Simone. She leapt up from the sofa and went over to her nightstand. She returned with a smile and a deck of cards.

Tarot cards.

Nathalie's shoulders fell into a slump, which made Simone tilt her head like a puppy. (Simone was good at that.) "It's almost half past eight. I told Maman I'd be home by nine."

"Louis will be dropping off a book about astrology any minute now, so this will be fast, I promise," Simone said, sitting next to Nathalie on the sofa. "You know I need the practice."

Yes, Nathalie knew. Simone's acquaintance with tarot card readings stemmed, like so much else, from her new life at Le Chat Noir and from Louis. One of the other showgirls did it on the side to entertain customers. Simone, having had a reading once from her, learned from the girl how to do readings of her own for her "favorites" at the club, as she called them.

Nathalie, hiding her reluctance, agreed. Simone giggled through a thank-you before growing serious. "Now. Single question or open reading?"

Simone had explained what this meant once before. Until the episodes at the morgue, Nathalie would have opted for a general reading. Not anymore. "Single question. What do these 'visions' mean?"

After shuffling the cards a few times, Simone asked Nathalie to cut and laid out three cards face down. "There are a few ways to do this, but I want to start with the simple version until I have more experience. This card is the past, this one is the present, and this represents the future. Ready?"

After a nod from Nathalie, Simone flipped over the card representing the past.

On it was a man in the center with two horses on each side.

"This is the Chariot," she said. Her tone was thoughtful, focused. "It means that you've overcome adversity and that you display perseverance."

"Starting off with compliments. Those tarot cards know how to flatter a girl, don't they?"

Simone looked Nathalie in the eye, grinning. "See? That one was sensible enough. It could be referring to your mother's accident and getting a job at the newspaper."

"Could be," Nathalie said, returning the smile. She didn't want to say it, but in her view, that card could be interpreted to explain most anything. "Although it doesn't seem connected to the question."

"No, it does! Your job at the newspaper is the reason you go to the morgue every day, so it's what led you to the visions."

Nathalie couldn't argue with that.

"Open your mind," Simone said. Her demeanor was so charming that Nathalie had no doubt she'd impress her "favorites" with this game. "Now for the next card, the present."

Simone flipped over a card with a moon on it. "The Moon means . . . confusion."

Nathalie felt Simone's gaze, but her own eyes didn't lift from the card.

"If I wasn't confused, I wouldn't have a question to ask," Nathalie said, sitting up straighter. "So I think this one is true for anyone who poses a question."

"That could be. But the Moon also means dreams."

Dreams while sleeping . . . or awake?

Much too strange.

Nathalie couldn't dismiss that one quite as easily. "We needn't do the third card."

"Too late," Simone said, turning over the card that addressed the future.

The card depicted a man hanging upside-down. His feet were crossed and hands were behind his back.

Simone grimaced. "The Hanged Man."

"Hanged?" Nathalie said. "I guess it could be worse. It could be a guillotine."

"It's not what you think. It has to do with self-sacrifice, I think." She bit her lip. "Yes, that's it. And it involves changing *how* you think."

Nathalie thumbed the sofa fabric. "In summary, then, I had perseverance, I'm confused, and I'll have to sacrifice something at some point. Or I already did, if missing out on a summer on the coast counts. It sounds like most everyone's life at one time or another."

Her voice was much shakier than she'd intended it to be.

Simone got up and came over to Nathalie, giving her shoulders a squeeze. "It's just a game," she said. Nathalie knew Simone was just trying to make her feel better.

She appreciated it all the same. With a peck on the cheek she left Simone and trotted down the stairwell. The outside door opened as she reached the landing, and an auburn-haired young man with a paisley frockcoat entered carrying a book. A generous waft of his lavender cologne filled the space between them.

His green eyes sparkled with recognition when he saw her. "I suspect by Simone's eloquent description that you are Mademoiselle Nathalie Baudin," he said, with a regal bearing. He held his hand to his cheek, as if taking her into his confidence. "And if you aren't . . . my apologies."

She laughed. "I am indeed."

He extended his hand and she met it with her own. "*Enchanté,*" he said, raising her hand to his lips and brushing it with a kiss. "Louis Carre."

Nathalie blushed. No one had ever kissed her hand before, except for men Papa's age striving to be overly proper, and they didn't count.

Louis turned her hand over and inspected her palm. "Ah, an Air Hand. Restless if that mind of yours isn't kept active, eh? Simone has a Water Hand, full of passion about life."

"Both are true," she said as he let go of her hand.

"My mother is, among other things, a palm reader," he said with pride. "She learned it from *her* mother and passed it on to me."

She smiled. "My mother is a seamstress, and she tried passing it on to me, but I'm not very good." They chuckled.

"Don't think me rude for asking, but I have an appreciation for fashion: Did she happen to make the skirt you have on? Magnificent craftsmanship."

Nathalie glanced at her beige-and-white skirt with intricate lacing. An old skirt but well-preserved and one of her favorites. "Yes, in fact, she did."

"Your mother knows her way around a sewing needle. I admire such skill."

Nathalie thanked him. Such compliments delighted her, not out of vanity but pride in her mother's talent. A talent that had been halted by severe burns.

Louis bid her farewell and told her to be safe.

"Interesting you should say that," she responded. "You're not the only one to tell me that in recent days. These murders have everyone on edge."

"You know what I think?" he whispered, again with that conspiratorial gesture. "Devil worshippers."

Her stomach wriggled like a serpent. "What?"

"Simone told me the two of you were talking through the possibilities. *I* think there's a Satanic cult behind the killings. The police don't think like that." He tapped his temple. "You have to explore even the most dimly lit paths."

Nathalie had never thought of anything along those lines, either. Louis had a most interesting way of thinking. That's what poets do, she supposed. See things differently than everyone else. "Anything is possible."

"Isn't it, though?" Louis bowed. "Enjoy your evening, Mademoiselle Baudin."

She left the building, particularly mindful of her surroundings as she walked to the steam tram stop. The tram arrived after a brief wait; she boarded and then got off at the Place de la République, as always.

Almost immediately she had the unmistakable sense that she was being followed.

9

Nathalie got off the steam tram, passed a man on a bench reading *Le Petit Journal*, and stopped to tie her shoe.

The man, who wore a British-style bowler hat, stood up when she bent over. He put his hands in his pockets and turned his back to her. When she resumed walking, she noticed—just barely, out of the corner of her eye—that he followed her.

He'd hesitated. Almost as if he were waiting for her to finish tying her laces.

She shook her head. There were other people on the sidewalk. Although it was smart to be alert, she could make herself crazy wondering if everyone whose path matched hers was a threat.

But at first he'd faced the opposite direction. Hadn't he?

She wheeled around to see the man face-to-face. He wasn't there. Two other men passed her, and the sidewalk was otherwise empty. She glanced across the street and saw the hat. The man, wiry and on the shorter side, was leaning against a gas lamppost beside the Place de la République monument. His clothes were dark, nondescript. All she saw was the back of him, again.

Nathalie put her hand in her pocket, squeezed her catacomb talisman, and continued on her way. At the next block she took a right, then looked both ways to cross the street.

That's when she noticed him again. He turned when she turned, and he crossed when she crossed, staying about a block behind.

This wasn't a coincidental stroll. No one would take this route unless they were headed to the same cluster of apartment build-ings.

And if they were, they wouldn't have crossed the road to lean against a lamppost first.

Why would someone follow me?

She tried to push aside the next question, but it pushed back. *What if it's the murderer?*

Goosebumps erupted across her skin. *Run home and he'll know where I live. Run to a public place and I might lose him.*

The latter made more sense; the Canal Saint-Martin was nearby, lined with gaslights, and often sprinkled with lovers and tourists.

She went from a walk to a run.

Her heart thundered in her ears, drowning out every other sound, even her own footsteps. She glanced over her shoulder. The man was still in sight, taking swift, agile strides.

Within a minute she was on the Quai de Valmy with people strolling along both sides of the canal. She slowed to a walk, peek-ing to see if the man followed. She couldn't see him in the crowd. Had he left? Was he hiding?

She spotted a carriage across the bridge. A couple seemed to be making their way over to it. She hurried to get there first, careful not to spook the horse.

"Monsieur," she said to the driver, "I need to get home. Imme-diately."

The driver cocked his brow, then looked past her at the approach-ing couple. "Samuel here has put in a long day of work," he said, patting the horse on the neck. "My rates are higher at night."

Nathalie scowled. Thankfully she'd gotten paid that day. She pulled some money out of her dress pocket and waved it at him. "That's fine."

With a shrug, the driver extended a hand and helped her up. He asked her, as she knew he would, why she was wandering along the canal alone so late. "I got lost," she lied, searching the crowd for the man until they were on quiet side streets. She made nervous conversation to keep the driver from asking questions, eyes darting the entire time. She asked about Samuel, spotted gray with a black mane, and told the driver a story: When she was four, Papa had lifted her up to pet a carriage horse on the nose. The creature snorted at her, with a good deal of noise and moisture, giving her a fear of horses she'd outgrown years ago. By the time she was done with her story, the carriage was pulling up to her apartment building.

After a visual sweep from one end of the street to the other, she stepped out of the carriage. She paid and thanked the driver, then entered her apartment building, not sure her heartbeat would ever slow down.

Nathalie paused at the top of the stairwell, drumming her fingertips on the bannister. How to explain her tardiness to Maman? The apartment door opened before she could give it much thought.

"I heard a carriage. That was you? Spending money on a carriage?" Maman retreated back into the apartment. She placed an empty candelabra on a small table with five white candles resting on it.

"I had to," said Nathalie, following her inside. She closed the door and locked it, then checked to make sure it took. "I didn't—I didn't feel safe walking."

Maman caressed her scars. Her mother used to intertwine her fingers when she was anxious, something which she could no longer do. Touching her scars took the place of that. "I don't want you to be out alone after dark, or even close to dark." Her agitated tone shifted into concern. "Not until all of this goes away."

"I don't think anyone is ever alone in Paris," Nathalie said with a tense chuckle. "I—I went to the canal on my way home."

Maman's brows creased. She put candles in the candelabra, one by one, each movement rougher than the last. "Why?"

As Nathalie rummaged through her head for an answer, it occurred to her that there were, in fact, two possibilities. Her interpretation of events since getting off the tram may have been correct. Or she may have gotten all of it very wrong.

Maybe the man wasn't following her.

Maybe it was a too-keen sense of alarm, a hasty conclusion.

Maybe it was the killer.

Maybe it wasn't.

After all, he'd never gotten close enough for her to get a good look. And when she'd gotten to the canal, she hadn't seen him.

Nathalie cleared her throat. "Have you ever had a little voice in your head that says 'Do this, not that'?"

"Many times," said Maman as she struck a match.

"My little voice said to take a carriage tonight, and that was the closest place to get one."

It wasn't the truth, but it wasn't a lie. It was something in between.

"Sometimes the little voice knows best," said Maman, lighting the candles. "Even if it did mean spending money on a carriage. What was it that prompted the little voice?"

"Just a . . . feeling." Nathalie kissed her mother on the cheek. "I'm sorry for worrying you, Maman. I promise to be home long before nightfall from now on."

"Thank you, *ma bichette*."

Maman took one of her half-finished dresses, a red chiffon one with velvet trim, off the dress form. By candlelight she worked on it—slowly, awkwardly, painfully—a while before bidding Nathalie goodnight. After Maman left the room, Nathalie waited a few minutes before peeking out the windows and checking again to make sure the apartment door was locked. She did it all a second time, too.

Then she settled down on the sofa, Stanley at her side, to write in her journal. In lieu of never seeing the wiry man's face—hidden under a hat, in shadow, always just too far away to see—she recorded every other aspect of her encounter, even drawing a street map. After finishing, she flipped several pages back to reread the last few entries leading up to tonight.

Then she reached one written just yesterday according to the date. That entry she read three times.

It was her handwriting. It was her style of storytelling, her use of words. The descriptions, which dove into everything she'd experienced this summer in minute detail, were certainly hers.

Yet she didn't recall writing a single word of it.

Nathalie wanted to hurl the journal across the room. No, throw it out the window. Or hold it over the candelabra and burn it. Or toss it into the Seine on her way to the morgue tomorrow. She could buy another journal. And maybe she should, because this one betrayed her, played a cruel game with her memory. After all the secrets she entrusted to it, the journal deceived her.

For now, however, she buried it under a pillow behind Stanley.

She walked her mind through the previous day, step by step, the way you'd guide a child across a rock-strewn creek. Then she encountered the gap.

During the night she'd gone up to the roof to escape the thought cage her dark, quiet room had become. She remembered sitting down on the roof and then . . .

Nothing again until this morning.

Oh goodness. She'd posted a letter to Agnès this morning. A letter she couldn't remember writing, just like the journal entry.

What did I say?

The bridge spanning the time on the roof and waking up had crumbled away.

As to why she couldn't remember . . . well, why couldn't she remember the bouquet? That first episode in the morgue yesterday, whatever she'd seen or imagined or dreamed up, had shaken her up more than she knew.

Then it'd happened again today in the morgue, and now she wondered if she could trust her own mind. Was she really followed tonight, or had her brain distorted that, too?

She reclined on the sofa, closing her eyes. Somehow she needed to anchor herself in a truth, any truth. It all came back to the morgue. Either her visions reflected reality or they didn't.

Again and again she called up the memories of what she'd seen for each victim. After a while, Nathalie fell into that strange place between thought and dreams.

Instead of hazy thoughts, she found clarity.

She sat upright, startling both herself and Stanley.

The silver ring. It was a minor detail from her second episode at the morgue, something that had eluded her focus. Until now.

In the vision, the girl had been wearing a simple silver band on her right little finger.

When the first victim was found, there had been two accounts in the newspaper. One was Nathalie's column about the morgue. The other was a report about the girl's death—where she'd been found and when, what she was wearing, whether anything had been in her pockets, how long she appeared to be deceased. Tomorrow's edition would have the same account for the second victim. That was the standard procedure for all the bodies on display.

If the ring was mentioned, then what she was seeing was real. Not because Simone said so, and not because Nathalie would prefer a supernatural explanation to madness. Not because, if she allowed herself to think about it, maybe even indulge in it, there was something powerful about it. Purposeful. Special.

It would mean she'd arrived at a truth. A mysterious one, but a truth all the same.

10

Nathalie woke up later than usual the next morning and rushed to get dressed. She was hurrying to the kitchen to get something for breakfast when the headline stopped her like a stone pillar.

First Murder Victim Identified

Maman sat in Papa's well-worn burgundy chair reading the newspaper. Nathalie came up behind her, resting her hands on the leather. It smelled of Papa's pipe and the spicy balm he bought in Morocco and wine and everything else that was Papa. She couldn't wait for him to come back.

"The girl was a nanny from Giverny," Maman said, adjusting her green robe. "Visiting Paris on holiday. Alone."

"A nanny. I hadn't thought of that."

"What?"

Nathalie bit her lip. She probably shouldn't admit to Maman that she tried imagining what the victims had been like, who they were, what their stories had been. It would only add to Maman's concerns about the morgue assignment. "Some people at the café said maybe she was a streetwalker. What was her name?"

"Odette," Maman said, putting her finger on the name. "Odette Roux."

Nathalie crossed over to the kitchen and sliced some bread. Something was unusual about that name. It sounded—*familiar,* somehow. Yet the only Odette she knew was a little girl who lived down the street.

Or maybe it was that a certain comfort existed in hearing the name. A name, any name, besides "the girl" or "the first" or "Victim #1." She was Odette with the freckles and the pink dress who tucked in little ones and sang them nursery rhymes. Odette who played hide-and-seek, standing in closets and ducking behind wardrobes as children searched for her. Odette who dried the tears of a little boy who skinned his knee. That's who she would be to Nathalie.

Maman folded the newspaper and put it under her arm as she stood up. She walked over to the kitchen window, her eyes following a bird that tottered along the sill to avoid the rain. "I'm going to the morgue with you. Then I'd like us to visit Aunt Brigitte."

Nathalie's heart sank before bobbing like a cork. "Why?"

Maman threw her a perplexed look. "If we don't visit Tante, who will? I'm ashamed to say it's been a while."

They'd been once to the asylum since the accident, but Aunt Brigitte had been upset by Maman's injured hands covered with bandages. She'd cried and cried because she didn't want Maman to be in pain, so Maman decided not to go again until her burns had healed some.

"I meant why are you coming to the morgue?" Nathalie put some blueberry jam on her bread. "You don't especially enjoy it."

She wanted to protect Maman like that little bird on the window might have protected her young. Her mother didn't need to see the murder victims, didn't need to stand in the morgue where the killer had lingered, watching the crowd stare at his victim.

But there was more to it than that. She also didn't want Maman in on her secret. Going to the morgue together somehow felt like . . . an intrusion.

An intrusion? Nathalie was instantly ashamed of the thought.

Maman handed her the newspaper. "I want to see what everyone else sees. What you see."

If you only knew, Maman.

Nathalie spread the paper on the table after Maman left. She searched the sidebar and found the sentence, mundane to the rest of Paris, that altered her view of everything.

> Deceased wore a blue-and-yellow frock with a floral print, undergarments, one shoe, and a silver ring on her right little finger.

Exhilaration fluttered through her body. Could it be that she didn't have to fear this "power" after all? That she could explore it like a new novel, every insight a fresh page? She didn't understand this gift but she was prepared to embrace it. Learn from it. Make it part of who she was and use it for good.

At least and at last, she was beginning to trust its authenticity.

When Nathalie entered the morgue, her gaze went right to where Odette used to be.

Not seeing Odette's lifeless body anymore affected Nathalie in a way she didn't expect. Although she'd never admit it to anyone and could barely acknowledge it to herself, Nathalie missed seeing her. The vision's intensity and all it released had made Odette more than a corpse on a slab, more than just the victim of a murderer. She'd become a soul amidst the soulless. Nathalie felt connected to her, to both of them, through the unexpected intimacy of witnessing their deaths. Like the first time she saw her grandmother take off her glasses, or the time she sat in the front row of a concert and watched the pianist lose himself in the music.

Like that. Only dark and terrible and full of rage and blood.

The rain kept the crowds away, so it was only Maman, Nathalie, and three others in the viewing room—two women and a man who waddled like a duck. Surely none of them was the murderer. Still she wondered: Had he come here to watch the crowd view his second victim yet? If so, had he come more than once?

After a glance at the curtain to note that M. Gagnon wasn't there, Nathalie watched her mother. Maman was still, her eyes focused on the body, unblinking. "I wonder how she ended up there," she whispered. "In that situation. Whatever it was that led her to her killer."

I watched her run from him, Maman. I saw it all. Backward at that.

Nathalie leaned in to her mother. "That's what makes it so scary. It could have been anyone." *Including me. Or Simone.* Nathalie stepped closer to the viewing pane, her mind drifting to the victim's silver ring. It might have been from a beau or might have been a family heirloom. Or she could have bought it with her own wages or found it on a bridge over the Seine. The ring had a story, like a thousand other things in this poor girl's short life.

Something shifted in the viewing room: the light, a faint sound. Nathalie turned to see a figure in the shadows behind her, just over the threshold and to the left. She couldn't make out anything other than great height and an umbrella, yet the presence was sinister. Intimidating.

She whipped around to face front and took Maman by the elbow. "We should go."

"What's the matter?" Maman turned to look, but her expression reflected neither curiosity nor alarm. "Roland, how nice to see you."

Nathalie let go of her mother and was never more relieved to be in darkness. It obscured her blush.

Not the killer. Overly imaginative, Nathalie. Just Roland. One of the tailors at the shop where Maman used to work. Nathalie greeted him with a smile, which bounced off his glasses back to her in the darkness. As Maman spoke to him, Nathalie faced the corpses again. *Don't be foolish.*

"Why were you in such a hurry?" Maman asked when Roland stepped away.

"I felt light-headed," Nathalie lied. "I thought I needed some air, but it passed."

They fell into silence. Nathalie focused on the second victim and thought about the vision from yesterday. After a moment she closed her eyes, trying to remember details. How the victim ran, what the space looked like, how the cuts were made. The only element she could think of that resembled a clue, something the police didn't already know, was that navy-and-gold hallway runner.

Probably hundreds, if not thousands, of hallways in Paris had a rug like that. She could examine five runners with those colors and not be sure which one she'd seen in the vision—it happened quickly, and she didn't *study* it.

How could that be helpful? It would show that the murder took place indoors, anyway, in a home of some sort. She wished she had something more substantial to share, but maybe it was still worth submitting. The public didn't know which puzzle pieces were in place and which were missing; even seemingly unimportant details might be worthwhile.

Maman nudged her, murmuring that she was ready to go. They emerged outside to find that the rain had subsided.

"I saw and I still don't believe," her mother said. "That's why I don't come—"

"Mademoiselle Baudin, how are you?" It was M. Gagnon, calling out from the steps behind them. Nathalie's belly turned to stone, as if that Medusa on the morgue door had petrified her stomach.

"Well enough, and you?" *Please don't say anything about the interrogation.*

"Bodies and more bodies," he said with an uneasy laugh.

Maman raised a delicate brow. M. Gagnon introduced himself as police liaison for the morgue.

Nathalie couldn't help but notice what an appealing grin he had. And how his imperfect tooth stuck out, just the tiniest bit.

He seemed much . . . *nicer* than he had been the other day. Something about his attention, the fact that he'd noticed her, baffled Nathalie. Yet it also pleased her.

M. Gagnon certainly had her attention, too.

"Enjoy your stroll before the rain starts up again," he said, tipping his hat as he walked in the opposite direction.

"How do you know him?" asked Maman. She moved a pin in her chignon and waited for an answer.

"He . . . said hello one day," said Nathalie. She shifted her weight. "He's often in the display room when I come."

Maman smoothed out her brows. "Why should he wish to make your acquaintance if he stands on the other side of the glass? Do the guards greet you?"

"No. Only him," Nathalie said. "Monsieur Gagnon is, uh, a gentleman. He urged me to be careful, nothing more."

Maman didn't reply, but it appeared to satisfy her, though you could never tell. Sometimes she'd wait a week before floating a follow-up question.

Nathalie glanced over her shoulder as they walked away. M. Gagnon was leaning against a lamppost, hands in his pocket. His eyes were on the ground and then, as if he could see her watching from thirty yards away, on her. She looked away, embarrassed.

And also intrigued.

All the way to the asylum, she thought about him. She didn't know what to make of his friendliness today, but she liked it. Very much.

Saint-Mathurin Asylum had been and always would be a place of nightmares.

Nathalie's cousin Luc once said there were rumors of haunted floors, hidden corridors that led to suicide chambers, and secret rooms where the violently insane were left to regulate themselves, with the hospital providing only food and water and services to remove corpses if the inmates killed one another.

Nathalie didn't believe any of that, not now, but as a child she'd lost many a night's sleep to such tales.

Where Aunt Brigitte dwelled was frightening in a different way. All the women in the hospital were confined to this floor; the severity of their cases varied such that the silent and forlorn wandered alongside the shrieking, quivering women in the halls. The woman Nathalie had seen during that forbidden foray years ago was, she discovered in time, far from the only one prone to outbursts of hysteria.

The walls and floors were cold stone; the air was putrid with sweat and filth. And the sound was a terrifying clamor of wailing and mad, incessant chatter. Nathalie couldn't imagine calling this home. Not even for a night. Mme. Plouffe's home, where Tante had a room before the asylum, was peaceful and homey. Saint-Mathurin was a cauldron of madness and dread.

And yet Nathalie didn't mind coming here, not now that she'd grown accustomed to it. The patients fascinated her, given that she pitied rather than feared them, and Aunt Brigitte, beneath her madness, had a childlike kindness.

Nathalie and Maman made their way down the corridor, passing a plaster statue of Saint-Mathurin behind glass. A pair of bloodied handprints—made, legend had it, by a patient whose escape was suicide—trailed from the middle of the wall to the floor. Maman always turned away when they passed that spot; Nathalie always studied it, trying to see in her mind's eye what happened that day.

They walked by a room of patients. A frail elderly woman stepped out of it and followed them down the hall. "Where is the key? Can you let me out? Father said I could go if you gave me the key." Over and over again she asked, softly and almost lyrically, as she tapped Nathalie's arm. They ignored her; the nurses told them never to engage the patients.

Suddenly she gripped Nathalie's elbow with a startling amount of strength. "WHERE IS THE KEY?" the woman screamed. Her voice was poison; her eyes teemed with contempt. Nathalie tried to pull away and the woman squeezed harder. Maman pushed the woman off just as a nurse hurried over.

"Estelle, do not touch anyone!" The nurse uttered an apology as she peeled the woman off Nathalie. The woman screamed even louder for the key; the nurse started to escort her back to her room and the woman dropped, as if her lower half had ceased to work, and twisted. A second nurse ran over to help as the woman flailed and yelled.

Nathalie didn't mind coming here. Most of the time.

"Look at this," Maman said, pointing to Nathalie's elbow. The red imprint of the woman's grip remained. "You'll have a bruise from that."

"I'm fine. It doesn't hurt," Nathalie said. Maman shook her head, and they entered the room Tante shared with three other women.

One roommate with shorn hair was snoring on her bed. The other two weren't in the room. Aunt Brigitte, Papa's older sister by five years, was curled up like an infant. Her brown hair was long, stringy, and streaked with gray. Her skin was full of fine lines, like cracked porcelain. She was staring at the window but not, it seemed, out of it. Her lips were moving and she was talking to herself.

They said hello, and Tante rolled onto her back. She gazed at them, face blank for a moment, before grinning. "Caroline! Nathalie! Thank you, thank you for coming to see me. Thank you."

Tante always thanked them profusely for coming. Nathalie used to think it was amusing, but then she realized, no, it wasn't. It was heartbreaking. Aunt Brigitte was locked in a horrible place with no human connection besides nurses, doctors, and other patients. Aside from a courtyard where patients could go for an hour a day in good weather, Tante's world was stark, empty, and devoid of anything meaningful.

"I had a nightmare last night," said Aunt Brigitte, her voice low, as if she didn't want her roommate to overhear. "I was a cobra in a basket, and a nun pulled me out. I sank my fangs into her hand."

Nathalie swallowed hard. Tante's dreams always evoked horrifying, vivid imagery.

Aunt Brigitte grinned before continuing. "When I bit her she turned into a dove."

Maman and Nathalie locked eyes for a second, and then Maman cleared her throat. "That's frightful, Brigitte."

Aunt Brigitte then ceased to talk, completely, and became as still as a statue with only her lips moving.

That happened often. Tante would go . . . elsewhere. Nathalie always wondered where: The past? The future? Deep into her imagination? After a few moments, she'd return to the present.

Maman broke the silence. "Nathalie works for the newspaper now."

Aunt Brigitte didn't answer, as if she hadn't heard, for a few beats. Then she looked Nathalie in the eye, with a grave expression, and touched her cheek. Tante spoke in a thin voice. "Trust no one."

Nathalie flinched.

Why would she say that?

Her mother, ever adept at moving past Tante's unusual behavior, continued on about what a good writer Nathalie was before mentioning Papa. Maman read his latest letter to Aunt Brigitte while Nathalie pondered why "trust no one" had come to Tante's mind.

"I miss Augustin," said Aunt Brigitte, her voice cracking. "He's a good brother. I wish—I wish." Tante's lip began to tremble and her face crumpled into tears.

As Maman hugged her, Aunt Brigitte's tears turned into sobs. Tante buried her face in Maman's arms like a child. She said something over and over again; Nathalie couldn't make it out.

"What's she saying?"

"'I wish he could make me better,'" Maman said.

Nathalie frowned, wishing she could help Tante. Papa did have a way of making things better, or trying to, and she understood why Aunt Brigitte would cry for him.

Maman soothed Tante until she calmed down. Moments later she said she was sleepy.

Madness. Peculiar, scary, and unpredictable.

They finished their visit shortly thereafter and found a downpour waiting for them outside. Hurrying to the tram stop, they huddled together, using their respective umbrellas to form one large shield from the rain.

"Tante said something strange to me." Nathalie leaned in closer. "Did you hear her? 'Trust no one.'"

"Most everything Tante says is strange."

Nathalie shook some raindrops off the umbrella. "I know, but that seemed very . . . specific. Don't you think?"

"I don't know."

That was how it was with Maman. If she didn't want to talk about something, you might as well converse with one of the gargoyles on the Notre-Dame.

Maman's dismissive silence only served to embolden Nathalie. "You and Papa never told me," she began. "How did Tante end up in Saint-Mathurin?"

"It's complicated, *ma bichette*." Maman looked her in the eye. "She thinks she sees things. And she tried to drown a man because of it."

11

Nathalie lost her grip on the umbrella and almost dropped it. "Things? What—what kind of things did she see?"

Maman glanced at the others waiting at the tram stop: a bespectacled young man reading Marx, a pair of lovers enamored with one another, and a mother holding the hands of her young son and daughter, singing cheerfully in what sounded like Polish. "It happened while she lived at Madame Plouffe's house," she said, dropping her voice. "She disappeared one night, and they found her trying to drown a man in the Seine. Fortunately a policeman was nearby and intervened in time."

Nathalie tried to picture that scene but couldn't. It didn't seem possible. Her aunt was bony and frail, and from what she could recall, always had been.

"How could Tante be strong enough to drown a man?"

"She jumped on him from behind, while he was peering over a bridge." Maman mimicked looking over a bridge. "There was a struggle, and somehow they both ended up in the river. He didn't know how to swim, and she tried to push his head under."

This Nathalie *could* imagine, because even in the asylum, her aunt showed a fierceness. Or the remnants of it, anyway. Aunt Brigitte's eyes flashed with intense emotion whenever she talked about her dreams.

"Aunt Brigitte was adamant," Maman added in a quiet, somber tone. "She claimed she saw the man throw a baby into the river."

"And?"

"They searched for three days. No baby was found in or around the Seine. Or reported missing. The man had no history of crime, either."

Nathalie absorbed the words like cloth soaking up a blood stain. "How ghastly. The poor man!" She wondered what became of him, and if he ever looked over a bridge after that without first checking to see who was nearby. "But Aunt Brigitte, locked away forever because of one mistake, appalling as it was? After all, she didn't kill him, just gave him a good fright . . ."

Her voice trailed off, replaced by the questions in her head. *Did Aunt Brigitte end up at Saint-Mathurin because she tried to kill someone? Or because of the reason why, because she believed her dream to be real?*

Maman watched the Polish children jumping over a puddle. "Your father thought it was best. Madame Plouffe was a delight but she—she couldn't give Tante the care she needed. And neither could we. You understand that, right?"

Before Nathalie could answer the steam tram pulled up, splashing muddy water on her mother's dress, purple with a gray swirling pattern. Maman leaned over to inspect the splatter and dropped her bag in a puddle. Then the tram door opened, with Maman lamenting her soiled dress and bag as she climbed on board. Nathalie sighed. She had so many more questions, yet she knew her mother wouldn't answer any of them, not while sitting on public transportation with other people within earshot. Maman was prim when it came to discussing family matters, even when the only people who could overhear were strangers.

Nathalie closed her umbrella and followed Maman onto the tram, wishing her aunt had said more, or less, than "Trust no one."

Over the next two days, Nathalie tried talking to her mother several times about Tante's commitment to the asylum. Maman continually, and skillfully, changed the subject. (Nathalie had once commented on her mother's ability to deflect questions, to which Maman replied, "You've given me many opportunities to practice over the years.") Her evasiveness only piqued Nathalie's interest more.

"Why is it such a secret?" asked Nathalie, after her third attempt to talk about it.

"Because your father wants it to be." Maman's tone, normally smooth as a gemstone, had a finality about it. The conversation was over. Not just at the moment, but completely.

The words struck her like little arrows of sympathy for Aunt Brigitte. Was Tante insane, misunderstood, or both?

"I'll bet my mother is sorry she told me," Nathalie remarked to Simone. They were sitting on Simone's sofa eating grapes. The woman next door sold grapes in a street cart and sold them to Simone for half price if they didn't sell in the first few days. During her last visit, Nathalie had suggested that Simone buy extra grapes sometime just so they could stomp on them, as if they were at a winery. Simone said it would be too messy for the apartment, but that she'd gladly stomp grapes if they ever took a trip to a Bordeaux vineyard.

"She probably is," said Simone, fishing a grape seed out of her teeth. "But you can't put the bark back into the dog. She'll explain eventually."

"Speaking of explaining," Nathalie said, pointing to the front page of *Le Petit Journal*, "this doesn't. I don't even know why Monsieur Patenaude printed it."

A second letter from the killer had been published. She huddled over the newspaper, rereading it yet again.

> *To Paris,*
> *Thank you for coming to my second exhibit. It was marvelous to see my pieces side by side, if only for a short while. The queues have been most impressive. I don't want to dis-*

appoint, and I promise to give you something fresh to look at soon enough.

Until the next one, I remain,

Ever yours,
Me

"These girls aren't people to him," said Simone. "They're chess pawns."

"Or works of art."

Simone raised her brows and sat back. "That's morbid, even for you."

"His words, so to speak, not mine. Think about it," Nathalie said, tucking some loose hairs into her wool felt cap.

"As if the morgue is an art gallery," Simone said. Her long-lashed eyes narrowed in thought. "Or a wax museum. Speaking of which, I'm taking you there sooner rather than later. You have to see the latest tableaux. Louis says they are among the best he's seen and that the attention to detail is astounding."

"What? You want me to have *fun*? Simone Sophie Marchand, what kind of friend are you?"

"The kind who wonders why you have sat here for an hour but have yet to write that anonymous letter. Don't think I'm letting you go turn in your article to Monsieur Patenaude until we have something."

The purpose of Nathalie's visit today *was* to write the letter to the Prefect of Police, and the sheet of paper had been giving her a dirty look since she sat down. Now that it was time to put pencil to paper, however, she was having second thoughts. Third and fourth thoughts, even.

"Here's my list of reasons *not* to do it: One. Information is minor. Two. Cannot recall any other details. Three. Not even sure what this ability is or why I have it. And four. Feel foolish sending this in. Here's what I have for reasons to write the letter: One. Simone said so."

"How about," Simone said with a chuckle, "you will remain anonymous, you could help them more than you know, and if you were one of those unfortunate girls being gawked at in the morgue, wouldn't you want your killer brought to justice?"

"Wouldn't anyone? It's not that. It's . . ." She finished the sentence with a sigh. She knew those were sound reasons, and she'd already thought of every one of them. Amidst all the excitement of having this power, the fear of uncertainty began to slither around her mind. What responsibility would this bring? What if her involvement complicated the investigation . . . or somehow made her a target for the killer?

She didn't confess these worries to Simone because she didn't want to appear selfish.

Besides, if nothing else, this ability meant she had to think beyond herself. Didn't it?

Simone crossed her ankles. "It's what?"

"It's daunting."

"Start simple, then," said Simone. She sifted through a box on the table and pulled out an envelope. "One sentence will do, won't it? 'The second victim ran from her killer in a hall with a navy blue rug with golden stripes on the edge.'"

"It's just so . . . factual. It almost sounds silly," Nathalie said, exhaling her weariness. "That's all there is, though, and I don't want to be dramatic."

They sat for a moment, thinking.

"I know!" Simone said, snapping her fingers. "I can't believe we didn't think of this before. Tell them how he killed her! In precise detail. They can tell from the autopsy, but no one else would know that. Except you."

"Except me," Nathalie said. "Or someone at the morgue, sending it in as a prank."

"Don't concern yourself with any of that. They'll wonder how anyone but the killer could know that. Or they might assume it's just a good guess. You have nothing to lose, because they might just throw it out. However, you *could* gain some credibility."

"I'll get their attention if nothing else."

"And," Simone said, folding her arms, "you remain anonymous."

Nathalie nodded and picked up the pencil. They spent a few minutes discussing how to word the letter, agreeing that direct and simple would be best. Nathalie closed her eyes and thought through the vision. It took a few minutes to write; she tried not to dwell on the incongruity of capturing a passionate act using aloof language.

> The second victim was killed in a hall that had a dark blue rug down the center; the rug had golden stripes along the side. The killer made three cuts along one continuous path: from the left corner of the mouth to the top of the jaw, the bottom of the jaw to the top of the throat, then from throat to collarbone. The deepest slashes were in the neck. The knife was approximately fifteen centimeters in length.

Neat block letters. Unadorned prose. Gruesome honesty. Nathalie didn't want to read it a second time.

Wax sealer in hand, Simone turned the paper toward herself and read. "Perfect. Shall I?"

Nathalie chewed the inside of her cheek. If she thought about this too much, she might change her mind. Again. "Yes."

Simone folded the paper, placed it in an envelope, and put a wax seal on it. She handed it to Nathalie to address. "Here you go, Mademoiselle."

Nathalie indulged in another handful of grapes before getting up to go, even though she wasn't hungry in the slightest. Simone gave her a longer than usual hug and said, in a whisper resonant with both comfort and affection, "You have a gift. This is the right thing to do."

The dead girl's murder, slice after slice after slice, flickered through Nathalie's mind as she nodded in agreement.

Relief passed over Nathalie, more like a breeze than a gust, when she mailed the letter. She was glad that it was gone, that someone else would now decide what to do with that information. And there was something satisfying about revealing part of her secret yet feeling protected.

As she exited the *bureau de poste*, she was fiddling with the button on her trousers and collided with a man heading inside.

Well. Of all people.

Nathalie couldn't say who was more surprised.

12

"Monsieur Gagnon," said Nathalie, taking a step back. "Imagine that our paths should cross here, too. Paris feels small lately, doesn't it?"

"Mademoiselle Baudin, is that you?" His ears turned as red as apples. "Small indeed."

Nathalie gave a brittle laugh. "Another delightful summer day perfect for strolling."

M. Gagnon tucked the letter he was carrying into his coat pocket, then eyed her from her shoes to her cap. "Your clothes," he said, using that official voice he'd used during their first encounter.

Nathalie straightened up. "What about them?"

"How come you have on, uh . . . why are you dressed like a young man?"

"Dresses aren't always convenient," she said, in a tone suggesting he should know that.

He turned his head askew without breaking eye contact. "That's why you're not wearing one? Convenience?"

"Yes. No," she said, her cheeks warming. She didn't want to talk about this, and frankly, it was none of his concern. "What brings you here?"

"Business." He glanced at the door and scratched his palm.

"Isn't that a sign you'll receive a letter?"

M. Gagnon returned his gaze to her with arched brows. "What?"

"Your palm." Nathalie silently thanked Maman for training her so well on the art of changing the subject. "There's an old wives' tale that an itchy palm means a letter is on its way. Or money. I forget which."

He patted his palms together and flashed a quick smile. "You're not going to explain the trousers and cap, are you?"

Nathalie folded her arms. She had never met anyone who was equal parts attractive and irksome. Each time she saw him, a different side emerged. What was this today? Was he being polite? Inquisitive? Awkward? Maybe he was all three. Simone had told Nathalie he was probably enamored with her, at least somewhat, but Simone often floated on a cloud of romantic thoughts. Not that Nathalie would mind if M. Gagnon *were* enamored with her. "I'd rather not."

"I won't pry," he said, shifting his weight. "Good day, Mademoiselle Baudin. See you at the morgue, I expect. Since you go every day."

"I—"

"It's understandable," he said. "There's a lot to see."

With that he turned on his heel and began to walk away.

"Monsieur Gagnon, weren't you on your way into the *bureau de poste*?"

He faced her again. "Oh yes," he said. He rolled his eyes in a deliberately amusing fashion. "Have a wonderful afternoon."

Nathalie grinned as he passed her and went inside. She didn't know what to make of him, but she was very glad he'd been noticing her.

When Maman brought in the letter from Agnès three days later, Nathalie tore it open so hastily she made Stanley jump. She had no memory of what she'd written Agnès—how much she had or hadn't told her about the visions—and had been anxiously awaiting her response these past few days.

Her heart pounded as she read.

Dear Nata,

Yes, I've heard about the murders and am astounded. First Pranzini, now this. What is becoming of our beloved Paris?

There are plenty of whispers in Bayeux about it, and Papa receives the Sunday edition of Le Petit Journal *by post once weekly. How can you be so casual about this affair? I can't think of anything more compelling, especially for the journalist who covers the morgue. Incidentally, your articles are superb—clearly expressed and thoughtful without lapsing into sensationalism. Consider yourself fortunate to experience this moment in journalism. I myself would be queasy seeing the victims, but you . . . Nata, you have the constitution for it. Are you not thrilled?*

It is hot here, but being a few kilometers inland, we have the benefit of an ocean breeze. We have gone to the beach twice thus far; once nearby, and once on a trek to the Deauville resort, where we stayed two nights. I met a strapping curly-haired boy from Rouen and flirted with him quite a bit. We had lunch together the first day, and he sang to me in Italian. You know what singing means to me—I do miss the choir at Notre-Dame—so this utterly charmed me. I was truly taken, ready to let him kiss me. Then he called me "Anastasia." I asked who she was, and after much prodding, he sputtered that Anastasia was a girl he'd met at the resort last week. He assured me she'd since gone home. I nevertheless sauntered off, pleased with myself for not kicking sand on him like I wanted to, and read Dostoevsky the rest of the trip.

As for the ocean, it is as breathtaking as ever. That's the thing about the sea, isn't it? It never really changes, and neither does its power to inspire awe. I suppose your father has a hundred stories to go with that sentiment. I cannot wait to see your face next summer when you lay eyes on the ocean for the first time.

Bayeux is small and intimate and full of history. Lace is produced here, and I have never seen so much lace in my life. (I am rather sick of it.) The cathedral is striking on the outside, though not as remarkable as some I've been fortunate enough to see. Vikings were here, can you imagine? And there's a tapestry depicting the Battle of Hastings. I saw it a few years ago. It's interesting, I suppose, but whoever sewed the horses did not concern himself much with accuracy.

The dialect here is unusual, but I've grown accustomed to it. There are several English-speaking shopowners here, so I have been practicing. We don't get to use German and English very often, but I'm still glad we have courses in them. I hope to become fluent in both. Then I can eavesdrop on tourists.

Oh, and there's a confectioner who makes the most delectable violet-flavored sweets. They are both smooth and crisp with some kind of jam. If you can believe it, Roger shared with me some he'd gotten for his birthday. I suppose he isn't completely terrible. Only mostly.

Are you taking part in the Bastille Day celebrations?

Tell me more about these murders—even that which you cannot include in your column. Could you send some newspaper articles, old and new, to fill in the blanks? Once weekly doesn't suffice.

Bisous,
Agnès

By the time she was done, she thought for sure both Stanley and Maman could hear her thumping heart. She held the letter to her chest.

So she hadn't told Agnès about the visions. That meant there was a part of her life, at least one part, that hadn't been tainted by them.

And she intended to keep it that way, for now.

Nathalie tucked the letter back into the envelope and sat down. She read through Agnès's letter one more time (of course Agnès would find a boy at a resort—the boys loved her), and before she went on about her day, she let herself daydream about the ocean for a while.

Paris took a breath, or perhaps heaved a sigh, for the next seven days.

Victim #2 would forever remain that, an unnamed sculpture in death: Her body was not identified. She had to be pulled from display in the morgue, despite the crowds coming to see her, because nature began calling her back to earth.

She was decomposing.

Le Petit Journal and the other newspapers did their best to keep the story alive that week, even during the trial of Henri Pranzini (sentenced to death by guillotine for the triple murder, Nathalie was satisfied to read). M. Patenaude referred to this recent slasher as "the Dark Artist" in an editorial, and the front-page illustration of the Sunday supplement imagined him as a monstrous, cackling brute. The artist depicted his face in shadow and had the Dark Artist standing alone in the viewing room at the morgue, wielding a knife in one hand and a painter's palette in the other.

The name took, even across the other daily papers. It also appeared to please the killer himself, who signed his third letter with the new designation:

> To Paris,
>   It's been silent, I know. I'm rather behind on my promise.
> I decided to write in advance of my next exhibit, should

you wish to queue up at the morgue early to get an adequate
place. I shan't keep you waiting long.

    Until the next one, I remain,

Ever yours,
The Dark Artist

Nathalie's bones had tickled from the inside out when she read it. The newspaper printed it a few days after she'd posted her anonymous tip. What if she had stood beside the Dark Artist at the *bureau de poste*? Or behind him in line? Just like the killer had been in the room the day she'd had her first vision.

She confided this, and other thoughts, to her journal (having since forgiven it about the memory gap). She wrote everything with as much belief as disbelief. Nothing came from her tip to the Prefect of Police, and while she hadn't expected it to, she still wanted to keep a record of details in case something else occurred. Observations about the morgue. Theories about the killer. Fragments of conversation she overheard here and there throughout the city. Her own woes and worries about the visions. Now that she'd made the decision to help from afar and didn't trust her memory, she wanted to be thorough. Just in case.

Something else nagged at her, too: what Maman had said about Aunt Brigitte seeing things. And since Maman refused to elaborate, Nathalie had but one choice if she wanted to find out what, if anything, that really meant. She needed to visit Aunt Brigitte alone.

After going to the morgue, an atmosphere infiltrated with dread thanks to the third letter, Nathalie made her way to the asylum. The sense of dread followed her; the hair on the back of her neck stood up more than once, and she found herself pausing every now and then, looking over her shoulder.

Perhaps because this was her first visit alone, aside from the childish excursion several years ago. She told herself it was no more or less unsettling just because Maman wasn't beside her, even as she stepped into the sluggish cage-door elevator with two nurses escorting a man in a straitjacket. Even as the three of them got off on a floor where a man with one eye gouged out tried to enter the elevator, only to be pulled back by a nurse. Even as Nathalie walked down the hall, past room after room of wordless melancholy and hushed isolation, save for the giggling woman sprawled on the floor outside Aunt Brigitte's room.

One of Tante's roommates was praying. Another stood at the window, tapping it like a telegraph and talking to a bird on the other side, begging it to bring her a worm to eat.

Aunt Brigitte was sitting on the edge of her bed, eyes closed, and fussing with her braid.

Nathalie whispered a hello to her aunt, who opened her eyes and smiled.

"Where's your mother?"

"Home. I was in the neighborhood today and thought I'd visit."

Aunt Brigitte scrunched up her face into a girlish grin and put out a bony hand to stroke Nathalie's cheek.

Her hand was so cold. So very cold. Nathalie didn't think you could be so cold and yet alive.

Aunt Brigitte went through her usual ritual of thanking Nathalie for coming and complaining about her roommates' eating and sleeping and praying habits. She did not, however, mention any dreams from the previous night. When Nathalie asked her if she'd had any, she grimaced.

"Nightmares," she said. "I don't want to talk about them."

Nathalie understood that well enough. No one cared to relive nightmares. Given the vivid nature of Aunt Brigitte's dreams and her fragile state of mind, Nathalie supposed her nightmares were doubly horrifying.

Her aunt sighed and fell silent.

As difficult as the next sentence was for Nathalie to say, she knew this was her opportunity. She cleared her throat.

"I learned only recently, Tante, that you—that you see things."

Aunt Brigitte's gaze fixed on her like an owl on the hunt.

"I mean before," Nathalie added, in a small voice. "Before . . . here."

Aunt Brigitte stared at her niece without blinking. "I know what I saw. I wanted to save the baby."

"What *did* you see?" Nathalie's tone was more apprehensive than intended.

Aunt Brigitte, after a quick glance at her roommates, motioned for Nathalie to come near.

"He was about to drown the child," she hissed. "The priest was getting ready to drown the child in the baptismal font. Do you know why?"

Nathalie was so close she wondered if Aunt Brigitte could hear her pounding heart. *Priest? Baptismal font?*

"It was his child. The mother was a nun. They were about to murder the child, right there in church, after baptizing it." She placed her hand on Nathalie's shoulder and pulled her closer yet. Her voice dropped to something just above a whisper. "If I hadn't trembled and dropped the knife, I could have slit both their throats. And saved the baby."

Nathalie stopped breathing.

It took her a few seconds to realize it.

"I ran away screaming. They didn't even come after me." Aunt Brigitte let go of Nathalie and sat back. "But they drowned the baby anyway. I hid in the bushes and watched them leave with the body. I would have tried again to kill them if I still had the knife."

Nathalie stepped back, swallowing hard. *This wasn't Maman's story.*

Aunt Brigitte clutched Nathalie's wrist. "Why did you ask?"

"I—I didn't know anything about this. Maman said you saw things, and she only told me about the Seine, and—"

"The Seine!" Her voice became as sharp as a sword. "Jealousy! Misunderstanding! He was a good man but they didn't see that."

Nathalie was even more confused. "He? The man you—"

She wanted to say the word "attacked" but stopped short. Aunt Brigitte's face fell.

"I know what I saw!" she cried.

Aunt Brigitte repeated *I know what I saw* over and over again, her cries erupting into heaving sobs. A nurse rushed in and tried to calm her down but it was too late.

The wailing only intensified.

Nathalie slowly retreated out of the room. *Trust no one.* Tante had a reason for saying that. It was somehow connected to this, her insanity, whatever it was that put her here.

Aunt Brigitte's roommate emerged from the room pulling her own hair, then reached for Nathalie's.

"No," said Nathalie, extending her hand. The woman frowned and began to moan. *She can't speak.* Nathalie hurried away from her and down the hall.

Aunt Brigitte's screams chased her right into the elevator.

13

Nathalie arranged the last of the newspaper clippings, straightened out the pile, and began to write her letter.

> *Dear Agnès,*
>
> *They are calling him the Dark Artist—and he has taken to the name. I needn't explain why, as the enclosed articles will explain everything. I would not advocate reading them prior to sleep, as you may have nightmares. I have had many.*
>
> *Do you think I have been casual in the sharing of it? Careful, perhaps. Or it could be that the journalist in me is accustomed to taking on the tone of reporting when I write. Thank you for your kind words about my articles (I have included others).*
>
> *You asked if I am thrilled. I have to say, this is without a doubt the most exciting set of experiences I have undergone directly.*

Nathalie paused. Would that suffice? Sending Agnès a number of articles, answering questions she asked directly . . . that should satisfy her curiosity. She hoped.

> *Bastille Day—I watched some of the parade on my way to work. It could have been my perception, but the crowd seemed thinner and more subdued this year.*
>
> *I've been thinking about the ocean. What does it feel like*

to stand in the sand, amidst the waves? Papa spends time on the sea, but rarely in it, and certainly not on holiday. I imagine the ocean water to be refreshing and powerful. How does it smell to you? Salty, I know. Papa says as much. What does that mean to you, though? It cannot be like the salt and water Maman makes me gargle when I have a sore throat. There must be more to it.

Those violet confections sound divine. Enjoy one on my behalf. I promise to dedicate my next pain au chocolat to you, in honor of sharing one together upon your return.

Bayeux sounds utterly charming. Vikings. I shall ask Maman to fashion a Viking hat for me for my visit next summer. What do you say of that?

Bisous,
Nata

A Viking hat. Nathalie chuckled as she put the paper and articles into an envelope. She could picture herself walking around a little town with it, Agnès laughing but mortified.

Maybe next summer would indeed be very different from this one.

The Dark Artist's third exhibit was far more grisly than the previous two.

If Odette appalled onlookers and Victim #2 magnified the savagery, then the atrocity committed on this girl's body spoke for all of them. Her inky hair was in a long, messy braid. It cascaded down her right shoulder and over her exposed breast, framing the deep, reddish-black ear-to-collarbone cut. She had the facial bruising of the others. What used to be her left temple was now a fist-sized cavity outlined in crimson and black.

Nathalie didn't touch the glass, however, because she and Simone had a plan. Yet she felt an unexpected tickle of desire. The vision was there, hers for the taking, if she wanted it. She shook her head forcefully, as if doing so would remove such thoughts.

She reached into her bag for the tube of catacomb dirt. For peace. For good luck. For something, whatever it could offer her right now. She wrapped her fingers around the glass vial, willing the perceived fortune to travel up her arm and spread throughout her body.

Suddenly Nathalie felt like she was being watched. Her eyes went to M. Gagnon, standing guard beside his black velvet curtain. He met her gaze without looking away and then smiled like someone who was in on a secret.

Nathalie returned the smile.

"If you want to gawk at him instead of the bodies," said a gruff voice to her right, "move over and let someone else see."

Heat slinked up her neck and onto her cheeks. She turned to see a stout man, a few days' worth of stubble circling his pout, behind her. "*Je suis désolée,*" she said, but he waved off her apology.

Nathalie peeked over her shoulder at M. Gagnon as she left the morgue. His eyes were fixed on the third victim. She'd never observed him studying the bodies before. If anything, he'd always seemed indifferent, probably so he wouldn't go mad seeing corpses all day. A colleague entered the display room and spoke, startling him.

The testy little man who shooed her along was coming toward the exit. He glared at her and opened his mouth to speak. Her priority was getting to Simone, not engaging with this undersized fool, so she hurried out the door and shut it before he could get through.

The flurry of curse words that followed her across the street told her, quite clearly, that she'd timed it just right.

Maman was at the tailor shop visiting her friends, so Nathalie took advantage of the solitude and wrote her column from home. After she changed into her trousers, she examined her reflection—not for vanity, but to make sure she was convincingly *not* a girl.

Her dark waves were tucked into a wool felt cap, making her long neck appear even longer. The trousers, tan and roomy, dropped over her sturdy shoes. This pair of trousers was several centimeters too short (she should have listened to Maman and waited until morning to hem them, but she'd mistakenly assumed she was skilled enough to do it in the dim candlelight). A straight-fitting white shirt, cuffs folded back, completed the ruse.

She grabbed her satchel, put it on like a messenger bag, and made her way to the steam tram depot.

Although Nathalie could pass as a boy from several meters away, a closer look would suggest otherwise; her features were undoubtedly those of a young woman. Dusted with freckles. A petite, slightly rounded nose, just like Maman. High, almost severe cheekbones, also from her mother. Inquisitive brown eyes, like Papa, but with long lashes.

From the chin down, she looked very much like a boy when she dressed the part. Being lanky and small-busted, for better or for worse, helped. A dainty chimera.

It was interesting, having to dress this way. Not every girl would have agreed to it. Agnès, always ladylike and well-dressed, envied the job but almost certainly wouldn't wear boy clothes for it or any other position. Simone probably would not only agree to it but embrace it unflinchingly, pretend it was a role (as she encouraged Nathalie to do), and somehow still be eminently feminine. As for Nathalie, she loved it as much as she hated it; wearing these clothes both empowered and embarrassed her.

Strolling freely across the floor of *Le Petit Journal* in costume, that part was amusing. She enjoyed playing a joke on dozens of people day in and day out. Not to mention, she was curious as to whether any of them guessed, or at least pondered, if that gangly "errand boy" was actually a girl. Writing a column that around a million people read made her proud. If dressing like a young man was what it took, then it was worth it.

Yet she hated obscuring her identity for no good reason. Dressing as a boy to earn respect, or to avoid disrespect, was not a *good* reason. It was an *unfortunate* reason.

Someday she would march through the doors of *Le Petit Journal*, head held high, in whatever feminine attire she wanted to wear. Maybe she'd walk into an important meeting wearing a long, flowing silk brocade skirt that Maman would praise, hair piled elegantly on her head, wearing ornate, graceful shoes with heels like she saw at Le Bon Marché. With the heels she'd tower over most of her fellow journalists and be eye-to-eye with the rest.

But today she was sixteen, in trousers and a cap, and walking quickly with her head down. M. Patenaude wasn't in his office, so she left her article with Arianne, who handed over some mail. The first few days Nathalie worked at the paper, she'd been excited to get mail, until she realized it was nothing more than advertisements, the occasional donation request, and internal memos that had nothing to do with her. She tossed the mail in her bag and left.

Finally she could go to Simone's. They'd devised a strategy: If there was a third victim, she'd get Simone and go back to the morgue. That way Simone could listen to whatever it was she mumbled during the vision and try to make sense of it.

Nathalie jogged up the stairs to Simone's apartment. She tapped on the door like a woodpecker, which Simone never found as amusing as Nathalie did.

Simone opened the door, pursing her lips before she spoke. "Normal people knock, you know."

"That's why I don't," Nathalie said, poking Simone's shoulder. She entered the apartment. "I hope I didn't wake you. Did I?"

Simone waved her hand. "The neighbors upstairs had a door-slamming fight about twenty minutes ago. *That* woke me. I was going to get up soon anyway." Studying Nathalie's anxious face, her eyes widened. "Are you here for the reason I think you're here?"

Nathalie nodded and spoke in a solemn whisper. "Another victim. With her skull bashed." She put her fingertips on Simone's left temple. "Here."

Simone mouthed a drawn-out "oh my," and less than fifteen minutes later they were on a steam tram heading back to the morgue. As they stood in the queue, Nathalie told Simone about her visit to Aunt Brigitte.

"Sometimes I wonder if those visions, the things my aunt claims she saw, were . . . I don't know. Real." Nathalie was relieved to share this thought, at last, with another person.

"You've told me stories about your visits," said Simone, a note of skepticism in her voice. "The woman who said she was painting a mural but she'd stabbed herself and smeared the blood across the wall. And that time a lady ran around shouting that the devil was chasing her and wanted to make her his bride. And a hundred other examples, not to mention your aunt's behavior."

This was true. Before her morgue visions, Nathalie was dismissive of the things Tante said and did. The ramblings of a crazy woman.

She reddened, ashamed of the reminder. "Lately I've been thinking it might be different with my aunt."

"Why? Because of your own visions?"

Nathalie adjusted the brim of her cap. "I don't know. I'm trying to figure that out."

"As sad as it is, remember that your aunt and those other people, they're locked up for a reason." Simone's tone was kinder than her words, which made them easier to take. "Most of them end up on the street or in the asylum because they can't tell the difference between imagination and reality."

Nathalie frowned.

What makes you so sure?

Simone had never met Aunt Brigitte. She only "knew" her

through whatever Nathalie shared. Nathalie turned away. "How do you know I don't belong in there myself?"

"Because you're you," Simone said, taking Nathalie gently by the chin. "Practical, smart, and, whether you like it or not, perfectly sane. A little weird and silly at times, but sane."

She answered with a bittersweet smile. Simone didn't know she'd stumbled on an uncomfortable truth. Nathalie knew from Papa's stories, and even her earlier memories, that Tante hadn't always been this way.

When did that moment happen, the shift from sanity to madness? Where was that final step, and did Aunt Brigitte know it was coming?

Would I?

The guard waved them inside, interrupting her thoughts. Simone patted her on the back as they crossed the threshold.

She was keen to touch the viewing pane, but Simone took more time to study the corpses than expected. Nathalie had to remind herself that what had become normal for her was still a spectacle for Simone.

Still a spectacle.

"These poor girls. Each one suffers more than the last." Simone stroked the viewing pane as if it were Céleste's cheek.

For a moment, Nathalie envied her for being able to touch the glass that way. No choice, no consequence. Just touching glass because it was there, a barrier between life and death.

Simone faced her. "I'm ready when you are."

Nathalie hesitated, fidgeting with the waist of her trousers. The scenes were in reverse, so would she speak backward? Demons spoke backward. That's what she'd read somewhere, anyway.

Louis had guessed that devil worshippers might be involved. Until they knew the Dark Artist's motives, nothing could be ruled out.

Then a thought chilled her. *This isn't some kind of possession, is it?*

She shook off the unwelcome thoughts and extended her hand, watching her fingertips meet the viewing pane. One breath later she was in the vision, looking down at two blood-spattered, white-gloved hands that were too big and powerful to be hers. And yet somehow they were.

The backward scene went from bloody to bloodless as the killer chiseled the victim's face. Steady, powerful strokes. This time Nathalie did more than see it. She *felt* the blade rip.

Everything continued in reverse. The knife disappeared. The girl's head bounced up like a ball into the killer's hands, then he tilted her to the side to inspect a deep wound on her temple. He pushed her toward the corner of a decorative wooden table and lifted her head in a swift, violent motion. The victim's eyes, full of tears, met his the moment before her death.

Then Nathalie was once again in the viewing room of the morgue.

Simone took her hand. "What happened?"

"I—*he* threw her down into the corner of a table," said Nathalie, her voice hoarse. "That's what killed her, so the slashes came after she was dead. And he was wearing white gloves."

"Knifing her after she was dead," said Simone, shaking her head. "How barbaric."

Nathalie took her hand out of Simone's. "I can't believe I didn't realize this all along. I'm not just watching like an outside observer. I'm not looking over the shoulder of the murderer. I'm seeing it through the eyes of the killer himself. And—and now I'm *feeling* it."

Nathalie shuddered. She'd rather have a thousand spiders on her body than have that feeling again.

Simone exhaled the way people do before delivering bad news. "Now it makes sense. The way you spoke, as if you *were* him. Inside him, almost."

Nathalie's stomach tightened. Somehow she was closer to the vision, more aligned with the murderer, than ever before.

"You said something that only could have come from the killer: 'My pretty, pretty Mirabelle.'"

Nathalie wrapped her arms around herself and gazed at the body on the slab. *Mirabelle.* Saying the name out loud . . . Was that why Odette's name had felt familiar when she learned of it? It must have been.

A man appeared beside them like an apparition, his spicy cologne filling the humid air around them. "*Pardonnez-moi!* Might I ask, what just happened?" His voice was honey dripping off a spoon into hot tea. Rotund and elegantly dressed, he tapped his white-gloved fingertips together with a grin.

When Nathalie turned to look at him, she had to stifle a scream.

White gloves.

Her heart became a rock inside her chest. Inanimate. She gasped for air and the rock became a heart again, beating faster than ever.

She'd seen him before. In line at the morgue. He was a detail, a face in the background. The day she had her first vision. The day the killer was in the same room.

And now, for no obvious reason, she'd had a vision that was stronger than ever. Closer than ever to the Dark Artist.

A shiver glided down her back.

No.

It couldn't possibly be.

14

Nathalie straightened up. "Who—who are you?"

The man, whose white mustache matched his gloves, cocked his head. Simone seized her elbow and yanked her toward the exit.

"Are you him?" Nathalie didn't care who heard. "Did you do this?"

The guard stepped between the gloved man and the girls. "Mademoiselle—"

"Let's go," said Simone, tugging some more. "You need some air."

"No, I don't. That's him, Simone. I know it is."

"He might not—"

"What are the odds?" Nathalie hissed. She glared at the man, who was now talking to the guard. "I've seen him here before and now I have this vision and then he comes up to us and—"

"It probably *is* a coincidence, Nathalie." Simone pulled her out the door. "You're being irrational. He's just a man wearing gloves."

"I *remember* him," Nathalie said. They walked toward a bridge, Simone still holding her arm. "He was there the day of my first vision, just like the murderer. I'll show you!"

They stopped at the edge of the bridge. Nathalie took out her journal and flipped to the page that described her first vision. "Look. Right there. I describe the crowd while I was waiting to get inside. Then I had the memory gap."

Simone stood beside her and read. ". . . 'A man wearing white gloves.' Yes, he was in the room, right, but—"

"You're the one who said to trust my visions. Today I was nearer than ever to the killer. *And* that man was standing right behind us. The gloves again, on a hot summer day? We should tell Gagnon," Nathalie said, pointing to the morgue.

Simone stepped back. "And what would we tell him, that the man was eavesdropping? Or about your visions?"

"No, I'd say—" Nathalie left the sentence in mid-air. Simone was right. "Well, we can't just walk away."

Now it was Simone who couldn't argue the point.

Nathalie tapped the side of her nose. *"J'ai du nez,"* she said. Her idea was both thrilling and ridiculous. "We'll follow him."

Simone looked over her shoulder. A couple with a puppy stood on the bridge, too absorbed in each other to notice anything. She lowered her voice anyway. "First, we can't be chasing every man in Paris wearing white gloves. Second, we're going to follow someone who, if your instinct is correct, is a killer? Only if we can go recline on the railroad tracks later, too, right when a train comes in."

"It won't be dangerous. What could possibly happen during the day with crowds everywhere?" Nathalie gestured to the streets, the shops, the cafés. People, people, and more people. With hurried steps she crossed the bridge and the street, Simone close behind, and pressed her back against a cobbler shop window. "And not *every man* in the city. Just him. We'll keep our distance. I just want to see if there's anything . . . unusual about him."

But there was something else. She knew all too well what it was like to be followed. Or *feel* like you were being followed. Something inside her hungered at the chance to reverse that feeling. To embolden herself against the memory of it.

Simone picked a thread off her blue polka dot dress and twisted it in her fingers. "I suppose it *could* be interesting to see where he goes from here."

"You know you're curious."

"I know *you're* curious," said Simone, placing the thread on

Nathalie's cap as if it belonged there. "I also think you're mistaken. I'll go along with this so you can get whatever proof you need that he *isn't* our man. How's that?"

Nathalie sulked. "You're quick to assume I'm wrong. Just wait."

A minute or so later the gloved man exited the morgue. They fell silent as he meandered across the bridge to the curb across from them, waited for a two-horse carriage to pass, and crossed the street.

Nathalie was about to retreat into the cobbler shop when the man, whistling away, took a right down the sidewalk. They peered around the corner. He passed a tobacco shop, a watch repair shop, and a butcher shop. Then he paused, inspected his pocket watch, and entered a confectioner's shop.

"Good choice, Monsieur Gloves," said Simone, who had a knack for assigning nicknames. "Pick us out a pair of bon bons."

Affecting a casual air, they strolled to the confectioner's shop. Sweetness floated under the awning, teasing passersby with notes of chocolate and caramel. Nathalie peeked through the window. M. Gloves inspected the candies in earnest delight and tapped his fingertips together.

"Is that how he views bodies at the morgue, too?" Nathalie muttered.

Simone either didn't hear her or acted like she didn't. Why was she so reluctant to consider him?

M. Gloves bought two large chocolates and popped one in his mouth. Simone and Nathalie wandered to the butcher shop window, pretending to read the price list on the door, until he left the confectioner's shop, still whistling. They watched him turn left and head down the sidewalk away from them.

"I suppose since we're here," said Simone, walking back toward the confectioner's shop, "we might as well get something. He's not in a hurry, and it's only right to be a patron of the shop at this point. My treat."

"*Merci*," said Nathalie, distracted. She didn't want to take her eyes off M. Gloves, lest he fade into the crowd. "I'll stay out here."

As Simone entered the shop, Nathalie watched the man settle onto a bench at a steam tram stop. Still whistling. He had the second chocolate in one hand, opened his jacket with the other, and—

Oh my.

There was a creature of some sort in his pocket, and he fed the chocolate to it. Nathalie moved closer to get a better view.

"Some partner you are." Simone nudged her from behind. "I come out with a chocolate-covered strawberry for you, and you're gone."

Nathalie took the strawberry from her without turning. "A rat. See? He's got a rat in his pocket, and he's feeding it."

Simone followed Nathalie's gaze. "I didn't know rats ate chocolate."

"I didn't know people kept them in pockets."

A steam tram pulled up before they could say anything else. M. Gloves tucked his rat away and headed for the open door.

"Let's go!" Nathalie hurried toward the steam tram, Simone at her heels mumbling something about tomfoolery. They hopped on and took a seat four rows behind M. Gloves on the upper level. He'd finally stopped whistling.

There they sat, stop after stop after stop for over an hour, with everyone getting on and off the tram except M. Gloves. They'd circled the route twice already.

"Maybe he knows we're following him and isn't getting off," said Nathalie.

"Or maybe he's just a strange man fond of gloves who has nothing to do but tour Paris via public transportation all day." Simone shook her head. "I'm sorry, Nathalie. I know you were hoping to discover something, but this was futile. I have to go to rehearsal. If I get off at the next stop and walk home, I'll just about make it."

Nathalie glanced at M. Gloves and back at Simone. "I can follow him myself."

"You're still not convinced?"

Nathalie didn't respond.

"I'm not getting off this tram unless you come with me," said Simone. Her mouth was twisted with exasperation. "I mean it."

Nathalie pressed her back into the seat. "I thought you considered him harmless."

"He is. But I still don't think it's wise to traipse around Paris all day. You're not thinking clearly, Nathalie. We're getting off the tram."

Nathalie knew that determined, big-sisterly look in Simone's eyes. This wasn't a bluff.

They were quiet as the tram took another corner and slowed to a stop.

"Well?" said Simone.

Nathalie pouted. She had no choice; she couldn't make Simone late for work going on an adventure that hadn't proven anything. Other than that the man kept a rat in his pocket and liked chocolate.

"The tram is going to move on if we don't get off now." Simone pleaded with her eyes.

Nathalie stood up with a slouch, taller than Simone and yet feeling much smaller. They stepped off the tram in silence.

"Please stop fixating on this man. It won't do you any good." Simone hugged Nathalie. "Also, the day after next is my day off. Céleste is sick again, and my mother asked me to look after her for a few hours so she can work at the market. Maybe after that we can go to the wax museum."

"I'd like that," said Nathalie, trying to sound engaged as she watched the tram. "I'll bring lunch to you and Céleste."

Simone crossed the street toward her neighborhood. Nathalie paused at the curb, watching people shuffle into the tram. A man startled her as he brushed by in a hurry to board.

She could just about see M. Gloves's head through the tram window. The tram pulled away, and right before it turned the corner, he turned around.

He met her gaze, staring at her until the tram went out of sight.

Nathalie remained unsettled for the rest of the day. She mostly moved her food around the plate at dinner (and fed some to Stanley under the table), claiming she and Simone had had a big lunch when Maman asked about her lack of appetite.

She hated lying to Maman, making excuses, telling her half-truths. She was bothered by the lies told and lies she prepared to tell; since the visions started, she'd chosen practicality over truth. The feeling of dishonesty sickened her.

Every day added another block of iron to the weight of this power. The luster of excitement was dulling, little by little.

Nathalie watched her mother, her scarred hands holding the fork awkwardly, the fine lines around her eyes and mouth that had grown more pronounced this summer. And while Maman complained that Nathalie was too thin, her own dresses hung more loosely these days. Her focus seemed to be understandably inward lately.

So there they sat, few words between them, each with her own set of worries.

She couldn't stop thinking of M. Gloves. It irked her that Simone had dismissed her suspicions. They were valid, and she didn't understand why Simone disagreed. That fingertip-tapping, whistling man. Were his eyes the ones through which she'd seen *My pretty Mirabelle*? Had she sensed his presence while having the vision? Was that why she felt so strongly about him?

Or maybe she'd made a mistake today about the white gloves in the vision. Perhaps she'd unconsciously seen M. Gloves on her way into the morgue. Her mind could have added that detail, the way Maman's voice sometimes became part of a dream if she was waking Nathalie.

No. She had to trust that the vision was real or else . . . or else she didn't know what. She'd become insane, that's what. She was under duress, but she wasn't *mad*. Besides, everything had been proven right and real so far. This episode shouldn't be any different.

Nathalie hated the idea of speaking the murderer's words during a vision. It made her feel unclean, intrusive. Too close to the mind of a killer.

She stared at the dull, benign knife in her hand, hovering over the plate. A knife. For cutting food. Meat. The face and neck of a young woman.

Her hand went limp and the knife fell, dropping onto the plate with a startling clang.

Maman and Stanley jumped. Nathalie apologized for the noise and excused herself from the table to finish a few chores.

Later that evening, when she reached in her bag for her journal, she pulled out a few papers and envelopes. She'd forgotten about her mail from *Le Petit Journal*. A charity, a reminder that the archive room was going to be reorganized, three advertisements. The last envelope was addressed to "Public Morgue Writer" like the advertising promotions, but had "A Fellow Writer" in the return address.

She opened it as she walked over to the wastebasket. *Ouch!*

The envelope sliced her finger. She licked the cut and unfolded the paper, ready to toss it in the trash, when her heart stopped like a painting, forever frozen in time.

My Dear Scribe,
  Bravo on the columns. Nicely done, though you're a bit shy with the descriptions of my work. Truly. Tell them about the sliced flesh, how it's red, black, and purple, except where the rot has set in, where it's of a brownish-green hue.

Tell them how the knife went in so deep it cut the bone.

Tell them how beautiful the girls once were, and how their delicate features have become grotesque death masks.

Tell them.

You would do well not to disappoint me.

Yours,
The Dark Artist

15

Nathalie practiced handing the letter to M. Patenaude a few times before leaving the apartment. At first she trembled during rehearsal, then she overcompensated by practically shoving it at the imaginary M. Patenaude.

When she actually stood there, in his office, she gave it to him almost as nonchalantly as she'd hoped. The paper shook only the tiniest bit as she offered it to him.

M. Patenaude took a long time to read it; clearly he reviewed it more than once. His glasses seemed thicker than usual today, and his expression was portrait-ready serious as he pursed his lips.

He looked up from the letter and put his glasses on top of his head. The motion was jerky, reminding Nathalie of a marionette. His words spilled out like water from a knocked-over glass. "We get a lot of mail from impostors."

"How do you know the letters to 'Paris' from the Dark Artist are real?"

He paused. Just a beat. Just long enough to make Nathalie wonder why.

"We don't know for certain," he said. He took a cigarette out of a case on his desk and lit it. "Instinct plus an educated guess. If you stay in the newspaper business long enough, you know what feels right and what doesn't."

On the one hand, she found his answer frustrating. *That's it?* On the other, it made sense. Policemen relied in part on instinct, as did chefs, bakers, and even seamstresses. Maman often spoke of making a dress as much from feel as from measurement. Why not reporters?

"Sometimes," M. Patenaude added, exhaling some smoke, "it's more art than science."

Nathalie peeked out the window. Building after building, boulevard after boulevard. Somewhere out there was a long hallway with a navy-and-gold runner and a room with a fancy table bloodied from a crushed temple and a killer who wore white gloves. "Do you think *this* letter is real?"

He took his glasses off his head and rested them on a stack of papers. He squeezed his eyes shut. "Yes."

Her skin prickled in response. "How do you know?"

"I know truth when I see it, and this is truthful." M. Patenaude opened his eyes and knocked some ash off his cigarette. "That being said, I need you to promise me something."

"What's that?"

"Don't tell anyone about the letter." M. Patenaude's tone was flat. "Why?"

He looked at Nathalie, away, and back at her again. He took a long drag from the cigarette and let it out in an O. "Because I said not to." His words marched out like patient, dutiful soldiers.

Nathalie's tongue tripped onto the start of a protest. Not that she knew what she was disputing other than the restriction itself. And his manner of delivering it.

"It's too risky," he added in haste, as if afraid he'd forget to say it. He cracked a smile that never reached his eyes. "You need to be safe. Do I have your word?"

"I promise to keep it to myself."

"Good." M. Patenaude tapped some ash into an ashtray. "I also think it . . . might be good if you took the rest of the week off. With pay. I'll get Kirouac to cover for you through Sunday."

"Why?" Her voice showed more distress than intended. She'd considered telling him about M. Gloves but was glad she didn't; if he knew she'd boarded a tram to follow a potential suspect, he might reassign her altogether. "I don't want to lose this position, Monsieur Patenaude. I am committed to writing this column and writing it well."

"You won't," he said, holding up his hand. He puffed the cigarette and placed it on the edge of the ashtray. "You're a model journalist-in-training, I assure you. This is only temporary."

Nathalie didn't want time off, but she nodded anyway. M. Patenaude was Papa's friend and was trying to protect her; he knew more than she did about these things.

"If another one of these comes in," M. Patenaude continued, picking up his glasses, "give it to me. I'll turn this one over to the police. I'd prefer that you stay anonymous."

Again he had a point.

"When I'm back on Monday, should I be more descriptive, like he said? It's rather off-putting . . ."

M. Patenaude dangled his glasses by the nosepiece. "Yes, as a matter of fact, I think readers will devour it."

She leaned back. That wasn't what she expected him to say. Or how she expected him to say it. She'd contemplated telling him about M. Gloves, to ask him his journalist-honed opinion. Now she decided against it.

"*Merci*," Nathalie said, looking down at her bag to tie it up. When she picked up her head, she caught M. Patenaude watching her in a way that was—well, she didn't know *what* to make of it. Odd, but he was an odd man. Penetrating, but he was evidently prone to such gazes. Curious, but he was a journalist, and journalists were inquisitive.

Even so.

It was only a flicker, but something about his expression told her he knew much more than he was saying.

The next morning Nathalie went to the morgue, just to see for her own self, and passed the time normally spent writing at the

Louvre instead. For the next few days, she'd pretend nothing had changed.

M. Patenaude's instructions meant she'd have to do exactly that. True, she didn't want to worry Maman anyway, yet the directive made her uneasy. More deception.

She was getting tired of it all. The visions, the strain she felt afterward, having to hide her power, and now this threat from the Dark Artist. For what? She should be gazing at the ocean that separated France and England, not gazing through the glass that separated the living and the dead.

Fortunately Maman was out with a seamstress friend when Nathalie returned for lunch. For today at least, she could avoid the discomfort of acting like she'd just returned from the newspaper. It was bad enough she'd left the house this morning in trousers to keep up appearances. The less she had to keep up the ruse, the better.

Nathalie changed into her normal clothes and took lunch, a cold tomato soup with chèvre, downstairs to share with Simone and Céleste, as promised.

"She's asleep," Simone whispered as she opened the door. Céleste was on the sofa, a miniature version of Simone but with dark brown eyes under those delicate eyelids. A wet washcloth was folded neatly across her forehead, and her face was flushed. "It's worse this time. Every time she gets a fever, it takes longer to break. She's had this one for three days. She's complaining of stomach pains now, too."

Simone kissed Céleste on the head as they walked past. The little girl stirred, a look of pain flashing across her face. She opened her eyes long enough to say a sleepy hello to Nathalie before rolling to the side to rest again.

"I—I didn't know she was this sick," said Nathalie. "I know you've said so, but to see her this way . . ."

"Upsetting, isn't it? This talkative little bunny, red-faced and unable to stay awake." Simone shook her head. "No one knows what it is, only that she gets better and then it comes back."

"She'll get better once and for all," Nathalie said, because what Simone needed most was hope, not a reminder of the uncertainty.

The two of them sat at the table, eating soup and talking in hushed tones, until Simone's mother returned from the market. Mme. Marchand, fatigued but pleasant, was most thankful for the soup.

A short while later, Nathalie and Simone rode the omnibus to the wax museum. Louis was so excited for Simone to see the newest tableaux that he'd gifted her with two tickets—one for her and one for Nathalie. He wanted, Simone said, for her to describe her impression to him rather than go with her. "He plans on writing a poem about our reactions," Simone said in a whisper, as if anyone on the bus knew Louis or cared about his poetry.

They followed four other people under the archway that had "Musée Grévin" written on it, presented their tickets, and entered the peculiar realm of wax figures.

Nathalie and Simone moseyed through a room of historical figures, musicians, and dancers. Simone yawned as they approached a cabaret tableau.

"Bored already?" teased Nathalie. "I thought the cabaret was never dull."

"It's not that," Simone said. "I just didn't sleep well."

"I didn't, either." Nathalie swallowed back the strong desire to tell her about the letter from the Dark Artist.

"Between Mirabelle and Monsieur Gloves and your aunt's baptismal font story about the priest and nun . . ." Simone let go of the sentence and pushed up her sleeves. "I opened the curtains wide and let all the light from the streets pour into the room. Too many thoughts in my wild imagination."

Nathalie paused before responding. Something didn't make sense.

"I'm not sure I understand," she began, drawing each word out with care. "I remember telling you the baptismal font story . . ." Dread tugged at her as she assembled the next sentence. "I don't remember hearing it from Aunt Brigitte. How could I tell you a story that I don't remember hearing?"

Simone cocked her head. "It happened the other day. When you visited her without Maman."

Nathalie stared at Simone, trying to figure out if this was a joke. But her demeanor was solemn, almost grave, and there was no spirited twinkle in her eyes.

"I remember being in the asylum," Nathalie said, recalling the moment she walked through the entrance the other day. "I—I don't recall that conversation with her."

Simone didn't blink. She studied Nathalie's face before speaking. "What *do* you remember?"

"She was braiding her hair, and she talked about her roommates. She usually talks about her dreams. That day she didn't because she had a nightmare and said it was too disturbing. Then—" Then what? A gap, like flipping ahead several pages in a book. The next thing she remembered was rushing home on the omnibus. She relayed all this to Simone, who filled in all the now-forgotten asylum details Nathalie had shared a couple days ago.

Nathalie's eyes fell on a wax version of Napoleon III. "I've been very forgetful lately. It wasn't just buying the flowers and having no memory of it. I went on the roof one night to write to Agnès and write in my journal. I don't remember coming back into my room afterward, but I woke up in my bed. I also don't have the faintest idea what I wrote to Agnès, and when I read my journal later, it was unfamiliar. And now this."

Simone put her hands on Nathalie's shoulders. "Something just occurred to me," she said. She bit her lip before continuing. "Yesterday you told me about visiting Aunt Brigitte, but today you don't recall most of the visit itself. You bought flowers for your mother while standing in line at the morgue—the same day you saw

Odette—and afterward didn't know how you got them. I wouldn't be surprised if that memory gap on the roof happened right after you saw Victim Number Two."

The thoughts in Nathalie's head slowed down. "They *were* all around the time I visited the morgue and had the visions. I thought it was—was just the strain of it all."

From there her mind sped up again. Too quickly.

She felt cold from the inside out, and the words echoed in her head as they came out of her mouth: "So every time I have a vision, I lose a memory."

Simone took a step back, her body tense. "It—it has to be. Why didn't we make this connection sooner?"

"Maybe on some dark, deeply buried level I suspected it." *But couldn't admit it to myself or anyone else.* "I don't know if I did or didn't. I don't know, I don't know."

"I mean, the only way to know is if it keeps happening," said Simone, tucking a tress under her hat, "although I can't think of another explanation."

If *it keeps happening.*

If.

"And," Simone added, "maybe it's only temporary. You might get those memories back after some time has passed. It's possible."

"It's also possible I won't." Her mind full of cutouts, like a string of paper dolls? She didn't need that.

Simone turned toward the tableaux. "Even so, is it really that disagreeable? Inconvenient, perhaps, but to forget that you've bought flowers isn't that disruptive. Every other old man forgets that, I'll bet."

"That's rather dismissive." As if Simone *wanted* the memory loss to be a minor detail worth overlooking. And now she had her back to Nathalie besides. "Especially when it isn't happening to you."

"For the incredible ability to see things? I'd give up a few memories."

Nathalie's ears got hot. This wasn't some stage show. It was her mind.

They moved to the next room behind a small crowd. As soon as Nathalie saw it, her limbs grew heavy. She couldn't move. She felt like she'd turned from girl to rooted tree.

There, in horrifying detail, was a wax depiction of Victims #1 and #2, Odette and the forever unnamed second girl, on a slab at the morgue. They were just as she remembered, mangled macabre siblings on a slab. The scene also included the viewing pane and, on the other side of it, a small crowd of people gawking.

"Can you believe it?" said Simone, who, Nathalie just now noticed, had been watching her.

"No," said Nathalie in an even voice, mustering a small smile. She uprooted her limbs to get a closer view. Every cut on the victims' faces was rendered carefully.

"They just unveiled it a few days ago. I was hoping you hadn't seen the posters. Louis was right. It's so realistic, isn't it?"

Nathalie had been to the museum many times before, just like she'd been to the morgue before she wrote for *Le Petit Journal*. She'd seen displays of crime scenes and battles and pieces of Parisian life. Everything was a potential tableau at the Musée Grévin; she should have expected it.

Who knows, thought Nathalie. The victims themselves may even have come here before they died. Or to the morgue itself, to gaze at the corpses they'd join.

"Almost too realistic." Had her own reports been used as a reference in its creation? She wondered if the artist who created the molds studied the morgue's photographs, if M. Gagnon himself handed him the documentation pictures. Or perhaps the artist stood there, in the viewing room, sketching. "Why—why did you want to show me this?"

"So you could see what you write about, what you experience, through the eyes of an artist, " Simone said. "I thought you might be impressed, maybe even find it thrilling."

Nathalie didn't answer. She felt redness spill across her cheeks.

"I meant to ask," continued Simone, "what did you send to the police—something about the gloves and the decorative table? Oh, and that her name is Mirabelle, naturally. Yes?"

"I didn't send anything to the police this time," said Nathalie.

Simone raised a brow. "Oh. When you do, then."

"I won't be." She made the decision as she said it. "I'm not doing this anymore. I—I can't."

"Meaning . . . ?"

"Meaning I'm tired of the ghastly visions, the constant what-ifs, the dishonesty, the realization that I'm seeing through a killer's eyes, feeling what he feels, and saying his words, all of it." *Including a letter possibly threatening my life.* "I'm not going to give up pieces of my memory now, too. That's losing my mind, Simone."

Nathalie closed her eyes, squeezing back the tears she was afraid would fall. She expected to feel Simone's arm around her shoulder or to be drawn into a hug.

"I don't understand," said Simone, shaking her head. "You're . . . giving up your power?"

Nathalie stood up straighter. The urge to cry disappeared like an extinguished flame. "I'm not *giving up.* I'm making a choice. Every peak is followed by a valley, can't you see that?"

Simone nodded, but it felt like she was humoring her instead of trying to understand. Simone seemed to be humoring her a lot these days.

"And now memory?" Nathalie folded her arms. "That's quite a sacrifice, and for what?"

"Because you have a chance to *help.*"

"We don't know that. So far it hasn't been much help to any-one. It's not like I've solved the case. Rugs and tables aren't going to solve a case."

"We knew this wouldn't be easy." Simone lowered her voice and rested her fingertips on Nathalie's wrist. "It even came up in the tarot cards. Remember the Hangman? Self-sacrifice, changing how you think?"

Nathalie jerked her wrist away from Simone. "They're only tarot cards, Simone. A parlor trick. Just because the cards mention sacrifice, that doesn't mean I should just accept losing my mind."

"I never said that!" Simone's voice rose so quickly that two women stopped talking. They stared for a moment before resuming their conversation.

"Not in those words." Nathalie folded her arms. "It sounds to me like I should be doing *what the cards* say I should be doing. Feeling what they *say* I should feel."

"That's not what I mean," said Simone, rolling her eyes.

I hate it when she rolls her eyes. "Then what do you mean?"

"If you'd let me finish a sentence, I'll tell you." Simone threw up her hands theatrically.

"No need for the flourish," said Nathalie, mocking Simone's gesture. "Just say what you want to say."

Simone gritted her teeth. "Stop interrupting *and I will.*"

One of the gaping women whispered something to the other. "*Occupez-vous de vos oignons,*" Nathalie snapped. Rarely did she tell people to take care of their own onions, so to speak, but these women deserved it. She waited until they turned away before continuing. "I'm done interrupting, Simone. Please explain to me whatever it is you want me to believe."

Simone looked from the tableau to Nathalie. "This is an atrocious set of crimes. *You* can do something about it. Not many people can; they just go to the morgue to gawk and gossip afterward. I don't think you should give up that gift so easily."

"Easily." Nathalie sneered. "*Nothing* about this is easy."

"I didn't say that it was!" Simone rolled her eyes.

Again.

"Where has sensible Nathalie gone?" Simone continued. "First you have us chasing an eccentric man with a rat all over the city, and now you're putting words in my mouth and arguing with me. Why are you *acting* this way?"

He threatened me! That's what Nathalie wanted to say, but she didn't. She couldn't. She'd promised she wouldn't.

Nathalie clenched her teeth. If she spoke, she'd burst into tears. She certainly didn't want *that* on display. The wax figures were the exhibit, not her personal fears.

Nathalie stormed out of the room, her heels thudding on the floor with an angry, determined pace. Simone followed her out, room after room until they reached the exit, all the way babbling about things like "persistence" and "special ability" and "destiny" and a slew of other phrases that climbed on top of each other.

Why me? "Why me? WHY ME?"

"Don't look at it that way."

"Don't tell me how I should look at it." Nathalie's whole body burned with fury, resentment, and a fear she wouldn't admit. "I cannot live like this. I *will not* live like this. I can't tell anyone but you about this bizarre curse. I can't wish it away or pretend it isn't there." She closed her eyes and sighed. "I can't unknow what I know."

"I understand, but—"

"*Non!*" Nathalie spat out the word like poison. "You wouldn't have brought me here thinking this would 'impress' me if you did. You don't understand. *No one* can understand. That's the point. I don't know, maybe my crazy aunt would. But that doesn't matter. I'm trapped. Trapped!"

Simone bit her lip for a long time before speaking in a calm voice. "You aren't trapped. We can—"

"Stop. Just stop." Nathalie held up her hand. She hoped Simone didn't notice the quivering. "No 'we.' I've had enough of you, too."

"What? What does that mean?"

Nathalie answered by pushing open the door and storming down the sidewalk.

Simone was going to follow her. She was sure of it.

Except Simone didn't.

Good. She's just in it for the adventure, anyway. And to impress Louis. And to make tarot card readings come true.

Nathalie couldn't see through her tears. Luckily her feet knew this pavement so well that it didn't matter.

16

Nathalie didn't want to go home yet.

She walked without knowing where she wanted to go. While standing next to some Spanish tourists, she noticed them studying a map. Her eyes fell to where they were pointing: Bois de Boulogne.

The perfect spot—a park where she could be alone among people and settle down on this hot-but-not-too-hot day. She'd gone there just before Simone had moved, on an unusually warm April day. The two of them had spent an afternoon there sprawled out on a blanket, eating fruit and madeleines and watching people. They'd invented stories about every young man who passed by and what their sweethearts might be like.

Already that seemed like ages ago.

She went to the nearest tram stop and hopped on right before it pulled away; her temper subsided with every *click-clack* of the tram. She had to change trams twice to get to Bois de Boulogne, and the trams were crowded, but she nevertheless felt a sense of peace by the time she stepped onto the grass.

All the trees were taken, with couples and families and solitary picnickers spread across almost every spot of shade. Nathalie strolled until she saw a mother and her little boy gather up their things, leaving behind a place in the shade just like the one she'd had in mind.

She reclined, limbs stretched out, and gazed at the sky framed by leaves of the nearby elm. She placed one hand on the grass, enjoying the feel of it through her fingers. With the other she loosened her top button and let her fingers rest on her collarbone. She didn't have the energy to move another muscle.

The sounds of the park, distinct and discrete, soon became a hum that was neither noise nor symphony. After running through the events of the day several times, her thoughts began to drift.

To Simone, and the last time they fought before today. It was just over two years ago and about a self-centered, brooding boy who was a bad influence on Simone. Simone disagreed, and they didn't speak for a month, which was when Simone decided that the boy was in fact both self-centered and brooding. Nathalie had felt regret rather than validation, though, swearing never again to pass judgment on Simone's beau choices. As for Louis . . . it didn't matter now, did it? Not if she and Simone weren't talking anymore.

She thought about Agnès. Her interest in the murders, and Nathalie's choice to keep the visions from her. Maybe now she'd tell her, now that it was an experience in the past.

Her thoughts drifted to Papa, too. She missed him, plain and simple. He'd been home several weeks before Maman's accident. And then he was off again, like he often was, for months and months. He wouldn't be back until September. Then he would be with them through January or February, and Nathalie was already thinking about how they'd play cards, visit the Louvre and Catacombs, and make soup together. And bread. Papa loved to make bread.

Then she thought about the last time she'd seen Aunt Brigitte "on the outside," prior to her committal to the asylum. Nathalie remembered wearing the bright red winter coat her grandmother had made her for Christmas. The coat was too big and too puffy. (She suspected that Mamie thought she was ten, not seven, because Mamie was very wrinkly and forgot stuff. At the time, Nathalie thought maybe wrinkles made people forgetful.) Maman insisted she wear it all the same. The only good part was that she also got to wear her new boots, which meant she could stomp in the slush when Maman wasn't looking. And even once when she was, which Nathalie pretended was an accident.

They'd gone to see Aunt Brigitte so they could help her pack and tidy up the room she rented from old Mme. Plouffe.

"Where's Tante going?" Nathalie asked as they approached the white stone house with ivy in the front.

"To a place where they can help her," Papa said.

"Why does she need help?"

"Because she has a sickness."

Nathalie didn't understand that. Aunt Brigitte was skinny, but she walked quickly, and she never coughed or said she had a belly-ache. She didn't *look* sick. "What's wrong with her?"

Papa and Maman talked to each other with their eyes, as Nathalie thought of it, and then Papa answered. "She forgets things."

"Like Mamie?"

"Somewhat."

Nathalie wasn't sure whether or not she could believe Papa. After all, Aunt Brigitte didn't have wrinkles and her hair was brown, not gray. "Then how come Mamie doesn't need help?"

"Your grandmother has Papi to take care of her," Maman said, taking her by both mitten-covered hands and stooping down to make eye contact with her. "Tante is lonely. She wants to be with more people, and the nurses will help make her stronger."

With that Maman kissed her hands (more properly, her mittens), a gesture Nathalie knew meant "no more questions."

Aunt Brigitte never had an apartment, not that Nathalie remembered. She just rented a room from a kind elderly woman who "helped women like Brigitte," as Papa described it. Mme. Plouffe had lots of rooms and lots of people living in her home—how could Tante possibly be lonely?—and she cooked for them. Sometimes she played the piano for them after dinner, Aunt Brigitte said. Whenever Nathalie visited, Mme. Plouffe gave her a cookie or biscuit. She was a very nice woman, Nathalie thought, and it was too bad Tante was leaving. Nathalie hoped the next place had a nice woman who gave out sweets, too.

Papa lifted her up so she could use the knocker ("only three times and not too hard," Papa said). Mme. Plouffe opened the door, an unusually serious expression on her face, and let them in. She whispered something to Papa while Maman and Nathalie took the stairs to Aunt Brigitte's room. Papa followed.

Aunt Brigitte sat at a small table playing solitaire. She got up to give each of them a hug and was all smiles, as though she were welcoming them to a party. The room, dark and smelling of flowers Maman called "gardenias," was covered with papers. On the floor, on the bed, even on the gardenia plants. Papa asked Nathalie to sit at the table with Tante so he and Maman could organize the room and pack the bags.

"Do you want to learn how to play?" asked Aunt Brigitte.

Nathalie bobbed her head. For the next few minutes she watched as her aunt played solitaire while explaining the game. She stole glances at the papers Papa was gathering as Aunt Brigitte spoke. Then Nathalie couldn't stand it anymore. Curiosity prodded her the way that toothy oaf Jacques poked her in class to try to get test answers.

"What are all the papers?"

"It's my story," said Aunt Brigitte, pride lighting up her face. "Let me show you." As she leaned over to pick up one of the papers, her blouse lifted.

Nathalie gasped. "Your stomach!" she hissed.

Maman and Papa were talking; they didn't hear anything.

"Just a few boo-boos. I'm okay." Aunt Brigitte patted her belly with a flinch and handed Nathalie the paper she had picked up. "I know you're a very good reader. Read my story."

She took the paper but her eyes were still on her aunt's stomach. Maybe that's what her parents meant when they said Tante was sick, because those boo-boos must have hurt. Nathalie looked at Maman putting clothes into a valise and at Papa stacking papers. *Did you see?*

She placed the paper on the table and sat on her hands. At the top was one word, written in big letters. INSIGHT. Nathalie didn't know that word, but she memorized it (she was very good at both memorization and spelling) and would look it up later. She tried to read the words below it and frowned. Aunt Brigitte's handwriting was too hard to read, almost like scribbling. Not neat like Maman's.

"Brigitte!" And like that Papa was at her side, his big hand flattened over the paper. "She's only a child. This isn't meant for her eyes."

He snatched the paper off the table, and before Nathalie could blink twice Maman had her by the hand.

"Come," Maman said. "Let's go see Madame Plouffe. I think she has a cookie for you."

Nathalie slipped off the too-tall chair. She waved to Aunt Brigitte, who smiled.

"Maman," Nathalie whispered. "Tante's belly."

Her mother crossed the room, her hand clasping Nathalie firmer with each step.

Nathalie whispered even more softly. "It's full of tiny red crosses, like someone pushed them on her and made her bleed."

And then Nathalie felt it. Gloved hands around her throat. She turned enough to see Aunt Brigitte's face hovering over her own and the grip growing stronger until . . . she tried to breathe—

Her eyes opened, and she saw a blue sky with leaves and branches around the edges. Nathalie blinked several times. It was all a memory, all save the very last part. Aunt Brigitte had never tried to choke her. Not ever. That must have been when she'd fallen asleep.

Nathalie's hand was on her neck, resting now, but her fingers felt tight, strained.

Anything but relaxed.

17

Nathalie gathered her satchel and headed to the Arc de Triomphe, where she took a crowded omnibus down the tree-lined Champs-Élysées avenue. She got off at the Place de la Concorde, beside the Louvre gardens, sick of passengers and of sitting. Going the rest of the way home by foot would take a while, but she needed to release some energy.

At first she didn't walk; she paced, like the restless black panther at the Ménagerie in the Jardin des Plantes. Whenever she went to the zoo she made it a point to visit that panther. It didn't matter what the weather, season, or time it was; the panther paced almost incessantly, stopping only for feeding time.

But she wasn't a panther and she wasn't confined, so there was only so much pacing she could do. She resumed walking. She wanted to tire herself out, to be fatigued enough to collapse when she got through the door. It would be a welcome relief from all of . . . this. There was no other term to describe it. *This.* All she had to do was give in to weariness.

She couldn't, and she wouldn't. Not yet, anyway.

Those papers in Aunt Brigitte's room preoccupied her after that memory-dream. She hadn't given the papers a thought in years; in fact, she'd forgotten about them entirely. Ever since she'd left the park, they'd consumed her thoughts.

After all, it was better than thinking about the Dark Artist, who may or may not be M. Gloves, what he was doing now, and whether he had his eye on her a week ago. Yesterday. Now.

It was also better than thinking of Simone, who, Nathalie decided, had simply changed too much since moving away. The old Simone would never have gotten so caught up in the idea of a "gift" that must be nurtured at all costs, even memory loss. No doubt Le Chat Noir and all its influences, including Louis, played a role in Simone's fantastical notions.

She took a route along the Seine. In her periphery she saw something in the river, floating. *Another body?* She whipped her head around.

A bather. Just a girl cooling off, lying on her back. The girl lifted her head and spoke to a friend sitting on the bank, who then plunged into the water with a splash.

Nathalie scoffed. *Au revoir, visions. I won't miss the paranoia.*

Tranquility had been rather standoffish toward her lately, and she hoped to reconcile with it soon enough. For good.

With a sigh, she reached into her bag for her vial of catacomb dirt. Her fingertips explored the bag until they bumped into the glass. She clutched the tube.

It felt different in her palm. Shorter, fatter, bulkier.

She yanked it out of the bag. A small jar containing dark red liquid.

Blood.

Nathalie stumbled and almost fell into someone. She moved to the wall, pressing herself against it for support.

Breathe.

Perhaps it wasn't blood. Just a rash assumption prompted by the sight of the girl in the river.

She raised the jar to eye level, tilting it to see the consistency. The sticky way it streaked against the glass, the slight thickness of fluidity—she was right. She wanted to be wrong because that would mean this might be harmless or a prank or even a mistake. And it would mean she wasn't standing here beside the Seine, with a jar of someone's blood in her hand, in this bizarre life that felt like it belonged to someone else.

Then she noticed something else inside the jar. Thin, opaque.

She unscrewed the lid and sniffed, cringing at the unmistakable metallic smell. A slip of paper was submerged in the blood, all except for a tiny corner.

Some leaves tumbled with the breeze over her feet. She picked up a few, making them into a cradle in her hand, and pulled out the paper by the clean edge. Blood droplets fell to the ground. Disgusting. She held it away from herself and placed it on the leaf cradle.

The paper had something written on it. Even with the blood, the ink showed through clearly. Just one word.

Inspiration.

She crushed the leaf cradle over the paper and made a fist.

Whose blood? Why? When? On the omnibus . . . no, she was far too aware of pickpockets and always held her satchel close in a crowd.

The park? It could have happened while she was asleep. She tried to picture M. Gloves, strolling up to her sleeping body, whistling with his rat in his pocket. The image didn't fit, and she couldn't say why.

Or . . .

No.

The thought was too much to bear and made her want to become water and seep into the dry earth. Like blood back into the wounds in her visions.

Maybe she had encountered the Dark Artist and couldn't remember.

He might have approached her. Threatened her. Done something to her. And she couldn't remember. Maybe the nap wasn't a nap—the dream started out as a memory—but a new kind of memory gap prompted by . . . by what? Seeing the wax figures of the morgue, the argument with Simone, something else? Something might have happened. Or it might not have.

She couldn't say for sure.

"Is that blood?"

Nathalie looked up to see a young woman in a black habit, frilly white cap, and black veil. She recognized the garb as that of the Sisters of Bon Secours who tended to the sick.

"It—it is," said Nathalie.

The nun glanced from the bottle Nathalie held in one hand to the fist she'd made in the other. Her inquisitive green eyes swept up to Nathalie's face.

"It isn't mine." She shrugged. "I don't know whose it is. Some-one . . . put it in my bag, I think." *I hope. Because as disturbing as that is, it's better than forgetting that I met the killer.* "I just discov-ered it."

The truth was absurd. She knew how she must have appeared, what she must have sounded like. But she couldn't lie to a nun.

The nun leaned in close. "Do you need help?" Her eyes searched Nathalie's neck and arms, presumably for signs of physical harm.

Nathalie shook her head.

"I can bring you to a hospital," the nun whispered. "I'll stay with you until your family comes. Do you have family?"

Her tone was compassionate, her expression caring. Yet also careful, the way Maman spoke to Aunt Brigitte when she wasn't making sense.

"I do have family, thank you. I'm on my way home right now. I—I don't need to go to a hospital," Nathalie said, glancing at the blood jar.

"Are you sure?"

"Yes."

The nun, gazing at her with a mixture of sympathy and pity, patted Nathalie's elbow. She closed her eyes slowly and then opened them again. "Very well." With a bow, she walked away.

"Pray for me, Sister," Nathalie called after her.

The nun turned and smiled faintly. "I already am."

* * *

Nathalie dangled her feet over the Seine. Sitting on the cement was uncomfortable, and she was still too anxious to stay put for very long, but she needed to think.

She hated her life. She wished that rather than touching the morgue glass that first time, she'd smashed it instead. If she could go back in time, that's exactly what she'd do.

The visions had ruined everything normal and good. Her sense of reality, and her imagination, blended together in the worst possible way. Her relationship with Maman. Her friendship with Simone. Her honesty in writing to Agnès. Her ability to sleep. To eat. To remember.

And the Dark Artist, what did he care? He had no way of knowing about her ability. Who did he think he was tormenting? The girl at the morgue or the anonymous journalist responsible for the morgue report? He couldn't know she was both.

Could he?

He could have been following her every move since that first vision. Or he could be playing a game like he did with the police and *Le Petit Journal*, sending in his stupid letters. He might know everything about her. Or nothing. Between falling asleep and her unreliable memory, she couldn't trust herself.

Now what?

Inspiration. Obviously she didn't understand what that meant. That was the point, no doubt. To confuse her and make her wonder what some deranged murderer intended with his ambiguous messages. But she wasn't going to do that anymore.

Why me? For all of this, why me?

The blood served no purpose other than to taunt her. If she brought it to the police, they wouldn't believe her, whether she claimed it was a stealthy deposit or an encounter about which she had no memory. Even if the police did, somehow, take her seriously, there wouldn't be anything they could do about it. They couldn't tell if it was the blood of a Dark Artist victim or a rat from the sewers.

Nathalie emptied the blood into the river and let go of the bottle. Then she threw in the lid, followed by the crumpled leaves holding the bloodstained paper. She watched the blood dissipate and the jar fill with water until the river swallowed it completely. The leaves and paper floated away a meter or so before starting to sink. She put her hands in the river, letting the current flow through her fingers. Then she stood up, wiped her hands on her dress, and walked home as quickly as her legs would take her.

18

The only solace Nathalie had for the rest of the day, aside from the comfort of Stanley at her feet, was a letter from Agnès.

Dear Nata,

Oh my. I have read those newspaper clippings again and again. Please send more. I want to know everything about the Dark Artist and these murders. What a tremendously exciting time to be in Paris. I dare say that my curiosity would outweigh my squeamishness and that I might be observing at the morgue right alongside you.

Do you have any guesses? Are you hearing anything at the newspaper that hasn't been published? How do you think he gathers his victims? You must be terrified to be alone on the streets. Be careful, my friend.

We went to an apple orchard the other day. Although the apples are not yet in season, walking along the rows and rows of stout trees was a delight. They are all lined up like sturdy dominoes. Lush and fragrant. However, bees are quite fond of them and Roger got stung. It probably makes me an awful sister, but I told him to stop crying and that he deserved it anyway. Just a few minutes before, Maman had told him to stop running about so wildly. Of course he didn't listen, knocked over my nearly full basket, and didn't help pick up the apples. I threw one after him and missed. I am glad the bee had better aim.

I thought of how to explain the smell of the ocean to you and still am not sure I have an adequate description. Salt and water, as you say, and life. Also death and rot—as with seaweed—but even then, it's a welcome smell. If movement and strength and beauty have a scent, it is the ocean. I suppose that's not entirely helpful, is it? You shall see for yourself next year, I hope. Adorned with your Viking hat perhaps.

Bisous,
Agnès

She wasn't sure how she was going to respond about the Dark Artist, nor did she want to think about that right now. For now she was just grateful for her friendship with Agnès and couldn't wait for her to come home.

Tendrils of regret crept toward her during the night.

Nathalie didn't notice them at first. Not as she lay awake, proud of wresting control from this ability, from the Dark Artist, and from Simone's misguided influence. They were there, in the shadows, but she was too defiant to see them.

Then they reached for her in dreams about Simone—good, happy dreams reminiscent of good, happier days. The sorts of dreams that would fool her, upon waking, into thinking all was well between them and she could spring out of bed to tell Simone about the blood jar. As if things were still that way.

Those tendrils came closer yet the next morning, when she read about Mirabelle.

An anonymous tip submitted at the morgue yesterday suggested that the victim's name was Mirabelle. This was confirmed hours later when the victim's cousin identified her as Mirabelle Gregoire, who'd quarreled with her husband and had left their home in Plaisir, nearly 30 km outside Paris, several days prior.

Nathalie's face grew itchy with heat. Simone. Who else would have given M. Gagnon the name?

That wasn't Simone's vision. It wasn't her detail to share.

To her this is exciting. Stimulating. A thrill.

Nathalie could trust no one. Aunt Brigitte, in all her delirium, was right about that.

Then the first wisp of doubt seized her. If she couldn't trust Simone to understand, then she couldn't trust anyone to do so. Especially without evidence. Disposing of the blood and the note had been rewarding at the time, but now who would believe that the bottle of blood had existed at all? She wasn't planning on telling anyone about it and had no reason to . . . not now, anyway. Someday she might. And then what? She'd be deemed hysterical or some such nonsense. Right back to where she started.

She cut the tendril back. What was done was done. It didn't matter.

Did it?

If the Dark Artist referenced "Inspiration" or blood in one of his taunting letters to the police, it might.

No. Speculation is one of the reasons I put an end to this absurdity. I'm tired of fixating on answers.

And wasn't that why she'd become so preoccupied with M. Gloves? Not that he flawlessly matched her ideas of who a killer might be, how a killer might look and act. The man drew attention to himself and seemed oblivious about it, for goodness sake. But she'd wanted an answer. Any answer. Because any answer was better than what they had now, which was no suspects and no theories and no anything but ripped-up girls on a slab. Maybe M. Gloves was the killer, but for the first time, she gave weight to the idea that maybe he really wasn't.

She sheared that tendril, too.

New regrets grew more quickly than Nathalie could keep up. It would take another two days for them to coil around her heart completely, a vine of doubt intertwined with other sentiments: anger and shame, uncertainty and fear. Relief. A longing to forget.

Maybe those cracks in her memory weren't such a bad thing. Maybe she needed more of them. Enough to forget all of this.

She'd heard of one way to forget something once and for all. Every day she saw the advertisement in *Le Petit Journal*.

Hypnosis.

Yesterday she'd read an account in the newspaper about a woman's experience with hypnotism. One day, she'd woken up *convinced* she'd taken a trip to London when in reality she'd never been. Lo and behold, the paper reported, her parents had made a voyage there when she was three. The memories were there, just buried. The hypnotist had made sense of it all.

If hypnosis could uncover a memory, maybe it could cover one back up.

The thought of ridding herself of this blessing-curse or curse-blessing once and for all suddenly called to her like a Siren. There was hope in the unknown, and it was worth a try.

An hour after reaching that decision, Nathalie was walking down a narrow alleyway on the Left Bank looking for *Étienne Lebeau, Hypnotist & Phrenologist*.

Phrenology. That had to be the most absurd practice in existence. The belief that you could "read" a person's character by studying the shape of his or her skull was preposterous.

It was so preposterous that it wasn't frightening. It was merely nonsense.

Hypnosis, on the other hand, wasn't nonsense. Nathalie believed it was quite the opposite. And, even though she felt apprehensive, hypnosis just might end this struggle.

She didn't have a precise address; the advertisement said Rue Xavier Privas and nothing more. The twisted cobblestone path sneered at her with fickle shadows and unexpected turns, obscuring all but the next few paces at a time. She walked past a wine shop, a dentist (she had never been and hoped never to go), a tanner, a milliner. Had she not pressed against the building a moment to step over a pair of cats, a chubby gray-and-white mother cat nursing her kittens and a tawny tomcat, she might have missed the small yellow, weather-worn placard altogether. No bigger than a book cover, M. Lebeau's sign had an illustrated finger pointing up a dark stairwell that looked like it hadn't seen a human in decades.

Nathalie reached inside her bag for the vial of catacomb dirt and put it in her dress pocket. With a deep exhale, she placed her foot on the first step.

"It will be fine."

She turned to the voice over her shoulder and saw a red-haired young man with a knowing grin.

"Monsieur Carre," she said, overly formal on purpose. She peeked over his shoulder to see if Simone was nearby. Thankfully not. "Fancy that we should meet here of all places."

"Oh," he began, waving his hand. "I followed you."

"You what?"

"Not like *that*." Louis smoothed his crisp white shirt collar. "I work at The Quill, the bookshop back there. I saw you pass by and called to you, although I suppose you didn't hear me . . ." His words ticked up the scale of uncertainty.

Nathalie remembered passing a bookshop. She hadn't heard anyone call after her, but then again, she'd been focused on her task. The area was raucous, with shop owners luring customers and women shouting conversations across the alley from one third-floor window to the next. "I didn't hear you."

"The street can be noisy at times. I—I was hoping I could talk to you for a moment. Simone told me that the two of you—"

"Please, Monsieur Carre—"

"Louis."

"Louis. Please. I don't wish to discuss Simone. And if you'll excuse me, I have—I have something to tend to," she said, glancing up the stairs.

His smile slipped from knowing to wry. Simone hadn't told him about the visions, had she?

"I went to him once," Louis said, in that conspiratorial way of his. "You're somewhere between dreaming and wakefulness. The old man puffs opium but is harmless."

Opium? Nathalie gazed up the stairs and took her foot off the step. Maybe this wasn't such a good idea. She'd heard stories of people smoking opium but didn't know much about it other than what Papa had shared from a trip to China: People gathering in rooms, lounging about on pillows, puffing away until they talked about things like flowers that cackled and houses that cried.

How could an opium smoker concentrate well enough to do hypnosis?

"I apologize for startling you, Nathalie. Simone is upset by the rift, and—maybe you two can talk sometime, that's all. Good luck with the hypnosis." Louis nodded a farewell and strolled back the way they came. Nathalie watched his fiery hair bob through the crowd, down the first turn, and out of sight.

A rat darted out from under the stairs, spooking her. It spotted the tawny cat and disappeared behind a sack.

Go. If he can make you forget you ever had visions at the morgue, then it's worth trying no matter what he smokes.

She marched up the steps and knocked on the door.

19

"Hypnotism or phrenology?" came a high-pitched male voice from behind the door. Before Nathalie could answer, the door swung open and a slender, gray-haired man with glasses, rosy cheeks, and a brown suit that had seen better days smiled at her.

"Uh, hypnotism," she said, glancing back down the stairwell.

"*Excellent!*" He invited her to enter. "I did three phrenology readings today and am ready for a good hypnosis. Étienne Lebeau, by the way, as you know from the sign."

Nathalie introduced herself and stepped into a cavernous room lined with columns of books. They resembled crooked little smokestacks, covering all but the windows. She glanced at the titles at the top of the piles closest to her. *Neurypnology.* Was that a word? *Suggestive Therapeutics: A Treatise on the Nature and Uses of Hypnotism.* Boring. *Enchanted Science or Science Enchanted?* Sounded like a riddle. *On the Origin of Species.* At least that one she'd heard of.

"Please, come sit," said M. Lebeau, gesturing to a gold damask sofa. "Have you ever undergone hypnosis before?"

"I have not."

"Splendid!" he said, clasping his hands. He then described the process: that he would guide her to a relaxing state of mind, that he would use the sound of his voice to reach her, and that she couldn't and wouldn't do anything that would violate her free will.

A white-haired woman with bulging eyes and dozens of beaded necklaces stepped out of the back room. "I'm Madame Geneviève Lebeau," she said, straightening out her floral dress. She then took

Nathalie's hand, warmly, and spoke in a near whisper. "May you find peace."

With that she beamed and shuffled over to the maroon drapes, closing them. Grayness swaddled the room like a blanket of mist. Sunlight crept around the edges of the drapes and created shadows where there hadn't been any before. Mme. Lebeau slipped into one of them and disappeared into the back room.

M. Lebeau took a seat across from her in a wooden chair and, placing his hands on his knees, leaned toward her. "Now for the most important question of all. What are you hoping to achieve in today's session?"

"I want to forget some events I experienced." On the way here, she'd explored all the possible ways to answer this question. This response seemed the most careful while still allowing her to be truthful.

"May I ask what kind of events?"

She turned her head to the side as if he'd sneezed on her. This, too, was deliberate. "Violent, criminal things. Please understand that it's difficult for me to discuss."

"Oh," he said, lowering his voice. "I won't pry. I should tell you, however, that forgetting an event doesn't mean letting go of the fear of that event."

Nathalie frowned. "Why?"

"Say you were afraid of snakes because you'd been bitten by one as a child. I could help you to forget that episode, but your mind would still fear snakes, though you wouldn't understand why."

"That's worse."

M. Lebeau nodded empathetically. "Perhaps you can use the session to try to make peace with those events."

"I doubt that," Nathalie said, but then she reconsidered. She'd come this far, and there was no harm in seeing if that was possible. "Let's try that, then."

"Good," said M. Lebeau. "Do note that during hypnosis you may share things you wouldn't in a fully conscious state."

"I understand. May we begin?"

"In a moment." M. Lebeau stood up, disappeared into the room where his wife had gone, and returned with a long pipe and a large, covered bowl. "Opium. I like to clear my head before each session."

Was that what his wife was doing back there?

"Doesn't that cloud your thinking instead?"

"Only if I have too much, which I never do while I'm working. With just the right amount my mind opens up like a butterfly emerging from its cocoon. That's how I prepare to set *your* mind free, make it even more open than my own. Would you like some opium as well?"

Nathalie shook her head vigorously.

"Very well." M. Lebeau tapped the sides of the bowl, studying her. "Are you ready, Mademoiselle Baudin?"

"No. I—I don't think I can do this."

"Why?"

"Because—" Her tongue tripped over the excuses and unfurled the truth. "Because I'm afraid."

"Close your eyes," said M. Lebeau in a placid tone, exhaling smoke. "And we'll work on helping you find peace. Shall we?"

There was a kindness about him, a tenderness in his voice, that was grandfatherly and reassuring. He reminded her of a sweet librarian, long since dead, who'd recommended books to her and Papa years ago.

"Yes," she said, reclining on the sofa, eyes closed. "I'm ready."

In a moment she heard nothing at all, as if the books lining the walls had shushed the sounds of Paris so Nathalie could, at last, retreat into herself.

"You are floating on a cloud. Carefree, comfortable, and safe," began M. Lebeau. His voice, melodic and serene, dissolved the silence. "The sound of my voice will guide you, show you where your mind can go. Relax on that cloud. Feel yourself, lighter than air. Your feet. Your legs. Your back, shoulders, neck. Your head. All are cradled by this peaceful, protective cloud. You are content."

Nathalie's breathing steadied into a calm, deep rhythm. The cloud was softer than any pillow she'd ever touched, the sky surrounding her was more beautiful than any blue she'd seen in nature or in art.

"I'm going to tap your shoulder. When I do, our journey will begin on a field of grass."

A hand touched her shoulder, then it was gone.

She stood on vivid grass, cascading green as far as the eye could see.

"Behind you there is a house. Go inside. You will see someone, someone close to you. Someone who helps you. That person will embrace you."

She turned around to see a small white house with black shutters and a red door. As soon as she walked inside Simone kissed her on both cheeks.

The voice, this voice that she somehow wanted to obey without understanding why, was peaceful. "Who is there?"

"Simone." Nathalie heard her own voice. Somehow she heard it, even if she didn't feel as if she were speaking.

"Simone is there to help you put things into a box. There's a large box in the center of the room, and there are rocks beside it. You are going to open it, and then you're going to fill it up with rocks. The rocks are your memories, the ones you wish to forget. If a rock is too heavy, Simone will help you."

Nathalie walked to the center of the room and knelt down. She picked up a small rock and put it into the box. A memory of standing in line at the morgue.

Then another, then another. Entering the morgue, walking up to the viewing pane. A rock into the box, a child crying behind her at the morgue.

A rock with more weight. A girl on the cement slab, viciously ripped by a knife. What was her name?

Another rock, heavier than the last. A child's screech of terror.

Another rock, this one jagged. Touching the viewing pane.

Another rock, this one too heavy. Simone extended a hand to help. Odette on the slab shrieking, bloody, getting bludgeoned by a knife.

She dropped the rock and screamed. Simone leaned in and turned into Aunt Brigitte with the word INSIGHT branded on her forehead. Nathalie stood up and the floor turned into sand and she stood knee-deep in the sea. A wave crashed at her feet and pulled her into the water, away from the beach and into the dark and frothy depths. She screamed until she went under and suddenly she was aware of M. and Mme. Lebeau holding her hands in the room full of books and telling her, in soothing tones, that she was safe.

Rawness spread in her throat. She stood up, just as she had during the hypnotic—dream? Vision? What *was* it? Something different than sleeping, different from the morgue visions. Yet another place her mind could go.

Her mind stumbled through the murky labyrinth of reality. "How long have I been under?"

"Not quite ten minutes," M. Lebeau said.

No, it had to be hours and hours. Her body said so. She approached the window. The shadows hadn't changed much. He was right.

"I don't believe you were truly under," he continued. "Very close, but you didn't let go entirely. Somewhere in between, it seems. You may remember much of what happened, rather like a dream."

Her legs were loose with fatigue. She felt as though she'd been running from something other than herself for the past few hours.

"Mademoiselle, please sit," said M. Lebeau, guiding her to the sofa. "I'm so sorry this happened."

Mme. Lebeau, who smelled of clove and something medicinal, placed a wrinkled hand on her cheek. The touch reminded her of Aunt Brigitte's.

"I'll get you something to drink," she said, vanishing into the mysterious back room.

Nathalie tried to swallow away the harsh sensation in her throat. "I feel like I was in a nightmare, but worse. Does this happen often? Someone being 'in between,' as you said, and then coming out of it terrified?"

M. Lebeau shook his head. "I'm afraid it doesn't. Only once before under . . . special circumstances. Are you . . . ?"

The question perished on his lips.

"Am I what?"

He picked up the opium vase and pipe, set them on a desk in the corner, and stared at her. Then he broke into a smile much like the one he'd greeted her with when she'd entered. "Are you feeling well enough to walk? That is, will you need help getting home?"

His tone had a drop of artifice in it.

That's not what you were going to ask.

"Am I what?" Nathalie repeated as though he hadn't answered. Because in truth he hadn't.

Mme. Lebeau returned carrying a silver tray with a teapot and cup. She set it down on the end table next to the sofa. "This will make you feel better."

"Monsieur, what were you going to ask me?" Nathalie tried again.

"Nothing," he replied cheerfully, crossing his arms. "I'm sorry, that's not true. I was wondering how old you are. A rude question, I know."

"Sixteen."

"Oh!" His eyes brightened. Was he surprised? She looked her age and was never taken for more than seventeen or eighteen. "To be young again. Eh, Geneviève?"

Mme. Lebeau smiled. "Indeed."

But something about the way he spoke, something about the way his face lit up, told Nathalie that wasn't the question he'd intended to ask, either.

He wasn't going to budge. Whatever he'd nearly asked faded into never.

Why?

Mme. Lebeau poured the tea and handed her the cup, decorated with blue and white stripes and some kind of exotic script.

Nathalie lifted it to her lips, inhaled its pungent earthy, floral smell, and immediately put it down. "What is this? It's not tea."

The elderly Lebeau couple glanced at each other before Mme. Lebeau responded. "It's similar to tea, and it will bring you back to yourself."

"Is it opium?"

"No," the old woman said, "but it does have poppy seeds and other herbals."

Nathalie prickled with unease. For a second she was tempted, very tempted, to drink the tea as quickly as she could swallow. But she didn't. She couldn't.

"I'd better be going," she said, standing up on legs that suddenly felt much better. "Thank you for trying to help me. How many francs?"

M. Lebeau waved his hand. "I would not take your money, Mademoiselle. My apologies that your experience was so unsettling. I can only conclude that—that whatever you came here to forget cannot be forgotten."

Nathalie straightened up, noticing for the first time how small and shriveled these two strange people were. Despite it all she found them likable in their eccentricity. There was a freedom about them, she decided. Something like what Simone wanted, only with the experience and confidence that age brings.

She took her satchel and said a hasty good-bye, with M. Lebeau's final words chasing her all the way home.

"Remember who you are," he'd said, "and then you'll know why you can't forget."

20

The hypnosis session, or whatever it was given that she hadn't actually gone under, affected Nathalie in an unexpected way: It sharpened her focus.

For the rest of the day, her thoughts kept returning to one thing. Not the visions, the Dark Artist, the letters, or the bottle of blood. Not even Simone or her unusual-but-engaging sweetheart.

Aunt Brigitte.

Nathalie had been determined, after that memory-turned-dream in the park, to look for Tante's papers. The blood jar discovery had pulled her onto a different path; besides, she hadn't had an opportunity to search the apartment the past few days. But Tante's appearance in her hypnotic reverie brought her attention firmly back to those papers.

Why were they so important?

They were the ramblings of a woman hanging on to the rim of sanity by her fingertips.

And yet.

Papa had made an effort to save them. Protect them, even. And of all the facets of Aunt Brigitte to filter into hypnosis, only the most prominent word on those papers came through.

INSIGHT.

Nathalie thought about that last day at Mme. Plouffe's. Several moments came back to her now, shards of glass reassembling into a window. Transparent. Distorted, but not entirely occluded.

Of course Aunt Brigitte hadn't tried to choke her; that was a dreamer's editorial. She and Maman had left Aunt Brigitte's room without incident. Afterward Maman had brought her to Mme. Plouffe, who'd given her warm milk and a raspberry thumbprint cookie. The next thing Nathalie recalled was the carriage ride home. Papa had held the stack of papers close to his chest in a way that had reminded her of the way she held her stuffed bunny, Silvain. Once home, Papa had carried those papers straight into the bedroom and never spoke of them again.

Had he kept them?

If he had, the papers would be in their bedroom. She had to search.

Yes, she could have waited until the next time Maman was out on an errand or visiting friends. She hadn't had that opportunity in several days, however, and she needed to know.

Inquisitiveness trumped patience, as it so often did.

After dinner, Nathalie sat in Papa's chair and read from her Poe anthology. Maman settled on the sofa to work on a blanket for the Cartiers, the family across the street expecting a little one this fall. Around half past nine, Maman said she was going to "rest her eyes," placed her knitting needles down, and fell asleep shortly thereafter.

Before long Maman's breaths were deep and rhythmic; she was just beginning to snore lightly.

Good. She wouldn't rouse for a while.

Nathalie rested the Poe book on an end table and stood up as quietly as possible. She took light steps toward Maman's room. Shadows enveloped her as she slipped through the doorway, a curious Stanley in tow.

She felt in the darkness for Maman's bedside lamp. *Clink!* Her hand struck the base. She pulled back her hand, listening intently until she heard the sound of Maman's sleep from the parlor.

Nathalie put the lamp on low, the flame equivalent of a whisper, and carried it—where? She paused, glancing around her parents' bedroom as if seeing it for the first time. She hadn't looked around at the nooks and crannies in their room for years, not since she got caught searching for Christmas presents when she was six. (That year she received a visit both from Père Noël, who gives gifts to well-behaved children, and from Père Fouettard, who delivers spankings to naughty children. She never searched for gifts again.)

She started with the closet, full of bags and boxes against the back wall. Looking through them took longer than it should have, between the dim lighting and her efforts to be soundless. She found nothing except a pair of her baby shoes. After some hushed coaxing, Stanley hopped out of the closet. Nathalie shut the door and listened for a moment, long enough to detect that Maman was still sleeping, and proceeded to the drawers.

There were six of them. Nothing was tucked away in the first two. The third drawer squeaked like a mouse. Nathalie's fingers danced along the interior and stopped on something long and flat with hinges on one side. A box.

The ideal size for documents.

She placed the lamp on the dresser and moved it to the edge, catching just enough light to see what was inside. Papers and more papers: her birth announcement, documents about her parents' marriage and Papa's work in the navy, and some papers related to money and the apartment. Her heart sank as the stack grew thinner.

The next three drawers held nothing resembling documents. A keepsake box containing coins from Papa's adventures overseas lay nestled in the last one. Nathalie had always been captivated by those coins because they told a story of their own about Papa's travels to places like America (she wanted to visit Boston one day) and Cochinchina and Algérie française.

An unexpected ruffle of emotion, mild yet inescapable, passed through her. *I miss Papa.*

His rumbling voice, his hearty laugh, even the way he looked when he was deep in thought. He'd seen much—it was etched on his face like a melancholy concerto—and spoke of it from time to time, yet Nathalie knew much more was left unsaid.

She took the lid off the keepsake box and grabbed a coin. Any coin. It didn't matter. Just something to make her feel connected to Papa there, in that moment. She put it in her pocket, patting the coin twice as if to safeguard it. Time to resume her search.

Stooping down, she scrutinized the space under the bed. There were two boxes there, but she knew one was for storing winter clothes and the other was for Christmas decorations. Lifting the lids confirmed it. Stanley climbed into one of the boxes and she gently nudged him out. She stood up to listen for Maman's deep breaths before moving on.

Two more places to inspect.

Nathalie stared at the outline of the wardrobe, dreading its creaky doors and drawers, and crossed over to it. She leaned in close to muffle that first *thud* when the doors were unlatched, cringing when it was louder than she anticipated. She listened again for Maman's breaths. Still heavy.

With the lamp at eye level, she peered into the recess of the top shelf. Bed linens on one side and the blanket her grandmother had knit on the other, with nothing in the space between.

Nathalie reached for the first drawer and pulled it back; the wood groaned like a weary old man who wanted to be left alone. She hesitated.

Everything was quiet. As quiet as a side street in residential Paris could be. Maman wasn't breathing audibly anymore, but she wasn't stirring, either.

Nathalie thumbed through some sweaters and, seeing nothing, pushed them back.

This search was far less thrilling and worthwhile than she had expected. Maybe that was the problem—expectations. Simply wanting the answer to an old and probably irrelevant question to assuage her desire to know about Tante didn't mean the world was going to comply.

She moved to the last place worth exploring: the desk. An inkwell, a small stack of books, and a paperweight lay atop it. Stanley jumped on the desk, weaving around the books to sniff the inkwell.

The first drawer turned up nothing but a ruler, some nails, and a hammer. The second drawer was noisy and took an eternity to open. It was strewn with scraps of paper and a folded-up page of *Le Petit Journal*. Just as Nathalie picked it up, Stanley leapt off the desk, knocking two books onto the floor.

The sofa jostled on the wooden floor, ever so softly.

She put the books back onto the stack, shooing Stanley out of the room to no avail.

Maman's cough burst in from the living room.

Nathalie extinguished the lamp. Maman's back would be to the bedroom, but if she stood up, she'd see the glow.

The floor creaked, distinctly, as it only did when bearing human weight slat after slat.

Oh no, no no no . . .

The noisy drawer was still open. Nathalie shoved the newspaper inside the front of her dress and pressed up against the drawer.

"What are you doing?"

She turned. Her mother held a lamp that threw just enough light to reveal a scowl.

"Nothing," Nathalie said, willing her voice not to crack. "Stanley came in here and I followed him."

"Are you sure it wasn't the other way around?"

"I'm going to bed and I wanted to take him with me, that's all."

Maman placed the lamp on her nightstand and folded her arms. "Was he in that drawer you just closed?"

Nathalie watched Stanley saunter out of the room. "He knocked some books off the desk. The drawer was open a little and I pushed it in."

The lie swelled like a lump of dough, pushing at the walls of her stomach.

"We'll talk in the morning. *Bonne nuit*, Nathalie," Maman said, her usual warm tone traded for ice.

She wished her mother a sheepish good night in return and went to her bedroom. She pulled out the newspaper—one sheet, pages nine and ten from April 27, 1869—and began reading.

"Marriage Announcements." Her parents were married April 24 that year. She read through the notices and spotted her parents' names on the list.

She'd never seen a newspaper so old. Beside the marriage announcements were birth announcements and obituaries. An advertisement for Café Maxime spread across the top of the page. The other side had two stories, one about an upcoming parliamentary election that was so dull she stopped reading after the fourth sentence. The other was continued from page two, with the headline "Effects Uncertain":

. . . has denied that the experiments are correlated with insanity. "I've brought magic into the world," said Dr. Henard, "not lunacy."

Still, Dr. Henard does not deny that many patients who have successfully undergone the blood transfusion have observed side effects over time. "I'm not at liberty to discuss individual cases, but there do appear to be treatment results that were not anticipated."

Although Henard offers no further comment, the Tremblay family remains adamant. "My wife was a good woman, a good wife," M. Tremblay said, shaking his head. "I've lost her to madness, just like the other four families who lost someone to the asylum after these experiments. And I have to wonder, what happens to my children if I'm next?" Tremblay shakes his head again. "Henard promised us that we'd 'gain insight.' Maybe in his mind insight is just another word for devastation."

Or, as we see it, sorrow.

Nathalie dropped the newspaper. It floated onto the ground with a quiet rustle.

Insight.

The parallel was too much. Too uncanny. Too everything to be a coincidence.

She didn't know much about Dr. Henard's experiments, only what she'd heard from some schoolmates who claimed to have a relative who'd been a patient. Henard had found a way to impart seemingly magical abilities—clairvoyance, mind reading, super-human strength—through blood transfusions. Then terrible consequences had come to light; people lost their powers over time, some died as a result of transfusions, some became physically ill. He'd fallen out of favor and, as far as Nathalie knew, disappeared from public consciousness over a decade ago. Few people talked about "that fraud Henard" anymore.

Nathalie had never before heard of a connection between the treatments and insanity.

Aunt Brigitte claimed to see events in her dreams that became real, or so she thought, and was judged to be insane as a result. Had Tante been one of his patients?

Nathalie sat on the bed as another thought seized her. The visions, the memory loss . . .

She shook her head; those things couldn't be related. She'd never gotten a medical procedure, not that she could remember.

That. She. Could.

Remember.

21

Nathalie arranged and rearranged the questions she had for Maman, writing them out in her journal before bed. Then she did something else that, she now decided, she should have done in the first place.

Told Agnès about the visions.

She couldn't be hypocritical, pressing Maman for answers while holding on to secrets of her own.

Using her nicest stationery, employed only on special occasions, she wrote the letter.

> *Dear Agnès,*
>
> *My friend, I hope you will forgive me. I have kept this from you long enough. I cannot withhold this from you any longer.*
>
> *I know far more about these murders than you can imagine, because I am experiencing something that is, in every essence of what the word means, unimaginable.*

Nathalie wrote slowly at first, choosing her words carefully. Then she let them flow and told her everything: what she'd truly meant in that first postcard, how the memory gap had stolen Nathalie's recollection of penning a letter, the trip to the hypnotist. She asked if Agnès had heard of Dr. Henard's experiments, and if so, what she knew about them. She wrote pages and pages. Alleviating the burden of secrecy liberated her.

*I promise to explain more and answer any questions when
we meet for lunch at Le Canard Curieux the day after your
return at 1 o'clock. I know we set this date and time before
you left for Bayeux. Does it still hold?*

Bisous,
Nata

*P.S. I do hope I remain in your good graces. I also hope you
understand why it meant so much to me to hear about your
summer. Many, many times I have thought about how much
I would rather be learning to make tarts or strolling through
town or teasing Roger with you or spending the day at the
beach. Instead of all this. My apologies again.*

By the time Nathalie finished the letter, she was exhausted and
fell asleep soon after. She woke up confident and prepared to talk
to Maman. At last she might have some answers about Aunt
Brigitte. About herself. She braced herself for the truth.

She tucked the newspaper she'd found last night into her journal and brought it into the kitchen, smiling. Maman was finishing breakfast and didn't pick her head up.

"What were you doing in my room last night?"

Apparently Maman had some questions of her own. Nathalie
had been hoping this was one of those times when Maman didn't
follow through on a we'll-talk-later warning. "I told you. I followed
Stanley in there."

"Don't lie." Maman looked up, her eyes brimming with disappointment.

Nathalie blushed. "I was searching for something. Papers that
Papa brought home once."

Maman raised a brow, beckoning her to continue.

"Something Aunt Brigitte wrote a long time ago. When she was
in Madame Plouffe's place, just before she went . . . away."

Whatever it was Maman was expecting her to say, it wasn't that.

Nathalie spoke in a calm voice. "Something made me think

of that day, and every detail came back to me. I couldn't help but search. I was embarrassed about getting caught. I didn't know what to do when you walked in, and for some reason I was afraid to tell you the truth. There was a newspaper in the drawer, and I took it. The one with your marriage announcement."

She handed the old newspaper back to Maman.

"You shouldn't have been poking about," said Maman, grimacing. "Especially when you could have asked me about those papers."

Maman had a point. Nathalie could have, should have asked her about those papers. Yet these visions, this curiosity that had turned into a curse, had Nathalie burying deception on top of deception. It had begun with evading M. Gagnon's questions from that very first life-changing day with Odette. Being evasive with Maman and ever so much more coy to Agnès. Even in the fight with Simone, who knew almost everything, she'd had to refrain from saying anything about the Dark Artist's threat. And wasn't disposing of the blood jar another form of lying, if only to herself?

"I'm sorry." Nathalie met her mother's gaze and sat down at the table. "Then . . . what about Aunt Brigitte's papers?"

Maman looked over her shoulder as if seeing into the past. "Most of what she wrote was illegible. Your father insisted on keeping the papers anyway and brought them home. The next day they were gone."

Something about the way Maman spoke those words—the cadence, the hollow tone, the bitterness of a swallowed hurt—told Nathalie she'd touched on an unwelcome memory.

"Gone?"

"He said he burned them."

She chewed the inside of her lip. "I never considered that."

"Why do you have to consider it at all?" Maman folded her arms. "All these years you just accepted Aunt Brigitte for who she is and where she is. Now all these questions."

"And I have one more," Nathalie said, struggling not to let her voice quiver. "Based on something I read."

She flipped over the newspaper and pointed to the story about Henard. "This."

Maman's face hardened. "What about it?"

"I think Aunt Brigitte was one of Dr. Henard's patients." Finally. Finally, the words that had nearly burned a hole in her tongue all night came out. "Am I correct? Did she have one of those blood transfusions? Is that why she's in the asylum?"

Maman still hadn't taken her eyes off the newspaper. Gradually she lifted her head. She clasped her hands with sluggish fingers and leaned back. "No."

Nathalie regarded her mother. "I don't believe you."

"We are not talking about this."

"Yes, we are!" Nathalie crossed her arms. "Why shouldn't we?"

Maman tightened her folded hands, thumbs pressing into her flesh. "Where did this come from? This interrogation? This behavior? I won't be spoken to that way. I am your mother, not Simone."

A twinge traveled through her heart. Maman didn't know about the quarrel with Simone, which made it even worse.

"Then maybe I'm the one who needs to be at Saint-Mathurin."

Maman threw up her hands. "Now that's a fanciful conclusion. What are you talking about?"

"Insight. Aunt Brigitte wrote it on those papers. It's here in the article, the idea of 'gaining insight.'" Nathalie tapped the newspaper. "Tante claims to have insight. She dreamed about future crimes and tried to prevent them. Then I guess she went mad somewhere along the way like the people mentioned in this article. Am I wrong?"

In one swift motion, Maman pushed her chair back and stood. She walked behind the chair and gripped it firmly, as if to steady herself. She stared at her scars and exhaled through her nose. "No. You're right. Everything you said is true."

"It is?" Nathalie asked, her voice laden with bittersweet awe.

"And now what?" Maman asked in a tranquil, even tone that

Nathalie found unnerving. "You know the truth, and you know the shame that was brought on our family. That your aunt is insane because she sought magical powers. She's considered a fool for taking part in those experiments. What else is there? That's everything."

"What about—"

Maman held up her hand and closed her eyes. She paused a moment before opening them again. "I said that's everything. You can do all the sleuthing you want, you can ask all the questions you want. I won't answer them."

"Why? Does it bring shame to the family to tell the truth?"

"How dare you?" said Maman, her face a mixture of indignation and hurt. "The decision is mine, not yours. You're sixteen. What do you know about truth?"

"Until today, I didn't know much at all," Nathalie said, hands on hips.

"Enough. I will never discuss this again."

That last sentence set a flame to everything else Nathalie wanted to know. Needed to know. *Am I one of Dr. Henard's patients? Did something happen to me in childhood that I don't remember?*

That might have come up in the hypnosis, had she gone under. Wouldn't it?

I see things, too, Maman. Like Aunt Brigitte.

Now she had to wait. For a better time, when she could try again to talk to Maman. She had to believe that they could talk, that she could tell her everything, some other day.

Maman went to her bedroom and returned several seconds later holding her shopping bag.

Then she locked her bedroom door.

Nathalie's heart descended into a basin of sadness. Maman hadn't locked that door in years.

Silence settled between them, a chasm full of more questions than answers and one that neither wanted to cross. Maman let out a sigh, composed of both frustration and weariness, and announced that she was going to run errands. Nathalie asked her to mail the letter to Agnès. Maman's eyes lingered on the envelope too long, Nathalie thought, perhaps wondering what Nathalie had written, what family secrets she'd spilled.

After Maman left, Nathalie approached the window. She watched her mother walk down the street and out of sight. Stanley nuzzled her shin and weaved in and out of her legs.

She retreated from the window and felt a lump form in her throat. Tears followed. So many that she went to her bedroom and cried into her pillow, weeping until her nose stuffed up and her face swelled.

When she had cried all she could cry, and maybe even more, she fell asleep. She awoke with a stabbing headache and lay there, petting Stanley. Maman still wasn't home. Good; Maman would assume that in her absence Nathalie had gone to the morgue and newspaper.

She wondered what Simone was doing. Whether she was at the club. Or sleeping, because she was keeping her "vampire hours." Or Simone might, at this very moment, be eating grapes. Maybe with Louis, who almost certainly would tell her about Nathalie's trip to the hypnotist. Or maybe Simone was with some other girl she'd befriended at the club, a replacement friend. After a while, when Nathalie was done imagining all the ways Simone might be spending her day, she drifted off again.

And so went the rest of the day, this hazy vacillation between sleep and wakefulness. One of the few moments she remembered afterward was Maman coming in to kiss her on the forehead just after nightfall.

The headache subsided by the next morning, which was good, given that it was Nathalie's first day back as morgue reporter in almost a week.

After a few bites of fruit for breakfast, she dressed in her boy clothes and left. She forgot to tie one of her shoes, though, and tripped down the last few stairs of the apartment building. The spill resulted in a tender ankle and a maddening splinter (thanks to the railing) in the palm of her hand. Maddening because she couldn't get it out, despite going back to get one of Maman's sewing needles and picking at it on the tram. She tried again while standing in line at the morgue.

She hated splinters, unlike blood blisters, which she almost enjoyed. They intrigued her, because sticking a needle through your skin and having blood come out painlessly was rather thrilling. But splinters were just aggravating.

"Nothing worse, eh?" said a throaty voice. A tall, striking woman with raven hair pointed to Nathalie's hand. "My beau gets splinters all the time."

"I'm right-handed and have to use my left to get it out. Most inconvenient."

The woman fussed with her hair, atop her head like a crown, and smiled. "Would you like my help?"

"No, no, thank you," she said. Something about the woman's demeanor was off-putting. Familiar and false all at once.

Nathalie picked away and finally caught the end of it as she crossed the threshold of the morgue. As she finished pulling out the stubborn sliver of wood once and for all, she bumped into the man ahead of her, causing him to drop his newspaper.

"*Je suis désolée*," she said, bending down to scoop up the pages. While handing them to him in a clumsy gesture, she noticed an illustration across the top half of the newspaper.

A tarot card with a man and a woman, with an angel hovering above. The Lovers. She knew this because the first time Simone had done a reading for herself, this card had come up. Simone had talked about it for a month, all but certain it boded well for herself and Louis, who at that time she only admired from afar.

DARK ARTIST SENDS TAROT, the headline read.

Nathalie knew, in that split second between seeing the

headline and looking at the viewing pane, that Victim #4 was on display.

And so she was.

This unfortunate girl, with Seine-bloated, olive skin and dark hair, was sliced worse than any of the others. Mirabelle Gregoire had been left with a gash on her temple. In Nathalie's vision, Mirabelle had been pushed and fell against the corner of a table. This victim had cuts in the same place where Mirabelle's wound had been. And on her throat and cheek like the others.

They were deeper. Stronger. Angrier.

Nathalie's stomach seized up. She reached inside her satchel and pulled out the vial of catacomb dirt. She clutched it with so much force her hand went numb.

The compulsion to touch the glass, to see a few moments of what happened, overwhelmed her.

You'll regret it. Don't do it. Pray for the girl and write your column. This is none of your concern.

The urge grew more pervasive, and Nathalie felt a change in her breathing.

Maybe I overreacted. Maybe I gave up too soon. Maybe I'm nothing like Aunt Brigitte.

Each breath was shorter and shallower than the last.

It was surprisingly hot in here, given the mild day. The room felt crowded, yet it wasn't any more so than usual.

It darkened inside the morgue, as though a black cloud moved over the building and blocked the sunlight. Bathing it in shadows that grew blacker and blacker . . .

The next thing Nathalie remembered was being sprawled out on a cold stone floor staring at the ceiling. Three people, including the man she'd bumped into and the tall woman who noticed her splinter, stood over her. The woman extended a hand. "You fainted. How do you feel?"

Nathalie knew she had to have been scarlet from head to toe because she had never, not once, been so embarrassed. She took the woman's hand and got up, carefully, because the only thing worse than fainting would be fainting again immediately afterward. "I'll be better once I get some fresh air. *Merci beaucoup.*"

Nathalie looked at the viewing pane again.

The visions have done enough harm. Don't.

She took a step and heard something crack at her feet.

Her vial of catacomb dirt, shattered. The dry soil spread out on the morgue floor in between bits of broken glass. A mess to anyone else, good luck charm and unexpected source of comfort to her. Nathalie's heart sank.

"We'll clean it up," whispered the guard. No doubt he thought he was reassuring her.

Cheeks burning again, she hurried out. She took long, fast strides across the bridge and went to Café Maxime.

"Mademoiselle Baudin," called a familiar voice from over her shoulder.

She turned to face him.

"I saw what happened at the morgue. You ran off before I could check on you. May I join you for a cup of coffee?"

Her heart fluttered. This was the last thing she expected this morning. Her instinct was to say no because . . . well, she couldn't think of a good enough reason, other than that she was self-conscious. "Please do, Monsieur Gagnon."

"Call me Christophe."

22

Her insides did a pirouette. "Call me Nathalie."

First names. Did that mean no more official questions?

And coffee. What did *that* mean?

They walked to the back of the outdoor café a respectable distance apart, with Nathalie wishing the whole time they were arm in arm. Christophe motioned for her to lead the way, and as she did, she once again picked up on his woodsy-orange blossom scent. As Jean cleared the table, Nathalie watched a man at the table next to them. He had *Le Petit Journal* open to the tarot card story. She tried to read over his shoulder, but he was sketching something—a music hall, it seemed—and obscured her view.

Jean seated them and brought over menus. Christophe ordered coffee. Nathalie got coffee and a plate of cheese, fruit, and bread even though she craved a sandwich. If for some reason he changed his mind and wanted some food, she could offer him a slice of brie or ham.

"I thought it was time we talked," he said, his tone much less formal than encounters past. His posture was relaxed, too. It was as if the switch to first names changed his demeanor, put him at ease. He had on a pale blue shirt (which, Nathalie observed, made his eyes even more exquisite) and his light brown hair was uncharacteristically disheveled.

Did he mess it up in the rush to see me?

As soon as she thought it, she blushed. *How ludicrous.*

"Sorry, I don't mean to embarrass you."

Which, of course, only made her blush more.

"I'm fine," she said, willing her cheeks to resume their normal hue. "And thank you for your concern. I appreciate it. I don't know what happened in there. The heat, I guess. Or maybe because I didn't have much breakfast. Oh, and I had a headache last night. It's happened before. Only twice. Once in the library studying for exams. It was about three o'clock and all I'd eaten all day was a *pain au chocolat*, which is what I would have gotten today, now, I mean, if I'd had breakfast this morning. It's my favorite pastry. The second time was last summer in a park when it was very hot and I stood up quickly after reading *Les Misérables* for several hours."

Why am I rambling? I am not one to ramble. I'm speaking as quickly as Monsieur Patenaude. My hands are quivering. Hands, please stop. Please.

And now my thoughts are rambling.

The left corner of Christophe's mouth curled into a half smile. *Breathe.*

Nathalie straightened up with a grin. "Talking, yes. As you can see, I've already begun."

The coffee and the food arrived. She gestured for him to help himself, and when he declined, she couldn't help but feel disappointed.

"So," he said, tapping the side of his coffee cup, "you're at the morgue every day, or at least, every day I'm there. Why?"

Nathalie cut herself a piece of bread. She stared at him a moment as she took a bite, wondering whether or not he already knew the answer to this question. "You alluded to this once before, too. The day we crossed paths outside the *bureau de poste*."

He smiled quick as a wink. "You might say I'm persistently curious."

"I think the same could be said about me," she said, chuckling. She picked up a few crumbs with her fingertip. "I . . . I write the morgue report for *Le Petit Journal*."

Christophe sat back and folded his arms. For a moment his

expression froze in thought, unreadable, before easing into one of bewilderment.

"You are welcome to go ask Monsieur Patenaude—he's the editor and a friend of my father's—yourself," Nathalie said, sitting up especially straight. "Or I can give you a phrase or two that I'll include in my article, and you'll be able to read it in tomorrow's paper."

"You—you aren't joking," said Christophe, uncrossing his arms.

"Not at all." Nathalie picked at some cheese as she told him how she got the job and how long she'd been there. "Speaking of that time outside the *bureau de poste*. You also asked me about my clothes, remember?"

He nodded.

"I wear trousers when I go to *Le Petit Journal*," she said with a shrug. "Monsieur Patenaude thought it best that I dress as a boy so I don't stand out."

"That's why?" Christophe threw back his head and laughed. "Good ol' Patenaude. I know the man well, actually. That sounds like him."

Nathalie frowned. "Why is that funny?"

"I'm not laughing at you or him. Or your trousers. I'm laughing at myself," he said, pointing to his chest. "I must admit, I was terribly embarrassed that day outside by the post, and I didn't know what to think . . . with the trousers and whatnot. I—I have never seen a young woman wearing anything other than a skirt or dress."

She snickered. He *had* acted strangely during that encounter.

After a few beats of silence, he sipped some coffee and cleared his throat. "I saw you didn't touch the viewing pane at the morgue today."

The statement fell on her like one large, all-encompassing raindrop that doused her in confusion.

"*Pardonnez-moi?*" It made her uncomfortable that he knew. Knew what? More than he should have, if nothing else. They'd just shared a lighthearted exchange, and now this. The legs on her chair could well have been kicked out.

He rested his hands under his chin. "It means I think something happens when you place your hand on the viewing pane."

Nathalie, briefly wondering if she'd imagined what he just said, replied by taking a sip of coffee. Those few seconds felt like fifteen minutes. "That's quite a claim, Monsieur Gagn—Christophe."

The next thought she had pinched her heart. This friendly, easygoing demeanor might just be a way to persuade her to give up information. Maybe he thought she'd be more cooperative if he came across as more relaxed; maybe this "talk" was all business, no pleasure. She clenched her jaw and pulled her plate closer, annoyed with herself for liking him so much.

He peeked over his shoulder before answering. "I've seen you. Not just the first time; every time there's a Dark Artist victim. A couple who stood next to you in the viewing room reported it once, too. They heard you say the name 'Mirabelle.'"

Hmmm. So it hadn't been Simone who supplied the tip about Mirabelle. Instead it was some people she hadn't even noticed watching her. Her stomach lurched as she recalled that older couple with the dog from the previous vision and how they'd moved away from her. Did everyone do that?

She traced a question mark on the table with her finger. "This is the part where I don't know what to say next."

"I apologize for surprising you. There was no easy way to start this conversation."

She looked down. A little bird was at her feet pecking away at crumbs. It reminded her of the first vision, and how she'd come to this café afterward to try to make sense of what had happened. How she'd fed the birds most of her croissant.

"I reacted with polite skepticism when the couple told me," Christophe added. "So as not to invite any questions."

Wait. He was *protecting* her?

Nathalie studied him, with his perfect nose and vigilant blue eyes. Unless he was a magnificent actor, he wasn't faking it. This friendliness was genuine—yet unexplainable all the same. "Why protect me? And why have you been paying so much attention to me?"

Indelicate, yes. But it redirected the conversation, which was all she wanted at this point.

"I think your privacy, everyone's privacy, deserves protecting. Whatever happens when you touch the viewing pane, you don't want others to know. I've watched you closely since our first encounter, although truthfully I'd noticed you even before then." Christophe took a sliver of brie from her plate, as if to confirm his sudden familiarity.

She blushed. "Thank you. It's nice to know I have a—a friend."

The crumb-catching bird half flew, half hopped onto the table and picked at a crumb. "I'm glad we could have this conversation," Christophe said, his eyes on the bird as it flew away.

Whether it was his softened tone or protectiveness or the appeal he held for her, she didn't know. She *should* have been upset by his questions. Yet she wasn't. All she knew was that her instinct told her she could trust him.

"Something happened the other day," she said, biting her lip. "I didn't tell anyone. I was angry and frustrated and just wanted it all to go away."

The expression on his face invited her, warmly, to continue.

And so she told Christophe about the jar of blood, the *Inspiration* note, and how she had thrown it all into the Seine.

When he responded with understanding rather than a lecture, she decided to tell him about the letter from the Dark Artist as well as the time she thought she was followed.

He listened with intensity, as if everything she said was the most important detail he'd ever heard. Nathalie liked that.

"Thank you for making that so much easier than I expected,"

she said, smiling with relief. She finished her coffee and wrapped her hands around the cup.

"You're welcome. I don't know how you kept that to yourself for so long. You are brave." He placed his hand on hers, resting it there a moment before withdrawing it to straighten his collar.

Nathalie flushed at his words and his touch, a soft touch that was there and then gone like a waft of beguiling perfume. She cast her eyes on the pebbles at her feet.

"So," he said, smoothing his collar, "what *does* happen when you touch the viewing pane?"

Ah, yes. Ever the interrogator. Hoping he wouldn't return to his initial curiosity was too lofty a wish.

A plank or two slipped out of the rapport they'd just built. She could lie and he'd know—because he just *knew* those things, it seemed—or she could tell the truth, which could garner any number of reactions. Nathalie pressed her thumbs into the cup. "You wouldn't believe me if I told you."

"I might. I've encountered more than you can imagine."

Nathalie scoffed. "This is different."

He glanced to the side. The man sketching the music hall appeared to be listening. In a hushed voice, Christophe continued. "What if I told you that as a police liaison, I've met someone who could communicate thoughts to someone kilometers away using animals, and someone else who could see a person's future by holding his or her hand? And yet another person who could smell blood and death like a hound?"

Nathalie's flesh tickled inside and out. "I would say those are . . . very extraordinary people."

"They are. I suspect you are, too." He leaned closer. "You can tell me, Nathalie."

Could she?

She could. He didn't treat her like a child, or a deranged person, or a storyteller. His honesty and willingness to talk drew her in—a sharp contrast to Maman, who'd tried to hide the truth and then ended the conversation. Christophe had understood everything so far. Maybe he'd understand this, too.

"I—I have a vision whenever I touch the viewing pane. It was an accident the first time, and for a while I didn't know what to make of it." Nathalie let go of the coffee cup, pushing it away. After a sigh, she proceeded to tell him about everything from that first vision through the third, including the tip to the police, her recent discovery about the white gloves, and the memory loss she'd been suffering after each vision.

She told him her theory about M. Gloves, too, imperfect though it was. Christophe wasn't convinced he was a possible suspect, and even though her own suspicions had begun to wane, at least the man represented a possibility. No one else so far had.

Once again he focused on her in a way that made her feel like the most interesting person in the world.

Here she was, telling him about the visions, and she felt normal.

"Those people you mentioned," she said, emphasizing the word *people*, "did they get their powers from Dr. Henard's experiments?"

"Yes."

Her heart danced with anticipation. "I found out recently that my aunt was one of his patients. She would have dreams where someone was about to kill an infant. She's in the asylum now, because of the transfusion and its effects, I think, so I can't talk to her about it. And my mother won't answer any questions."

Christophe grimaced. "About Henard?"

"About anything," Nathalie continued. "She refused to talk about it before I could ask a single question. I don't know for sure, but I'm assuming that I received one of these blood transfusions as a child. How else can this be explained?"

"They had reasons to avoid telling you. To protect you, most likely." He squinted in concentration. "What year were you born?"

"1871."

"So you're sixteen?"

"I am."

Strange. The hypnotist, too, had asked about her age.

"Nathalie, I don't know how to tell you this," he said. He opened and closed his mouth several times, presumably searching for the right words. "You could not have been one of Dr. Henard's patients. He was murdered in 1870."

23

Nathalie didn't speak for a moment. Instead she examined everything around her besides Christophe. The man sketching at the next table, whom Jean the waiter addressed as Walter, and his now-folded-up newspaper. The other patrons in the café, the dishes on their tables. The trees around the perimeter, the scrap-hungry birds.

Everything fit in. Everything had its place.

Except for her.

"Are you sure?" she said, when she could once again look at Christophe.

"I'm afraid so. He was found in his laboratory, poisoned. Some think it might have been a former patient, some posit it was a colleague, others still think it was a lover. Nothing points to one over any other; it was a clean murder, so to speak. A few days later the Germans surrounded Paris, as it were, so the mystery surrounding his death just dissolved into the chaos."

The war between France and Prussia had been over in nine months or so, as Nathalie recalled from her studies, and the German blockade lasted four of them. One dead doctor, even a famous one, was nothing compared to tens of thousands of starving Parisians.

One girl with unexplainable powers, similar to Henard's patients yet not one of them, *that* was something different.

"What does that make me?"

He shook his head in sympathy.

"Ever since this started, I've been wondering what I am. Who I am. Then I think maybe, finally, there's an answer. Or the beginning of an answer." She waved her hand. "And just as quickly, it vanishes like smoke. I'm a freak."

"No, you aren't. You're smart and resilient, and you have an incredible power. Just because *I* don't have an explanation doesn't mean no one will." He drummed the table in thought. "Talk to Monsieur Patenaude. He—he knows more than I do about the Henard experiments."

M. Patenaude? He was pleasant enough, and yes, he'd given her the job. He was also strange; she couldn't imagine opening up to him, friend of Papa's or not. "Why?"

Christophe pressed the sides of his coffee cup. "Well . . . newspaper stories and whatnot. There was no shortage of press about the Insightfuls."

"They have a name." She declared it, resentful that it was *they*. Not *we*.

"An insulting one, at least initially. Once Henard's credibility went on a downward spiral, anyone who was part of his experiments became a laughingstock," he said, flinching as he delivered the last word. "I mean no offense to your aunt. That's just what happened. It's interesting how words change, nevertheless. 'Insightfuls' was derogatory at first, and over time it became rather neutral. Even Insightfuls themselves use it now."

A defiant redefinition. Nathalie liked that.

Jean came over with the check. Christophe, who insisted on paying, settled it and stood up. "I must be going. As it is I'll have to explain my sudden departure from the morgue."

She smiled, rising from her chair. "Departure."

He met her smile and pushed in the chair. Walter the sketch artist had gone, leaving *Le Petit Journal* behind. Nathalie grabbed it and followed Christophe into the street. As they stood outside the entrance, he spotted the newspaper under her arm. "If you choose not to touch the glass anymore, I understand and would not fault you. If you change your mind, please make me aware of anything you see."

She still wished to be rid of the visions, now more than ever. "I appreciate it."

"For the sake of the investigation, I'll classify you as an Insightful. If that's acceptable to you, that is. I recommend it only because they're treated as credible witnesses if their power reasonably assists an investigation. Most prefer to keep their magic a secret these days, so they're granted the option of anonymity. Since we don't know for sure . . ."

His voice trailed off. *Since we don't know for sure what you are, we'll make believe you fit into a category we understand.*

What else was there to do? "I suppose that's a good idea. Practical, anyway."

"Very good. And one more thing," he said in a softer tone, stepping closer. "Once before, I told you to be safe. The blood jar, letters, being followed—if anything else happens, come to me. It may or may not be the Dark Artist. But always come to me from now on. Whatever else you choose to do, please promise me this."

"I promise," she said. Her voice caught in her throat, just a bit, because she'd never been so attracted to anyone. And only in that moment, when he bid her good-bye, did she realize it.

She sat on a wall outside Notre-Dame to read the newspaper and write her article. The Dark Artist sent "Paris," via *Le Petit Journal*, nothing other than the Lovers fastened onto a paper with his signature. A tarot card reader who asked to remain anonymous suggested that the Dark Artist "might be mocking the idea of choosing a romantic partner" and "doing this to sneer at the idea of love," both of which sounded like reasonable interpretations to Nathalie.

She felt a pang of sorrow for the fourth victim. Had she been a lover? A woman who once rejected him? She might have been a stranger who reminded him of a lost love. Or she might just have been in the wrong place at the wrong time with nothing at all connecting her to the Dark Artist except chance.

What story does her death tell?

Nathalie folded the newspaper and shoved it in her bag. *It's not mine to know. I've already spent too much time in the Dark Artist's head.*

Leaning back, she noticed a mime performing for a crowd a short distance away. He was dressed in black with a painted white face and white gloves, standing on a small platform.

The mime was contained in an imaginary box and made a great show of trying to break through the top lid. Once he did, he indicated a ladder above the open lid and climbed it, triumphant as he reached the top. However, in his victorious joy, he lost his balance. He took a pretend tumble onto the ground, only to land gently, dust himself off, and stand up again with a bow.

Her attention snagged on his gloves. What if the killer was a mime? What if that was the Dark Artist, right there, performing for people, while his latest victim was on display on the other side of the cathedral?

She thought about going over to him to see . . . to see what? If the mime looked like a murderer? As if she could tell. As if she had anything to go on but gloves. Yet again. At least with M. Gloves, she could place him in the morgue the day of the first vision, just like the killer.

What do I know? What do I know about any of this? I'm just a girl with a gift like the Insightfuls, without being one of them.

Turning her back on the mime, she wrote her article. Inspiration. Was that what the Dark Artist meant? Was that blood jar a way to underscore his letter, his demand that she be more gruesome?

She didn't want to play his game. She also didn't want any more blood jars in her satchel. Or worse.

Nathalie added to the article, despising the space on the page dedicated to flattering him with exaggerated statements ("cavern-ous slashes from a vicious blade," and "bruised flesh like fruit under the skin, waiting to burst").

When she was done, she made her way to the newspaper head-quarters, planning what to say to M. Patenaude as she rode the omnibus. She decided to act like a journalist about it: ask questions about Henard's experiments without saying anything about her own visions. For now she wanted to do research, and she could at-tribute it to inquisitiveness.

She hurried upstairs, nearly colliding with one of the newspa-per boys on the stairwell. After whispering an apology, she trot-ted down the hall to M. Patenaude's office. Her stomach clenched as she raised her hand to knock on the closed door.

"He left early today," said Arianne, picking her head up from the ledger. "I think something he had for lunch was spoiled. I told him not to get bouillabaisse from the Brasserie Candide because she keeps her food out too long. He doesn't listen."

Of all days.

Her gut twitched. She hadn't counted on this.

Arianne extended her hand.

Nathalie stepped back. *"Oui?"*

"Your column," said Arianne, raising a brow. "Isn't that what you're here for?"

She'd been so focused on talking to M. Patenaude about In-sightfuls that she almost forgot. She reached into her bag, tore the article out of her journal, and handed it to Arianne.

"I don't know about you," said Arianne, tapping the desk with her fingernail, "but I refuse to walk alone in the city right now. My father accompanies me to work, and my brother meets me at the end of the day. Some of my friends have similar arrangements. Do you have someone to escort you?"

Nathalie shook her head.

"I don't know how you do it," Arianne said. She wrapped her

arms around herself. "And reporting on the morgue besides? You have a lot of courage, my dear."

"Or maybe just the foolishness of youth," said Nathalie with an awkward titter. Papa was at sea and she didn't have a brother, but she wouldn't have taken their protection anyway. Would she? She'd like to think she wouldn't mill about in fear, but who could say? The fourth victim might have felt the same and walked right into the path of the Dark Artist.

"You are anything but foolish," said Arianne, smiling. She held up the article. "Kirouac is in the archive room, but I'll give it to him to review."

Archives.

An idea slinked into Nathalie's mind.

"Speaking of the archive room, could I have the key and go in there for a bit? I have some research to do."

M. Patenaude wasn't available, but countless newspapers were. Some of them must have had stories on Henard's experiments.

"I'm afraid not," said Arianne. "Kirouac has had a whole crew in there for the past two days. They're moving cabinets around and cleaning up some things. They don't want anyone in there until they're finished, which should be this evening."

"Tomorrow?"

"As long as they're done, you're more than welcome to go."

Tomorrow couldn't get here soon enough.

A delectable fruity scent greeted her in the hall as she approached the apartment. Nathalie inhaled deeply, savoring the smell before walking through the door.

She entered to see Maman making raspberry jam.

"Good news!" Maman said, beaming. "I went to buy raspberries to make a pie at Marchand's market, and Simone's mother asked if I was going to make some jam. The jar I gave them last

Christmas was the best she'd ever had, she said. We talked for a while and she offered to sell my jams at the market." Maman bounced on her toes. "She said whatever I make, she'll put on the shelf. She's going to talk to some of the other shopowners in other parts of the city, too, to see if they'll sell it as well. We agreed on a price, and now all I need to do is supply her. Isn't that wonderful?"

Given their argument yesterday, this was among the last moods she expected her mother to be in this afternoon. Nathalie had anticipated coolness or a round of inquiry or even some worry in the aftermath of the daylong headache. It took her a moment to shift her thinking to reflect this version of Maman, who was happier than she'd been in months.

"*Parfait!*" Nathalie said. Jam-making wouldn't replace sewing, neither in terms of fondness nor of income. Yet it was clear Maman was overjoyed to do *something* with her hands. "I'm so happy for you!"

She walked over to hug Maman and kissed her on both cheeks. Part peace offering, part congratulations.

"Nathalie . . . that reminds me. How is Simone? You haven't mentioned her in a while."

Simone. Just hearing the name made Nathalie's heart cry and tighten all at once, like one of those flowers that folded into itself if you touched it. "Our schedules are very different. So are our interests these days, it seems."

Nathalie didn't mention the argument they'd had. She didn't need to; both of those "reasons" were accurate and, most likely, what contributed to the tension between them.

At least on Nathalie's side.

Right?

"I understand that," said Maman, her voice empathetic. "My friends from the tailor shop . . . it's different now that I'm not there. I saw Simone this morning when I was heading to the market. She didn't see me, but I saw her getting off the omnibus at our stop. Probably to visit Céleste. The poor girl is getting worse, and they still don't know what kind of illness she has."

Céleste, innocent and at that perfect age where she should enjoy being a child, with none of the responsibilities of the adult world. No little one should be robbed of that through sickness, Nathalie thought. Yet it happened again and again. Last year one of her classmates had died from tuberculosis over the summer, and even now it didn't seem real.

"That's horrible," she said, sitting at the kitchen table. Stanley hopped onto her lap. "Céleste is a sweet girl."

Maman shook her head the way people do when a child is sick and you wish you could do something about it. It was the universal gesture of feeling powerless. Nathalie had observed it many times at the morgue—in the sag of a shoulder, the whisper of a prayer, the piteous shake of a head.

Her thoughts shifted to Simone. Was she downstairs right now?

Nathalie sat with Maman a while longer, waiting to see if her mother would bring up yesterday's quarrel. Maman did nothing of the sort and talked only about jam and fruit and any number of things that weren't Aunt Brigitte, Dr. Henard, or the Insightfuls.

How could Maman act as if yesterday hadn't happened? There was so much left to discuss. Nathalie seethed for a good long while before giving up; she was too tired to push her mother into conversation at the moment.

Her theory had fallen apart, and she had no explanation for the visions. For now, it was nice to feel normal.

Even if it was only a pretend version of normal.

24

When Nathalie stood in line at the morgue the next day, Christophe came out to meet her. He stood several meters away from the queue and motioned for her to come near. Her face flushed with warmth as he stepped close to her.

"I told one of the guards to let me know when you arrived," he whispered. "I've met with the Prefect of Police. He's arranged for a police officer to follow you while you're out in the city. He's in the morgue now and will follow you when you leave. I've sent another to watch your apartment building. Both will be in ordinary clothes, as will anyone who relieves them. We'll be doing this around the clock."

Her skin tingled. She wanted to resist, to say she didn't need an escort, but only because she didn't want to admit that she might be in danger, even if only in theory. Christophe would never put this in place otherwise.

She'd read about this sort of thing in serial novels. And now it was happening to her. This wasn't in her head anymore. It was *real*.

"You're not to acknowledge them," Christophe added. "But you'll be able to identify them. They'll have a white walking stick with a black handle."

Nathalie nodded. "Thank you, Monsieur Gagn—Christophe. That's very kind of you."

"We can't protect everyone in the city, but we can do our best to protect you. I prefer to err on the side of caution," he said with a grin, his imperfect tooth poking out.

She thanked him again and returned to her place in line as he went back inside. Several minutes later, the line moved and she entered the morgue. The same corpses were on display as the day before. As much as she pitied the fourth victim, she again refrained from touching the glass. Nathalie apologized, silently, to the girl on the slab.

I'm sorry. I can't. I need to take care of my own self, my own sanity. I hope you understand.

After a subtle acknowledgment to Christophe, she left. The temptation to turn around was strong, and despite intending to wait until she crossed the bridge, her curiosity got the better of her. She paused on the bridge to look into the Seine and peeked toward the morgue. A burly man, carrying a white cane with a black handle just as Christophe had said, strolled toward the bridge as casually as any other urban wanderer.

A feeling of power coursed through her blood. It was thrilling to be protected and to push back the Dark Artist's influence on her.

She finished crossing the bridge and settled on a bench to write her article. Afterward she took a steam tram, and the man with the walking stick boarded as well. She relaxed into a seat toward the back. At the next stop, several people got on.

Including a man with a white mustache and white gloves.

M. Gloves took a seat in the front row with a prim expression on his face. He hadn't noticed her. She was grateful (for once) for a crowded omnibus.

Could he be the Dark Artist? Time had diminished her suspicion; he seemed too old and lacking in agility. She'd wanted to have a suspect, someone to consider, because it was better than having a faceless face and a nameless man haunting her. Right now, with M. Gloves on the same omnibus, she questioned herself yet again. Was it the desire for a suspect, or was there something else about him—and not just the concept of him—that nagged away at her?

Today she intended to find out once and for all.

The policeman was observing the passengers, unaware that the portly man two rows in front of him, the one telling the ticket collector that his rat gave him "someone to talk to," might be the Dark Artist.

Nathalie planned to get off when he did and, once she was sure her protector was behind her, follow M. Gloves.

Several stops later, he exited and walked through the gate.

Père Lachaise Cemetery.

She hesitated in the aisle; if it weren't for an impatient passenger jostling behind her, she might have missed her chance to disembark.

Of all the places to go in Paris, she wouldn't expect a murderer to stop here.

Then again, why not? Maybe he did his work in the cemetery. Or found new victims among the graves.

Nathalie got off the bus. Out of habit she reached for her vial of catacomb soil before remembering its fate on the floor of the morgue. One of these days she'd have to take a trip to the Catacombs to fill another tube. She didn't like being without a good luck charm.

After a glance to make sure the policeman was close enough behind, Nathalie entered under the arch.

She and Simone had been to Père Lachaise several times in the past few years, with every visit inadvertently turning into a game of hide-and-seek. It was a densely populated city of the dead, a netherworld version of Paris, with its regal mausoleums and snaking pathways and elegant memorials. Most recently they'd gone in May, thrilled at the notion of seeing the composer Rossini's remains exhumed for reburial in Italy. They couldn't get close enough to see the coffin, but it was nonetheless exciting.

She followed M. Gloves. When he stepped off the path to a cluster of tombs, she halted. Being inconspicuous was easy enough along the main pathways. Among the gravestones and mausoleums themselves, she couldn't possibly follow without being noticed.

She jumped as a couple stepped out from behind a mausoleum. The thin, clean-shaven man wore a light gray waistcoat and the woman, a white lace tea dress and a hat with a red flower on it. Her pretty eyes peeped over an ornamental red-and-gold fan. They were so well-groomed they could have emerged from an illustrated fashion periodical. Nathalie felt like she'd seen them before. Were they the couple from the morgue who witnessed her vision and told Christophe she said "Mirabelle"? Or maybe it was only one of them she recognized. Or maybe neither, because here she was, skulking through a cemetery after someone who probably wasn't the killer but could be.

"Mademoiselle, are you lost?" asked the man.

Nathalie glanced past them to M. Gloves. The tombs of Abelard and Heloise, famously tragic lovers from the Middle Ages, were in that direction. "I was heading to, uh, Abelard and Heloise. I think I see the monument from here."

"Don't forget to leave them a love letter," the man said. "We once did." He nudged the woman, who giggled.

The couple bid her good day and moved on. As soon as they were a few steps away, Nathalie peeked over her shoulder. Seeing the policeman with his walking stick, she swelled with confidence and trailed M. Gloves.

He wound his way through tomb after tomb, taking so long Nathalie wondered for a moment if he was luring her somewhere.

No, that couldn't be. He hadn't seen her.

Had he?

At last he stopped and paused before a grave. She moved over to the left a few rows in order to approach and observe from the side.

He took off his gloves and reached into his pocket, opposite the one with the rat. Carefully he pulled out a white rose and placed it on the grave.

Pretending to gaze at the markings on the tombs, Nathalie drew closer, stealing glimpses every few steps. When she was several gravestones away, he knelt on the grass and blessed himself.

She narrowed the gap between them until she could see the gravestone better. The white marble, with scrollwork all along the border, had a faded inscription. She sidled nearer to see.

JANINE THÉRÈSE DUBRAY
BORN 7TH MAY 1862
DIED 20TH OCTOBER 1875
IN HIS WILL IS OUR PEACE.

M. Gloves buried his head in his hands and began sobbing.

She was suddenly ashamed of being here, intruding on him this way. She'd been mistaken. Entirely, utterly mistaken. She should never have considered him, not for one moment.

Those weren't the bare hands of a killer who wore gloves. Only the shaking, desperate hands of a man still grieving. Not the hands that wielded a knife in rage, not the hand that held down screaming girls until they were sliced to death.

Flushed with shame, she turned to go. She kicked a rock into a gravestone, startling M. Gloves.

"Hello?" He peered behind him, tears streaking his round face. If he recognized her, he didn't show it.

"Hello, I—I thought you were someone else," she said, hoping the humiliation wasn't as obvious as it felt. "I'm sorry. And . . . my condolences."

"Thank you." He gestured toward the grave. "My daughter. Lost her to cholera. Tomorrow her best friend from childhood is getting married, and . . ." His shoulders slumped.

Nathalie gave him a somber nod and left him, this man who plainly was neither the Dark Artist nor even M. Gloves. He was M. Dubray, a father still very much in mourning twelve years after his child's death. He deserved to grieve in private.

25

Within a half hour Nathalie was immersed in the archives at *Le Petit Journal*, having spent the entire trip from the cemetery to the newspaper issuing mental apologies to M. Dubray. She chastised herself for being foolish, for having fixated on him at all. It was time to adjust her thinking and take a different approach.

More than ever she needed facts.

M. Patenaude was in an editorial meeting, which she didn't mind so much, because she wanted to find out as much as possible on her own before talking to him. She was embarrassed that she'd known so little of Henard's experiments and of the Insightfuls when she talked to Christophe. People who had or once had magical abilities may have walked by her on the street or stood next to her in the morgue room. There was so much to learn that she felt like an explorer discovering a new land.

Obviously her parents had avoided the topic because of Aunt Brigitte.

The archive room, a maze of soaring wooden cabinets, had at least one copy of every daily newspaper since its founding in 1863. Given that she didn't know when Henard or his patients first made headlines, she began at the only place she knew for certain. The end. After searching just a week's worth of newspapers—during September 1870, when Henard was killed—she knew she'd underestimated the enormity of the task.

Nathalie pulled out the article about Henard's death and leaned against a drawer, sizing up the rest of the row. Hundreds and hundreds of newspapers. It would take days to sort through them all.

She unfolded the newspaper dated September 17, 1870 and began to read.

Pierre Henard, Doctor of "Insight," Found Dead in Laboratory

Dr. Pierre Henard, 58, was found dead in his laboratory Friday morning. Henard, who briefly rose to fame with his now-infamous blood transfusions, was likely poisoned, says Prefect of Police Émile de Kératry. Signs of a struggle were also evident; much of the doctor's equipment was destroyed. Dozens of glass vials containing blood were shattered throughout the laboratory. Henard's neck and face were covered in cuts made with a glass shard found at the scene; de Kératry said these were likely postmortem.

Vials containing blood. Like the blood jar. *Was that a coincidence or a connection?* Nathalie continued searching backward. In July 1870, there was another article of note.

Henard to Resume Transfusions

Advertisement posters spotted throughout Paris yesterday made an announcement: After a six-month hiatus following the accidental death of a patient during a transfusion, Dr. Pierre Henard is resuming his practice on August 1.

Despite the controversy surrounding Henard's experiments, people continue to ask for the procedure.

"It's not as busy as it once was," said the owner of a nearby business, "but people are still coming out of there with bandages every now and then."

In 1866, Henard conducted an experimental blood transfusion, blending science and, as some claim, "magic" to bestow "magical powers." The procedure entails drawing blood, adding Henard's proprietary chemical concoction to it, then reinjecting the blood into the body.

That first patient: the doctor himself.

Henard, who will no longer speak to members of the press, reportedly still possesses his power—the ability to diagnose disease through smell. He claims never to have experienced side effects, unlike all others who have received his transfusions, though rumors suggest he periodically loses his sense of taste.

Several patients have gone mad, and many say their magical abilities were temporary, some lasting as little as two months.

Has Henard refined his formula or procedure? Or, as one distraught former patient says, is it simply that "there are always people imprudent enough to ignore the lessons learned by others"?

She folded the newspaper and filed it back into the drawer.

"Nathalie? What are you doing?"

She jumped. M. Patenaude stood at the end of the row, hands behind his back, a modest smile on his lips. He rocked slightly on his heels.

"I—I was waiting to talk to you," she said, leaning against the drawer.

"Yes, Arianne told me." He pointed to the cabinet. "I meant what are you researching?"

"Dr. Henard."

M. Patenaude's caterpillar eyebrows arched. He took slow, deliberate steps toward her. "Why so?"

"Well, that's why I wanted to talk to you, too. Monsieur Gagnon said you knew a lot about Henard. And, um, Insightfuls."

"Insightfuls. That's quite a topic." He removed his glasses and pinched the top of his nose. "Let's . . . continue this conversation in my office."

Nathalie closed the drawer gently, tucking away the people

and events of everyday Paris, preserved in ink. She followed M. Patenaude to his office in silence. When she stepped in, he held up his finger and stepped back into the hall.

He sent Arianne away on an errand and entered his office, closing the door behind him. "Monsieur Gagnon told me you'd want to talk."

The heat rose to her cheeks as she settled into a chair. "Did he?" *How much did he tell you?*

M. Patenaude put his hands in his pockets and walked over to the window. He stared through it for so long Nathalie thought he'd forgotten about her. She glanced at the closed door, uncomfortable with his prolonged silence.

"He didn't offer many details, only that you found out that your aunt was one of Dr. Henard's patients and that you had some questions he couldn't answer." M. Patenaude turned away from the window and faced her. "Also, he didn't send you to me because of any newspaper stories. He sent you because I'm an Insightful."

The words coming out of M. Patenaude's mouth didn't match Nathalie's understanding of the man, the editor-in-chief of *Le Petit Journal* who was prone to restive gestures and always in a hurry. *He* had a magical power?

"I—I never would have guessed." Her entire perception of him had changed with one sentence. Might she have an ally? She bubbled with excitement. This was it, her first chance to talk to someone who lived this experience and wasn't insane. She appreciated that unlike Maman, he was direct. He wasn't afraid to *talk* about it.

"We're everywhere," he said, spreading his palms out. "Men, women, all classes, religions, professions. You don't often know it, not anymore. The rest of society has . . . varying opinions about it. Some of us boast about our abilities, others hide them, and most are somewhere in between, I think. Whether or not they still have their powers."

"What's *your* gift?" She leaned forward. "Do you still have it?"

"Yes. I can tell whether or not someone is telling the truth."

She hesitated, halted in surprise, as if he had cast a spell. "You . . . can read minds?"

"No," he said. "It's more subtle than that. I can understand the intentions behind what people say and write. I hear words and voices in a way similar to music. Truth is melodious; lies are full of wrong notes, a blatant mistake in a symphonic piece. The bigger the lie, the more off-key it sounds to me."

The admission sounded ridiculous yet plausible. As with her own mysterious ability. "Would you show me?"

"I'll ask you some questions," he said, tenting his fingers. "Lie in response to some, be truthful in reply to others."

"Go on."

"What's your middle name?"

"Frances." Truth. It was her grandmother's name. Although she didn't love it, she had loved Mamie very much.

"What's your favorite color?"

"Pink." Lie. She disliked pink.

"What is the last novel you read?"

"*Frankenstein.*" No, she'd yet to finish it, in fact.

He gazed out the window once again. "You told the truth, lied, and told a half-truth. You haven't read the book in its entirety, I'm guessing."

"All correct." Nathalie paused, crossing and uncrossing her legs. She could trust him. "Monsieur, I have to tell you something."

"Yes?"

"I have a special ability, too."

He whipped his head around. "*You* do? I thought you were asking because . . . well." He adjusted his glasses. "What do you mean, exactly?"

So Christophe truly *hadn't* told M. Patenaude, just as he hadn't told Nathalie about M. Patenaude's gift. Until this moment, she hadn't been able to tell if M. Patenaude already knew and was just waiting for her to come out with it; his reaction was too sudden, too honest to be an act. Christophe earned even more of her respect by not telling her secret or M. Patenaude's and for merely setting a conversation in motion.

"It started shortly after I began doing the morgue reports." Then, just as she had with Christophe, Nathalie took some time to tell him everything about the visions.

"Of course," he said, clasping his hands. "Now it all makes sense."

"It does?"

He nodded. "You once wrote that one of the victims 'suffered' before her death. I had you qualify that, do you remember?"

"I do."

"I knew you were writing from a place of honesty." M. Patenaude got more animated with every word, like a scientist happening upon a new discovery. "That is, I could tell you weren't merely assuming—it would have been a sensible guess anyway—but that somehow you *knew*. I couldn't figure out how, needless to say, and I confess to being . . . wary of you."

She remembered well his strange behavior and how it had unsettled her. Never would she have guessed it was a reaction to her own conduct.

"Apologies if that came across at the time," he added quickly.

"It's understandable," she said. And then, after pausing long enough to collect her thoughts, she told M. Patenaude how she'd learned more about Henard's experiments, and how she'd deduced that Aunt Brigitte was an Insightful. She told him about the blood jar, too, and how Christophe had since assigned her police protection. He listened, bobbing his head and fidgeting incessantly with his glasses. "When I told Monsieur Gagnon all of this, he explained that Henard died in 1870, the year before I was born. That's what I was searching for in the archives. More information about that and about Henard's experiments. I—I need to know how this happened. Did someone else continue to do the blood transfusions after him, maybe something secret?"

M. Patenaude shook his head. "Unlikely. He was very protective of his work, especially when people started criticizing him. He made a ceremony of burning his notes once, claiming his knowledge would die with him." He walked to the front of his desk and leaned against it. He didn't seem to know what to do with his hands. Tenting them, pressing them against the desk, folding his arms, all in the course of a few seconds. "Nathalie, there's something else you need to know. I shouldn't be the one to tell you, but at the moment, I don't think I have a choice. I'm sure your father will understand."

"Papa? What does he have to do with this?" Yet as soon as the question left her tongue, she knew.

"Your father got one of Henard's transfusions, too." M. Patenaude's words echoed Nathalie's thoughts; in her mind she recited the answer right along with him.

Confusion and happiness spun her in a circle, pushed by the very unusual feeling of discovering a tremendous secret that had been kept from her.

Then he lowered his voice. "He has the gift of healing. And I'm forever grateful to him for it. My youngest son had scarlet fever, and if it weren't for your father, he would have . . ."

Nathalie's breath caught as the weight of M. Patenaude's unfinished words, and of Papa's gift, rested on her soul. "That's— that's beautiful."

"It is. I have a lifetime of gratitude and debt to pay your father, though he's too humble to acknowledge as much."

Nathalie took in the profound significance of that sentiment. She could imagine no greater bond between two people than a life saved, and so many things fell into place at that moment. M. Patenaude's willingness to give her an unorthodox job for a sixteen-year-old girl. His sense of loyalty to Papa and, by extension, to her. And her own blood tie, literally, to the Insightfuls.

"Somehow he passed it on to me," she began, almost to herself. "Do you agree? It's only logical. As much as magic can be logical, although I suppose together with science it *is* logical, or can become logical. Why didn't I think of it before? I almost feel silly for not coming up with that idea." Even as she spoke the words, tumbling one on top of the other before M. Patenaude's shaking head could interrupt her, she recognized the hollowness in them.

"Insightfuls don't bestow their gifts on their children, not that I know of," M. Patenaude said, still shaking his head. His words were laced with empathy. "My wife and I both have gifts, but our sons have no magical abilities. And the same is true for the dozens of other Insightfuls I know, and the accounts I've read of still others, so—"

"I don't care what you say," said Nathalie, her demeanor stiff as a tree. First she had an answer, then she didn't. No. She had to be right, and M. Patenaude had to be wrong. "You don't know every one of Henard's patients. Maybe some of them did give birth to children like me. There could be hundreds of us for all you know."

"Nathalie, I'm so sorry—"

She stood up, bristling with annoyance. "We should talk about this again. I have as many questions as you're willing to answer."

He opened his hands toward her. "Anything. I promise."

Now it was she who shook her head. "Not now. Maman is expecting me. I have to go."

With a nod to M. Patenaude, she excused herself and hurried out of the building. Not until she was almost home did she even remember to look for her policeman, who sat in the back of the steam tram. Once she spotted him, she straightened up with even more resolve.

Time to explain everything, Maman. Everything.

For some time Nathalie had been dreading the possibility of running into Simone at the apartment building. When it finally happened, this day of all days, when she had so much else on her mind, the encounter was in some ways exactly what she'd imagined.

In other ways, it was not.

Nathalie opened the door to the foyer just as Simone was about to do the same from the inside.

Simone emitted a tiny "Oh!" while Nathalie lost the ability to make any sound at all. Instinct jumped in as Simone crossed the threshold to go out; Nathalie felt a rush of longing to tell Simone everything that had happened since their fight almost a week ago but forced it back.

They walked past each other in tense silence. Nathalie took one more step and caught the door so it didn't close between them. She turned back to Simone, whose blond curls obscured half her face. "We should . . ."

We should talk sometime. That's what was supposed to come out. Instead her words turned into weak, sightless baby mice when Simone wheeled around and threw her a cold look. Nathalie hadn't noticed it before, but Simone's face was tear-stained and her eyes puffy.

Nathalie hadn't seen Simone cry very often. For all her exuberance, Simone protected her tears. "I keep them in an imaginary jar that only comes out when I'm alone," she'd once said.

"What's wrong?" Nathalie blurted out, taking a step toward Simone.

Simone turned her back to Nathalie, hurrying out and down the stairs without a word. Nathalie let go of the door and stood there a moment as it closed, leaning her head against it.

She didn't feel as upset toward Simone anymore and thought perhaps the feeling was mutual. "Maybe it's for the best," she said out loud, because if you said something out loud it was easier to convince yourself.

Wasn't it?

26

Nathalie entered the apartment to the sound of Maman humming cheerfully and the smell of boiling strawberries. Stanley greeted her, as he always did, and for a moment she took in this scene of what should have been domestic contentment. She looked around the apartment. Everything was so familiar. Yet everything was also different.

Papa was an Insightful.

And her parents had never told her. Never said a word about Henard's experiments, such that Nathalie scarcely knew anything about them until recently. Like some ignorant child in a rural town where people couldn't read instead of a young woman living in a magnificent city full of culture. Entrusted with the duties of a journalist, besides.

Do they think I'm a fool? That I would never find out, that they could hide it from me forever?

She reached for her catacomb dirt, forgetting for the second time that day that it wasn't there anymore.

"Come try this jam!" Maman called from the kitchen.

She tossed her bag on the sofa and approached Maman, who stood with a spoonful of jam, ready to feed her.

Like a child.

Nathalie took the spoon and sampled the jam. With a forced smile, she handed back the spoon. "This will sell out in no time."

Nathalie's eyes went to the jars of jam, lined up in a row.

They resembled blood jars. Larger, of course. And she knew

the dense, dark liquid and streaks inside the glass and even the droplet on the table was only jam.

"That's my wish." Maman turned back to her strawberries and stirred them.

All the way home, Nathalie had thought about what she wanted to say, how she wanted to bring up her powers and what she'd learned from M. Patenaude. She was tired of playing games.

"I found out some things, Maman. About Papa. And about myself, I think."

Maman paused for a moment, and then continued stirring even more vigorously than before. "Things."

"Aunt Brigitte isn't the only member of this family who was one of Dr. Henard's patients," Nathalie said, her voice steady and clear. "Papa was, too. He's a healer. Monsieur Patenaude told me."

Maman placed the wooden spoon on the counter and reached for a lemon, the muscles in her arm taut. "That's absurd, Nathalie. M. Patenaude peddles gossip for a living. You should know better."

"He has no reason to lie. For what?"

"Who knows why people do what they do?" Maman said, cutting the lemon. She squeezed some into the pot of strawberries and stirred some more.

"Are we going to dance with one another again, Maman? I was right about Aunt Brigitte, and I'm right about this. What I don't understand is why you're lying to me."

"Lying?"

"That's what you'd call it if I evaded the truth, changed the subject, answered questions with questions, and dismissed the facts because they weren't convenient."

Maman slammed down the spoon. "What you call lies, I call protection." She whipped her head around, a hawk alerted to prey. "I told you how embarrassing it was that Aunt Brigitte ended up in the asylum. It's a disgrace to admit to being any part of that."

"Monsieur Patenaude doesn't seem ashamed to be an Insightful."

Maman stepped toward Nathalie. "Do not ever use that term. It's an insult."

"It's only an insult if you want it to be."

"You don't know what you're talking about," said Maman, moving so close she was practically under Nathalie's chin. "You don't know how Tante was ridiculed and how your father was mocked when Dr. Henard went from hero to fool. Yes, I kept it from you, and I'm not sorry that I did."

Nathalie's face erupted with heat. "Maybe you should be. Because Papa passed it on to me."

"What?"

"I have visions, *Maman*." Nathalie spat the words as if they were sour milk. "At the morgue. Every time the Dark Artist has a victim on display, I touch the viewing pane and I see the murder scene."

"You're lying." Maman took a step back.

"Now *I'm* lying? No, I'm not. I see the cuts he makes in their faces, Maman. I see the blade sink into their flesh, I see the girls scream until they die, I see the blood pour out of them. I see it as if I'm killing them with my own hands."

SLAP.

Maman, quick as a wasp. Maman, who hadn't struck her in the face. Ever.

Nathalie looked away as her hand went to her cheek, cradling the sting. Hot tears trickled over her fingers before she could stop them.

She pulled her hand away, eyes no longer tearing up, and wheeled to face Maman.

The fury she expected to see wasn't there. Instead her mother's face reflected fear. Terror, even.

Maman retreated, her back to the stove.

"Why are you backing away?"

Her mother stuck out her chin. "You're not acting like yourself."

"Neither are you!"

Maman clutched her apron. "Something is wrong with you. You're either making this up or you have magical powers you have no right possessing. You and Simone, always exploring something. Her mother has mentioned tarot cards. You . . . are you two involved in something? The occult?"

Nathalie narrowed her eyes to slits. "I am not dignifying that absurdity with an answer."

"I ask because *this* is not possible," said Maman, more to herself than Nathalie. "No one has ever . . . unless you're mad."

"That's your answer? Slap me and then go stand by a pot of strawberries?" Nathalie flailed. "You can't run away from this, Maman! I'm *not* crazy. I *do* have powers. Being scared of me is about the cruelest response you could have. *Merci* for your understanding. And then you wonder why I don't tell you anything."

"Perhaps it's better that way for both of us."

Nathalie turned on her heel and headed to the apartment door. "Oh," she called, her hand on the doorknob, "and you'll be happy to know that I'm never going to touch the morgue glass again. Maybe that will ease your fears."

"What do you mean, never again? Why?"

Nathalie stormed out of the apartment without answering. She stalked down the hall toward the door that led to the roof and felt for the key above the threshold.

Where is it? Did someone take it?

She looked back toward the apartment, dreading the thought of going back in. Then she spotted the key on the floor, in the corner. She opened the door, locked it behind her, and climbed the stairs. She sprawled on the flat roof and lay there thinking and crying, and at one point contemplated the idea of throwing herself off. It wasn't a serious thought; when she ran through the scenario, her imagination halted as soon as she pictured walking up to the edge.

The sky went from blue to yellowish blue on the horizon to

brilliant orange. Darkness trickled in, and at some point, she noticed stars. Eventually she drifted off to sleep and awoke with a start.

Thunder.

She went downstairs to the warmth of the bed, Stanley curled up beside her. The thunderstorm came through, louder and more powerful than any other this summer, or so it seemed.

27

When Nathalie woke up in the morning, there was a note from Maman on the kitchen table.

At Mass. Will return before noon.

Nathalie crumpled the paper and threw it on the floor. Mass? They went to church for holidays and funerals. Otherwise Maman never went to Mass, only to prayer services at Notre-Dame from time to time.

Maman had never slapped her in the face before, either.

After a quick breakfast, Nathalie returned to her bed. She wrote in her journal.

Waiting.

Wondering.

A short while later she heard the key turn in the apartment door lock.

Her heart thumped. She listened as Maman opened the door and cleared her throat. Next she heard paper crinkling; Maman must have picked up the note. Every mundane sound rustled with suspense, each one a ghost of uncomfortable possibilities, startling her, then skulking into the shadows.

As if she could avoid conversation with Maman forever.

In the next moment she heard Maman's footfall draw closer. Nathalie's heart pumped faster and she leaned over the side of the bed, sliding the journal underneath.

Maman cleared her throat again, this time at the bedroom doorway. She took off her white-flowered hat. "May I come in?"

Nathalie shrugged.

"I went to Mass today."

"I saw the note."

"I prayed for you," Maman said, her voice neither soft nor sharp.

"In case I'm some kind of monster? Maybe I need an exorcism." Nathalie made the sign of the cross in the air, then let her arm drop to the bed, dead weight.

Maman entered the room and sat on the corner of the bed. "I prayed for myself, too."

"So that you know how to handle your demon child? Or mad daughter? Or science experiment freak? It must be one of those."

"Stop it. You're in your bedroom, not on stage." Maman's tone had an edge to it for the first time since she'd begun talking. She exhaled into a weary, troubled sigh. "Please tell me what's been happening. All of it. I will listen without getting upset. I promise."

Nathalie propped herself up straighter. "*Non.*"

"*Ma bichette.*" Maman drew closer, placing her hand on top of Nathalie's. "Please."

Stanley jumped off the bed. "Giving us privacy, are you?" Nathalie watched him leave the room. She paused, staring at the empty doorway for a moment, before facing Maman.

"It started a little more than three weeks ago."

Nathalie described the visions and the memory loss. She didn't mention the hypnosis or the fight with Simone, and she left out anything having to do with the Dark Artist's threats. Sharing this secret with Maman was challenging enough; she didn't need to throw that onto the pile. As for her choice to stop eliciting the visions, she explained it as something she didn't want to torment herself with any longer. Maman understood.

When Nathalie was finished, Maman stood up. "If I didn't know better, I'd say you were one of Dr. Henard's patients."

"That's what I've been trying to say."

"I don't understand any of it. This has never happened to any-one before, not that I know of, but maybe something else brought this on." Maman traced her scars several times before continuing. "I received a transfusion, too, Nathalie."

"What? *You* have magical powers?"

"No, I don't. It—it didn't work on me. A handful of people tried the experiment and failed to acquire any special ability. I was one of them. No one other than your father knows that."

She felt as though instead of speaking those words, Maman had punched her in the stomach with them. Was that the reason? If both of her parents had gotten a transfusion, then maybe whatever didn't work on her mother was passed on to Nathalie.

Yet there was no way they could ever know, was there?

Perhaps I inherited the magic she was supposed to acquire. "What happened?"

"Your father and I met shortly after he and Brigitte received transfusions," said Maman, her voice almost apologetic. "It was a different time. You don't understand. This was a promising new discovery, a chance at something incredible. Superhuman."

Nathalie shook her head. "You didn't think there would be risks. You trusted that something so inconceivable was real without consequences."

"Yes, we did," said Maman, and her voice was more sure than it had been so far. "We did believe it. The proof was there at first, and magic was a new, enticing discovery. With the exception of the very religious and very old-fashioned, most everyone in Paris thought this was the next big step for the human race. It's hard to comprehend that now, but for a time, Dr. Henard was praised for his work. He tried to be a good man, I think." The last few words caught in Maman's throat, and she paused.

Nathalie folded her arms. *If I had been alive at that time, would I have tried it?*

"I was enamored with the gifts Papa and Brigitte had," said Maman, a sentimental shine in her hazel eyes. "I wanted that, too. When I got the transfusion and it didn't take, I was devastated. Hundreds had been successful, and fewer than twenty hadn't.

I pitied myself for being unlucky. And I was jealous, very jealous, of your father and Tante. I felt inferior to them and almost ended the relationship with Augustin because I didn't think myself worthy."

Nathalie loosened her folded arms and put her hands over her heart. She beckoned Maman to continue.

"Not long after that, the stories started cropping up. We thought the problems were anomalies, just like I was among the few anomalies in the experiments." Maman fussed with her hat. She pinched the silk flowers and tugged at the fabric. "We were safe for a while, until your father's symptoms emerged. Then Brigitte's behavior started to change little by little."

"Like what?" Nathalie asked. "What did you notice first?"

Maman placed the hat beside her. "She began having trouble distinguishing between reality and dreams, what had happened and what was going to happen. When she started taking matters into her own hands, violently at that . . ."

Nathalie knew the rest. From Mme. Plouffe's to the asylum. She wondered how many other women at Saint-Mathurin had been among Henard's patients.

"What about Papa?" Nathalie asked in a whisper, stroking her bed linens.

Will he go mad?

Will I?

"He uses his power to tend to sailors who have fallen ill in a subtle way, such that people often don't know he's healed them."

My goodness. Such humility. She loved Papa more than ever.

"Whatever they have," Maman continued with a sigh, "he takes into himself—just a small part. A broken leg, his leg will be sore. Whooping cough, he'll develop a cough. Never deadly, thank the Lord. Henard's patients suffer, but they don't die from their symptoms. Even so, he has to restrict how often he heals or he'd be constantly sick, and he cannot heal himself."

"He'll be able to heal your hands."

"Not completely. He can't make them perfect again." She examined her hands, sadness darkening her face. "But he can take the pain away, maybe help me move them better. He can prevent someone from getting too weak, and he can help someone's body get stronger, healthier. I suppose you could say he helps the body heal itself."

A surge of pride swelled in Nathalie as she took in what that really meant. Her father helped people, better than a doctor, better than anyone. And he did it even though it temporarily diminished his own health.

She thought of the many times growing up where he'd touch her skinned knee or kiss her forehead when she was sick, telling her he'd make her stronger. She thought that was just the kind of thing fathers said, a playful game, but he really had been helping her. "That sounds like a marvelous gift. I don't understand why it's a family secret or a source of shame."

Maman closed her eyes, then opened them. "Along with Henard's disgrace came the disgrace of his patients. One time," she said, shaking her head, "a crowd marched down Champs-Élysées saying Henard's patients were diseased, or unnatural. 'Henard is not your God,' they shouted, and 'You're less than human, not more,' and worse."

Nathalie swung her legs over the side of the bed and stood up. She gave Maman a hug.

She'd held back telling Maman some things, and she had no doubt Maman was doing the same. Maman's eyes held on to something—reasons, perhaps, and explanations she was too ashamed or uncomfortable to share. She still resented Maman for hiding all of this, but it was the kind of resentment that, she realized for the first time, might become more tepid with mutual understanding. Anger wasn't going to get her anywhere.

A cautious peace settled around them for the rest of the day, fatigue slipping into the cracks. Nathalie could trust her mother with some, but not all, of her secrets. For now these would have to do.

28

The next morning, on her way to the morgue, Nathalie stopped at the mail box. When she saw Agnès's fluid penmanship, her insides became gnarled tree roots. Did Agnès forgive her? Surely she'd be understanding. But Nathalie had expected Simone to be understanding, too. What if Agnès was just as lacking in compassion, or worse? Nathalie couldn't bear another conflict this summer.

She stashed the letter in her bag, opting to read it later. When she was ready.

That decision lasted scarcely a minute.

Biting her lip, she leaned against the wall and retrieved the letter.

> *Dear Nata,*
>
> *I confess that my first response was not a very kind one. Upon reading your letter about this ability of yours, I wrote one promptly.*
>
> *Then I did what Grandmother recommends. I put it to the side and slept on it. When I woke up, I read it again. I tore it up and disposed of it.*
>
> *It does not matter what I said, because that letter was selfish and impulsive; I only tell you about it out of guilt. These are the words that reflect my thoughts.*
>
> *I do not hold this against you at all, my beloved friend. A secret such as that is neither easily kept nor easily shared.*

You have endured more this summer than all of our school-mates together, and that you can speak of it at all, with any semblance of normality, is stunning. I would be a heap of sorrow and nervousness. You are, even at our age, a pillar of both pluck and resilience.

Hypnotism is not something I believe in—or rather, I didn't before your letter. Now I am not sure what I think of it. I suppose it may not be the fraudulent parlor trick I assumed it to be.

As for the Dr. Henard experiments, I know only what my parents have said. They are critical of those who partook in them, I'm afraid, and believe only those who fancied themselves better than the rest of us sought to be patients. I do not share their opinion. Do you think your power is related to that somehow?

Our date at Le Canard Curieux still holds. This shall be my last letter of the summer, for by the time you receive this, we'll be within a day or two of leaving. Aside from packing, I plan to spend my time with my hands in the earth (Papa still insists on it) and in dough—not at the same time, of course.

I very much look forward to our meeting. It is splendid to see your words, but I am eager to hear them in person. Despite the tone of our recent letters, I predict much laughter between us, too. Not all our moments should be solemn, even in the darkest of circumstances, and I know you agree.

Until then.

Bisous,
Agnès

Nathalie sighed audibly. *Thank you for understanding, Agnès.* She'd learned so much about herself and the world around her that it was hard to believe a letter sent less than a week ago could be out of date. So many things different, so many new discoveries, already.

She couldn't wait to share them all with Agnès.

Nothing new occurred at the morgue; the fourth victim was still on display. When Nathalie took a seat on the steam tram afterward, an abandoned copy of *Le Petit Journal* lay on the empty seat beside her.

Streetwalker Charlotte Benoit Identified as Fourth Victim

Charlotte Benoit. She had a name, yet her corpse was still on display.

Nathalie didn't feel the same connection to this victim because she hadn't touched the glass, and now she felt guilty about it. She hadn't given as much thought to her as Odette, the nameless second victim, and Mirabelle.

Wasn't that the point? To avoid being consumed by the madness of the Dark Artist?

She felt different this time, learning Charlotte's name. The feeling was new, something mixed with a soft brushstroke of remorse, a drop of curiosity unfulfilled, and a pinch of liberation. Maybe that's how she'd feel from this point on, now that she'd distanced herself. Or maybe that combination would shift—more of this, less of that, all of this, none of that—over time.

Or maybe the Dark Artist would stop. Or get caught. Then she wouldn't have to think about it at all. And what would happen with her gift once the murders stopped? Would it emerge again? Would she see other murders? Why *these* killings in particular? Was there something special about them that brought out her ability?

None of these questions matter. I'm never going to use this power again anyway.

Yet they did. She still wanted to understand as much as possible.

A short time later, as she handed M. Patenaude her article, she asked if he had a few minutes to continue their conversation from the other day.

"Happy to," he said, closing his office door. Arianne was away from her desk.

"I probably shouldn't be telling you this, but . . . you're the only one I can talk to right now. After everything we discussed the other day, I can't keep this from you," she said, pressing her knuckles together. With a sigh she settled into the chair across from his desk and explained how Maman had gotten a Henard transfusion but didn't succeed in obtaining magic. Despite the modest amount of guilt she felt betraying her mother's secret, she didn't see any way around it. M. Patenaude had the ability to discern truth, and he'd know if something wasn't quite right.

"I keep a lot of secrets, Nathalie. I promise not to say anything to anyone."

She regarded M. Patenaude, with his not-so-thick glasses today, and thought about just how difficult that must be. To know the truth when sometimes it might be easier to accept a lesser version of it.

Nathalie cleared her throat. "I realize I may never know how or why I have this ability. I like to think what Maman didn't get, I did, and that Papa's magic added to it somehow. Whatever happened, and whether it's correct or not, I consider myself one of you. An Insightful."

Maybe Maman didn't like that term, but Nathalie did. She liked choosing whether or not she touched the viewing pane, and she liked the idea of deciding what to call herself.

He smiled. "It's human nature to want to make sense of things. We've talked about that with regard to journalism—it's one of our truths, to be sure. So first, I think your theory is an excellent one. Second, I'd consider myself an Insightful, too, if I were you."

Nathalie took off her cap and let her walnut-colored waves fall onto her shoulders. While she was in here with M. Patenaude, peeling back a layer of her identity, it felt absurd to be dressed as a boy.

Then she asked the question that had been bothering her since she saw that headline earlier. "Do you think it's wrong of me to reject the visions? Am I being selfish?"

"Not at all." His tone was decisive, which made her glad she asked. "No two people experience this the same way. Ability, symptoms, what it means to bring magic into your life . . . it's very personal."

It occurred to her that she didn't know what side effect, or symptom as he called it, M. Patenaude endured. "What's it been like for you?"

He walked over to his desk and sat behind it, moving a stack of newspapers to the side. "Sometimes a blessing, sometimes a curse."

That's exactly how Nathalie had thought of it. She nodded.

M. Patenaude pushed his glasses up the bridge of his nose and continued. "The blessing is the feeling of clarity, of cutting through the nonsense when communicating with people. That's also the curse. Believe it or not, there are times when it's easier to hear a lie than the truth."

Easier to hear, easier to tell. Sometimes.

"And as you know," he added, "we all have something taken from us. For me, it's loss of vision to varying degrees. It comes back, but it wavers."

She stared at his glasses. That's why sometimes they seemed thick, sometimes they seemed thin. He really *had* been wearing different glasses at various times; she hadn't been imagining it. "Would you have done it if you knew you'd struggle with eyesight?"

"I've asked myself that question too many times, and the answer changes. So I've stopped asking." He pinched the stem of his glasses. "More often than not, I think yes."

"You've done a lot a good with your gift, like Papa. I'm sure that's rewarding."

"It is, but I can't take too much credit for the gift itself," he said. "You don't choose the ability. It comes from who you already are."

Nathalie hadn't thought about this, and as soon as she did, her stomach knotted up. Seeing murder came from within? "That's not comforting."

"It should be; you're learning something about yourself, what's important to you." He leaned back in his chair and crossed his legs. "You have your father's height and eyes but your mother's nose. No one can predict which physical features a child might inherit. The magic works sort of like that—some intangible attribute that makes you 'you' weaves into your ability. For example, truth has always been interesting to me, and words captivate me."

"So those are the things that manifested your power," she said, intrigued by the conclusion. What did the visions say about her?

A knock at the door interrupted them. "Mail," called a voice from the other side.

M. Patenaude rose from the desk and opened the door. After a fleeting, somewhat muffled conversation, he came back with some mail. "I asked for your mail, too," he said, handing her several unimportant pieces before halting. His eyes rested on the envelope a moment before holding it up to show her.

Uncomfortably familiar handwriting. Addressed to the Morgue Reporter with "A Fellow Writer" in the return address.

Her pulse climbed like a frightened cat up a tree.

"May I?" asked M. Patenaude.

"Please do."

M. Patenaude opened the letter and read it out loud. "'My Dear Scribe, I see you found my present to be most inspiring. Bravo on this most recent description of my latest exhibit. I am pleased. Be sure to continue.'"

Nathalie felt as if a cool breeze passed over the back of her neck. "He's disgusting."

"He is," said M. Patenaude with a nod, "yet his sentiment,

revolting as it is, is also genuine. That makes me think the safest choice remains to comply."

"I hate it." It was one thing to read Poe. It was another to write about real people and real crimes to please a killer.

M. Patenaude tucked the letter back into the envelope. "I could assign—"

"*Non.*" Nathalie pushed her chair back. She took some hairpins out of her trousers, tucked her waves back, and put on her wool felt cap. "I'm a journalist. I've already given up the visions for my own well-being. I'm not giving this up, too."

It wasn't necessarily a pleasant compromise, but it was one she could accept. For now.

As the days passed, she found peace in her decision to refrain from touching the glass, and she found strength in her trusty always-in-sight policemen. Regaining some control brought her confidence.

No worries about visions, memory loss, or entwining secrets with her soul. She would just be Nathalie Baudin, anonymous reporter of public morgue displays. Not Nathalie Baudin, odd girl who went into a *trance macabre* whenever the Dark Artist sent another victim or who felt like she was being watched by the other morgue visitors.

Right?

I feel safe.

I feel normal.

To celebrate the first week of her newly regained sense of freedom, she bought Maman flowers from Mme. Valois. She was pleased to think that this time she'd remember buying them.

Nathalie carried the bouquet of yellow, pink, and white daisies into the morgue. She almost expected fate to jab her with the irony of another victim, but thankfully, no butchered young women lay on top of the concrete blocks. All the unfortunate men and women there, except for the man whose neck and face signified a suicide by hanging, simply appeared to be swollen but asleep. Their deaths were cold, pitiable, and alone—the opposite of dramatic. Forgettable. That was in part why Nathalie found them to be so tragic.

Five days after Charlotte's body appeared in the morgue, Paris had wondered aloud if the killer had stopped. Although he'd gone more than two weeks between killing his second and third victims, the public appetite had been whetted. He'd teased them, trained them to expect more, cultivated a sense of urgency. You couldn't pass a tram stop or stand in line at the morgue or sit at a café without hearing someone speculate as to whether or not there would be any more murders. Maybe he was killed. Maybe he left the city. Maybe he'd been found out and was being blackmailed. *Le Petit Journal* asked, HAS THE DARK ARTIST PUT DOWN HIS KNIFE?

Whether or not the Dark Artist was done, *she* was.

Nathalie glanced at Christophe, who gave her a courteous nod.

As she daydreamed about meeting with Christophe and discussing subjects other than death and visions and magic, she smiled. She wanted to talk to him, truly talk to him, and was working up the nerve to invite him for coffee and a sweet.

Yes. She'd made the right choice, and she was ready for new and joyous experiences. Life should be—would be—better now.

29

The next afternoon, Nathalie stepped into the shopping arcade and paused to let her eyes adjust. As much as she enjoyed being outside, a stroll through the bustling passage, with its vaulted glass ceiling and granite floor, was equally stimulating. The plethora of shops and restaurants on either side brought the boulevard indoors, which Nathalie thought to be a clever concept.

She made her way along the walkway, passing underneath the decorative wrought-iron signs that arched overhead. Somewhere between the stationer's shop and a perfumery, she halted. People ambled to and fro, but something didn't feel right.

Was someone following her?

She turned and saw her policeman the usual distance away. No one loitered or pretended to look away; nothing seemed out of the ordinary. (If anything, people were annoyed that she didn't keep moving along.) After examining every face in view, she concluded that she'd been mistaken. It must have been the combination of her policeman and this confined, crowded space.

Shaking her head, Nathalie continued along the passage. As she approached Le Canard Curieux, Agnès arrived from the opposite direction. She was tempted to burst into a run and scoop petite Agnès into her arms.

They met at the entrance, bubbling with hellos and hugs and cheek kisses. A waiter seated them inside the restaurant and presented them with menus.

"You seem so refreshed!" said Nathalie. "If Summer were a sixteen-year-old Parisian girl, she would look like you."

Agnès's dirty blond hair had grown lighter over the summer, and her peachy skin was a few sun-kissed shades darker than usual. Her clear blue eyes sparkled more than ever, and her pink cotton dress with white peonies framed her summer look perfectly. Nathalie was suddenly aware of her own drab hair and sunburned cheeks.

"Thank you," said Agnès, beaming. "And that dress of yours is divine. I like the yellow, but I especially like the beadwork. If you weren't so much taller than me, I'd be asking to wear it."

Nathalie made a mental note to ask Maman to show her how to make a similar dress for Agnès. If she had a few months to work on it, she could give it to her for Christmas.

"I brought you something," said Agnès excitedly.

"Oh!" Nathalie's eyes lit up. "One of those violet-flavored candies?"

Agnès's face darkened. "I was supposed to bring you *two* somethings. That was to be the first. But Roger the Rascal got into my bag and took the candies I'd bought you."

"He plays his role as aggravating younger brother well, doesn't he?"

"Too well," she said, rolling her eyes. "Fortunately your inedible gift fared much better."

Agnès reached into her bag. She pulled out a bluish-green jar, similar in size and shape to what Maman used for jam, and handed it to Nathalie. "Since you couldn't come to the beach, I brought the beach to you."

"And I don't even need a hat! Good, because they're bothersome," said Nathalie with a laugh. Inside the jar was sand and seashells. She took out the three reddish-gold shells, not yet bleached from the sun, and ran her fingertips over the delicate ridges. "What stories these could tell." She then pinched a few grains of sand

and let them sift through her fingers. It wasn't the coarse sand and gravel of Paris. It was finer, subtly multicolored, and complex.

The waiter interrupted them to ask for their orders. Neither had read the menu yet, so they made their selections hastily—*quiche au fromage* for each of them—and continued talking before the waiter even left the table.

Agnès leaned in. "We had a family picnic on the beach at Deauville. Which, as enticing as that sounds, amounts to sand in your food, no matter what." She wiped off her empty plate to demonstrate. "I scooped that up from beside our blanket."

"Thank you, Agnès." Nathalie was touched that Agnès had done her best to connect her to the holiday she was supposed to have shared with her. "That means a lot."

"Don't thank me too much. It's only a temporary gift. You have to give it back next year."

Nathalie raised her eyebrows.

"Not to me. To the beach itself. I want you to bring it when we go next summer. Pour it out on the beach and get some of your own!" She laughed her Agnès laugh, one that sounded like gemstones clinking in a wineglass.

Nathalie smiled. She didn't know if she'd be able to go on holiday with Agnès next summer; it would depend on Maman's ability to work and money and a host of other things. Yet she didn't want Agnès to think otherwise, not for a moment. "That's a delightful idea. I promise to do exactly that."

The waiter came over with their meals shortly thereafter. The egg and cheese on the buttery, rich crust were fresh and flavorful, and the dish was perfectly cooked. As they ate, the conversation turned from the carefree talk of Agnès's one-day beau from Rouen to the heaviness of Nathalie's visions, the Dark Artist, and the Insightfuls. Nathalie apologized yet again for keeping Agnès in the dark and more than made up for it, telling her everything that had happened since that first touch of the glass.

"You're blessed, Nathalie," Agnès said, her voice measured with awe. "I don't care how you obtained this gift. Don't worry—I'll never tell my parents any of this. I don't share their perspective, as you can guess. Your power is incredible. It's meaningful. You're doing great things as a journalist already. And you're going to do great things with your gift."

"You are too good to me," Nathalie said with a warm smile. "I've given up my gift, though. And you know how it was with those Henard experiments. Sometimes the magical ability fades away or changes."

Agnès shook her head. "It's still there. If you want it and need it, you reach inside for it. It's become such an intimate part of you so quickly that I bet it will never leave." She tucked her hair behind her ear as she paused. "It's who you are, even if you don't use it. Like a flower that disappears into the soil over the winter. It's still a flower."

Nathalie had never thought about it that way. The analogy was sweet and comforting. She could say the same of her friendship with Agnès, too.

They spent the rest of the day together, even making a trip to the morgue. (Christophe was just leaving the display room and didn't see them. Nathalie pointed him out all the same, admitting her fondness for him. "What are you waiting for?" Agnès asked.) After the morgue they shared a *pain au chocolat* at Café Maxime, as was their custom. Agnès was in such good spirits that she began to sing. She had a voice like a songbird and was a choir member at Notre-Dame, but she didn't sing church music now. No, Agnès playfully sang some traditional French songs, got Nathalie to join in, and got the people at the neighboring table to sing along. Soon half the café was singing and laughing.

Nathalie took in the joy around her, wishing she could make it last forever. This was the best day she'd had in a long time.

They made plans to meet up again at Le Canard Curieux in a week. Simone might be out of the picture, but Agnès was here, and Nathalie appreciated her companionship more than ever.

And she had almost a year to convince Maman to let her go on holiday to the Normandy coast for a month next summer. After all, she had a mission. She had to return some sand to the sea.

Several days later, after going through the morgue, Nathalie moseyed over to the Seine. She stood on the nearby Pont de l'Archevêché and watched for a while as boats sailed under the bridge.

"Good afternoon, Mademoiselle Baudin."

Her favorite voice this summer.

"Hello, Christophe." She turned, hoping he wouldn't notice the blush in the bright sun. "Stepping out for some fresh air?"

"Fresher than bodies." He rested his elbows on the railing. They both faced the river and spoke of the boats and bathers and how nice it would be to have some *glace à la vanille* on a day like this. Then he paused and looked behind them. "I see your escort is nearby. Everything is going well, I assume?"

"It is," she said, stealing a glance at his handsome profile. "I've never had anyone look after me this way. I'm flattered."

Christophe spread his hands out on the railing. "It's part of what we do, particularly in times of heightened awareness. More importantly you . . . remind me of someone dear to me. You have her curiosity and wit."

"Do I?" Nathalie's body tingled with anticipation. She wanted to place her hand on his but refrained. "Who?"

"My sister. I became a police officer to honor her life," he said. "Her husband came home in a drunken rage and beat her, as he often did. One time he pushed her out a window, and . . ."

He didn't have to say the rest.

"I'm sorry. I—I had no idea." She felt sorry for him, and she also felt foolish. "Paris is very lucky to have you protecting it."

He half smiled. "Insofar as I can. This is the most sinister set of crimes I've ever seen—and unpredictable. There's no pattern as to how or why the Dark Artist is picking them. At least two men spend their days trying to figure out what connects all these young women and there's still no clear answer," he said, shifting his weight. "My betrothed is in America with her family for the summer. Although I miss her, I'm very glad she's not in Paris right now."

Nathalie found herself gripping the railing tightly. "Betrothed?"

"Ah, yes. I've not mentioned her? I proposed just prior to their departure in May."

Several feelings surrounded her, partnering in a *quadrille* dance around her heart. Pity for Christophe, sorrow for his sister, admiration for his pure heart, and embarrassment that his heart wasn't for her, not in that way, despite her deeply buried hope.

"No, you hadn't." Nathalie kept her focus on the river. "How exciting for you."

He said something after that, but she didn't hear him. If he noticed the tears in her eyes, she'd have blamed the sun. Fortunately an acquaintance approached him, giving her an opportunity to leave, and she didn't have to explain.

Visually the morgue was always a screaming, macabre kaleidoscope of deaths both violent and passive. Yet the place itself was quiet—somewhere between a church and an empty restaurant. People stared at the corpses, bearing expressions of horror, and often fell silent. Sometimes they gasped or prayed; sometimes they murmured to their companions or the stranger closest to them. All in all, however, the morgue was generally a place full of thoughts and respect accompanied by little sound.

But not this day.

Eight days after the fourth victim, Charlotte Benoit, was identified, and six days after her corpse was removed from display, the morgue echoed with sobs. It was a devastating sound; Nathalie was wearing a black skirt and caught herself bunching up the fabric as the sobs intensified. The room was the fullest it had been in a while, and Nathalie couldn't see the corpses just yet.

She did, however, see the back of a woman Maman's age, heavy-set and wearing a hat. The woman stood near the viewing pane, face buried in her hands.

Mme. Jalbert?

Her mind started to form questions about why and what a co-incidence when Nathalie's hands, as if possessed, pushed through the crowd. She didn't bother to apologize, because when she made her way to the glass, a piece of her soul disintegrated.

There on the slab, with a jaundiced old man on one side and a toothless woman on the other, lay a girl with sun-lightened hair and sightless blue eyes and gentle hands that would never write another word. The corpse of beautiful.

Beautiful.

Agnès.

30

No, it was a dream.

She'd had nightmare after nightmare about the morgue.

This was only a dream. The worst one yet, but a dream. Or an illusion of some sort. She'd only seen her a few days ago. Agnès was very much alive. Very much *Agnès*.

Then Nathalie heard Mme. Jalbert sob. Agnès's father came out of the Medusa door and embraced his wife. The two of them stared at their bloated, dead daughter and held each other close.

It was real.

Nathalie looked at her hands. She couldn't feel them. Couldn't feel anything. The black-and-white striped blouse she wore seemed be on someone else's arms. Her bones and organs melted and her body collapsed in on itself and she spilled onto the floor of the morgue like liquid.

Only when someone's satchel brushed her elbow did Nathalie solidify into a human made of flesh and bone once again.

She'd averted her gaze from Agnès instantly but now forced herself to look again. Heart in her throat, she made the sickening observation that Agnès had the facial cuts of the others, the temple wound of the victim Mirabelle Gregoire, and something the Dark Artist hadn't done before: two slashes ripped across the stomach.

Agnès's father began to escort his wife toward the exit. Nathalie didn't know whether to go after them or afford them privacy. She hesitated for a moment before deciding in favor of consolation, even though she herself had no voice, no means to verbally acknowledge what happened.

She'd just taken a step toward them when Mme. Jalbert broke away from her husband. She dashed toward the viewing pane, threw her heft against it with a thud, and bawled.

"My baby!" She pounded the glass several times, each strike weaker than the last. In a voice wrought with defeat, she leaned into the glass as if it were an ear for the dead. "You're still radiant, Agnès."

Acid crawled up Nathalie's throat.

I have to. I have no choice.

Agnès's father approached his wife, tenderly pulling her away from the viewing pane. Christophe appeared in the display room with two men. One carried a sheet, and the other, a stretcher.

"*Non!* Don't take her away. Don't!" Mme. Jalbert screamed, tears streaming down her cheeks.

For Agnès.

Christophe put his hand on the curtain, ready to close it.

You're blessed, Nathalie.

"Why?" Agnès's mother cried. "Why *my* girl?"

Nathalie did the only thing she could. She touched the viewing pane.

Something was different this time.

The vision didn't take place in reverse, nor was it soundless like the previous ones. Everything played out as if it were a theater scene, pulling Nathalie deeper into the Dark Artist than ever before.

She felt with his hands.

Breathed his breath.

Agnès was drowsy and coming to, as if she'd fainted. "Where am I?" She mouthed the words; Nathalie couldn't hear her.

"Somewhere safe. You had a little accident when you stepped

off my carriage. Nothing serious." That she heard; the Dark Artist's own voice, with remarkable sharpness and nuance. Through his ears.

Agnès shook her head, confused. "I don't remember." Again, soundless.

She moved to get up and he pushed her down by the shoulders. Fear shone in her eyes. She screamed so hard her neck pulsed, but it was silent.

The Dark Artist straddled her, pinning her wrists with his left hand.

She squeezed her eyes shut and turned her head. Tears streamed down her face, pooling into the blood oozing from her mouth.

The Dark Artist pressed one white-gloved hand into her neck and reached behind himself with the other. The blade led his hand back into view.

"No!" she mouthed, jerking her head.

The Dark Artist snorted. "Yes, of course!"

He plunged the knife into Agnès's throat and Nathalie snapped to the present.

She was overcome with nausea. The curtain had been drawn across the viewing pane. She braced herself against the glass and looked toward Agnès's parents. They were gone.

"Agnès." She said the name of her friend. Now a corpse. She knocked on the window, as if she could wake Agnès up, as if Agnès could just hop off the slab and walk out with her.

Nathalie began to shake. She might as well have been standing outside naked in the middle of winter.

No one noticed her. The rest of the crowd huddled together, strangers bound through the dramatic outburst of Agnès's mother.

Nathalie inhaled and exhaled carefully until the pulse hammering in her neck stopped. The questions battered her from within. Why wasn't this scene in reverse like all the others? Why could she hear the Dark Artist but not Agnès? Was this vision different because it was Agnès?

Agnès, her beautiful friend who had spent her summer near the sea, in the kitchen, in the warmth of her grandmother's home.

And now ending it in the morgue.

Nathalie was still too shocked to cry, and she was afraid that when she did, she wouldn't be able to stop.

Someone—not Christophe—pushed the curtain open again. She stared through the morgue glass to study the other eleven corpses, but all she saw was Agnès.

I will find him for you, Agnès. Find him and bring him to justice.

She walked over to the wooden Medusa door and knocked. One of the guards let her in, closing the door behind her. She was just about to explain her business with Christophe when he stepped out of one the rooms, removing his gloves.

Did he just handle Agnès's body?

"That's my friend. Agnès Jalbert."

Christophe pointed to the room he'd just exited. "The—the victim?"

She nodded, because she'd lost the ability to speak. It felt like a sponge was in her throat, swollen with the tears she cried on the inside.

"Oh goodness. I . . ." He hesitated, trying several times to say something and stopping short each time. Then he cleared his throat. "I'm so very sorry, Nathalie. Shall we talk in my office?"

Again she nodded. The sponge was still too dense with sorrow to let words pass through.

The walk along the corridor differed so much from her first time here, the day of her first vision. Back then she'd been fascinated by the workings of the morgue, intrigued by every sight and smell, devouring every detail of its antiseptic morbidity. Those things were in the periphery, and given all that had since happened, she felt almost guilty for once thinking that way. Now her life was nothing but death.

Nothing but death.

Agnès is dead. "Agnès is dead."

And that was it. Saying those three words released the tears from the dam.

She didn't want to cry in front of Christophe, but she couldn't help it. Everything in her being just poured forth. He helped her to a chair and pulled his own next to it. She took the handkerchief he offered and soaked it with her tears. She cried, with shoulders shaking, as Christophe tentatively patted her hand.

Nathalie composed herself just enough to tell Christophe about Agnès. About their time together the other day, about coming into the morgue today. About her decision to touch the viewing pane and what she saw. "Could I have helped catch the Dark Artist? Could I have *saved* Agnès?" The questions hung there like mist; she didn't expect Christophe to answer them. They were impossible to answer. "I will do whatever it takes to help catch him. I want to watch him march to the guillotine."

The strength in her voice, a voice that had vanished just a short while ago, surprised even her.

"I understand," he said, and everything from his eyes to his tone to the way he sat in the chair conveyed empathy. "That's a selfless, meaningful way to honor Agnès's life. If it becomes too much for you again, that's fine, too. Whatever you'd like, Nathalie. You can come to me anytime. For help or to—to talk. And of course we'll be keeping the patrol in place, no matter what."

She thanked him and fell silent. It wasn't a comfortable silence. The nagging thoughts she'd kept at bay used the quiet to break through to the forefront of her mind.

Did the Dark Artist kill Agnès because of Nathalie, or perhaps instead of her?

The query sat on Nathalie's tongue a moment, then rolled back into herself. No. She didn't want to say it out loud. Christophe knew the question was there; he had it, too. She was certain of it.

She thanked him for being so kind and assured him again that she would continue to help. He escorted her out, urging her to be safe, like he had the day they met. She was about to step away when Christophe put his hand on her shoulder.

Nathalie faced him, startled by the gesture.

"I'm—I'm very sorry about Agnès," he said. He extended his arms tentatively and embraced her with strong yet tender arms.

The moment was brief, but she held it close like the cherished gift it was. She hoped that whatever was taken from her memory on this harrowing day, this alone would be spared.

31

In the days that followed, a series of emotions stormed through Nathalie like an invading army, row after row. They left behind a pitted landscape, a battle-weary spirit forever altered.

And once they passed through, these waves of sadness and anger and denial and guilt, they disappeared into a void. Alongside the intense feelings was a parallel emptiness.

Everything or nothing. Noise or silence.

The crescendo of this terrible dichotomy peaked at the funeral visitation for Agnès, where Nathalie stepped into and out of herself several times.

The Jalberts' apartment was a boiling pot of black attire. People filtered in and out, pulling out black lace handkerchiefs and crying and bringing food. The din of whispers cut through the air like the wingbeats of a thousand birds.

Nathalie ignored all of it. She spoke to no one, not even Maman, as they stood in the parlor. Her eyes stayed on Agnès, laid out in a white silk dress trimmed with elaborate lace. Nathalie was relieved to see the death mask, cast in wax at the morgue. No cuts, no bruising, no horrible disfigurement. Agnès had dignity in death and somehow, despite all that had happened to her precious body, beauty.

Those who didn't know she was ripped to death might have thought she'd passed in her sleep.

A horde of *if only* thoughts rushed Nathalie. If only Agnès had spent that night with her cousin Marie as planned. If only Marie hadn't become ill during the music concert they attended and gone back to her apartment; if only Agnès hadn't chosen to stay and return to her own home that evening instead. If only she had made it here.

Surely the cousin was here, in the room now. Nathalie didn't want to know which of the morose young women lining the walls was Marie.

Nathalie and her mother approached M. and Mme. Jalbert, swathed in black wool and crêpe, and said all the things you say to those in the depths of indescribable grief. Roger stood beside them with great solemnity, staring at his older sister's corpse. His black clothes made his white-blond hair and pale complexion seem hollow, almost ghostly.

She decided not to tell the Jalberts about her vision, not here, not ever. There was no benefit to confessing it or telling them she'd seen the moment of Agnès's death or that she inhabited the gaze of the monster who did it.

After paying their respects, Nathalie and Maman approached the casket. Maman knelt in prayer. Nathalie did, too, and after praying to God, she spoke silently to Agnès. She'd done so many times since seeing her in the morgue, and probably would talk to her forever. The funeral was to be hundreds of kilometers away at the cathedral in Bayeux, and the burial in the yard of Agnès's grandmother. So this, this was the last time she'd see Agnès outside of her own memories.

My Agnès.

I did this to you. Don't forgive me, because I will never forgive myself. I promise to seek justice for you, and I promise never to cast off my gift again. All that it entails, the penalty that I pay . . . it's a just reward for my guilt.

She caught sight of Roger, blinking quickly and trying so hard not to cry. *I promise to keep an eye on Roger, too.*

Nathalie stood up and touched Agnès's cold hands, folded in prayer. *Thank you for everything.*

Maman made eye contact with her and Nathalie responded with a nod. As they made their way out of the crowded apartment, someone tapped her on the shoulder.

Simone.

She wore a black lace dress that fit her silhouette perfectly, and she smelled of rose water.

How Nathalie had missed that scent.

"I'm so very sorry," Simone said. Louis stood at her side and somberly uttered the same.

"I—I . . . thank you." She swallowed back the tears. This was too much. Simone, here, now. "Thank you both."

Afraid that she would erupt into tears and make a fool of herself, she turned abruptly away. Maman hadn't realized she'd stopped and had already gone out.

"I'll be watching Céleste during the day tomorrow," Simone called after her. "Please . . . please come by."

Nathalie bit the inside of her cheek and faced Simone once more. "I will."

After lunch the next day, Nathalie knocked on the door of the Marchands' apartment. She reached in her dress pocket for the catacomb dirt that wasn't there, like she had so many times since shattering it. Tomorrow she resolved to go to the Catacombs for more. She'd take comfort anywhere she could get it right now, even in the form of an earth-filled vial.

Simone answered the door quickly, almost too quickly, as if she'd been waiting with her hand on the knob. The brightness in her eyes had dimmed and her faint smile of greeting lacked the usual Simone sparkle.

Nathalie was unprepared for the grimness of the apartment as she stepped inside. Unwashed dishes, clothes strewn about the chairs and sofa, papers scattered—this in a home normally tidier than her own. Candles were lit in front of a small painting of the suffering Christ and another of the Blessed Mother, with a halo. A dark mood hung in the air, grief mixed with apprehension and dwindling hope.

The door to Céleste's room, which Simone used to share, was open a crack. Nathalie could hear the raspy, measured breathing of the sleeping child within. "I'm so sorry about Céleste. My mother told me she's even sicker than before."

"*Oui*," said Simone, her voice flat. She sat in a tapestry chair, moving a rolled-up blouse to the side. "For a while she would get better, then worse again, then better. Now it's just worse. The doctor comes by daily, but we may need to bring her to the hospital at some point."

Nathalie sat in the middle of the sofa. Not right next to Simone's chair, not too far away. "I pray for her every night."

"Thank you," said Simone.

Uncertain silence drifted between them. Minutes passed.

Or only seconds, perhaps.

Nathalie knit her fingers together, studying them as she wound them around one another.

"So," began Simone, "Agnès. I—I don't even know where to begin. I didn't know her well, only knew her through you, and yet I see her face every time I close my eyes."

Nathalie's throat pulsed with sorrow. "Me, too."

"As soon as I heard about Agnès, I realized how foolish this quarrel was . . . and I'm ashamed it carried on as long as it did."

"I agree." Nathalie couldn't bring herself to look at Simone, because she was afraid she'd cry. And she'd done too much of that in recent days. She stared straight ahead. "I didn't touch the glass for Charlotte. I needed to clear my head. But then for Agnès . . ." Her voice cracked.

Simone came to her side and put her arm around her, and Nathalie rested her head on Simone's shoulder. They were quiet for a while. A comfortable quiet. When Nathalie felt like she was able, she told Simone everything that had happened, from her day with Agnès to her vision in the morgue to her conversation with Christophe afterward.

"So much has changed this summer," said Nathalie.

Simone undid the bottom of her braid and weaved the blond strands again. "At least I'm still me and you're still you. We grew up together. We're still growing up together."

"When will we finish that?"

"Never, I hope."

Nathalie shook her head. "If we're in our sixties and you're still doing cabaret and I'm still dressing as an errand boy, we're in trouble."

They shared a laugh, probably a heartier one than the joke deserved.

It felt good.

"Did Louis tell you he ran into me?"

Simone nodded. "On your way to the hypnotist. What—what was *that* like?"

When Nathalie explained that Simone was actually "with" Nathalie during her almost-hypnotized state, Simone got choked up.

A tacit carefulness framed the healing moments between them, the way a timid pianist holds back during that first attempt to play Mozart or Chopin. Each sentence brought them closer.

Eventually, each told the other all that had happened since their quarrel at the Musée Grévin—an argument which, despite lasting a few weeks, seemed as long as one of Papa's sea excursions. The more they talked, the easier it became. At one point, Céleste awoke, and Simone sang her and Nathalie a nonsensical ditty about the tiger and the puppy that she'd learned for a new act at Le Chat Noir.

Céleste propped herself up and giggled. "Can you teach me the words?"

"And me," Nathalie chimed in. "I'll sing it to Stanley. I'm sure he'd be happy to hear about tigers and puppies."

Simone laughed. "For my sister and for my dearest friend's cat? *Absolutement.*"

As she taught them the song, guilt seized Nathalie like a cramp. Agnès's slain body was being transported to Bayeux to be subsumed into the earth, and here they were, learning silly lyrics. Was that wrong?

Maybe. Or maybe it was just a way to get through all of this and remember, for several fleeting moments anyway, what normal felt like.

32

She hadn't written the morgue report the day Agnès was there. Christophe had sent word to M. Patenaude, and Kirouac covered for her that day. She still hadn't read the article.

Her hands had been heavy writing the subsequent morgue reports, and the trek to *Le Petit Journal* now seemed eternal. Perhaps because of her vigilance. Even with a policeman around, she found herself studying the face of any man she could get a good look at, wondering if *he* was the one who'd taken Agnès from her. And she kept reaching for a vial of catacomb dirt that wasn't there.

The day after her heartfelt conversation with Simone, she dropped off her column and searched the mail room for a small box. She found one with a cover. Exactly what she needed.

When she went back outside, there was some commotion surrounding a carriage accident. Onlookers flooded the street, including the steam tram depot. Nathalie walked several blocks to a different one and confirmed with a professorlike man that the route went through Place Denfert-Rochereau.

Thirty minutes later she disembarked, next to the Lion of Belfort monument, which she quite liked (mostly because it was a lion, but its symbol of French resistance in response to the German blockade was impressive, too). There was no queue outside the Catacombs entrance, and she hoped that meant no tourists, either.

Not that she would notice, unless she happened to be within earshot of a group. Paris's underground crypts, full of the bones of souls given up centuries ago, was the final resting place of six million. Papa said you could go from Paris to Germany if the tunnels were end-to-end in a straight line.

One step onto the spiral-stepped descent into the Catacombs, one breath into the stale, damp air that hummed with death, and Nathalie retreated many years to the first time she'd visited the underground crypt.

Papa had brought her. Both he and Maman resisted, despite her pleas for months on end. But once Juliette Lavigne bragged about having gone, Nathalie just *had* to go. (Juliette boasted about all her exotic "grown-up" experiences, and when she switched schools a year later, Nathalie was both relieved and sorry that her daring rival had left.) It wasn't just envy that drew her. It was also, and even more so, the stories she read about or heard at school—spirits roaming and skeletons dancing and, according to Simone, who'd been there twice before Nathalie, curses falling on those who followed a particular route through the Catacombs.

Nathalie simply had to see for herself.

She pled in many ways and on many occasions. Finally, when she'd almost made a game of asking because she expected refusal, Papa conceded. *For my birthday, Papa. I'm eight. I'm not a baby anymore.* That one worked.

To Nathalie's surprise, Maman didn't object, either.

So they went into the Catacombs on her eighth birthday, just her and Papa. She was proud, practically skipping through the entrance.

The darkness in the Catacombs was heavier, blacker, than any she'd ever known. Candles affixed to the walls offered little pockets of light on some of the paths, but Papa had a kerosene lamp and led the way, with confidence, down some of the smaller, unlit paths. She followed him from several meters behind.

Stacked-up bones lined the walls. Skulls. Limbs. Ribs. Hips. All swirling in different shapes and patterns. She took a fistful of dirt from the floor near a skull display and put it in her pocket. You weren't supposed to do that, according to whichever adult made up "don't touch this" and "don't touch that" rules in Paris. She made sure Papa didn't see.

Every centimeter from floor to ceiling. More bones than she could ever count, room after room. A hotel for the dead.

The morbidity enthralled her.

At first.

After a while she drew in closer and closer yet; then she got so close she stepped on Papa's heels. He stumbled and the lamp swung around, flashing light on a group of intact skeletons, lined up like an audience before a show. Then Papa regained his footing and the skeletons disappeared into the blackness.

"*Ma bichette,* hold on to me."

Tentatively she reached for his palm and felt relief the moment her tiny fingers wrapped around his strong, calloused hand.

Then she heard voices in the crypt's pathways. They spoke another language—Spanish, maybe?—and were probably tourists.

What if they're ghosts?

Nathalie's imagination wouldn't and couldn't rest after that. *Millions of skeletons had been piled here. How could it not be haunted?*

Even with Papa's sure hand clasping hers, she didn't trust these Catacombs. There had to be ghosts everywhere. *Everywhere!* They'd sense her fear and drag her away from Papa into one of the dark, twisting paths where no one ever came out and—

She stopped walking as if someone had tied her shoes to the floor.

Papa turned to her. "What is it?"

"I want to go."

"Are you scared?"

"No, but I—I think we're lost. I don't want to get lost in here." She didn't want Papa to think she was too young to be here.

"You don't have to worry about that!" He gave her hand a squeeze. "I know the paths in here. I promise we won't get lost."

Papa *would* keep her safe. He always kept her safe. Besides, he wasn't afraid, so why should she be?

She put her free hand in her pocket and let the coarse dirt sift through her fingers. After a few seconds a feeling overtook her, coldness followed by intense warmth followed by the sense that she stood outside her own body.

Then something had happened to her mind.

She could see, as clearly as if it were happening in front of her, a young woman getting strangled. Then an old man getting struck with a rock to the head. Then a man shot. Then a little boy getting an arrow to the chest and a little girl getting pushed into a well, one after another, image after image . . .

Nathalie shook off the memory and inhaled the cool, still air of the Catacombs.

Had that been her imagination as an eight-year-old? Or the first inkling of her power? Or a supernatural punishment for taking the dirt?

At the time, she'd screamed and cried for Papa to take her out. Then she'd spun a tale to her classmates, Simone, and herself about how brave she'd been at the Catacombs. It made her feel guilty, however, so she'd begged Papa to take her again in several months, just to prove to herself that she could be there without fear. That time she didn't imagine seeing people dying or spirits pulling her away, and she hadn't ever since.

Would she today?

As she reached the bottom of the stairs, she heard the burly policeman on the steps above and voices ahead, in the tunnels. Italian, it sounded like, with a tour guide. Nathalie crossed paths with them at the stone portal that led to the tombs, stepping to the side so they could exit. While they passed her, she stared at the inscription etched onto the portal.

Arrête! C'est ici l'empire de la mort.

A warning to stop that seemed more like an invitation to explore. Who wouldn't be curious about the "empire of the dead"?

She walked several minutes down the main, candlelit pathway, looking left and right. No one else was here.

It was quiet. Too quiet.

Deathly quiet.

She turned to look at her policeman. He was standing way down by the portal, leaning on the white walking stick with both hands. He nodded. If her eyes weren't fooling her, he was grinning, too. It was the first time he or any of the policemen acknowledged her. She gave him a subtle wave before turning her back to him once again.

Nathalie peered down the next lit path to her left. This one was as good as any.

She stepped into the alley, tucking her hair into her cap. Neat columns of vertebrae, separated halfway to the stone ceiling by a line of skulls, lined the walls. She reached inside her bag for the little box she'd found at *Le Petit Journal*. After removing the lid, she kneeled near the wall and scooped up some dirt. She poured it into the box.

And waited.

And waited some more.

Nothing. No hallucinations, no ghosts, no voices, no anything. Whatever had happened when she was eight was either imagined or connected to her power. It wasn't some kind of catacomb soil curse.

She put the lid on, checking it to make certain it was secure, and put it in her bag.

A scream.

This is it. It IS the dirt. Leave it here.

But the scream wasn't a ghost or a vision, it was real. It was a man's yell.

Another scream, cut short.

She ran to the main alley. A slim man in a hat stood over the policeman, holding the walking stick. Except it was a long blade now, not a cane. A hidden weapon all along.

The man looked up at Nathalie.

He had no face.

The man bolted toward her.

She turned back down the tunnel she'd been in, sprinting until she reached a three-way fork. Unlit to the left and right, lit if she kept going straight. She looked over her shoulder; he hadn't turned the corner yet.

Disappear.

She hooked right onto an unlit path. After a few yards she stopped and whipped around, taking soft steps backward down the path. It had to open up at some point, and she'd be facing him if he followed her.

Soon she backed around a curve and the fork was out of view. Footsteps thundered and came to a sudden halt; he must be at the fork.

He's the one who followed me before. Same hat, same body shape.

What about his face?

Trembling, she retreated deeper into the darkness, winding around another curve. Farther and farther back she went until her hand struck something cold. Bones? No. Metal.

A gate. A closed one.

She crouched down, biting her tongue to keep from screaming, coated in a layer of sweat. She waited for seconds or minutes or hours or days.

No, minutes. Just minutes.

Maybe he was gone. Maybe he gave up.

A speck of flame appeared on the far wall near the curve. Nathalie balled up her fists, watching the flame dance across the wall until the man came into view holding a candle.

"Why, hello there."

33

He wasn't faceless after all.

Yet it was easy to think so from afar. His face was swathed in a white scarf, wrapped like a mummy. Slits for his eyes, nose, and mouth, nothing more.

A disguise.

He's the Dark Artist.

Nathalie stood up and slid to the right, pressing herself against a wall of bones. She reached behind her and felt a skull. She tried to wrestle it loose.

It didn't budge.

"No need for a weapon, my dear Scribe. You won't be able to get one of those things loose anyway. Packed tighter than firewood." His voice was smooth, almost indulgent. "I'm not going to hurt you. I have some questions, though." He set the candle into a sconce, casting a flicker of light on his hand.

White gloves.

Nathalie shivered, her eyes darting to the space beyond him.

Can I make it past him?

His eyes trained on her. "No, you won't escape. And even if you did, you wouldn't be able to hide. I'd hear you."

She glared at him. This couldn't be real. This couldn't be *him*. This man had to be an imposter, playing a joke, a cruel and terrifying hoax. The policeman wasn't dead. Just knocked out. It was all part of the ruse by some disgusting man who wanted to chase her and threaten her and wear gloves to give her a fright and—

"Are you the Dark Artist?" Fear shot the words out of Nathalie's throat in a high-pitched, angry tone.

The man tipped his hat and bowed slightly. *"C'est moi."*

Nathalie's intestines turned to liquid. She began to quiver uncontrollably, then channeled that into a yell as loud as her voice would go. "You killed my friend!"

The words echoed out of the chamber, along the bones, and into the darkness.

"You killed my friend," she said again, her voice barely audible. "My sweet friend who loved life and brought some of that to everyone she met."

"She was rather impressive," he said, "for the short time I knew her. At least you had a nice lunch together beforehand."

That feeling she'd had when she'd entered the arcade. Of being watched.

Nathalie wanted to kill him. Cut him to pieces with a shard of bone.

"It was her idea, not mine."

"Her idea? Agnès didn't ask to be killed. You're mad."

The candlelight flickered across his shrouded face. "No, I'm rather sane. Next topic. I have a question for you. Two, actually."

"I have about fifty for you."

"Very amusing, Nathalie."

Her name sounded horrible coming from him. She wished it had choked him before coming out.

He cleared his throat. "Something happens when my exhibits are on display and you touch the viewing pane. You go into some sort of trance and say the name of the victim."

She frowned, ready to deny it, but the Dark Artist cut her off. "I was there for Odette, remember? Now tell me: What exactly takes place?"

Nathalie wiped her sweaty palms on her trousers and straightened up. "Why—why should I tell you anything?"

With demonstrative nonchalance, the Dark Artist reached into his overcoat pocket and unsheathed a knife.

The same knife she'd seen in her visions.

"I thought you weren't going to hurt me."

"I might change my mind." He gripped the knife firmly and took a step toward her. "Answer the questions."

Distract him by talking.

She kept her eyes on the knife while answering. "Yes, I have an ability."

"And the details?" The Dark Artist shifted his weight.

Nathalie felt dizzy, more disconnected from reality than ever before. "I—I see parts of the murder scene. Through . . . your eyes, it seems."

"Too bad you can't include *those* details in your morgue report, eh?" His lips parted the scarf, grinning. "So you don't see me, you see *as* me. Perfect. I obscured my face before stepping into the Catacombs, just in case. Although that abhorrent policeman was a problem." He shook his head.

"Is he dead?"

"I'm asking the questions," he sneered, holding up the knife. "Now. You seem a touch too young, so forgive me if I seem perplexed, but are you one of us?"

Us?

"Well, based on that expression, I suppose it's fair to say we're both perplexed." The Dark Artist laughed. "And here I thought you knew. Or guessed."

She clenched her jaw.

"Insightfuls," he said in a stage whisper.

What? She pressed her back and hands even more firmly into the wall of skulls.

The Dark Artist chuckled. "I have extraordinary hearing, courtesy of one Dr. Henard. My parents were deaf, so I had to have ears for three as a youth. Exquisitely circular, isn't it?"

Nathalie didn't respond.

"It was especially useful today," he continued. "I heard you ask that man at the depot if the tram went to Place Denfort-Rochereau. From a block away." He twirled the blade handle with eerie gracefulness. "I've had my ear on you for some time and have tried to get you alone. I almost succeeded one time, and if it weren't for my clumsy lack of subtlety, I might have caught up to you before you hopped on that carriage ride."

She stifled a gasp. *I knew it.*

"After that I had to be much more careful," he continued. "You didn't notice me on most occasions—although you came close in the arcade—but what difference does it make now? It hasn't been easy. Those damn policemen and those damn public spaces with all those damn Parisians."

Her fingers crawled backward to reach for the skull once more.

"Once more," he said. "Are you one of us?"

The muscles in her legs twitched, ready to spring. "My parents were Henard patients. My father has a magical ability. My mother doesn't; she—she had a transfusion but nothing ever emerged. So I . . . inherited it somehow."

The Dark Artist cocked his swaddled head. "You're a *natural?*"

"I suppose so." *I'm much taller than him. One strike to the head and I can get past him.*

"What must your blood be like." A declaration, a thought out loud. Not a question.

Nathalie had bats in her ribcage, bursting to get out. She grabbed the skull, her fingers looping through the sockets.

"May I have some of your blood?" The Dark Artist stepped closer. "Just a few drops."

She tugged lightly on the skull, a subtle shift rippling through the stack.

"Don't worry. It's not what you think. I promise not to kill you." He sidled up to the candle he'd placed in the sconce and blew it out. "If you promise not to use that impressive power to turn me in."

She jerked the skull out of the wall and swung it into the chasm of darkness between them. The skull smashed onto his head with a satisfying crack.

"Witch!"

The blade came at her quick as a viper. She felt it catch her bag as she stumbled past the Dark Artist onto the alley floor.

Blackness, shocking in its purity, swallowed her as she regained her footing. Not one candle, not one glimmer in sight.

"I snuffed them all out," he hissed.

She charged into the darkness, dragging her fingertips along the left wall, feeling for an opening to a path, any path.

At last she found one and turned into it. She wasn't two steps in when she fell headlong onto a pile of sharp rocks.

No.

Not rocks.

Bones.

"Wrong turn." His whisper drifted over her like a spirit.

Her hands scuttled over a long, solid bone. She grabbed it, flailing in every direction as she stood up.

"Shall I show you the way out?" The whisper seemed to be everywhere at once.

The Dark Artist was in front of her.

Or to the left.

Behind her?

Utter silence. She couldn't hear anything but her own labored breath.

Then the tip of the blade kissed her cheek.

Maybe the Dark Artist thought Nathalie would give up. Maybe he thought she'd be too scared to move.

He was mistaken.

Lightning possessed her. She thrashed her weapon and heard the knife bounce off some bones. She darted right; he lunged after her. He gripped her elbow for a second before slipping and falling onto the bone pile.

Nathalie put her arms out, feeling along the wall until she found the opening again. She turned left, back on the path she'd been on in the first place. She ran and ran, finally spotting a speck of muted light at the end of another tunnel on the left.

His footsteps rumbled behind her, louder and closer with every step.

She sped down the dim path, eyes on the tiny flame, arms pumping, legs moving faster than they ever had.

The Dark Artist was so close she could hear his shallow, wheezy puffs of breath.

Nathalie reached the flame and wheeled around the corner to the right.

The main tunnel.

She kept running but heard nothing behind her. No footsteps, no wheezing. Not a sound.

Why? She allowed herself a quick glance.

He wasn't there.

She ran toward the entrance with as much speed as her lanky legs could manage and saw some tourists descend the stairs with a guide. Screams erupted when they discovered the policeman's body.

The Dark Artist heard them coming. He's hiding.

"Go!" she yelled in between gulps of air. "Get out of the Catacombs!"

Five or six people ran back up the spiral staircase; the guide and several others hovered around the body, as if they were afraid to leave it unattended.

"The killer is behind me! Run!"

They scrambled up the stairs with the guide at the rear. He kept his eyes on Nathalie until he disappeared from sight.

She charged down the tunnel, halting a couple of meters from the body.

The burly policeman lay there, eyes open, limp hand resting on his chest. His throat was slit with the blade from his own walking stick. There it rested beside him, in the aftermath of its treachery, surrounded by a pool of blood.

Nathalie turned away. A heavy blanket of sadness draped around her heart. *He died because he had to protect me. It's my fault he's dead.*

First Agnès.

Now him.

I don't even know his name.

She surveyed the tunnel. Empty. Deceptively still.

Nathalie knelt down and closed the policeman's eyes, then made her way up those endless stairs as quickly as possible. Once she emerged into daylight, she saw the tourists in a group to the side and two policemen approaching with the tour guide. She ran up to them. "The Dark Artist followed me into the Catacombs and chased me. He's still there!"

They looked at her askance.

She pointed to the Catacombs entrance. "Your colleague was killed keeping watch over me! I'm Nathalie Baudin, from the morgue. Christophe Gagnon assigned a patrol to me."

Recognition hit them, thunder after a lightning strike. Her words came out in a torrent, explaining what happened before they had a chance to ask. One of the policemen assured her that she was safe now.

Nathalie didn't believe him. As long as there was a Dark Artist, Paris would be smothered in danger.

She refused to let it choke her.

34

The next two hours were a flurry of policemen, questions, and answers.

But no Dark Artist.

Christophe was with her for all of it, even holding her hand, which made it both easier and more difficult to handle.

The Catacombs were full of hidden escapes, Christophe later explained, that led to churches and taverns and apartments. By the time she left the police station, investigators were canvassing the city for known secret entrances to the tunnels.

"It doesn't appear promising," Christophe informed her at one point. "Unless someone comes forward and admits to seeing something, he likely emerged unnoticed in an abandoned place."

So close to the Dark Artist. And for nothing.

He outsmarted me. He was going to win. Hurt me. Kill me. Watch me escape. He was going to be able to get away no matter what.

She hated Dr. Henard for endowing the Dark Artist with super-human hearing.

When she went home that night, she told her mother about the Dark Artist, from the first time she was followed home to the blood jar to the letters to the Catacombs. Maman became fran-tic, swearing Nathalie would never leave the house alone again until the Dark Artist was caught.

Her mother wasn't wrong.

Nathalie didn't fault her for being furious terrified hysterical

overwhelmed and every emotion that bridged any of those feelings.

She would have been, too.

In a way she envied Maman for being able to feel anything at
all, since she herself did not. Nathalie was numb, in a stupor, practically, by the time it was over.

And it was a good thing she'd told Christophe and Maman
everything, because as she got ready for bed that night, she sat
down to write in her journal.

The details eluded her.

Something was missing. Many things. She remembered the
Dark Artist tipping his hat and saying *C'est moi.* The next thing
she recalled was running down the main tunnel toward the people
standing over the policeman's body.

She hadn't been spared memory loss after all, and it had been
delayed by a few days. But this time she didn't mind nearly as much.
There was something to be said about forgetting.

Nathalie's eyes fluttered open. She was inside a room, reclined on
something cold and damp.

A concrete slab with water to keep the bodies cool, like they
used to do.

She was in the corpse display room.

With a controlled, careful movement, she turned to the right.
Odette Roux stared at her through dead eyes. She faced left and
saw the nameless second victim doing the very same.

Sisters in death.

She sat up. A cluster of people gaped at her through the viewing pane. Face after face after face. Dozens of Parisians gawked.
Pointed. Whispered. They shook their heads in pity and disgust
and the secret gladness they got from knowing that *they* weren't
there, in a chilled room, a prop in the unwitting performance of
the dead.

Nathalie's eyes shifted to the other slabs in the front row. Mirabelle Gregoire and Charlotte Benoit on the left. Agnès to the right, on the other side of Odette. Each one faced her.

Then they blinked.

All of them.

Odette, the anonymous girl, Mirabelle, Charlotte, and Agnès. One by one.

The nameless victim tried to talk. Her tongue, black as pitch, struggled to create a word. Nothing came out.

Nathalie felt more water flow over the slab. It was warmer now. Almost comfortable, like bath water. She looked down at her hands and shrieked as loud as she could, but not a sound escaped.

She was wearing white gloves.

And the water wasn't water. It was blood.

She jumped off the slab and turned to the back row.

Another soundless cry.

There, on the five slabs in the back row, were five different versions of her own bloated, bloodied, carved-up corpse. Out of the corner of her eye, Nathalie saw movement. She watched as Agnès got up from her slab, walked slowly to the back row, and pulled a sheet over each body, one by one.

Nathalie ran to the door the way dreams forced you to run—hardly moving, never quick enough, too sluggish to escape whatever it was you were fleeing.

Finally she reached the door. With great effort she pushed it open and ran through the door only to find herself holding a lamp and standing in the maze of the Catacombs. It was silent, so silent that she heard only her heartbeat and nothing more. She took lefts and rights and went straight but couldn't get anywhere; everything looked the same.

Footsteps behind her.

Nathalie started to run but it didn't matter, couldn't matter. She didn't know how to leave. When she turned around, all she saw was darkness. The footsteps got closer.

She couldn't see anything but blackness.

Then she stopped.

She extended her right arm to the side. Through the dim light she saw an orderly stack of bones—skulls, leg bones, arm bones—several meters back. She extinguished the lamp and curled up next to the dismembered skeletons, resting her head on the dirt.

The footsteps got closer and closer. She shut her eyes tightly but soon a glow shone through her eyelids.

She opened her eyes but was no longer in the Catacombs. Again she was on her back, this time staring at the sky. Maman and Papa came into view. Maman held a withered yellow bouquet and Papa clasped her vial of catacomb dirt in his hand. She sat up.

"I'm not dead!" she yelled. This time it wasn't mute.

She woke up screaming.

35

The scent of cooked cherries drifted into Nathalie's bedroom the next morning, an airy counterpoint to the horrors of the previous day.

Nathalie took her time getting ready, then opted for one more task before joining Maman in the kitchen.

The catacomb dirt. The stupid, meaningless soil that had cost a man his life and nearly cost her own.

Nathalie didn't care to carry it around anymore, yet she didn't want to get rid of it, either. She took the small box from her satchel and put it on her bookshelf, next to the bird skeleton. It could stay there.

She took the little jar with the sand and the shells from Agnès and put it on her nightstand. Her most treasured possession deserved its own place.

Maman had a baguette and a bowl of fresh fruit waiting for her. "I have some good news," she said with a tentative smile. "We received a telegram. Papa is coming home much sooner than expected! Sometime this week."

"He is?" Nathalie grinned on a day when she didn't expect to smile or laugh. "This is the happiest news all summer. I *need* happy news. So do you." She gave Maman a kiss on the cheek and sat down to eat.

As much as her mother tried to be cheerful, she couldn't hide her weariness. And Nathalie didn't blame her. Maman was calmer than Nathalie expected, both last night and as they talked about it again now, but it was obvious she hadn't slept. Nathalie hadn't, either.

"I haven't read the newspaper in days," Nathalie said as she cleaned the table after breakfast. "Do we still have the old ones?"

Maman spooned jam into one of the jars. "*Ma bichette*, are you sure that's a good idea? Monsieur Patenaude said you needn't worry about doing the morgue report until you're ready to return. If you're ready."

"I will be ready, maybe in a few days." Nathalie's tone was muted, resigned. "I can pretend to think of something else, but we both know that won't work."

Maman sealed a jar, then sighed. "They're in the rack beside Papa's chair."

Nathalie retrieved the newspapers and settled down at the kitchen table. She unfolded an edition from earlier in the week.

The one about Agnès.

Splashed across the front page was an artist's depiction of Agnès's grieving mother with the headline:

Heartrending Scene Inside Morgue

Her own heart shattered before she read another word.
Beside the illustration was a letter from the Dark Artist.

> *Dear Paris,*
> *My work continues to improve, and the crowds continue to show their support for my exhibits. I couldn't be more pleased.*
> *I do believe I'm just getting started.*
>
> *Yours,*
> *The Dark Artist*

His written words crawled on her skin like insects.
Agnès, an exhibit.

No. She was her friend.

Why, hello there.

It was both good and not good that she'd forgotten most of what had happened with the Dark Artist in the Catacombs. She remembered the words she'd used to describe it all, but they rang hollow in her memory, as if she'd recited someone else's story. And what if she'd left something out? Now her imagination would fill in the blanks.

Did he touch me?

She let go of the uninvited question with a shudder. Her fingers climbed to a miniscule cut on her cheek. From the tip of the Dark Artist's blade, as she recalled telling Christophe. She'd had worse scratches from an overly frisky Stanley when he was a kitten. Yet she'd somehow escaped a murderer who sliced women.

Sliced Agnès.

Was it the same knife?

He'd sliced Agnès from cheek to collarbone. But all Nathalie had was a cut on her cheek and a rip in her satchel.

Despite him wanting her blood.

She exhaled loudly, inviting a concerned glance from Maman. "I'm reading the article about Agnès," she said, smoothing out the paper. She resumed reading.

> This was an especially short-lived mystery, as Mademoiselle Jalbert's parents identified her body mere hours after it was placed on display.

The article went on to describe the scene, complete with quotes from bystanders, the guard, and Christophe. Her thoughts went to the morgue tableaux at the Musée Grévin that depicted the first two victims. Had they continued to change it, to add corpses?

Would a likeness of Agnès be there?

She didn't want to know.

Nathalie folded the paper neatly and turned it over so she

wouldn't have to see the illustration of Agnès's mother. It was too accurate. Too real.

She pulled today's *Le Petit Journal* closer. Again the headline attacked her.

POLICEMAN KILLED IN CATACOMBS

Agent de Police Sébastien Ethier was murdered by an unknown assailant yesterday at the entrance to the Catacombs.

His name was Sébastien. And she never knew, never even asked Christophe the names of the men who'd protected her.

Neither the Dark Artist nor Nathalie were mentioned in the article. Christophe had prepared her for this, saying the police wouldn't want to incite panic. To every other Parisian it would read like an act of violence perpetrated at random.

Sébastien deserved better. He died because of me.

She stood up and went to the parlor window where Stanley was perched. She gazed across the street to where a policeman, her policeman, sat. *You will be protected until we catch him,* Christophe had told her. But she'd never thought to consider *their* protection and the sort of risk they'd undertaken for her.

"Ask him his name, Maman. When you go out later."

Maman furrowed her brow. "Him who?"

"The policeman watching the apartment." She gestured toward the window. "I want to know his name. I'm not to address them, but there's no reason you can't."

"I understand, *ma bichette*. I will."

Tonight she would pray for Agnès, Sébastien, and the policeman outside the apartment, by name.

Later that morning, while Nathalie was folding clothes, Simone knocked at the door. "If you like profiteroles, open up."

Nathalie went to the door and greeted her. Simone swept into the apartment with two crème-filled pastries on a plate. "I thought I'd bring the two of you some food for a change. Someone was kind enough to bring us some, and I thought I'd share." Her glance darted between Nathalie and her mother. "Did—did I come at a bad time?"

Maman shook her head, thanked Simone warmly, and took a profiterole. Nathalie closed the door and took the second profiterole off the plate. "Thank you. I'm going to save mine for later."

"My dearest friend putting aside a profiterole?" Simone eyed her with a frown. "Something *is* wrong, isn't it?"

"I have a lot to share," Nathalie said, pointing her finger upward. "Maman, we're going to be at the Rooftop Salon."

Maman wiped her fingers with a cloth and tightened a jar. "Be careful."

"We will," said Nathalie.

"Why did she say that?" Simone asked as they exited the apartment.

"Because of yesterday."

Several minutes later, as they sat near the inside edge of the roof for shade, Nathalie told Simone all that had happened.

"Do you think he'll come after you?"

"Maman said Mathieu, the policeman watching from the street, is especially vigilant." Nathalie hugged her knees. "Who knows? I don't want to leave this building anytime soon, I can tell you that. And last night I slept with a chair propped under the doorknob." Even as she said it, she knew it wasn't a viable long-term plan. But it was a good one for today.

"First the jar, then his curious remark about *your* blood. I wonder if that's what drives him, some sort of fixation on blood."

"He's a lunatic," Nathalie said. She touched the cut on her cheek. "That's what drives him."

"I know, but maybe there's a connection to what he's doing and Henard's blood transfusions." Simone pressed back against the bricks and pulled her feet out of the sun.

"I wish I'd asked him another dozen questions. Not that he'd have answered them, but . . ." Nathalie let her voice fall away. "I'm exhausted."

She rested her head on Simone's shoulder. They sat like that, quietly, until an ant crawled up Nathalie's leg. She stood up and brushed the ant away. "The sun is catching us anyway. Shall we head back downstairs?"

When they entered the apartment, Maman was not alone.

Christophe sat on the sofa, petting Stanley, and greeted her with a weak smile.

"If it's not too much to ask," he began, "I'd like you to come to the morgue with me. Please. There's another victim."

Nathalie squeezed her nails into her palms. "Another one already."
And it could have been me.

After introducing Christophe and Simone, she crossed over to
Papa's chair, where Maman sat tracing her scars. Nathalie stood
beside the chair, fingertips grazing the leather.

Christophe leaned forward. "I know it's asking a lot, given everything that's happened, but we'd be most grateful. And Madame
Baudin, I assure you, she will be under protection the entire time."

Nathalie glanced down at Maman, who closed her eyes and
nodded.

"Of course. Whatever I can do," Nathalie said, pressing her
knuckles into the leather.

"I'd go with you," Simone said, "but my mother is leaving for
the market in a little while and I need to look after Céleste."

Maman put up her hand. "I'll watch her, Simone."

"Would you? Thank you, Madame Baudin."

Not since that fateful day at the wax museum had they been
out together, and if there was ever a time Nathalie wanted
Simone at her side, it was now.

A short while later, they arrived at the morgue. The queue was
lengthy and Christophe escorted them inside through the morgue
exit. A colleague whisked him away, but not before Christophe
promised to meet them at Café Maxime afterward.

Nathalie's mouth was dry. "Last time I did this . . ."

It had been for Agnès. She left it unsaid. Simone knew; there was no need to say it.

"Do you want to go home?"

Nathalie shook her head. *I promised Agnès.*

Simone hooked her elbow around Nathalie's and they shuffled toward the crowd. They couldn't yet see the corpses, but as always, the cluster of people told them where the victim lay. They waited for an opening at the viewing pane, slipping in when some people stepped aside.

The victim had pockmarked skin and a mess of caramel-colored ringlets that snaked across her breasts. Her swollen face was slashed so badly it was impossible to discern her features, and a deep, uneven gash stretched across her stomach. Nathalie pulled Simone closer.

What did he mean that getting murdered was Agnès's idea?

Once again she was lured in by his games.

"Each one is worse than the last," whispered Simone.

Sweat began to dot Nathalie's neck and forehead. "I saw him yesterday, Simone. It doesn't matter if I don't remember much. It just happened. *Yesterday.*"

Simone took her hand. "You really don't have to, Nathalie."

"What don't I remember? Maybe it's worse than what I do, or what I told you." Nathalie stepped back from the viewing pane. "I'm going to be 'seeing' through eyes that saw me. From the man who killed Agnès. Chased me. Pulled a knife on me. Killed Sébastien the policeman."

"*Pardonnez-moi,*" said a soft-spoken young woman behind them, "but might you two make room for others if you're done?"

"Are we?" Simone said, then turned toward Nathalie. "Christophe will understand. Everyone will understand."

Nathalie gazed at the sixth unfortunate girl, at what used to be her face, what used to be her stomach. "You've been right all along. I have this gift for a reason." Before she could hesitate another moment, like plunging into cold water, she reached for the viewing pane.

The victim was already dead.

Her mouth was open, mid-scream, and blood ran from her mouth. One eye was open; the other was shut. She was a bloody, shattered doll.

The Dark Artist, gloves soaked and scarlet, caressed the victim's cheek. One singular, angry cut traveled from her ear to her throat.

"Too late," he said.

Blackness fell like a drape over a birdcage.

But Nathalie didn't find herself standing in the viewing room next to Simone. Instead the vision continued. She no longer saw a room; she was outside.

Everything was white, in every direction.

Fog.

The Dark Artist opened the rear door of a covered cart and pulled out the girl's body. Nathalie felt the weight, heavier than anything she'd ever lifted before.

He carried the corpse a few steps and laid it down.

The river.

The Dark Artist knelt down, kissed the dead girl on the forehead, and slid her into the water gently, like a father bathing a child.

He arranged her, face up, hands lightly clasped. With a firm push he sent her down the Seine.

When he stood up, he took off his gloves. "Enough already."

Then he started choking.

His fingers flew to his neck—rope. It grew tighter. He gasped and stood up, pulling at the rope. It loosened slightly, then completely.

He turned in time to see a wrought-iron bar come toward his head.

Blackness fell again.

Nathalie still wasn't in the viewing room.

She was reclined and saw an enormous pane of glass in front of her. A dense crowd stood behind it. Simone was there.

And Nathalie's own self, next to Simone.

In the viewing room.

Nathalie came out of the vision with a start, hands jerking. Her eyes locked on the viewing pane.

Simone put her arm around Nathalie and hugged her close. "You're with me now. You're safe."

"*Mon Dieu.*" Nathalie tried to stop shaking. Simone pulled her closer and motioned for someone to go away.

"What happened?" Simone whispered.

The words were hard to form; she coughed on the first attempt to speak. When she did, she whispered so quietly Simone had to lean in. "Simone—the Dark Artist . . ."

Nathalie wriggled from Simone's embrace, struggling to get some air, and pointed to a corpse off to the side in the second row. "He's right there."

37

Simone looked at the man on the slab and then back at Nathalie. "Are you sure?"

"Very." She relayed her vision to Simone and stared at the Dark Artist, his slender physique repulsive in its newfound familiarity. She focused on his hands. The same hands that had held a knife to her cheek yesterday. The same hands that had killed Agnès and five other young women.

How strange to reconcile this pathetic corpse of today with the frightening killer who'd chased her in the Catacombs. He was nothing anymore. Nothing at all.

A purple stripe crossed his neck. His temple was gouged, leaving a blackish-red canyon on his skull. Even bloated, he had strong, precise features, as though he himself had been carved from something. Short, side-swept brown hair. Neatly kept beard. Even the clothes displayed behind him were well-cut and fashionable.

He was a most handsome man.

Nathalie had wanted him to be ugly.

As she glared at his corpse, a slow, uncomfortable realization spread across her like lava. "I've seen his face before. I don't know where, but I have. Not in a vision."

"He did follow you that time; you said he admitted it. Perhaps you caught a glimpse of him then?"

"I remember that night very well, and that doesn't seem to fit what I'm thinking. I feel as though it were more direct than that," Nathalie said, rubbing her temples.

"The blood jar?" offered Simone.

"That either happened while I was asleep in the park or is a lost memory. It doesn't match the pattern of the other memory gaps, though. That can't be it." Nathalie shook her head. Could she be so sure? "I don't know. What difference does it make now, anyway? He's taken his last memory from me."

She looked back and forth between the sixth victim and the Dark Artist. She'd wanted to help stop him before he killed again. And she hadn't. This girl with dreams and sadness and hope and sorrow, like Agnès and Odette and Mirabelle and the others, was gone. "I'm sorry," she said, fingertips grazing the glass.

"You didn't fail her," said Simone, her voice both tender and adamant. "They'll know the body on that slab back there is the killer. Because of you, they'll know. And he's gone."

Just like that, this threat, this menace, was gone. So were his secrets. Frustration needled her as she thought about the Catacombs, how he'd asked the questions when it was she who had so many. Had she asked him anything at all? Anything that might cast the smallest glint of understanding as to his motives? No, she would have told Christophe. The Dark Artist manipulated her, scared her, found her secrets while protecting his own.

She detested him even more.

Nathalie suddenly felt crowded. She turned to see that three or four people had gathered around her and Simone; the moment she made eye contact they retreated as if commanded.

She wanted to scream at them. *Your killer is right there. Right there!*

"If they only knew," she muttered. "Instead they stare at me."

"Never mind the corpse-gazers. Let's go." Simone took her by the hand and led the way toward the exit.

Nathalie stopped at the Medusa door, the one that had hissed at her that first day in the morgue. Or so her confused mind had thought. "We should tell Christophe."

"We'll see him in a few minutes."

She stared at the Greek monster and her unruly snakes. "He shouldn't have left us."

"Nathalie." Simone touched her shoulder. "He's doing what he has to do. Now let's go get a table. He'll join us soon."

As soon as they left the morgue, Nathalie looked behind them. A man with a walking stick came into sight just as they crossed onto Quai de la Tournelle. "Wait until Mathieu finds out. The Dark Artist is a corpse, not a threat."

"And isn't that a splendid sentence?" Simone said, nudging her ribs.

They took a secluded outdoor table at Café Maxime, with Christophe joining just as a waiter filling in for Jean was taking their orders.

"*Pain au chocolat* for you, Nathalie?"

"*Non.*" She couldn't. Not yet. "An éclair."

Christophe asked for a coffee and, once the waiter left, managed little more than a greeting before Nathalie spilled every detail of her vision. Clearly struggling to stay silent, he erupted with fiery satisfaction when she was finished. "This is it! You confirmed what I suspected. Better yet: He's already been identified."

Simone flattened her palms on the table. "Wait. What?"

"Not as the Dark Artist, but as Damien Salvage."

Nathalie's skin prickled. Knowing his name made him real, made him human.

Gone was his mystery, away went the countless other identities he might have had. There was no need to *imagine* who he might be anymore. And as monstrous and depraved as he was, he was also just a man.

This made him both more and less terrifying, even in death.

"That was the business I had to tend to when we returned."

Nathalie blushed, embarrassed that she'd taken offense when he couldn't be at her side during the vision. She felt Simone's gaze but didn't acknowledge it.

"The sixth victim's body floated up the Seine. So did his,

almost at the same time. The coincidence got my attention. I left word with my colleagues to let me know immediately if anyone identified the man." Christophe tapped the table with his finger, a tap for every word. "A well-to-do industrialist recognized him. The man had commissioned Monsieur Salvage to make an armoire a few months ago. He even had Salvage's calling card on him."

"Imagine having furniture carved by the Dark Artist?" Nathalie made a face. And then she remembered something. "Oh goodness. The ornate wooden table in the Mirabelle vision. Finely made, medium-dark wood, decorative work on the corners. He—he must have created it himself."

She felt guilty for having thought the details unimportant at the time.

"Practice for what he did to those young women," said Simone, knitting her brow. "But not anymore."

How delightful it was going to be to walk the streets again, Nathalie thought, and not wonder if there was malice in nearby footsteps or ill intent in the heart of every man who passed by.

The waiter came with their "celebratory meal," as Simone put it. Nathalie broke off a piece of her éclair and offered it to Christophe. She tried to ignore the tingle her limbs felt as he took it from her. "So whoever killed him dispatched of him in the river the same way. On purpose. Who? Why?"

Christophe finished chewing and then spoke. "He wants credit for it, which makes me think he—the Dark Artist's killer—knew about the murders. Or at the very least, observed him disposing of the victim and executed some justice of his own. Rope isn't hard to find near a river."

Nathalie crossed her arms. "I wish I saw more. Stupid fog."

"What you saw is enough to pull everything together," said Christophe in a kind voice. "Speaking of which, I'll relieve Mathieu of his duties on my way out. Nathalie, I'm very happy to say that you no longer need protection."

"'Mathieu,'" Nathalie began, imitating Christophe, "'you

needn't follow Mademoiselle Baudin any longer. While she thanks you for your service, I'm pleased to inform you that she doesn't need you anymore. Because the Dark Artist is dead.' Oh, I like the way *that* set of words feels on my tongue."

Christophe bit into a cube of bleu cheese. "As soon as I get back, I'll dispatch a team to the residence of one Damien Salvage to verify. Paris will know who the Dark Artist is in no time."

"I'll be buying a few copies of *Le Petit Journal* tomorrow," said Simone with a wicked grin. "I look forward to that headline. *The Dark Artist, Unmasked and Killed!* Or DEAD: *The Dark Artist, Damien Salvage!*"

"Well . . ." said Christophe, holding up his hand, "there's a good chance this won't make it into the papers yet."

Nathalie stared at him. "You're going to let people continue to think the Dark Artist is alive, even once you confirm that it's him?"

"The chief investigator will make that decision, but possibly. He may want to withhold that from the public until they investigate the matter of who killed him. Several days at most, I'm sure."

Nathalie glanced at Simone, whose horrified expression no doubt mirrored her own. Another day of fear in the city, another day of selling newspapers, another day of morgue visitors. And another, and another, as long as the police deemed necessary.

"It's . . . an unfortunate truth of the business," said Christophe. They spoke for a few more minutes as he drank the rest of his coffee. Then he excused himself, putting enough money on the table for all of them. He said a warm good-bye and departed.

Nathalie sat back a moment watching her fellow Parisians. At the café, on the street, going by in an omnibus, walking in and out of shops. When she'd learned about the Insightfuls, she'd thought there were two kinds of people in the world: those who had magic and those who didn't. But it was really two other kinds of people: those who knew what was really going on and those who didn't.

As to which were the lucky ones, she couldn't say.

38

Nathalie wrote a descriptive journal entry that night. The vision. The bodies at the morgue. The conversations with Simone, Christophe, and her mother. Maman was so relieved about the Dark Artist news that she held Nathalie a good long time and wept.

Some element of the day, or possibly the next day, would be forgotten. It was like flipping over a tarot card and wondering what it would be, or going to a hypnotist and wondering what she'd say. Some piece of reality would be extracted, removed by a clumsy, invisible surgeon. Eventually some part of this, something she wrote down with such a clear head, would seem foreign.

Indeed, the next morning she discovered which passages might well have been written in Chinese or Russian or Greek.

The memory loss this time was the vision itself.

Bitterness burned through her as the realization sank in. Why couldn't it be the vision of Agnès that she forgot? No, no. That one stayed with her. Fragments of the vision passing through her head whenever they pleased, day or night. That was the one she needed to forget most of all. Instead she would carry it for the rest of her life, a sack of bricks tethered to her soul.

Nevertheless.

Nathalie ran her finger along the journal's spine. She was grateful to be spared at least one distressing memory, even if it wasn't the one that haunted her most.

Did it mean something more?

To forget the very thing that the gift bestowed . . . was this a sign that her gift might be ending?

Several hours later she shared these thoughts with M. Patenaude. She went to tell him that, with the Dark Artist gone, she was eager to do the morgue column again. (She was also eager to see how Maurice Kirouac, unaware that was the Dark Artist when he'd done today's report, described him.) He was pleased to hear it and said she could resume the following day.

"I can only speak of my own experience and those I know," he offered, steepling his fingers, "but I don't think your ability is fading. Sometimes our power shifts slightly as we grow into it, like how your visions aren't taking place in reverse anymore."

"And how they've gotten longer." When she said it, something else occurred to her. "Did that have to do with—with Agnès? Did my closeness with her change this?"

M. Patenaude adjusted his glasses, which were thinner than they'd been in a while. "I don't know."

"Or maybe my encounter with the Dark Artist himself? Did being in proximity to him—to his power—affect mine? Since my ability is connected to his murders?"

"Again, I don't know. It shouldn't, not from what I understand. But who can say? That was part of the controversy about Henard's experiments; the results weren't as predictable as everyone hoped." M. Patenaude put his elbows on his desk. "Magic and science together became something else that was neither magic nor science. That's why I want to give you this, to help deepen your knowledge."

He opened up his desk drawer and reached inside.

"My wife found it at the bottom of a box of books," he said, handing her a booklet. "It's from 1866. I forgot this existed, or I'd have told you about it. It's yours to keep."

Enchanted Science or Science Enchanted? by Dr. Pierre Henard.

Nathalie gasped. She felt like she'd just been handed a map to a buried treasure.

"*Merci beaucoup!*" She held the thin little book gingerly, as if holding on too tightly would squeeze the secrets out and scatter them onto the floor. Something was familiar about this, so much so that she could have sworn she'd seen it before. Or maybe she'd heard someone mention the title once?

"It's a somewhat dry read," M. Patenaude said, "but you may find some answers there. What's interesting to me is that, despite all the controversy, the facts are truthful. That is, the truth as he understood it at the time. To that I can attest, thanks to my gift."

Nathalie slipped the booklet into her satchel and pressed her back against the chair, her gaze drifting outside the window and back to him. "You told me once before that the way the abilities manifest says something about the individual."

M. Patenaude opened his cigarette case and tapped one onto his palm. "Without fail," he said, striking a match. He lit the cigarette. "And sometimes not what we expect."

"I think I know," Nathalie began, "what the visions say about me. I have an appetite for the macabre, as you might have guessed, so I'm sure that's part of it." She took a breath and let it out as a sigh. "I also think I'm the kind of person who wants to see life for what it is. And death, too. No matter how brutal or ugly."

"All of which make you a superb journalist, I should note." M. Patenaude smiled as he took a drag.

"Thank you," she said. She watched him exhale, transfixed by the ephemeral quality of the smoke. Existing and then not, in a blink.

"Also," he added, "little moments of truth, particularly those about yourself and who you are, are worth celebrating. Remember that."

Those words provoked something in her memory, like a string bringing a puppet to life. The last thing the hypnotist had said to her: *Remember who you are, then you'll know why you can't forget.*

Then it came to her. M. Lebeau, the hypnotist. He'd had stacks and stacks of books, and she'd glimpsed some of the titles. That's where she'd seen Henard's work before. *Enchanted Science or Science Enchanted?* A booklet with a title that reminded her of a riddle.

When she'd gone to M. Lebeau, she hadn't known who she was, so to speak. Even after she'd come to understand her gift, she hadn't fully known. She probably still didn't. But this, this was enough.

This and, of course, Henard's own words.

The last thing Nathalie did before going to bed that night was to reread the sections of *Enchanted Science or Science Enchanted?* that she'd underlined. She had read through the booklet twice that evening. The first time on her own, and the second time she'd read parts of it out loud to Maman, who'd never read it. Nathalie was glad about that; for the first time since she'd told Maman about the visions, they were learning something about Insightfuls together.

The booklet was twenty-one pages, some of it mired in scholarly language that Nathalie did not find to be all that interesting. The parts that did appeal to her were riveting.

She turned to the beginning of the booklet.

> The idea for these experiments did not present itself to me at a single hour on a single day. Instead it was, I believe, the accumulation of years of observation (I shall return to that below) together with my great affection for Greek mythology and what one might call the magical elements of the Christian faith. The aftermath of an age where our greatest thinkers (Descartes, Voltaire, Locke) relied solely on reason cried for something less stark, to my mind. The spirit of mankind needed adornment.
>
> Regarding that which I found worthy of observation, it was not the commonplace. It was the unusual, the elements of this world that were of nature but somehow deviated from

it, that seized my attention most. Those who possessed musical, literary, and artistic genius as well as the cat with extra toes; Chang, the kind Chinese giant of two-and-a-half meters who appeared in London last year; a tulip exceedingly brighter than the others in a garden. I wondered if it was possible to harness in science the greatest possibilities of human nature and add to them the essence of one's distinct self.

Then he went on (and on, Nathalie thought) about his research, using complicated terms and formulas that she skimmed over. He wavered between specifics and vagueness in presenting his work ("secrecy is essential to most areas of my research") and talked in academic terms about science and medicine and alchemy and rites both ancient and modern. Dull.

The next part that intrigued her was Dr. Henard's discussion of his earliest experiments.

As of this writing, eight people have undergone a transfusion. The length of time since their respective transfusions ranges from two weeks to three months. Seven have been successful in displaying magical abilities, and the usefulness of their talents vary: (1) a man age 19 who hears through someone else's ears by touching the person's hands; (2) a man age 41 who can perfectly mimic any voice he hears; (3) a woman age 46 who can heal by making eye contact; (4) a man age 55 whose dreams can foretell illness; (5) a woman age 27 who can discern a person's financial situation by smell; (6) a man age 22 who can communicate thoughts to other people using animals as a vessel; and (7) a woman age 39 who can read a person's past by stroking his or her hair.

The eighth subject (age 33) is a mystery. His transfusion failed to bring about any magical ability. My examination of his body and mind before, during, and after did not suggest a reason as to why. I have marked this as an area for further study.

I have met with the subjects once weekly for the first month, then once monthly relative to their duration. All but the eighth subject are pleased with the results. All including the eighth subject are in good health.

Note that there is a slight variation in intensity of magic. Four patients report a greater clarity in the development of their powers over time; three maintain that their ability has been consistent since the transfusion. One patient is now with child and has inquired as to whether the child will inherit the magic. My theory proposes that the child will not, just as a child does not possess a broken finger should the parent have one or a preference for the color blue should the parent exhibit one.

However, the human body has many components. Just as I do not know why the eighth subject did not acquire magic, I cannot be certain that a circumstance will not arise whereby a child possesses a power indicative of magic.

That was the sentence Nathalie underlined more thickly than the rest. She had to read it through several times to make sure she understood it correctly. Maybe she was the only child of an Insightful to manifest a power. Maybe she wasn't and others remained hidden. Simply because M. Patenaude and Christophe and her mother hadn't heard of other examples didn't mean they didn't exist. What did it matter now? She was here. She was proof of what couldn't be proven.

She flipped to the end of the booklet, to the final section she'd marked as important.

Those who have objected to my work have said I am playing God. I am not playing God; I revere Him and pray to

Him and thank Him for giving me the gift of insight such that I devised these experiments.

I suspect some people will be envious of those who have undergone transfusions. The more one has, the more others begrudge him for having. Man is a jealous and at times petty creature. Man is also a creature with tremendous abilities, some free and some trapped behind our own small and limited thinking. It is my hope that this is the beginning of an era: one where the faculty of reason weds magic and the two create a new way to manifest the human spirit through gaining insight.

Until reading Henard's work, Nathalie had thought he was deceptive and arrogant and indifferent, the sort of man who didn't care about his patients or the consequences they eventually suffered. She understood now that there was more to him than that, or at least there had been, at one time.

39

The Dark Artist was rotting away, even as people bought newspapers awaiting his next letter or stood in line at the morgue wondering if they'd be among the first to see his latest "exhibit." Some of them had seen his corpse in the two days since it had been on display in the morgue. Even more read about it in the morgue report, which said he "resembled a plaster sculpture smashed in the temple by a hammer." The report also noted that his "clothes were of fine quality, with one exception: a section missing from his silk burgundy cravat."

If they only knew that the real question on their minds and lips should be, *Who killed the Dark Artist?*

Nathalie regarded the bodies in the display room, including the sixth victim and the Dark Artist, and touched the viewing pane. She didn't expect a vision, but she chose to continue placing her hand on the glass, just in case. Maybe she'd find out who killed the Dark Artist that way.

She also watched those beside her in the morgue—a young couple with children, a group of women—and wondered what they thought of the handsome man on the slab before them.

Christophe was in the exhibit room beside the black velvet curtain. When she made eye contact with him, he gestured toward the Medusa door. Within a minute she was seated across from him in the drab office down the hall.

"Why is he still on display?" Nathalie tugged on her cap.

"He's been identified—several more times, in fact—but no one has claimed his body for burial." Christophe put some papers in a stack.

"And the sixth victim?"

"Unidentified."

Nathalie's chest tightened with sorrow. She didn't want the final victim to be anonymous, to be dumped into a grave next to her murderer.

"I have some news, though," said Christophe, his expression serious. "We know for sure Damien Salvage *is* the Dark Artist. His home matches the description you gave of the hall and living room, including the rug and the table. What's more, he had a cart for his business, and they found a cedar chest with bloodstains inside. Presumably that's what you saw in the vision."

"Little by little it's making sense." Relief shaded her words.

"Somewhat," said Christophe. "They've only just begun sorting through his things. He lived beside his shop, with an alley in between. Not one of these tall, modern Hausmann-style buildings. He was his own neighbor, so to speak. Lots of privacy."

Nathalie leaned forward, resting her hands on his desk. "Any clues about who might have killed him? Someone who knew what he was doing and took matters in their own hands? Someone seeking revenge?"

"The police are exploring every possibility—nothing so far. We did receive an anonymous tip about the 'attractive young man on display,'" he said, "and it supports your vision. Someone was strolling along the opposite shore and overheard an abrupt struggle between two men, followed by a choking sound and shortly thereafter, a splash."

"That's it?"

Christophe shrugged. "As you know, the fog was thick."

Fog that shielded him as he stole into the night to blend in with the rest of Paris, Nathalie thought. Just like the Dark Artist had. "Hidden in plain sight, both of them. Like Poe's purloined letter," she said, referencing one of her favorite short stories.

"It happens more often than you'd think."

After a few minutes, Christophe excused himself to return to the display room. Nathalie wrote her article in his office (he offered, and who was she to decline? She felt close to him, sitting in his chair). She went right to *Le Petit Journal* afterward. From there she stopped at Simone's to let her know what the police had discovered.

When Nathalie finally got home, she caught Stanley sniffing an exquisite arrangement of flowers, every hue imaginable, in a vase on the dining room table.

A voice called from her parents' bedroom. "Is that *ma bichette?*"

Joy hugged her heart, letting it go just long enough for her to respond. "Yes, Papa!"

Nathalie spent the rest of the afternoon enjoying time with her family. They talked about many things, good (Nathalie's marks at school, Maman's jam-making, Papa's stay in Martinique) and horrible (Agnès's murder, Maman's accident, Papa's ship having a yellow fever outbreak) and even some of the mundane that had shaped their lives since the three of them were last together in April.

Except for Nathalie's magical ability.

Maman had taken her aside and asked her to wait until after dinner to tell Papa. She wanted one last dinner as a family, she said, before "everything changed."

Even though everything already had, Nathalie wanted to say.

Nevertheless, she knew how important these family moments were to Maman. Not to mention, she was glad Maman hadn't already shared her secret. She wanted to tell Papa directly.

She kept her mind occupied by helping her mother make dinner (ratatouille, her father's favorite). As they cooked, Papa told stories of his recent months at sea, and Nathalie watched her mother's hands, more dexterous than before. At dinner Papa's strong hands were uncharacteristically stiff and maladroit.

He'd already healed Maman.

After dinner, they played cards. Nathalie couldn't relax, however, and kept making mistakes. They played hand after hand, and by the time Maman served a torte, Nathalie's stomach was so stuffed with dinner and expectation alike that she couldn't eat. At some point a thunderstorm broke out, inspiring Stanley to find shelter on her lap, while her parents enjoyed a bottle of wine Papa had brought back from South America.

Then Maman pushed her cards into the center of the table and finished her glass of wine. "I think you two have some catching up to do," she said, standing up. She tousled Papa's bushy hair and leaned over his broad shoulders, kissing his cheek. With a wink at Nathalie, she retired to the bedroom.

Nathalie gathered the cards, tapping them into a neat stack. She continued straightening it longer than necessary. "I have something to tell you, Papa. Something . . . good, I think. Maman knows and wanted me to tell you the news myself."

"That you're the best journalist Monsieur Patenaude has ever hired?" he asked, his eyes giving away his smile.

"I can't say he's quite told me that." She chuckled and set the cards to the side, looking her father in the eye. "I have a magical ability, Papa. Like you and Aunt Brigitte and the other . . . Insightfuls."

"Insightfuls. I didn't know you knew—" Papa's jovial demeanor melted into incredulous surprise. He peeked over his shoulder at the closed bedroom door. Perhaps he wondered what Maman had thought, how she'd reacted, when she found out, what she'd told Nathalie. No doubt they'd discuss it later. "What sort of ability?"

"Visions. Of the Dark Artist murders," she began. Papa clenched his jaw and released it, and his "worry vein" appeared in his forehead. She was suddenly cognizant of how staggering a revelation this must be for him.

He gestured for her to continue, his face a reflection of both compassion and trepidation.

Nathalie spoke carefully at first, measuring her words as if she were only rationed so many. When she sensed Papa's true understanding and even truer support, her words came out like a waterfall.

She shared with him everything about her visions and how it had all unfolded over the summer, at one point showing him the copy of *Enchanted Science or Science Enchanted?* during their discussion about the Henard experiments. He gave her his full attention in the way that Papa did, making you think you were the only person not only in the room, but in the world.

Then she asked him a question she could have asked Maman. She'd saved it for him, though. "Maman said she wanted a transfusion because you and Aunt Brigitte had gotten them. Who went to Dr. Henard first? You or Tante?"

"We went together," said Papa, and Nathalie noticed his shoulders drop, just a little. "It was my idea. She—she was in a very melancholy state, and I thought this would help."

Silence folded into the space between them for a minute before Nathalie continued in a subdued voice. "Do you regret it? The transfusions, the magic, the consequences . . ."

Me. My ability. My singularity.

Papa smoothed his mustache with his thumb. He exhaled and sat back, regarding her before responding. "I think of regrets as small, slippery creatures. If you have one you must grasp it securely; it squirms and thrashes about and isn't comfortable to hold." He squeezed his fists and winced. "So you have to either hold it more tightly or let it go, yet even if you set it free, it leaves something behind, a stain on your hand."

Nathalie waited for him to say more but he didn't. "That's clever, Papa, but not a proper answer."

"Because there isn't one." He reached for her hand. "After all these years, I still don't know if acquiring magic is right or wrong.

It's both, maybe. What I do know is that whatever you do with your power, do it for yourself. Not for other people, not for Maman or me or Monsieur Gagnon or anyone else. Having other people tell you how to use your gift . . ." He shook his head, eyes unfocused. Nathalie supposed a thought or a memory had taken him elsewhere.

". . . will never bring me peace. Is that what you wanted to say?"

Papa regarded her once again, smiling. "Yes. Something much like that."

The sixth victim, Lisette Bellamy, was identified the next day. Her sister Liberté, with whom she lived, had been on holiday in Ireland. When Liberté came home to find her sister missing, she ultimately made her way to the morgue. Nathalie cringed when Christophe told her about it. She'd always felt something for those who made that soul-shattering discovery; now that "something" bore a tragic context her blackest nightmares couldn't have portrayed.

The Dark Artist was pulled from display several hours after Lisette. No kin had come forward, but the morgue needed room. The Dark Artist, anonymous on the slab, was unceremoniously dumped into the mass grave because other corpses needed display. Nathalie relished the irony.

She was eager to discuss it with M. Patenaude—and to ask him how long it would be before *Le Petit Journal* released the story. If they didn't find Damien Salvage's killer, then when would Paris learn that the Dark Artist ceased to be?

Sooner than she thought.

M. Patenaude was in a meeting when she submitted her article, so she left it with Arianne. Nathalie wished she could tell her not to worry about the murderer anymore, not to worry about being escorted to and from work. She wondered if M. Patenaude had already told her, sworn her to secrecy perhaps. Or if he let her go on believing, like the rest of Paris, that a throat-slashing killer was among them in the crowds.

Nathalie had many reasons to hate the Dark Artist. One of them was this, the fear that made women panic and look over their shoulders and think twice about every unfamiliar man who shared their footsteps.

She thanked Arianne and was about to leave when Arianne lowered her voice. "I shouldn't tell you this, but it will be published tomorrow anyway." She surveyed the room and continued. "The Dark Artist is dead."

Guilt draped itself on Nathalie's shoulders. "I—I know," she said, unable to meet Arianne's eyes. Sometimes she'd rather proclaim to the world she was an Insightful than keep secrets that were uncomfortable to keep. "I've been involved with the case. As . . . part of my column."

Again Arianne eyed the room to make sure no one was watching. "We—the newspaper—received a note. Even Monsieur Patenaude doesn't know about it yet." She pushed an envelope across the desk to Nathalie, who promptly took out the slip of paper.

The Dark Artist is dead.

I am not.

As Ovid wrote: "He has lived well, he who has lived in obscurity."

Nathalie grimaced. "What *is* this?" She reread the handwritten note several times, running her fingers over the ink, like rubbing your eyes after a dream. "I know Ovid was a Roman poet, and the quote is a boast about hiding in plain sight, I assume. Quoting a Roman poet about hiding in plain sight . . . why? What's the boast?"

"I don't understand it at all. Look—look at what else is in there," Arianne whispered, pointing to the envelope.

Nathalie examined the envelope and saw something wedged in the corner. She tipped the envelope into her hand. Out came a piece of maroon cloth.

Maroon. Did the color have significance? A symbol of blood, perhaps?

"I opened that envelope almost an hour ago and can't stop thinking about it. I can't get any work done." Arianne chewed a fingernail. "What do you think it means?"

Nathalie read the note one more time, as if it might say something different now, and put it back in the envelope. She pressed the cloth between her fingers. Silk.

Silk, just like—

"Oh! I know what it is!" said Nathalie, rapping a knuckle on Arianne's desk. "From his cravat. It had a piece missing, like someone cut it off."

The only probable "someone" was the person who'd killed him. Who else?

She dropped the silk on the floor, stooped down to get it, and fumbled getting it into the envelope. Was the cloth a souvenir? A symbol of power? Or maybe it was just to taunt Paris, like the Dark Artist had done. Why follow in the footsteps of the man you murdered?

Arianne sat back primly and arranged a stack of articles. "Perhaps it's just a hoax," she said, her tone unconvincing.

Nathalie was about to protest, to tell Arianne it seemed very real indeed, but then she noticed the young woman's hands trembling as they hovered over the pages.

M. Patenaude will use his gift and know. He'll convey it to Christophe. An actual errand boy would deliver the materials, and M. Patenaude's interpretation, to the morgue. The irony.

"A fraud, well . . . that's for others to decide." Nathalie placed the envelope on the desk as Arianne shuffled through the pages, lips pressed together. "We needn't worry. *Tout va s'arranger.*"

Nathalie didn't know if everything would be fine, and in fact, she didn't think that to be the case at all. She knew she'd be turning this over and over in her mind the rest of the day and probably well into the night. But if it gave Arianne even the slightest degree of reassurance, it was worth saying.

As she walked away from Arianne's desk, she paused. Maman was healed and would be returning to work soon, but Nathalie would be staying on at the newspaper anyway. It was time to act like it.

She removed her cap and let down her hair. Standing up to her full height, she turned back to Arianne. "Please tell Monsieur Patenaude that from now on, I'll be showing up in my normal clothes. We'll figure out how to explain it to the gentlemen."

"I will tell him," said Arianne with a compliant nod. She seemed grateful for the subject change. "And good for you."

Nathalie had seen and heard things no one else had, and she'd had experiences this summer few could conceive of, never mind live through. If she was good enough to help solve a case, then she was good enough to walk into *Le Petit Journal* as herself.

Whoever wrote the letter and quoted Ovid wanted to go unnoticed. Nathalie, from now on, aimed to be utterly indifferent to anyone's inquisitive gaze.

40

PARIS NIGHTMARE OVER
Dark Artist Dead, Killer at Large

Le Petit Journal's headline the following day told Paris about the current state of affairs, with an article covering the Dark Artist's murder and identity, complete with morgue photographs, as well as the search for his unknown assailant. The newspaper also published the letter with the Ovid quote and described the silk fragment as a "thread-for-thread match—though even this doesn't make the cravat whole."

Nathalie wished it were a prank. She wanted to think the Dark Artist's killer was acting out of bravery or principle, someone who caught him in the act and imparted his own sense of justice. The witness from across the shore had overheard a struggle; Nathalie had imagined a man walking alone in the fog, horrified by what he stumbled upon and disposing of the killer in a fit of fury. Or something happened when her vision of the scene cut out. Or the man was connected to one of the victims, stalked the Dark Artist, and confronted him.

But not this. Not a killer who sent letters and cravat pieces. Who was playing games now, and to what end?

By the evening, a special Dark Artist issue of the newspaper was out. She spread it on the sofa to read and provided an abridged version to Papa, who'd misplaced his reading glasses. Maman was changing out the drapes in the bedroom. "The police picked up a man seen near what's believed to be the vicinity of the murder."

"Based on what?"

"The estimated time the body was in the Seine compared with how long it took to . . . drift to where it was found." Nathalie leaned forward as her fingers ran along the column. "Also, they have quotes from a woman, identity withheld, who spoke to a reporter outside the morgue. She said she'd known Damien Salvage from an opium den they both frequented. She'd first encountered him in February, shortly after the triple murders by Pranzini, and said Damien 'possessed something akin to respect for the murderer.'"

"And here he is," said Papa, "dead before the guillotine drops on Pranzini. With even more blood staining his soul."

"Both fair and unfair," Nathalie said. She, Simone, and Papa planned to go to the Pranzini execution, less than two weeks away. Too bad it wasn't the Dark Artist's death sentence. "The paper also says the woman didn't think anything of it at the time: 'Who with an iota of reason, even in a cloud of opium, would?' That's a direct quote."

"Augustin," Maman called from the bedroom, "could you help me reach the top of this drape?"

Papa reluctantly got up from his chair, which Stanley occupied in haste (the two of them had an ongoing disagreement as to whom the chair belonged). Nathalie moved on to another article that recounted the Dark Artist's crimes throughout the summer—in spirited, exhaustive detail—and provided an account of each of his victims. The article spilled over to the next page, and when Nathalie turned it, she gasped.

Agnès's photograph.

A thorn of sorrow pierced her heart.

Even in a newspaper account referencing her brutal death, even in a picture hazy in its reproduction, Agnès looked irrepressibly vivacious.

If Paris was going to have one final, visual reminder of Agnès, before everyone moved on with their lives and forgot the names and faces of the victims, Nathalie was glad it was that one.

She reached for Maman's sewing box on the end table and found the scissors. Carefully, as though slipping would hurt Agnès herself, Nathalie cut out the photograph. Then she brought it to her bedroom, propped it up against the jar of beach sand and shells, and said a prayer for her friend.

The next evening, Maman, Papa, and Nathalie visited Simone's family. Maman brought dinner, and as Simone and Nathalie put everything in the kitchen, Papa knelt next to the sofa where Céleste lay. M. Marchand told him about her condition while Simone's mother changed the girl's blankets.

Only Simone knew what Papa was going to do.

The Marchands didn't know Papa was an Insightful, and Nathalie's parents wanted to keep it that way.

Nathalie and Simone set the table.

"Did you read the newspaper today?" asked Nathalie.

Simone nodded. "It didn't take them long to dismiss the man they brought in for questioning, did it? The search continues."

Maman cleared her throat from the parlor. The girls stopped talking and looked over to Maman signaling with her eyes to watch Papa.

Céleste smiled feebly at him as he told her a story about a stow-away monkey on his ship. Nathalie moved closer to them. Papa winced, just barely, as he clenched his fist (to show how upset the captain was at the monkey).

Nathalie then gazed at Maman watching Papa, proud and content.

Papa gently put Céleste's tiny hands into his own for a few seconds. He flinched, so quickly and so slightly that no one who didn't know of his power would have noticed. He kissed Céleste on the forehead and stood up, glancing at Nathalie as he did so.

And that's when she felt it more deeply, more profoundly than ever. Being an Insightful wasn't a source of shame, embarrassment, or worry. To witness strong and sturdy Papa using his gift with such tenderness illuminated her. Having this magic was an honor.

The families enjoyed dinner together a short while later. At one point, Simone started speculating about the Dark Artist's killer and the letter to the paper; a stern look from her mother brought that to an immediate, mid-sentence halt. ("Not in front of Céleste," M. Marchand mouthed when the little girl wasn't looking.) After dinner, Nathalie and Simone excused themselves to meander around the block. They were scarcely down the front steps of the building when Simone hugged Nathalie at the waist.

"I've been bursting to tell you this for hours!" she said, her voice giddy. "Louis asked me to extend an invitation to you for tomorrow evening."

"Oh?" Nathalie's tone was cautiously polite. If it was to attend a poetry reading or some such, she'd have to find an excuse to graciously decline. "For what occasion?"

"To attend a *séance!*"

Ever so much better than a poetry reading. "Truly?"

"Truly. You'll go?"

"Of course!" Nathalie used to think séances were nonsense, but several months ago she would have said murder scene visions were nonsense, too. And hypnosis. And the magic of Insightfuls. "You've been, so how does it work? Do we . . . choose someone to contact or wait to see what happens?"

"Well, Louis did have someone in mind."

Nathalie's heart quivered. "Agnès?"

"If she's—willing, yes." Simone bit her lip. "But I think for your sake and theirs, not any of the other victims."

Nathalie was overjoyed by the idea of talking to Agnès. To plead for her forgiveness, to tell her she loved her and missed her. "Not any others, like you said. May they rest in peace."

They began walking down the sidewalk. "Although we do want

to disturb another," said Simone. She threw Nathalie an impish smirk. "The Dark Artist."

Nathalie gripped Simone's forearm. "We could ask who killed him!"

"Precisely. Who knows what other secrets he'd give up?"

The idea of wielding power over the Dark Artist from the side of the living appealed to her. Yet she also wondered whether resurrecting a ghost who'd haunted her while alive wouldn't cause a problem, like give her nightmares or visions or somehow interfere with her gift. Or worse, the memory loss that accompanied it.

Nevertheless, Nathalie couldn't resist one last triumph over him. "Whoever killed him is pleased with himself, if that Ovid quote is any indication. Who do you think is behind it?"

"My guess is someone connected to either a victim or a near-victim," said Simone, tucking her blond curls behind her ears. "Think about it. Maybe someone escaped and her husband or father tracked him down."

Nathalie hadn't considered the latter. Did anyone elude the Dark Artist? Surely it would have been in the newspaper. Then again, her own encounter in the Catacombs was kept from the public. Were there others, perhaps even that Christophe or M. Patenaude didn't know about or didn't tell her about?

They turned the corner and side-stepped an eager squirrel. "I thought it might be out of revenge, too, but now I don't know. The letter and the piece of silk? It's almost like someone wants the notoriety he had. Someone who's proud of himself for defeating the great Dark Artist."

Simone hooked her arm around Nathalie's elbow. "With any luck, we'll get an answer tomorrow night."

Simone and Louis arrived smartly dressed, she in a white lace blouse and poppy-red skirt, he in a dark gray suit with a lighter gray, check-patterned ascot tie. Maman, having never met Louis before, was not at all immune to his charms (he was particularly effervescent). She responded with a coquettish grin as he admired her fabric creations, unfinished though they were, that hung in the parlor. He gave Papa, who'd spent most of the day in bed with a fever and headache, a hearty handshake. The three of them made congenial conversation as Simone helped Nathalie finish pinning up her hair.

Nathalie didn't say they were attending a séance but rather a social gathering. This was half the truth, because Simone said there would be food served and a party beforehand. Maman herself was setting out soon for vespers at Notre-Dame. To pray, she'd said, for Papa's safe arrival home, his swift recovery from healing her and Céleste, and for the blessings his healing ability bestowed.

After bidding her parents good-bye, Nathalie stepped into the hall, sparkling with anticipation. "Where to?" she asked.

They walked down the stairwell. "We are going to the home of one Madame Zoe Klampert." Louis announced it like he was presenting a stage act. "I have no doubt she will astonish and astound."

"If she can bring us the ghosts of Agnès and Damien Salvage," Nathalie said, "I'll sing her praises to London and back. Where does she live?"

"In Louis's neighborhood," Simone said, pointing in that general direction. "Near the Université."

Simone had, with Nathalie's permission, told Louis about the visions after their reunion in the aftermath of Agnès's death. He was sworn to secrecy but had been intrigued from afar. This was the first time he'd had a chance to talk to Nathalie since then.

"What's it like?" asked Louis. "That very moment. Is it like a dream? Or like you closed your eyes and ended up in another room?"

"Both," she said, impressed with how he seemed to understand. He peppered her with other questions; the more she spoke, the more comfortable she was sharing her experiences. A measure of pride flowed through her veins like her magic-infused familial blood.

"What about the day you found a jar of blood in your bag?"

She frowned. That was a grim day, right after the fight with Simone, and she regretted spilling out the blood. It was a day she wished she could live over again. "I—I never sorted that out. Even now I wonder, every time I reach inside my satchel, if another one will be there."

Simone nudged Louis. "You've asked enough questions. Leave her alone."

Soon they arrived at Mme. Klampert's apartment building. Grayish white with flowerboxes on every balcony, it seemed too bright and modern for a séance. Somehow Nathalie had always pictured them taking place in dirty Gothic buildings recessed in the shadow of overgrown trees.

When they stepped inside, Louis led the way to the second floor. It was unusually quiet, and when they approached Mme. Klampert's door, the only sounds were their own footsteps. Nathalie had expected half a dozen voices from within, the jubilant noises of a party. Perhaps they were the first to arrive.

Instead of knocking on the door, Louis pulled out a key. He unlocked the door and gestured for Nathalie and Simone to enter. He followed them in and closed the door, locking it.

And then it was immediately obvious.

No one else was in the apartment.

As she watched Louis tuck the key in his pocket, unconcerned, the sick realization overtook her.

There was no séance, and there was never going to be.

It was all a trick.

41

The room they stood in resembled both a parlor and a laboratory.

Striped wallpaper, tapestry sofa and chair, kerosene lamps, a sun-faded rug, a bookshelf. No vases or trinkets or flowers. Only a candelabra on the bookshelf across the room.

And hundreds of jars.

Shelf after shelf of them lined the walls. Filled with liquid, they were all arranged by color. Black, brown, red, purple.

Blood. At least some of them. Nathalie was sure of it.

Her lungs emptied entirely, as if she'd taken a slow-moving cannonball to the stomach. She stole a glance at Simone, who seemed equally as stunned.

"Louis," Simone began, voice brewing with alarm, "what is this? Where are we?"

"Madame Klampert's apartment, as I said." He leaned against the door and eyed them both.

Trapped.

Nathalie scrutinized his face, his demeanor. Those regal, if exaggerated, manners, his lively nature, his congenial expressions . . . did they cover up a sinister side?

He's bookish and fashionable. Ovid and the silk cravat.

She banished the thought. No, not him. Not Simone's beau. That wasn't why he had brought them here. Maman and Papa knew they were with him.

Yet when he shifted his weight, she flinched. Her eyes found the candelabra on the bookshelf. Just in case.

"Why is the apartment empty? Why are we here?" Nathalie pointed to the bottles. "You asked me about the jar of blood in my satchel on the way here. That's some coincidence."

"She's right. I don't like tricks, Louis." Simone folded her arms. "Why *are* we here?"

Louis gazed at them, a satisfied cat indulging his audience. "Because," he began, eyes darting around the room, "*we* have some investigating to do. I suspect we're standing in the room of the Dark Artist's lover."

"His lover?" The next words hung in Nathalie's throat a moment before she could sputter them out. "Are—are you daft?"

"Mademoiselle Baudin, do you think you're the first person to ask me that?" Louis said as he straightened his tie, smirking. As Nathalie and Simone stared at him with folded arms, he held up his hands. "I'm not deranged or lying or trying to scare you. Trust me."

"We'll trust you when you stop talking in riddles," Simone said through gritted teeth. She took him by the elbow and pulled him close. "Explain this right now."

"You can begin," Nathalie said, "by telling us why you have a key to this apartment."

"We share a landlord, Madame Klampert and I. The man is a drunkard. He's not entirely faithful to his wife, either. I happened to come upon him at Le Chat Noir once with another woman." Louis cleared his throat. "I reminded him of this and we . . . reached an agreement."

Nathalie's jaw slackened. "You blackmailed him for a key."

"I did. And—my apologies, Simone, but please understand—I told him Madame Klampert was my lover."

Simone let go of him and scowled. "Sweet."

"Just a ruse, *mon chou*. I said I wanted to surprise her." Louis kissed Simone on the cheek.

"Less kissing, more explaining," said Simone.

His gaze searched the room as he spoke. "The woman who

lives here, Zoe Klampert, comes to The Quill from time to time. She asked for a book on tarot once, three months ago."

Tarot. *The Lovers*, the tarot card that was sent to the paper from the Dark Artist.

"Given my interest in fortune-telling," Louis continued, "I remembered her. Whenever she came in, even to browse, we talked for a moment or two. At some point we discovered we were nearly neighbors, and once I even delivered a few science books to her—that's where I got a glimpse of the jars."

Nathalie approached the nearest shelf. She peered at a jar with brown liquid and read the label out loud. "Rat placenta plus iron."

Simone came up beside her for a closer look. "Mine plus ink," she said, picking up a nearby jar with blackish liquid.

"Blood mixtures? Experiments?" Nathalie shook her head in disbelief. "And yet no equipment for measuring, no droppers, no chemicals. Only glass bottles."

Simone dropped the jar and swiped to catch it but missed. It hit the floor and shattered. The surrounding pool of blackness spread as if escaping the pile of shattered glass.

"Oh *mon Dieu!*" Simone's pallor turned to milk. "Now what?"

"We clean it up," said Louis, producing a linen handkerchief embroidered with his initials. "And search for evidence. There's got to be something here."

"I still don't understand the leap," said Nathalie. "You couldn't have known what was in the jars at the time."

Louis finished wiping up the mess, making a little bloodstained and shard-filled bundle. "No, but it was a memorable detail, to say the least." He stood up. "She said they were tinctures and that she used to work in an apothecary. I wasn't here very long and, taking her word for it, didn't think anything of it. Until I saw the Dark Artist in the morgue."

Simone, who was now inspecting jars on another shelf, turned to him. "You recognized him?"

"At the time, no, not exactly." He took measured steps around the room, inspecting every horizontal surface and everything except the jars. "However, he was very familiar. For days I couldn't figure out why. I thought I'd run into him at the club or the book shop. Then I read the account in the newspaper the other day and remembered. I'd seen his picture recently."

"When you came here," Nathalie ventured.

Louis nodded. "Indeed. Madame Klampert asked me to put the books on this table," he said, pointing to a well-crafted wooden table. "Except last time, there was a framed photograph of the two of them. Right here. They were standing before the Medici Fountain in Luxembourg Garden—we even exchanged a few sentences about it."

The marble and bronze statue of Acis and Galatea, lovers surprised by Polyphemus the giant. Again, lovers. A favorite theme of theirs, it seemed.

Nathalie suddenly felt dizzy. This couldn't be real. She couldn't be standing in the apartment of the Dark Artist's companion. In fact, she *shouldn't* be. The police should be here, not the three of them.

"You didn't have to investigate," said Nathalie. "You could have gone right to the police. Even if it didn't turn out to be accurate. They get false leads all time."

Louis put his hands on his hips. "Now where would the fun in that be? Worry none. If this plan of mine fell through this evening, I had every intention of going to the police in the morning. But I figured some evidence might help to back up my theory."

Nathalie was both aggravated and impressed with him for devising this scheme. He was much more clever than she'd perceived. She'd taken him as a poet with an interest in the occult. Beneath all that flamboyance was a shrewd, observant mind.

She turned to Simone, but Simone wasn't listening. She was transfixed by the jars. "This is it. Proof of her involvement. Look— look at those jars. Girl #2. Girl #3. Girl #1 is missing, but the rest correspond. All dated this summer. What else could it be?"

Agnès's blood. There. In a jar, like a science experiment or natural history museum exhibit.

Nathalie's finger trembled as she touched the one labeled Girl #5. "Agnès was Agnès, not Girl #5."

"I'm sorry," said Simone, stroking Nathalie's back. "I'm sorry you had to see it and think it."

They searched in silence for a few minutes. Nathalie joined Louis at the bookshelf as he pointed out the science books he'd brought her. She wasn't listening to him, however. She was trying to find Ovid. "What if she's working with whoever sent the letter? Or sent it herself?"

"For what, though?" asked Simone. "She could just disappear and no one would ever know she was collecting blood with the Dark Artist."

"No one does." Louis pulled out a book and leafed through it. "Yet."

The books were mostly science books, a few philosophy, and a handful of novels. Virgil's *Aeneid*, a volume of Cicero's works. No other ancient Roman literature.

Nathalie's eyes danced around the room. She walked over to a wooden cylinder desk and rolled back the curved cover. To the left stood a framed *carte de visite,* the small photograph slightly faded with a tattered corner. A pretty, dark-haired young woman sat in a chair; a slim, older man who resembled her stood behind. Zoe and her father, presumably, or an uncle? Nathalie picked it up to show Louis. "Is this her?"

He examined the photograph. "Her face is leaner now and she wears her hair up, but yes. That's her."

Simone came over for a look. "Pretty girl," she said, tracing the outline. "I wonder if her father, or whoever that is, warned her about murderous men?"

"Or imagined she would grow up to collect bottles of blood." Nathalie returned the *carte de visite* to its place, her feelings vacillating between disbelief and disgust. She couldn't reconcile this image of Zoe with the grim peculiarity of the apartment. The girl in the photo could have been a schoolmate, a friend to her and Agnès. Instead she was an inscrutable woman, obviously unhinged, who preferred jars filled with the blood of murder victims to figurines made of Limoges porcelain.

Nathalie scoured the desk. Envelopes, receipts, scraps of paper, financial documents, and two notebooks, all in neat piles, took up the rest of it. She began thumbing through a notebook when Louis walked over to one of the jar-lined shelves.

"So we know she was an accomplice," he said. He plucked a bottle marked "Mine, +1, with laudanum" off the shelf and slipped it into his pocket. Casually, as if breaking into someone's apartment and taking a blood jar off the shelf was a perfectly normal thing to do. "And we know she experiments with blood somehow. But we don't know how or why."

Footsteps came down the outside hall. Nathalie held her breath.

"It's not her," said Louis, waving his hand. "She won't be back for hours. She's at a séance."

Simone narrowed her eyes. "How do you know?"

"Because there is indeed a séance tonight—one of my acquaintances is the host, and I arranged for him to use the back room of The Quill. I saw the guest list a few days ago, and she was on it." He tapped his fingertips together. "She won't be back until late tonight."

Nathalie felt an unexpected stab of disappointment that they themselves weren't at the séance. What if she could have contacted Agnès?

She returned to the notebooks. The first one appeared to involve banking—numbers involving dollar amounts and transactions. The second, with faded ink and yellowed pages, contained symbols she'd never seen before and extensive notes. The penmanship alternated between long, flowing script and crisp, narrow text; it had to be that of two people. "Who *is* this woman?"

"Madame la Tuerie,'" said Simone after a pause. Madame of the Massacre. "I'm going to call her that. Never mind Klampert."

"Brilliant," said Nathalie, wishing she'd thought of it.

They started walking toward the bedroom when Nathalie spotted a table covered in lace and red silk at the end near the dining area. In the center of the table, surrounded by three unlit pillar candles, was a statue of a Roman centurion holding a lance in one hand and a crucifix in the other. A prayer book rested near the edge of the table.

Prayer. Maman was at vespers right now, praying for Papa and probably for Nathalie, too.

She opened the book, which reminded her of Maman's, and a red and gold prayer card fell out. One side depicted a Roman soldier with a spear and "St. Longinus" underneath. It wasn't a saint she recognized. She flipped it to the other side and read the prayer.

O Blessed Saint Longinus,
You who pierced the side of the crucified Christ,
You whose blindness His Precious Blood then cured,
Intercede for us.
Aid us in our suffering, strengthen the weakness in our faith.
Keep us on the path to true understanding
Lest we falter into the darkness.
Through your intercession and the mercy of God, the
    Almighty Father,
Amen.

Nathalie was repulsed by the thought of Mme. la Tuerie praying and hoped that no saint interceded any prayers for her whatsoever. She started to crush the prayer card but changed her mind.

A box of matches lay near one of the pillar candles. She lit a candle and held the prayer card over it, watching it disintegrate as she tossed the last piece into the flame. Nathalie murmured a quick prayer of apology to the saint, hoping he would understand.

"Is something burning?" Simone poked her head around the

corner. Nathalie started to explain when Louis called from the bedroom.

"Ladies, you won't believe what I've found."

Nathalie and Simone rushed in to see him standing over an open drawer. The bedroom was ordinary—street art paintings on the wall, a brass lamp, a quilted bedspread, a vanity with perfume bottles.

Louis took something out of the drawer and held it up.

A pair of white gloves covered in an unmistakable brown stain. Old blood.

Simone let out a squawk and slapped her hand over her mouth. Nathalie's muscles went rigid.

"Come see," he said, leaning against the mahogany bureau. When they joined him, he pointed to five more pairs of gloves.

"A trophy for each murder," said Nathalie, her stomach twisting more with each word.

"We'll bring this to the police," Louis said. He began to stuff his pockets.

"Wait," said Simone, placing her hand on his wrist. "Only one should do. What if she notices? It's bad enough we took two jars. So to speak."

"Out of hundreds." Louis put back the blood-soaked gloves and pocketed a pair. Nathalie wondered whose blood it was. Odette's? Mirabelle's? Charlotte's? Lisette's? The unnamed victim's? She hoped it wasn't Agnès's.

Nathalie turned away, and her eyes landed on the vanity. She noticed something long and thin among the bottles and leaned in for a better view.

She put her hand to her throat as an acidic taste rested on her tongue. It all sank in at that moment, all of this. The madness of it. The horror. The reality.

"You finish. I'll be standing by the door in the parlor," Nathalie said, backing away.

Simone took a step toward her. "Whatever you'd like."

Nathalie retreated a step and bumped into the dresser. As she caught herself she looked down at the vanity. With a shaky hand she picked up a gold-plated syringe with enamel inlay. "Is this . . . what she used to draw the blood?"

She put it down and turned away, not waiting for an answer. She knew the answer was yes. They all did. "I don't know why I didn't demand for the door to be unlocked and run out as soon as we saw the bottles." She struggled to get the words out over trembling lips. "This is madness. You're mad for bringing me here, Louis. My goodness. My beautiful friend's blood in a jar? The gloves that madman wore when he killed her? I want to leave."

Both Simone and Louis approached her warily, and this time she didn't retreat. Instead she let them embrace her as she sobbed, on the threshold of Mme. la Tuerie's bedroom.

When the moment passed, they stepped apart. Louis, who was facing the parlor window, tensed up. "Oh no."

Nathalie wasn't sure if he said "She's here" or if she just knew it instinctively.

They ran for the door and Louis pulled the key out of his pocket, dropping the gloves. He stopped to pick them up.

The hallway stairs creaked.

"Bedroom window!" he hissed.

They bolted out of the parlor. Simone unlocked the window and flung it open. She stepped onto the balcony first, then Nathalie.

The apartment door opened, followed by the squeak of the floorboards. Louis froze, his stricken face revealing the words he couldn't utter.

There was no time.

"Gagnon," Louis whispered, licking his lips. He tossed Simone the bloodstained gloves and put his hand on the window latch. "I'll catch up."

With that he pulled the window shut.

42

Nathalie and Simone stood on either side of the window, backs pressed against the cut-stone wall.

"Madame Klampert!" Louis's voice ascended like a musical scale. "M. Genet told me you were . . . having some difficulty with a window latch?"

Nathalie eased away from the window, worried she might be visible from a certain angle. She eyed Simone, tense and motionless.

"Not at all. You work at the bookshop. How do you know the name of my landlord?" Her muted voice, suspicious yet under control, came closer with each word.

"He owns the building I live in as well," said Louis. Nathalie imagined him giving an amiable smile to go with his tone. "I do odd jobs for him every now and then."

Silence followed. The kind of silence that sends your imagination to a dozen places in the span of two blinks.

"You must have the wrong apartment," Mme. la Tuerie said.

Was it fear or memory that made Nathalie think she'd heard that voice before?

Louis tittered. "I have to say, he wasn't entirely sober when he gave me the key." His voice faded further away as he spoke.

Mme. la Teurie's response was too muffled for Nathalie to make out. Louis responded; again she couldn't hear it.

Nathalie patted the side of the building to get Simone's attention. "Let's go," she mouthed.

"I can't leave him," Simone whispered. She looked at Nathalie and then back toward the window, as if Louis were going to come out of it and join them on the balcony. Her hands were balled up into fists.

The voices inside continued. Muffled, unintelligible, and in a normal register. No shouting, nothing to indicate an altercation. Why was Louis still in there?

Nathalie spoke in a firm whisper. "*We* are going to Christophe, then I'm going Notre-Dame. My mother might still be there. You wait for Louis at the morgue."

Simone pushed her shoulders against the wall. "I feel like a cat who can't get out of a tree," she said quietly as she tugged at her sleeves. "He's in there with a crazy woman. I don't know what to do."

"Trust him. And me. We have to go," said Nathalie, trying very hard to keep her voice calm. "Now."

Simone met Nathalie's gaze and nodded.

They climbed over the window balcony and dropped onto the running balcony below. They hurried along until they reached a tree branch, gripping it for balance as they slid down an awning. Nathalie, being much taller, jumped onto the sidewalk and helped Simone make a soft landing.

"Ready?" Nathalie gave Simone's hand a reassuring squeeze.

"Ready."

They ran as fast as they could.

Christophe listened to their account, with his customary balance of acumen and concern, and hastily escorted them to the nearby *Préfecture de police*. Louis's sly methods of apartment entry aside, the police appreciated the gloves and bottles. Nathalie and Simone were questioned separately, then thanked and dismissed. Louis was in the waiting area.

"Gagnon sent me straight here," he said, standing up. Simone nearly jumped into his arms for an embrace.

"I was so worried!" said Simone. She buried her face in his shoulder. "I was ready to stand out on that balcony until I knew you were safely outside."

Louis took her hands in his and kissed them. "Everything is fine. I made polite conversation with her, went upstairs to pretend to check another apartment, and after a few minutes, left."

Simone embraced him again.

A policeman emerged from one of the rooms. "Louis Carre? The inspector will see you now."

"I'll wait for you," said Simone as she sat on the bench.

"Thank you, Louis," said Nathalie. "I can't believe I'm thanking you for this wild adventure, but I am."

"Louis Carre Detective Agency, at your service." He winked and followed the official through the door.

Nathalie turned to Simone, who was much more settled now. "I'm going over to Notre-Dame. Thank you, too, for being such an incredible friend."

Simone blew her a kiss and grinned as Nathalie left.

The cathedral was less than five minutes away, and Nathalie's quick pace brought her to the entrance in far less than that. She went inside the middle door, the portal of the Last Judgment.

Fading light poured in through the stained glass windows, over the wooden pews and around the colossal stone pillars. The South Rose window, still catching the late-day sun, glimmered in every hue. There was no priest bellowing the Divine Office, no cluster of worshippers following along in their prayer books. Vespers had already finished. Maman was gone.

Gothic arches paraded up the nave of the church on either side toward the altar, where a small choir rehearsed. She heard the voices of men and women, young and old.

Was that the choral group to which Agnès had belonged?

The thought pinched her soul.

Nathalie decided to stay. Coming to Notre-Dame for Mass or to pray wasn't something she did as often as she meant to, but today she felt drawn to reflection. To calm down. To think and to tend to her spirit.

She lit a candle in one of the vigil alcoves near the back, the Chapel of Saint Charles, because she'd always been struck by the harrowing picture of Saint Paul blinding a false prophet. As she extinguished the match, a short, bald priest ambled up the aisle toward her.

"*Abbé*," she addressed him. "I have a question about a saint."

"*Oui, Mademoiselle?*" He turned to her with a civil nod.

"Saint Lon . . ." Nathalie struggled to remember the name. Something unusual and certainly not French. "Longinus. I think that's it. With the sword."

"Oh yes! The Roman soldier." His thin lips stretched into a smile. "He put a lance into the side of Jesus Christ on the Cross, to make sure he was dead. Blood and water poured out; the blood that spilled on him cured his eye disease. He converted to Christianity and, as you know, is honored as a saint."

Blood.

She shivered. "I see. Thank you, *Abbé*."

Nathalie stepped past him and walked down the aisle. She slipped into a pew halfway to the altar and settled onto a kneeler.

She buried her head in her hands and prayed. For the Dark Artist's victims and their loved ones—for everyone had them at one time, she believed, even if they died alone or, like the second victim, unknown. She prayed for Sébastien and Mathieu and all the policemen who'd stood guard for her. She prayed for Céleste. She prayed for her parents and Aunt Brigitte. For Simone. For the man she'd mistakenly thought was the Dark Artist, weeping for his daughter in Père Lachaise. For Christophe and M. Patenaude and Louis and the hypnotist and his wife and the nun who'd wanted to help her. She prayed for everyone else who'd touched her life these last few months.

She prayed for Agnès, whose lyrical voice she'd never again hear. She thought about their smirks in class and their secrets in the schoolyard. Nathalie would treasure those letters forever but never read them again; it would be too painful, a year from now or fifty years from now. But she'd always keep them close.

After losing herself in prayer for some time, she picked up her head. Placing her chin on her folded hands, she leaned forward on the pew. As the choir finished a hymn, Nathalie heard rustling behind her. She glanced back to see a woman holding a prayer book and donning mourner's garb—a black hat, black veil, a black dress, and even an old-fashioned mourning brooch—shuffle into the pew and kneel.

Once again Nathalie buried her face in her hands. She wondered who the woman mourned, whose lock of hair was in that brooch. She prayed for both the woman and the person for whom she grieved.

The choir began their next hymn, a quiet piece in a minor key. It was soothing to be contemplative here, in this sanctuary of peace. Nathalie wished she'd thought to come here for solace weeks ago. Why had it taken so much pain for her to seek this comfort?

After a few minutes, she slid back into the pew.

And found herself sitting on something. She reached back and her fingers felt something small, solid, and angular.

A box.

It hadn't been here before.

Had it?

She'd come in and knelt right away, so she couldn't be sure.

No, she was sure. This was new.

She peeked behind her. The woman was gone.

Nathalie picked up the box, wooden and masterfully crafted, and lifted the lid. Two jars were inside. She knew these jars. She'd seen them an hour ago.

Both jars had notes inside. One jar was otherwise empty, and the other was full of blood.

She turned around, every sense sharpened. No sign of the woman. Nothing out of the ordinary.

With clumsy, quivering fingers she pried open the lid of the blood jar and took out the note. She put down the jar and unfurled the note, her thumb unraveling the bloodied half. The word impaled her.

Agnès.

Nathalie stifled a cry and rolled the note back up; her fingers trembled so violently she was afraid she'd let go of the bottle. She put the note inside and the lid on, blood smearing on her hand as she tightened the lid.

She took out the empty jar and pulled out the note. Again, one word.

You.

43

Nearly in a trance, Nathalie dropped the note back in and put the small bottle on the pew. It clinked, startling her. Blood rushed through her ears.

She couldn't hear.

Couldn't think.

Instinct. That was all she had.

Wild-eyed, she looked in every direction for the woman.

She detected movement in the rear of the church. She turned. A figure in partial shadow scurried between columns.

The woman. Zoe Klampert. Mme. la Tuerie. A malevolent trinity.

Nathalie bolted from the pew. Mme. la Tuerie dashed out the exit before Nathalie made it down the aisle.

"HELP!" she yelled as she ran past some people coming in. "Get her! She—she attacked me!"

They spoke German among themselves and stared at her.

She got outside in time to see the woman run across a bridge to the left. Nathalie began to race after her but lost her footing on a wobbly stone; she tumbled and rose up in almost one motion. Mme. la Tuerie, weaving in and out of the crowd, extended her lead.

"She's insane!" Nathalie yelled, pointing as she ran. "Woman in black! She attacked me!"

Over and over and over again.

And no one helped, not one.

Everyone either ignored Nathalie or regarded her with alarm.

As if there was something wrong with her for screaming for help.

"What's she going on about?" someone asked.

"She's chasing a widow!"

"I bet she's from the Home for Wayward Girls."

The words struck her like bullets as she continued the chase. She stopped, crestfallen, when Mme. la Tuerie boarded a steam tram. Not until it turned the corner did Nathalie finally find a policeman.

It was, of course, too late.

Nathalie called out to the policeman. "A woman on that tram! She attacked me in Notre-Dame!" Gasping for air, she looked over her shoulder, as though the steam tram might derail and return the woman.

The policeman didn't seem much older than Nathalie. "Attacked you how?"

Nathalie hesitated. She'd said *attack* to get everyone's attention. "Not attack. She *threatened* me. I was praying and when I sat back I found a box with two jars, one with blood and one without and both had notes in them and . . ."

Her stomach churned. She suddenly felt off balance and steadied herself on the policeman's shoulder.

"Where are these . . . jars?"

Nathalie stepped back from him with a scowl. "In the cathedral! Do you think I tucked them away neatly in my pocket before chasing her?"

The policeman's brow arched upward.

"We can get them later." Nathalie put her hands on her hips. "That woman in the black dress. We need to go after her! NOW."

"Mademoiselle, you need to compose yourself." He held up his palm. "Did you see her place this box?"

"*Non.* But it couldn't have been anyone else."

"Did she touch you in any way or speak to you?"

"*Non.* Listen, she was the Dark Artist's lover—and partner!"

The policeman cocked his head. "How do you know that?"

"I do. Never mind how." She gestured toward the tram route. "We're wasting time!"

"Mademoiselle, she could be any number of places by now, and I suggest you file a report. We don't have the manpower, and—"

Flames shot up to Nathalie's face. *"Idiot!"*

She stormed away from him and went back to Notre-Dame, entering through one of the side doors. An older man with a formal coat was at the pew, holding the box and inspecting the area. An usher, she guessed.

"Pardonnez-moi, Monsieur."

He turned to her, eyes wide. As if she were an apparition instead of a girl. "I was at the front of the church when you ran after someone. What happened? What—what are these?" He lifted the lid to indicate the jars.

She explained what took place, as absurd as it was. His face was stoic, but under the mask she detected an undulating disquiet. He handed her the box, seemingly grateful to get rid of it, and offered to accompany her to the morgue. She didn't feel safe going alone—would she ever feel safe again?—and accepted.

They hastened out of Notre-Dame as the bells pealed, and the gentleman walked her to the front door of the morgue. She thanked him, annoyed a few people by lightly pushing them to get inside, and waved frantically at Christophe.

Minutes later they sat in his office and, for the second time in as many hours, she told him what happened. "Here's the . . . the box with the bottles." She pulled it out of her bag and placed it in the center of his desk.

He opened it up and examined the contents, including the notes in both.

"Why would she do this—and why to me? Because of my blood,

like the Dark Artist wanted in the Catacombs?" said Nathalie, voice cracking in distress.

"It—it would seem so. But of course I don't know." Christophe covered his eyes with his palms. "Nothing about this makes sense. Including how she knew where you were."

"I assumed she followed Simone and me . . . and then just me."

He shook his head. "By the time the police arrived, she'd vacated the apartment. The notebooks, gloves, some of the jars, clothing. Even the photo you mentioned. She couldn't have done that and followed you. We're watching the apartment to see if she returns, but this helps explain the lack of chemistry equipment. She likely has another place or is staying with someone."

"What kind of someone?"

"Family member, friend. The Dark Artist's killer for all we know." He let out a sigh. "We simply don't know enough about her yet."

"Only enough to know that she's crazy and revolting and pre-occupied with blood."

"Nathalie, I've said this before—too many times this summer, unfortunately—but I'm sorry you're under such duress." He pushed the box of jars to the side and patted her hand. "I wish I could take these wicked events away from you."

Even-tempered, sensible Christophe, who always made her feel safe. Where would she be without him? She thanked him and patted his hand in return. He was a colorful sprout among black, jagged rocks this summer.

He withdrew his hand and smiled. "I'm sure it's dark by now, or will be soon. Shall I walk you home?"

"It's more than a walk. It's an omnibus or tram ride away." She told him the area in which she lived. "Where do you call home?"

"Also the eleventh arrondissement," he said.

"I—I can't believe our paths haven't crossed before."

"It's, uh, somewhat recent."

"Oh?" And as soon as she uttered it, she regretted it, that little too-inquisitive "oh."

"The woman I intend to marry, her family lives in that area. It's a surprise for their return from America next month."

Nathalie cast her eyes to the floor. "Thank you for the offer, but I do believe I can make my way home well enough. I'll . . . hire a carriage."

He stepped two paces back and stared at her. "Are you . . . envious?"

She hoped he didn't see the heat race up her neck and settle into her face.

"Oh, Nathalie," he said, taking her hand. "I—I wish you didn't feel that way."

She couldn't look him in the eye yet and it was all she could do to avoid running away like a child. But she wasn't a child. "It matters not, Monsieur Gagnon." She stood up to her full height, gaze still cast to the side. "I wish you the best in your nuptials."

"Thank you," he said. He kissed her hand and let it go, gently. "I think at another time, in other circumstances, I should have liked to know you better. And differently."

Nathalie looked him in the eye for the first time since this conversation took its turn. "You . . . you should? I mean, you would have?"

He nodded, the serious expression on his face melting into a smile. His crooked tooth, seldom seen unless he smiled broadly, winked at her.

"Thank you, Christophe." She, too, smiled. "I appreciate that. I—I'd still prefer to see my own way home, however. I have too much blood on my hands to want protection anymore, and if it were anything more than that between us . . . I think it would only break my heart to see you walk away afterward."

He understood, or so he said, but a shade of disappointment clouded his face. "May I at least pay for your carriage?"

She was about to decline, but his slightly wounded expression touched her. With a polite smile she accepted, sad that he wasn't hers to have, but utterly elated that the affection was mutual.

He called a carriage for her, paid the driver, and kissed her on the hand before helping her ascend. All the way home she pressed the back of her hand, still tingling from his kiss, against her cheek.

44

The staccato knock at the door the next morning was swift and deliberate; it was a knock that meant serious business. Nathalie, still in her nightgown, peeked out from her bedroom.

"Who's calling on us so early?" asked Maman, putting down the teapot.

Papa rose up slowly from his chair. His fever had subsided the previous night and his hands were better; he said the fatigue would last for a few more days. "Charity request, maybe," he said on his way to the door.

"Wait!" Nathalie cried. "What if it's—" She swallowed. She felt silly putting it into words. *Madame la Tuerie.* She'd told her parents everything; it had been a late night of conversation and grateful embraces as well as admonishment and promises (not to undertake dangerous feats that were "for the Prefect of Police to handle"). Papa's reassuring look told her he understood. She cleared her throat and called out, "Who is it?"

"A courier on behalf of Saint-Mathurin Asylum."

Papa opened the door a crack, then swung it open. "Please come in."

A slender young man with glasses stepped over the threshold. "My apologies for disturbing you at this early hour. I'm afraid I have some unpleasant news about an accident involving Brigitte Baudin."

"Oh goodness." Maman covered her mouth with her balled-up handkerchief.

"Brigitte tried to take her own life this morning." The courier stood with his hands at his sides. "She's alive but badly wounded. I'm afraid the asylum did not ask me to relay any more than that."

Maman's face turned as white as her bonnet. *"Mon Dieu!"*

Papa thanked the courier and showed him out. His hand lingered on the doorknob. After a pause, he shook his head. "She—she seemed well enough during my visit the other day."

"I thought she was long past that," Maman said in a heavy voice as she settled onto the sofa.

"Past that? This isn't the first time?" Nathalie took a step into the parlor. "You never told me."

Maman shot her a look of disappointment. "Do you think talk of suicide is appropriate for a child?"

Nathalie blushed. *"Non."*

"It happened shortly after they took her in at Saint-Mathurin," Papa said, joining Maman on the sofa. He put his arms around her. "She made thirteen sets of rosary beads into a rope of sorts, and . . . fortunately someone heard her kick the chair away. They found her in time."

Maman buried her face in her hands. "Poor troubled, sensitive, unpredictable Brigitte."

Nathalie hesitated, wanting to choose her words carefully, then spoke. "I understand. Why you kept some things from me. About our family, about being Insightfuls and what all of that meant."

She studied them, her hardworking parents who'd given her a home of love and happy memories, when she knew all too well many girls had no such thing. The Henard experiments had changed their lives and hers forever, and yet they didn't crumble under the weight of their memories. They were fatigued and genuine, burdened and good. She was proud, so very proud, to have them as parents.

As soon as they stepped through the doorway to Aunt Brigitte's floor, rosemary and juniper pervaded their nostrils. "To purify the air," Maman had once explained. Sometimes the asylum staff used it to cover up accidents, like the time a patient threw up in the hall, or the day one of Aunt Brigitte's roommates dumped every chamber pot she could find until the nurses restrained her. So it was rarely just rosemary and juniper. It was usually rosemary, juniper, and some horrid, not-quite-masked stench.

Today there was no repulsive odor. The air was, if not quite pure, fresh. Rosemary and juniper wafted through the hall.

Nathalie wondered if it was intended to cover up the smell of would-be death.

Nurse Pelletier, lips pursed and strides brisk, approached Papa. They conversed briefly, and then the nurse walked away with steps as rapid as before.

"They put Aunt Brigitte in a different room for now, alone," said Papa, pointing to a room farther down the hall than Tante's usual room. "She woke up screaming from a nightmare. Nurse Pelletier calmed her down, and when she returned later to check, Tante was chewing on her wrist and bleeding."

Maman gasped and Nathalie winced. Maybe it was her imagination, maybe it was the visions, but she pictured the terrible scene all too sharply.

"Also," Papa continued, "she claims a demon dog came to her in her sleep, attacked her, and left her bleeding. That's the story Aunt Brigitte is telling, and . . . they don't want us to acknowledge it as a suicide attempt."

"We're to pretend it's just another visit?" Maman's hand flew to her throat.

Papa shrugged. "The doctor thinks that's best for now. I'm going to meet with him before we go."

They walked into Aunt Brigitte's new room to find her bundled up and under the covers. She looked small, so very small, in that bed. Every time Nathalie saw her, Tante seemed tinier and tinier, like someday she would disappear into the bed altogether.

Aunt Brigitte held up her bandaged wrist. "One of the hounds of Hell got me last night." Then, in a whisper: "It isn't safe from them here."

They approached the bed slowly and greeted her. Aunt Brigitte thanked them for visiting, as she always did. "Last night I dreamed I walked through the halls of this place and everyone was dead, mauled by an unseen creature. I knelt down to pray and a red-eyed demon dog appeared. 'Your prayers mean nothing,' it said, then attacked my folded hands. I woke up and . . ." She extended her wrist and let it drop.

Quiet settled among them all, and after a while, Maman coughed. "Because Augustin is humble, I suspect he didn't tell you: Not only did he heal me, but he healed our neighbors' daughter. She had some unknown ailment that had her feverish most of the summer."

Aunt Brigitte's face brightened as she beamed at her brother.

Nathalie observed Maman, impressed by how she excelled at helping Tante shift moods. Papa patted Maman's hand; he was probably thinking the same.

Aunt Brigitte launched into a story about how Papa had tried to teach her to skip stones, but she never did master it. "Of course it's too late now," she lamented. Her expression abruptly switched to concern. "Augustin, take the box home. The demon dog is a sign that the box shouldn't be here anymore."

"What box?" asked Maman. She began to look around Tante's sparse area, hastily remade from her other room. A set of wooden rosary beads without a crucifix. A worn prayer book. A stuffed cat Nathalie had given her one Christmas years ago, back when Aunt Brigitte lived at Mme. Plouffe's, because it resembled Stanley. "There's nothing here."

"Ask Nurse Pelletier," whispered Aunt Brigitte. "She put it in the vault years ago."

"Where they keep patient possessions?" Maman darted a look at Papa. He glanced away.

"And goodness knows what else," said Aunt Brigitte, waving her hand. "I don't trust anyone here."

"I'll get it," said Nathalie. Before anyone could object she left the room and found Nurse Pelletier feeding someone two rooms down. Once she finished up with the patient, she acknowledged Nathalie's request. After muttering "Now, where's the key?" several times to herself, she disappeared.

Nathalie watched the woman who'd just been fed, an elderly woman. She stroked a filthy rag doll as though it were a child. Another patient shuffled down the corridor toward Nathalie, murmuring. She stopped beside Nathalie, who pretended not to see, and stood on her toes. The woman leaned in to Nathalie as if to tell her a secret, and spoke in a whisper. "Where's the key?"

The woman shuffled away. Nathalie stared after her, suddenly recognizing her and contemplating the filter of madness.

"Here you are." Nurse Pelletier, returning sooner than Nathalie expected, handed her the box. "One of your parents needs to sign a document attesting to its receipt. Have them see a nurse in that office." She pointed to a room at the end of the hall and disappeared into another room to feed another patient.

Nathalie strolled back toward Tante's room and removed the box cover to see what was inside.

The papers.

The papers, the ones Nathalie had searched for, the ones scattered all over Aunt Brigitte's room at Mme. Plouffe's that day. The papers Papa so fiercely guarded. The papers Maman said had been burned.

MY STORY was written across the top of yellowed paper. Nathalie picked up the box and began to read.

My name is Brigitte Catherine Baudin and I am an Insightful. I am blessed, I am cursed, and I am proof that magic is real, beautiful, and devastating.

45

Nathalie's grip on the box stiffened. *This could be it. Finally.* Answers no one else could or would provide, to questions she'd never had until this summer. Questions she didn't think existed.

She heard footsteps behind her and instinctively closed the box. A white-bearded doctor with glasses muttered a greeting as he passed; a nurse holding bandages trailed him. They turned into Aunt Brigitte's room.

She leaned against the concrete wall and resumed reading in the hallway.

> I was twenty-six when I got the transfusion, and the magic transformed me, made me love life and Paris and God Himself more than ever. After twenty-five years I was ALIVE. The gift bestowed on me was clairvoyance through dreams. It was like a little surprise each day . . . which of my dreams would I see in real life the next day? Sometimes it was a scene in the park, sometimes it was a meal I enjoyed, sometimes it was a conversation with a stranger. Every day something from my dreams became a piece of my reality.
>
> I gave birth to a dead baby when I was twenty. His diminutive corpse haunted my dreams for five years. I received magic and the haunting stopped.
>
> No. It changed forms.
>
> When there were whispers of CONSEQUENCES, I pitied those who had them, including Augustin. He heals people

and takes some of their sickness into himself for a time. I believed myself to be fortunate. I didn't suffer from any effects.

Until I did.

It happened slowly. I think. Perhaps. I realize now as I write these words these words these WORDS that madness is stealthy and comes like a thief in the night (1 Thessalonians 5:2). Isn't that what Saint Paul said or meant or wrote nonetheless?

My dreams became reality and reality became dreams and violence came to me in dreams and then I came to violence when I woke up. BUT I HAD TO BECAUSE I HAD TO. I know what I saw. Babies, innocents. Killed. Being killed. Killers killing innocents. And I tried and tried and tried to save them and I tried I did to save them.

No one believes. No one believes. No one no one no one no one no one no one no one no one no one no one no one no one no one no one

Then the words became even more nonsensical—they were arbitrary and ill-placed, as if someone who didn't speak French had taken a list of phrases from a language book and copied them at random. That went on for another couple of pages and then the handwriting became sloppy, too. Soon the letters themselves became meaningless loops and lines and curves. By the fourth page it was utter gibberish.

Another twenty or so pages of senseless writing followed. Then, on the last page, Aunt Brigitte signed her name in large, clear script.

Nathalie lifted her eyes from the papers. Tante had borne a dead child? She realized then that she didn't know much at all about Aunt Brigitte other than what she saw during asylum visits and what she remembered from childhood. Nathalie would never pretend to comprehend the entirety of Tante's madness. These words offered a sliver of understanding for Nathalie to perch upon, something authentic in which to root her empathy.

She fanned the pages between her thumb and index finger, marveled and horrified by what they contained.

"That's probably the last thing she ever wrote," said Papa, appearing in the doorway. His voice was sad. Nostalgic.

"Maman said you burned them."

"I intended to," he said, lowering his voice, "because it was a difficult time for Insightfuls, and I didn't want any record of Henard's work in our home. When the time came, I couldn't do it. Out of respect."

Nathalie placed the cover on the box. "You told me you took Tante to see Dr. Henard because she'd become melancholy. Is—is this why?" she asked, hugging the box.

Papa nodded. "She'd been ashamed that the child was out of wedlock and was convinced its death in the womb was punishment. The man who fathered the child left her. The sorrow never did." He gazed over his shoulder, his expression forlorn. "Henard's magic was going to give her—us—a new path to take. I wanted her to feel alive again.'"

"She did." Nathalie saw the guilt in his eyes. "She wrote that, Papa. She did feel alive again."

"For a while," he said, his smile bittersweet.

She gazed into the room at her aunt, withered beyond her years.

Will that be me? Papa? M. Patenaude? Do we all become you, Tante?

Or were you just unlucky?

If magic and science had never met in Dr. Henard's laboratory, who might you have been?

"Augustin?" Maman called from inside the room.

They returned to the room. Aunt Brigitte had her eyes closed as the nurse gathered the old dressing. Papa spoke to the doctor, who addressed him in a stiff voice and led him out of the room.

"Maman, Nurse Pelletier said we have to sign a document for

this," Nathalie said, holding up the box. "I'll show you what's in it later."

"You can come with me to do that," said the nurse. She rolled up one last bandage and motioned for Maman to follow her.

Maman was no sooner over the threshold than Aunt Brigitte sat up. "It was about you, Nathalie. She sought *you*."

Nathalie's heart leapt. "Who? Where?"

"In my dream. You were sleeping under a tree in a park. The woman in black had a bloody knife in one hand and a little glass bottle in the other."

"Woman in black?" Nathalie felt her chest contract, a bow string pulled back. Was this more madness? Or was this . . . somehow real?

Aunt Brigitte beckoned her closer. "Her hands were so full of splinters, it hurt her to hold the knife. She stabbed a man on her way to you—near Augustin's age, splayed on a gray-striped blanket. He was face down so I couldn't see him. And from here to here," Aunt Brigitte said, dragging her hands from Nathalie's elbows to fingertips, "she was soaked in blood."

She quivered. Aunt Brigitte was more lucid, more clear-eyed than she'd ever seen her. Not tempestuous or angry.

Authentic.

"This woman," Nathalie began, fighting the dread that clawed at her throat. "What—what did she look like?"

"Stunning visage, dark braids that sat high on her head. She wore an unusual headpiece, red and gold, that looked like a fan. Height like yours."

The room spun around Nathalie like a carnival wheel.

Why hadn't she put it together before? It was all right there. All of it.

Splinters.

Red-and-gold fan.

Red-and-gold prayer card. To a saint whose conversion story involved blood. Of course blood. Always blood.

She'd seen Mme. la Tuerie not once. Not twice. Three times. And once had been with the Dark Artist.

Nathalie sat down on the floor. She didn't care if was filthy or smelled like chamber pots. Her legs wouldn't support her. She hugged her knees as she thought it all through.

The woman who'd talked to her in the morgue about splinters, the day she fainted. *My beau gets splinters all the time.*

The couple in Père Lachaise, the day she followed M. Gloves. Asking her if she was lost. A handsome clean-shaven man who'd had a beard when he was on the slab at the morgue. That's why he seemed familiar. She'd seen him. Talked to him. About the lovers statue in the cemetery.

The lovers, like the tarot card. Like the photograph at Medici Fountain that Louis had seen.

But one lover killed the other. She alone killed the Dark Artist. The man in the dream on the blanket. It represented the Dark Artist.

Somewhere on the edges of Nathalie's mind she heard Tante call her name, but she couldn't respond.

46

Nathalie trembled and made her way to her feet, using the wall for support.

"Why did you sit on the ground like that?" asked Aunt Brigitte. "There's a chair in the corner."

"I just—just needed to for a moment." Nathalie looked in the hall to see if either of her parents were on their way back yet. "Tante, did the woman kill me?"

"I don't know. I ran toward her and grabbed her wrist, but my hand slipped on the blood," Aunt Brigitte said, mimicking an elusive grasp. "You woke up in time to see her coming for you. And then you did the strangest thing."

She positioned her hand for a handshake. Nathalie tentatively met Tante's hand with her own.

"After you shook her hand, I woke up." Aunt Brigitte heaved a sigh as she gently let go of Nathalie's hand.

Nathalie stared at her own hand, as if it could tell her the rest of the story. "What about the—the demon dog? How was that part of the dream?"

"It wasn't," Aunt Brigitte said in a low voice. "That was a dream from days ago. An excuse. I bit my wrist as hard as I could to make *this* dream go away. To make them all go away. Forever." She closed her eyes. "I don't trust the people here. They never understand. No one does. Except your father. Where is he again?"

"With the doctor, remember? He'll be back soon." Nathalie stole a look over her shoulder. *Should I?*

I have to, and I have to now. I should have long ago.

"Tante. I need to tell you something. Quickly," she said in a soft voice. "Somehow I—I was born with Dr. Henard's magic. I have visions, too."

Aunt Brigitte's eyes shot open. She stared at Nathalie as if terrified of her. She screamed, a powerful bellow from a petite, bony body, and tugged hard on her braid. "No, no. NO! Not you. NOT YOU!"

Moments later the doctor and nurse hurried into the room with Maman and Papa close behind. The nurse asked Aunt Brigitte what was wrong.

"Protect her. Protect that beautiful child. Take care of her, Augustin."

"I will," said Papa. He tucked the blanket neatly around his sister. "Please don't worry yourself, Brigitte."

"She's free from danger," Maman added, brushing back Aunt Brigitte's unruly hair. She gave Nathalie a questioning glance.

"No. She's not." Tante moved her head side to side like a child refusing food. "The woman wants her dead."

Nathalie started to shake, even though the room was warm. "I'm—I'm well, Tante. Truly," she said, despite being nothing of the sort. She whispered to her parents that she'd explain later.

The nurse massaged some chamomile oil on Aunt Brigitte's temples and neck, then left the room. Maman sat on the bed and held Tante's hands as Aunt Brigitte closed her eyes with a moan.

Nathalie folded her arms to stop the shaking. How long were they going to stay? She needed to go tell Christophe. He might even want to come talk to Aunt Brigitte himself.

Her shaking got even worse. She folded her arms tighter.

"I'm afraid I'm going to have to ask you to leave," said the doctor, with a nod to Papa. "Brigitte needs her rest."

Maman kissed Aunt Brigitte on the forehead and said goodbye; Nathalie and Papa followed suit.

As they walked out, the nurse came back in, carrying restraints and a syringe.

During her trek to the morgue an hour later with Papa, who was unusually quiet, Nathalie thought through all the visions. Again and again, quicker every time, like a chant to assuage her nerves.

Due to her copious notes, she had everything memorized, even the experiences wiped from her memory. Two things had never made sense to her, but Aunt Brigitte's dream helped her piece it together.

Twice the Dark Artist had spoken words that seemed out of context. One was "Yes, of course!" after Agnès pled "No." Yet the visions hadn't allowed Nathalie to hear anyone except the Dark Artist. Why add the "of course"? And just before he met his own demise, he said, "Enough already!"

To whom?

To Mme. la Tuerie. The final time, if not the time with Agnès, too.

"I'll wait here," said Papa wearily, stopping at a restaurant near the morgue. He'd insisted on coming. After Nathalie recounted Aunt Brigitte's dream, her parents said she wasn't to go anywhere, not even the morgue or the newspaper, alone. ("It's the drop of water that made the vase overflow," Papa had said, invoking a favorite saying.)

Nathalie didn't object. She was relieved. Part of her felt like a little girl again, following Papa along like she did in the Catacombs—although this time it was she who led with speedy, resolute steps. The rest of her knew this was the only option, the only way to stay out of danger short of locking herself in the apartment.

She hurried toward the side entrance of the morgue and saw Christophe outside having an animated conversation with two police officers. He gesticulated with excitement—something she'd never seen before—and nodded attentively as they spoke. He looked the way she felt.

The three men finished talking as she drew closer. When Christophe saw her, he trotted over to her with a grin.

"I have news!" he said.

"So do I!" Her heart threatened to pound straight out of her chest.

"You first."

Her breathing escalated so quickly she couldn't get the words out on the first try. Drawing a steady breath, she tried again. She stumbled over words, eyes looking everywhere but at Christophe, and barely kept tears from interrupting. Eventually she managed to convey Aunt Brigitte's attempted suicide and the early trek to the asylum. As she pointed out where Papa was sitting, her voice caught. How could this be her day so far, her life right now?

Nathalie smoothed out the waist of her dress several times before continuing. "Tante had a dream, a disturbing nightmare, about Zoe Klampert trying to kill me."

"You don't have to worry about that," said Christophe, shaking his head vigorously.

"Yes, I do!" She repeated the dream and the vivid comprehension she gleaned from it, waving him off when he tried to interrupt. "Christophe, she wasn't merely a partner who collected blood. She's a murderer in her own right. I'm sure the man she stabbed in the dream was the Dark Artist. It had to be. Who else?"

"Nathalie, the news I wanted to share—"

"The only thing that doesn't make sense is the handshake," she said, scratching her temple. "Why would I shake her hand? Unless it represented the day I fainted in the morgue and she extended her hand to help me up—"

"We think we have the man who killed the Dark Artist. And Zoe Klampert might be dead."

Blood. All of it. Every drop in Nathalie's body felt as though it drained away and onto the sidewalk and into the streets of Paris. "What—what of Tante's dream? I know she's in the asylum because of those very dreams, but she's right; I feel it in my soul. She didn't know anything about the Dark Artist or Zoe Klampert. She's closed off from the world."

"I don't know." Christophe sat down on a bench and beckoned her to join him. "The man who claims responsibility, Raymond Blanchard, turned himself in today. He admitted to the letter, the silk tie fragment, all of it. He didn't kill the Dark Artist over any sense of justice but rather unrequited love for Zoe Klampert."

"He *loved* her?"

"Apparently," said Christophe. He began talking with his hands. "Blanchard saw his cart and followed him to the Seine that night; by the time he caught up to him on foot, the body was dumped. Or so he claims. The confrontation was over Zoe; they struggled and . . . you know the rest."

"I do. And I don't. I don't know what to believe." Nathalie squeezed her eyes shut then opened them again. "What did he say about killing Madame la Tuerie?"

"Shot her and buried her in a shallow grave. He told us where we could find the body—in a cemetery. Police are on their way there now." Christophe held his finger up. "I almost forgot: He said Zoe Klampert wasn't her real name but that he didn't know more than that."

Nathalie pressed her back against the bench, defeated. She should have been happy, should have absorbed Christophe's initial enthusiasm. Why wasn't she?

Because in spite of everything Christophe said, she wanted to believe Aunt Brigitte's dream. And she wanted him to as well. "You don't think there's truth to my aunt's dream?"

Christophe gazed at her for a long while before responding. "Some of the details are astoundingly accurate, but we have a suspect right under our noses. The police know of your ability and trust it. I—I don't think they'd grant that same confidence to Aunt Brigitte. Even though she's an Insightful—"

"She's also not well," said Nathalie. She thought of Aunt Brigitte's written words, how coherence became drivel. "That's why she's there. We don't know what's madness and what isn't."

"Instead of being disappointed, I wish you were able to feel happy. Relieved. Delighted that it looks like this will all be over soon." Christophe bit his lip. "I don't think you've been genuinely relaxed or content since I've known you, and my wish for you is . . . peace."

Nathalie cracked a smile. Peace? She'd forgotten what it was like to have a life of relative tranquility and ordinary worry. "In the meantime I suppose it's time to be a reporter," she said, rising from the bench.

Christophe walked with her to the morgue entrance and, assuring her that this was nearly over, bid her *adieu*.

Afterward, Nathalie joined Papa at the restaurant and wrote her morgue report over lunch. From there they went to *Le Petit Journal*. Papa had been to the newsroom before but was nevertheless amazed by the noise and intensity and movement throughout.

"M. Patenaude?" she said, knocking on his half-open door. He was shuffling through a stack of newspapers and told her to come in.

Papa led the way. "I have a lead for you on a good restaurant, but it's in Morocco."

M. Patenaude was so surprised to see Papa that even through the thick glasses his eyes noticeably widened. "I could certainly use a long lunch," he said, leaning back in his chair with a laugh.

Nathalie put her article on M. Patenaude's desk and settled into a chair. She and Papa told M. Patenaude the events of the last day or so, and he sat with creased brows, pensive. He knew about the suspect—he'd be meeting with the police later to interview

Blanchard—but was much more intrigued by Aunt Brigitte's dream than Christophe had been.

Christophe's lack of faith in Tante still bothered her. She understood it, and in the same position, she'd probably think the same. That still didn't take away the disappointment of his skepticism.

"Brigitte hasn't had a predictive dream in quite some time, correct?"

"Not that we know of," said Papa. "Certainly not anything this specific."

"That alone makes me think it's valid. And this has nothing to do with my own gift. Madness has tainted her ability, yes, but—"

The door burst open and slammed into a wall. They turned to see a man holding a sketch pad, cheeks flushed.

"M. Patenaude, I'm sorry to interrupt. This is urgent."

The man, presumably a sketch artist, raised a brow at M. Patenaude. Papa thanked M. Patenaude, and he and Nathalie left the room. The door closed behind them, but Nathalie lingered.

Just long enough to hear.

"A murder," said the sketch artist. "Throat cut. Our man on the scene mentioned a bizarre detail—something about a small bottle of blood next to the body."

47

Nathalie implored M. Patenaude to let her go to the crime scene with the sketch artist, but he firmly said no. As did Papa.

"You can wait here, though," M. Patenaude said, opening his cigarette case. "Be one of the first to know what happened. We'll run an edition tonight."

She graciously accepted his offer, then paced around his office in and out of smoke clouds as he and Papa talked. Despite being in the same room, Nathalie heard very little of what they said. They tried bringing her into the discussion at times, to distract her from worry. And themselves. They spoke of everything *but* the murder and what it might mean and the Dark Artist and everything else important.

Questions flitted around her mind like skittish birds.

The man who turned himself in, Blanchard? Did he kill someone else and then go to the police?

No, Blanchard was wrapped up in jealousy, not swimming in bottles of blood. That didn't fit.

Only Mme. la Tuerie made sense.

Did Blanchard kill her? Lie about killing her? Kill her after *she* killed someone?

Or was she working with someone else? What if she had another Dark Artist, another partner?

The questions spun faster and faster.

I thought I was going to be the next target.

And then the query that came back again and again, like a pesky gnat.

Why?

After M. Patenaude had gone through several cigarettes (two at least, possibly three), a harried reporter came in and dropped a draft on his desk. "This is all we know right now. Still a lot of details to work out."

Finally.

The reporter rushed out with a wave of acknowledgment as M. Patenaude thanked him.

Nathalie watched her boss read. It took hours. Wasn't he in a hurry? She'd never seen anyone read so slowly, much less M. Patenaude, who—

"Victim was a man, lived alone. An invalid who couldn't get out of bed."

A man wrapped in a blanket.

Nathalie sat down on the edge of a chair. "The man in the dream wasn't the Dark Artist after all."

Papa murmured in agreement.

M. Patenaude continued. "A jar full of blood was next to the body, as we know. No note in it but one on the body: 'I killed him, too.' And . . . a piece of burgundy cloth."

"It's not a hoax and it's not some mystery man. Madame la Tuerie—I mean, Klampert," said Nathalie. "All of it."

M. Patenaude put the article to the side and folded his arms. "I agree. For many reasons, but most of all these two." He sighed. "First, a witness saw a tall, dark-haired woman exiting the back of the building last night, right around the time they think the murder occurred. Second, the victim was an Insightful."

Nathalie sat on her bed perusing the article and making notes. The ink was barely dry on the special edition, which featured a longer version of the article and included a colored sketch of the crime scene: The bloodied body of the victim, Hugo Pichon, was under a gray-and-white striped blanket.

Not that Nathalie needed another reason to trust Aunt Brigitte's dream.

The Prefect of Police wanted "to gather more evidence before naming the suspect, but we will release the identity soon." Zoe Klampert, presumably. And what of Blanchard?

"I'll get it," Maman called out. Someone must have knocked on the door; Nathalie hadn't even heard it. Stanley hopped off the bed to investigate.

"Nathalie?" Maman's voice again. "You have a visitor."

Not Simone, or she'd have said so. Louis, perhaps, or someone from the newspaper?

Nathalie stepped out of her room and blushed. Christophe, holding a small cloth bundle, greeted her. He offered the bundle as she came closer. "Something to supplement my apology."

She took the bundle and unwrapped it.

Pain au chocolat.

Nathalie smiled. "Very kind. Thank you. But . . . why?"

Maman excused herself, saying she was going to organize her fabrics in the bedroom. She was starting work again at the tailor shop soon and wanted to be well-prepared. Nathalie sat on the sofa and invited Christophe to join her.

"Blanchard was a fraud," said Christophe as he sat down. "His story unraveled under scrutiny, thanks in part to M. Patenaude. It turns out that Blanchard didn't kill Zoe Klampert, but he was indeed in love with her."

Nathalie cringed. "Does he know who she is? What she's *done*?"

"What she's done—no. He does know who she is." He lowered his voice. "The place he told us he buried her? It was her father's grave."

"What?" Nathalie scowled. "That's cruel."

"It is," Christophe began slowly, "but it proved useful in another way. Her father was Dr. Pascal Faucher—and her given name is Faucher, too. We don't know why she goes by Klampert; we can't find any marriage record for her—or anything at all in her adult life. It's as if she ceased to exist years and years ago."

Nathalie thought about the photograph in the apartment. "That's probably who was in the photograph I saw."

"The one that was gone when the police arrived? Possibly," said Christophe. "I didn't know this until today, but Dr. Faucher was a scientist who experimented with blood and magic, like Henard. He didn't have the same breakthrough, but he was on the same path."

Nathalie could barely get the words out. "Her father was another—another Henard?"

Christophe nodded as Stanley hopped on the sofa between them.

That fact changed everything and nothing. Unless they caught Mme. la Tuerie, all they had were unwoven threads strewn across the floor.

"Also," Christophe began, drawing out the word as he glanced away. "I should have given weight to Aunt Brigitte's dream—and more important, your belief in it. I wanted so badly for this to be over that when we had a plausible suspect, I couldn't see any other path. I apologize for any false hope and distress I caused."

Nathalie wanted to be upset with him, even just a little. Then she looked at that crooked eye tooth and those blue eyes, listened to that kind and reassuring voice, and let everything he said filter through her heart and mind. No, she couldn't be angry with him.

"I forgive you," she said. "We've otherwise made a—a good team."

A careful smile spread across his lips. "And I brought you *pain au chocolat*."

"And you brought me *pain au chocolat*."

Nathalie broke off a piece and offered it to him with a grin. They spoke for a while longer, and after he left, his woodsy orange-blossom scent remained. She wished she could bottle it and put it on the shelf beside all the other things worth remembering.

48

The following day, *Le Petit Journal* identified Zoe Klampert as the primary suspect in the murders of Damien Salvage and Hugo Pichon.

More details emerged about the victim: Pichon, age 40, had no next of kin and had lived with his mother until her death in 1884. Since then his only company were the caretakers who visited him once daily—one of whom discovered his body.

"The door was unlocked when I got there," said Pichon's nurse [name will be withheld for privacy]. "I reached for the key above the doorframe. Gone. And M. Pichon always called out to greet me as soon as I walked in, unless he was sleeping. Then I would go straight up to him and he'd take me by the hand and thank me for coming. He didn't call out and he wasn't snoring. I—I was afraid to look."

At this point in her recitation of events, the nurse became tearful and required several moments to recover. "I walked carefully into the bedroom and didn't know what I was seeing. His neck, chest, arms were covered in blood, almost like someone bathed him in it. When I got closer, I saw one deep cut here"—here she pointed to the base of her throat—"and I shouted and ran downstairs to the landlord and pounded on his door."

The nurse identified M. Pichon as an Insightful, according

to his own admission. He never revealed the nature of his ability to her, saying it "didn't matter anymore."

But it did, thought Nathalie as she read, or Mme. la Tuerie
wouldn't have killed him. She wanted—needed—his blood for
some reason. Did she choose him for his gift, his inability to put
up a struggle, or something else?

The article identified Zoe Klampert, also known as Zoe Faucher, as the sole suspect.

Faucher. As she read the article, something else occurred to
her. Those notebooks. The older one that had strange writing and
looked to be penned by two people. Dr. Faucher's work? Was she
building upon it? Trying to create another generation of Insightfuls?

Murder played into it, though. And Henard hadn't been a killer.

Classically featured and attractive, Zoe Klampert stared at hundreds of thousands of Parisians from the front page of *Le Petit
Journal,* courtesy of a sketch artist. Nathalie and Louis had given
a description, and no doubt the faux killer Blanchard and the witness who saw her leave Pichon's building had as well. The portrait was masterfully rendered.

Omit the headline and she could have been taken as a mother
or a theater actress or a beloved schoolteacher. That wasn't the
face of a killer.

And then four days passed.

No one had reported seeing her. Not one resident, not one
landlord, not one shopkeeper, not one train conductor. A few mistaken leads were explored and discarded; otherwise it was as if
Mme. la Tuerie vanished like night at sunrise.

People speculated that she fled Paris. Illustrated posters with
Zoe's name and face on them were nevertheless all over the city.

Nathalie looked over her shoulder every few steps and didn't
walk the streets unaccompanied. Just in case everyone was wrong

about the disappearance of the murderess. Just in case she still wanted Nathalie's blood.

As the search languished in futility, Paris's attention shifted to another murderer: Henri Pranzini. Before the Dark Artist and Zoe Klampert stole headlines, Pranzini slashed two women as well as the twelve-year-old girl who witnessed his brutal crime. He had been the killer everyone talked about in cafés and on steam trams and omnibuses. Now, with his execution slated for the last day of August, the ink was spilled for him once again.

Nathalie would be among those to spill it: M. Patenaude had asked her to write an account of the execution. He'd assigned several journalists to do the same, each with a different focus. Hers was to be a reflection piece through the eyes of someone witnessing their first execution.

And it was a strange thing. Initially Nathalie had been looking forward to this when the death sentence was announced in July. At the time she was merely intrigued and anticipated satisfaction in seeing a murderer beheaded. It was something to witness, to be part of, to take part in like the morgue and the wax museum.

Death meant something different these days, though. She'd been so immersed in its grim, heart-wrenching, and terrifying realities that the spectacle of it had become much less palatable. Would she go to watch Pranzini die if M. Patenaude hadn't assigned her to it? Her answer changed every time she posed the question to herself.

The day before the execution, Nathalie was dusting her shelves and moved the bottle of sand from Agnès to the side. Bottles and jars, jars and bottles. Who knew containers could hold not only things but also significance?

The Dark Artist never had justice handed to him, she thought. He never had to account for his crimes, never had to take responsibility for killing Agnès and five other girls. She remembered wishing for his capture and execution someday. A sentiment that seemed so very long ago, and yet it wasn't.

At least he was dead. Mme. la Tuerie was not. As she so cleverly reminded everyone in her letter with the silk.

That woman was somewhere, and her crimes would follow her. The truth would stalk her.

Nathalie slid the bottle of sand back to its normal place, leaving her hand there a moment.

Bottles and jars. Jars and bottles.

Her uncertainty about attending an execution for entertainment would never be extended to Zoe Klampert. Not now, not ever. Nathalie didn't care if she herself was fifty years old when Mme. la Tuerie got caught. She'd be there, witnessing the guillotine drop.

The day before the execution, late in the afternoon, a gaunt, uniformed man with a skinny moustache showed up at the apartment. "I'm a courier from the pneumatic post. Are you Mademoiselle Baudin?"

Nathalie nodded. She'd never gotten a pneu before; sending a capsule through the underground system of air pressure tubes was expensive. Only urgent, important messages were sent that way.

The courier handed her a *carte télégramme* and stood with his hands behind his back as she read.

> *I need your help—your ability. I have an idea that I hope will bring us closer to catching ZK. If you're inclined, meet me at the bank on Rue Gerbier after the execution. From there we'll go to the morgue.*
>
>

Respectfully,
C.

He needed her to have a vision? Why at that hour? She'd be going there anyway later in the day, as usual. Maybe there had been another murder, another Insightful, and Zoe Klampert was the suspect.

The courier handed her a pencil and a reply card.

Of course. I assure you it would be my honor to assist. Until tomorrow.

With warm regards, I remain,
N.

49

"I can't believe we have cards for the inner circle," said Simone. "Louis was disappointed you couldn't get one for him, but he'll be watching with his Guillotine Boys, as he calls them, in their usual spot. I told him I'd meet up with them afterward."

It was four o'clock in the morning—by custom executions took place before sunrise—and they were heading by foot to La Roquette Prison. It was near Père Lachaise, not far from the apartment. Papa escorted them, trailing a few steps behind.

Nathalie and Simone bubbled with conversation, both about the execution and about the meeting with Christophe afterward. They were in the midst of making plans for tomorrow night— Nathalie was going to sleep over at Simone's, and Louis would escort her there—when Papa interrupted them.

"I'm going up this way," Papa said, pointing to a side street. "*Ma bichette*, you're sure you want to go to the morgue? You can say no."

"I want to do it. I'm certain."

Papa kissed her on the cheek with a shrug, promising to meet her at the bank, just in case she changed her mind.

The crowd outside La Roquette Prison swelled with apprehension and grim excitement. Gaslights stood above them like watchmen. Most people were pushed to the side streets, but Nathalie and Simone showed credentials and were admitted to an area with a better view.

They merged with the mass of people seeking the best vantage point and finally settled on a spot. It wasn't as close as they'd hoped—how early had *those* people arrived?—but it was near enough that they could see the guillotine well. Little flames from kerosene lamps in the crowd danced throughout the square like ill-mannered, nervous guests.

They waited for an hour that seemed like two. Then the executioner appeared. Broad and tall, just as Nathalie expected an executioner to be. She wondered who he was. Why he chose this profession. If he liked it. If he slept well.

The executioner tugged a pulley and drew up the angled metal blade, then secured it. Ominous and horrible, the guillotine rested there, waiting for release.

The crowd went silent as the gate creaked open. Some people raised their hats, others blessed themselves. One man made the sign of the cross in the direction of the guillotine blade.

The gendarmes raised their swords, then Pranzini came into view. His hands were bound behind his back and his ankles fettered.

Simone nudged Nathalie. "Is he *smiling?*"

"That sounds like something the Dark Artist would have done. Or Madame la Tuerie." Nathalie squinted. "He *is!* How defiant."

A priest, walking backward with a crucifix extended, led Pranzini onto the scaffold. The murderer kissed the crucifix.

Nathalie crossed her arms. "I'm surprised that crucifix didn't burst into flame."

"It might yet," said Simone.

The executioner placed Pranzini into position.

"SHAME!" yelled someone from the crowd. Others chimed in, and a wave of whistles and hisses overtook the crowd.

The blade released and Pranzini's head tumbled into a trough.

Simone clutched Nathalie's arm.

Nathalie's mouth went agape. She clutched Simone's hand with her own, never taking her eyes off the scene. "I expected it to be fast, but . . ."

"Life. Then . . ." Simone took her hand off Nathalie and snapped her fingers. "Death."

A guard retrieved Pranzini's head and tossed it into a basket. Sawdust, if Nathalie remembered what she'd read correctly. One minute he was breathing, the next he was in a basket of sawdust beside the rest of his body.

"My goodness, we were close enough to hear it fall! Louis is going to be so jealous when I tell him." Simone hooked her elbow around Nathalie's. "What did you think of it all?"

Nathalie shifted her gaze from the scaffold to Simone. "I'm repulsed."

"By him or the guillotine?"

"Both," said Nathalie. The execution was appalling, yet somehow a relief. She felt it in the crowd. "Despite my reservations, seeing it *was* satisfying."

The crowd flowed like water afterward, people slowly moving in every direction. Nathalie and Simone filed into the herd and shuffled along for a few minutes when Nathalie's eyes started to wander. The cusp of dawn bathed everything in shadows and orange-gray hues. She watched a squat man who walked like he was moving furniture, a bent-over beggar woman in a brown cloak, then observed a haggard man having a heated argument with himself.

"There's Louis," said Simone, nudging Nathalie. "If you make an incredible discovery at the morgue, consider making a special trip to the club to share it with your good friend Simone. Otherwise, I'll see you tomorrow night. Good luck!"

Nathalie smiled and said good-bye, waved to Louis, and turned onto Rue Gerbier. She spotted Christophe a few dozen meters ahead, leaning against a gaslight as the stream of Parisians passed. Papa wasn't there yet.

The man arguing with himself wandered back in her direction and walked against the crowd. Someone pushed him out of the way, and Nathalie stepped back to let him pass. The beggar woman came up next to her, shaking her cup. Nathalie, taken aback by her stench, ignored her and kept going. The woman was persistent. Papa always said not to engage beggars, because he'd been robbed by them on two occasions. But sometimes a beggar would follow and follow until you gave them something.

Nathalie reached in her pocket for a few centimes. She tossed them in the cup and the woman clasped her hand in gratitude. Nathalie pulled her hand away and for the first time, looked the beggar in the eye. Her face was coated in soot and dirt but her eyes—

She'd seen those eyes before.

Eyes she saw peeping over a fan at Père Lachaise, and eyes that glared at her every day this week from the pages of *Le Petit Journal*.

And then you did the strangest thing. Aunt Brigitte, extending her hand to show Nathalie what happened in the dream.

Time became solid and ceased to be. Or turned into water and disappeared into the earth. It was no longer time in that moment.

Zoe Klampert narrowed her eyes with a sneer.

A challenge.

Nathalie grabbed her wrist. The woman writhed out of her grip with surprising force. *She's strong.*

Zoe shoved her off balance and raced away.

Nathalie gave chase to her; an elderly woman blocked her way. "Shame on you. What kind of person goes after a beggar?"

"That's Zoe Klampert!" She wriggled herself free and ran into the dim light. Everything was shadows and half-lit faces and tricks of the light. Then she saw Zoe pass under a gaslamp. Nathalie weaved in and out of the crowd, gaining on her.

Several people turned their heads in confusion as Nathalie sprinted by. Zoe crossed a street and Nathalie stepped off the curb, just meters away. "Help! Zoe Klampert the killer!"

A dozen or so young men cut off her path, laughing and yelling and smelling of alcohol. One of the men hooked his elbow around hers. "Pranzini is dead! Come celebrate with us!"

Nathalie unhooked herself and stumbled away as they laughed. She searched the street and saw the swish of a robe disappear into an alley. Nathalie dashed in after her.

Zoe halted, back turned. She hesitated for a moment then faced Nathalie again, thrusting a vial of colorless liquid between them. "Hydrochloric acid. It'll burn a hole through anything it touches. Including skin."

Nathalie took a step back.

"You want to scream now." She tilted the vial from side to side. "I do know what you're thinking. One touch of the hand, and I can read a mind. Thanks to that invalid whose misery I ended the other day and a refreshing injection of his blood."

Nathalie's voice died in her throat. *Think.*

"No, don't think. I'm in your head, remember?" Zoe pulled the cloak off her head. "I spent the last few days in Monsieur Gagnon's mind—he's quite fond of you, by the way—and what an advantage that has been. That and the fact that beggars are invisible to most people. Otherwise I never would have known about Christophe's plan."

"You're bluffing."

"I'm not," Zoe said, putting her hand over her heart. "The invalid hasn't been buried yet. Body is still in refrigeration. Christophe had it put on a slab to give you a private showing this morning. To see if you'd have one of your visions. I don't know what exactly you see, but I couldn't have you learning anything about me."

Nathalie's brow furrowed. *I hate you.*

"Well, I don't much care for you, either. Useful gift, isn't it? I think I might have managed to replicate it in the lab, too." She pointed to Nathalie's head. "And I plan to stay *there* a few days before killing you. I need context for the blood experiments I need to run on the rare species *Natural Insightful.*"

"Nathalie?" Simone's voice behind her. Nathalie turned to see

Simone and Louis gathered at the entrance to the alley, little more than silhouettes in the emerging light.

"One step toward her," Zoe hissed, "and I shatter this at her feet."

Nathalie cleared her throat. "Do—do as she says. It's acid."

Louis ran away.

Coward.

"He *is* a coward," said Zoe. "Most men are, when you look closely."

Nathalie faced Zoe again. "You could have killed me in Notre-Dame."

"And collect your blood in the middle of a church?" She shook her head. "No, that was just a warning. I was upset about the apartment—fleeing was inconvenient. But you told me you were going. Well, you told your friend over there."

Nathalie was still formulating the question in her mind when Zoe answered it.

"Extraordinary hearing," she said, tugging at an earlobe. "A gift from Damien. Or as you call him, the Dark Artist."

"Here." Nathalie pulled back her sleeve and exposed her wrist. "Take my blood now. You—you don't have to kill me."

Zoe held up the vial. "I'd need to fill about thirty of these to do what I want to do."

"Stop." Another voice from behind.

Fear sailed across Zoe's face. A ship in a storm.

Nathalie turned and saw a policeman with his pistol raised. Christophe and Louis stood behind him.

That's why Louis ran. To get help.

"Not a coward after all, *Madame la Tuerie*," said Simone.

Zoe dashed down the alley and out the other side, smashing the glass tube somewhere along the way. They barreled after her, leaping over trash and a pile of clothes, closing the gap quickly. Zoe hooked a right into the crowd. Nathalie sprang forward and grabbed a piece of her robe to slow her down. The police-man reached them and took Zoe by the arm.

A man with a kerosene lamp stopped by and shone his light on them. "*Mon Dieu!* Is that Zoe Klampert?"

"What's that?" said another man. "Zoe Klampert?"

"Stay back," said Christophe, putting his hand up. "Albert, use the whipcords."

Christophe pinned her wrists behind her back as Albert took out the handcuffs. The name Zoe Klampert rippled through the crowd. She flailed and kicked as Albert tried to secure her. The crowd pressed in, surrounding them.

"*Excusez-nous,*" said Christophe, raising his voice.

Albert spoke even louder. "Give us room."

But the crowd drew closer.

Nathalie burned with panic, worried that the people would get in the way, that somehow Zoe would escape and outrun all of them in the darkness and go on tormenting her and Paris and—

"Murderer!" someone yelled.

A young man charged Zoe, flanked by two women, and knocked her off balance. More people joined the fray and yanked Zoe away from Christophe and the policeman.

Zoe thrashed like a fish. The gaslight nearby threw just enough light for Nathalie to see her expression.

Pure terror.

Good.

She stepped closer to get an even better look. Their eyes locked briefly as Zoe screamed for help. A plea? *How dare she?*

Nathalie lunged to join the attack and was jerked back by both arms.

"No," said Simone, pulling Nathalie close.

Louis adjusted his grip. "You don't want any part of that."

Someone from the mob lost his balance. He fell at their feet, bounced up, and reentered the chaos. Christophe took an elbow to the chin trying to peel someone away. Nathalie winced.

Zoe was invisible; so many people surrounded her Nathalie could only hear her cries.

"My work will change the world! Don't kill—" The crowd swarmed over her like hungry ants. The revelers from the other block passed by, saw what was going on, and joined in.

Zoe was cowering on the ground when the frenzy of violence and anger burst. Nathalie heard garbled, futile repetition of "My work!" before the murderess was silenced.

The crowd devoured her. They stepped on her. Slapped. Spit. Kicked. Pinned. Punched. Cursed.

By the time more policemen came over and broke it up, Zoe Klampert was beaten, bloodied, and limp.

And dead.

50

Nathalie gawked at the corpse.

She'd stared at and studied dead bodies all summer. She'd had visions and nightmares about them.

Yet for a second, she wasn't sure if the puddle of flesh and limbs and blood that used to be Zoe Klampert was a corpse at all. When is a body no longer a corpse?

Christophe placed his hand on her back and asked how she was doing. Dazed, she answered with a shrug. How was she doing? She didn't know. She wouldn't know until enough time passed for people to stop asking her. "I'm glad she's dead. How—how did you find us?"

"Louis's red hair, actually." He touched a cut on his chin. "I saw some activity in the crowd and moved toward it. Then I saw Louis get Albert and followed. Louis told me you were with her in an alley."

He shrugged in defeat, as if this were somehow his fault.

"I was so close I could *see* you when she came up to me." Nathalie felt like she was describing a strange dream. Had this really just happened? "At first I didn't know what was going on, then I had this horrific moment of clarity. All—all I could think of was chasing her."

"Clarity?"

She guided him off to the side, where there were fewer people, and explained everything. Zoe had been right, she learned, about Hugo Pichon's body in the morgue. Christophe admitted, with no small measure of embarrassment, that he didn't recall a specific encounter with a beggar because they were everywhere.

As Nathalie spoke, he soothed her with reassuring words, reminding her how brave she was, had always been. When she finished talking, he gave her shoulders an understanding squeeze. "It's over, Nathalie. Finally."

It was and it wasn't. Would any of this truly be over, in her mind? She turned to the corpse. "I'm looking at her body and I still can't believe it."

Simone and Louis came up beside them. "I can," said Simone. "Show them your foot, Louis."

He winced, showing them the bottom of his shoe. A hole went right through it, exposing tender, pink flesh. "Stepped in the acid."

"Maybe Papa can heal you," Nathalie said. Papa. He must be worried she hadn't met up with him yet. How much time had passed, anyway? "I should get back to him now."

Christophe bid her farewell and joined the other policemen; Louis and Simone said they'd walk with her back to Papa.

Nathalie paused as they walked by Zoe's body. Her left arm, broken and askew, was near Nathalie's ankle; for a brief moment she envisioned Zoe grabbing it and pulling Nathalie to the ground.

Zoe's brown robe was torn, exposing punctures like bee stings inside her elbow. Injection sites.

She had taken the blood of the Dark Artist and Hugo Pichon. Who else? More Insightfuls?

Agnès. Girl #5. Had her blood ever coursed through those veins? That of the other victims?

No more injections, no more experiments, no more death. Nathalie reached for one of the lesions and covered the hole with her fingers.

Instantly she was transported to another place. She was beating someone, pounding hard. People were all around her. She got a glimpse of the body she was thrashing.

Zoe Klampert.

Here. Moments ago.

Nathalie returned to the present and scrambled onto her feet. Simone looked at her, perplexed.

"I touched her and had a vision of what just happened. From the perspective of someone who helped kill her."

It was neither the morgue.

Nor the glass.

Her magic was connected to the murders and bodies themselves.

51

The next day, *Le Petit Journal* published a letter from Zoe Klampert to Paris.

I write this knowing I may get caught someday, and until then I shall keep this on my person. I will add to this page the names of the Insightfuls whose lives I take.

Damien Salvage—exceptional hearing ability; consequence of overuse is temporary ringing in the ears. (Have experienced)

Hugo Pichon—ability to read the mind of the last person whose hand he touched; consequence of overuse (i.e., not "pausing" at all) is temporary inability to comprehend the written word. (Experienced moderately, quickly rectified)

[new page]

Damien was faith and art and imagination. I am reason and science and fact.

What started out as a flirtation in an opium den became a splendid partnership.

I am a woman of great means because of my father, a brilliant scholar and researcher at the University of France. My father, deaf and mute but a genius through his quill. My father, my teacher. My father, swindled out of his scientific findings by the fraud Henard, who ignored my father's warning that the work on magic through blood was incomplete, untested. My father, who bid farewell to this earth with wolfsbane and a glass of Bordeaux.

I didn't kill Henard. But I did pay someone—a stranger, a mercenary—to kill him. Or assassinate him. How important must a man be to have an assassin rather than a killer? I paid the man to poison him and slice him with the glass used in his transfusions. To ruin his work. The dolt I hired was supposed to take a sample but thought he heard someone and fled.

Oh, how ironic! Damien never got caught because he always knew when someone was coming. Twice he heard someone approach just prior to abducting a girl and abandoned the effort.

Few charmed like Damien. After following them from a considerable distance for a day or two, he could be whatever he needed to be to gain their trust—to get someone to walk through a door or enter a room or accept a lift in the carriage. From there he did what he had to do to carry out the deception, sometimes with my help, sometimes not. Ask for directions. Feign illness. Beg for assistance. Show his workshop to a curious girl. Night and fog were our dearest accomplices.

I should have hated Damien for being an Insightful, but I didn't. I loved him. Profound and morose, angry and passionate—he was enchantingly damaged. He became more damaged as his magic started to slip away. A horrendous ringing in his ears, something he described as a tempest in his head, was the disadvantage of his power. As time passed it became more frequent, more prevalent, more pronounced.

He grew increasingly bitter. His magic dwindled and left behind a void nothing could fill. Food. Drink. Me. Opium. Woodworking. Nothing.

I wasn't there when he killed the first one. We'd gotten

into a row and I didn't call on him for nearly a week. When at last I did, he told me what he'd done to the girl the day prior. "I had a moment of clarity at the opium den," he'd said. "And I've found something to make me feel more supremely human than my hearing ever could."

I never assumed he meant murder. *Who with an iota of reason, even in a cloud of opium, would?* (Astute investigators might recognize that quote from when I gave it to a reporter on the condition of anonymity following Damien's death.)

His eyes were full of something—mischief, satisfaction, voracity. He was delirious with glee, proud to see her on display at the morgue.

I was angry with him. Not for killing the girl—Paris is full of meaningless lives—but for not taking her blood. He deprived me of a sample by shipping her body off so soon.

I have been studying my father's work for years, and now I dwell in a well-hidden lab he established long ago at [address redacted]. I aim to perfect the magic so that no one suffers like Damien ever again. Regular injections, I think, rather than a single transfusion.

I need samples to conduct my studies. Damien provided the girls, I did the research on myself using the victims' blood. We wedded his compulsion to kill with my desire to experience magic. We chose the girls we chose because of some quality they possessed, something I wanted for myself.

I was stronger one day, smarter the next. Prettier. Swifter. The nuance was gone but I was getting something, something from each of these girls, if only for a day or two. I continued to make discoveries and refinements; once confident, I tried Damien's blood. It was so powerful the ringing in my ears had me bedridden for days. The setback reinvigorated my fervor, however, and I eventually discerned how to alter it for my own self. Near perfection.

That one girl, the strange one Damien called a "natural,"

would have been the crown jewel. Instead Damien killed her friend, in a moment of recklessness, out of frustration that he couldn't get the natural. She did endow me with a lovely singing voice, however, for a few days.

Our interests began to diverge. I was annoyed with his stupid, risky letters to the newspapers. He wanted pretty girls and I wanted Insightfuls; he wanted to choose them based on their appeal, and I reached a point where I didn't care if the victim was a young woman or an old man—I wanted to pursue Insightfuls.

We did not agree. And so I took control.

I gave the anonymous tip about the alleged struggle between two men.

I sent the Ovid quote because living in plain sight was a thrill. I sent the fragments from Damien's cravat to make myself credible.

I am not done experimenting; with any luck, the list on the other page will be quite lengthy by the time you read it.

I have penned this because when all is said and done, I'm a vain woman. I want everyone to know who I am and what I achieved.

52

Nathalie woke up in the darkness on the floor. Something moved beside her.

A body.

She jumped up, her feet tangled in bedsheets, and yelled.

The body sprang to life.

Nathalie recognized the familiar outline and tried to calm down.

"What's the matter?" asked Simone. She stood up, leaned against something, and turned on a kerosene lamp.

They were in Simone's apartment.

"Why . . . why am I here?" asked Nathalie.

Simone picked up the lamp and carried it over to her. She raised the lamp toward Nathalie's face, casting an eerie glow on her own. "You're sweating. Nathalie, what's wrong? Did you have a nightmare?"

"No, I—I didn't. Why am I in your apartment?"

Simone swallowed. "You—you slept over."

"Oh," said Nathalie. She must have been in a deep slumber. Maybe she did have an upsetting dream, something that pushed her from sleep to confusion. Something wasn't quite right. She felt awake yet not awake.

And then it struck her why she must be here, because really, she didn't recall making plans. But here she was, in Simone's apartment. "What time is it? We didn't oversleep, did we?"

"For what?"

For what? They were supposed to get up in the middle of the night for the Pranzini execution.

Weren't they?

Nathalie paused to think.

No. It didn't make sense.

She noticed something on the dresser. "Could I have the lamp?"

Simone handed it to her. She hovered it over a newspaper dated August 31.

Klampert Killed by Mob After Pranzini Execution

Klampert? Pranzini?

It couldn't be.

"She's dead?" Nathalie cleared her throat. "What, uh, what day is it?"

"The very early morning hours of Friday, September second."

The realization exploded, a Pompeii that leveled her from the inside out.

"I—I don't remember," she said, sitting on the floor. She bunched up her knees and hugged them.

Simone knelt down beside her and stroked her back. "What . . . is the last thing you remember?"

Nathalie squeezed her memory. Strangled it. Only one thing came forward. "Waking up—in the middle of the night, like this, with Stanley at my feet. From a nightmare about what happened at Notre-Dame. I kept running and running and never got out of the cathedral."

"A dream from earlier tonight?"

"No," Nathalie said, hugging her knees even tighter. The next word trickled out like a drop of water. Or blood. "Tuesday."

She had no memory of the last three days.

Why?

ACKNOWLEDGMENTS

Ask a debut writer to write her acknowledgments, and the first thought that goes through her mind is, "I hope I don't forget anyone." The second thought is, "I should probably have chocolate and then reflect on the acknowledgments some more." And so on.

I would like to thank my wonderful agent, Ginger Clark of Curtis Brown Ltd., for offering (I still remember the moment that email came in), for believing in this project in all its iterations, and for being such a superb advocate and attentive, steady-minded professional. As I often say to her, I'm in good hands and grateful she has my back. She's also introduced me to the world of wombats and therefore regular doses of animal cuteness, which we all need. My thanks as well to Tess Callero for endorsing this manuscript wholeheartedly and being a cheerleader from the start.

This book wouldn't be what it is without my fantastic editor, Melissa Frain, whose vision complemented and enhanced my own. Her extraordinary brainstorming ability is topped only by her enthusiasm for bringing out the best in me and in this story. That she took a photo of herself where the Paris morgue once stood and included it in her first post-offer email to me was just frosting on the gâteau. (Almost a year and a half later, I visited the same spot and took the same photo.) I appreciate the thoughtful commentary, kind approach, and ongoing affection for Nathalie and the reimagined Paris in which she dwells. My gratitude as well to Zohra Ashpari, who is a pleasure to work with on all those behind-the-scenes elements of book production.

I would also like to thank the Curtis Brown team working on my behalf, foreign rights agents Jonathan Lyons and Sarah Perillo and film rights agents Holly Frederick and Madeline Tavis.

Tor Teen has taken a Word doc and a dream and made it into a book. Thank you to publisher Kathleen Doherty; production editor Melanie Sanders; copy editor Amanda Hong; and everyone else on the production, marketing, and sales teams at Tor Teen and Macmillan.

Other people make me look good in other ways: Seth Lerner, for designing such a compelling cover, and the incredible duo of Scott Erb and Donna Dufault of Erb Photography for my author photo.

This novel is my third written, first sold. My writing roots therefore run deep, so a shout-out to the Absolute Write Water Cooler, the hub for writers before Twitter. In addition to the Purgatory thread regulars (you know who you are), I'd like to thank a few people I "met" there. Bruce Pollock, for taking a newbie writer under your wing back in the day and showing her what critique partners were all about. Donna Cummings, who supported the idea for this novel when it was little more than that, back in our Starbucks days. Libby Kontranowski, who was a best friend at first (virtual) sight. I appreciate your valuable feedback (especially on the romance side of things), your willingness to take the seat next to me on the writing coaster, and the fact that you also liked *Golden Girls* when we were ten. Rachel Mork, to whom Libby introduced me on AW; Rachel thought I was funny and wanted to connect. Flattery gets you everywhere with me, so Rachel, too, was a best friend at first sight. I'm grateful to Rachel for being in the query/submission/revision trenches with me, for keen input over more drafts and scenes than this wordsmith can count, and for supporting me in so many ways great and small.

I'd be remiss without a shout-out to my fellow Novel 19s, my fellow dreamcatchers. Here's to our debuts. And Twitter: I appreciate everyone who interacts with me and supports me from afar, particularly Scott D., Don B., David K., and Karen F. To my Facebook family and friends, thank you for your support and enthusiasm in celebrating my authorial achievements.

Thank you to those who were my colleagues at The MacDuffie School when the offer came in (and to Jonathan B., who survived being in my office when I got the news). Special thanks to Dina L., office neighbor, listener to my publishing play-by-plays, and friend.

And now for family and friends, those who've been the closest witnesses to this writing life. To Jessica T., who couldn't love this book more or be happier for me. You are a true friend and lucky charm. Thanks to Janice for the duration of this friendship (goes back to the '40s, right?) and to Kate for rooting me on so sincerely. Thank you to John, who told me to just keep going and was with me the first time I set foot in Paris. I'm grateful to you for all our adventures.

My brother Kenny is in a multiway tie for #1 fan. Thank you for the brainstorming, for being proud, and for being such a big part of this. Thank you to David for bragging about your favorite (and only) sister and for the many laughs, in general. Thank you to Ursula, Julia, and Matthew as well for taking genuine joy in this accomplishment.

I've been blessed with incredible parents. Thank you to Ma and Dad for being everything a daughter needs her parents to be and for making me feel so very lucky throughout my life. I'm the person I am because of you, and I'm thankful for your support, life lessons, and unwavering confidence in me.

I'm also fortunate to have an amazing, brilliant partner. Thank you to Steve, for loving me, supporting me, being my creative collaborator, and having explanatory conversations with the cats when they get stressed about my lack of availability during revision periods. You're an extension of my mind and heart, and I don't know where I would be, where this book would be, or where my soul would be without you.

Thank you all, for everything. Time for more chocolate.

* * *

For nonfiction works on the cultural history of Europe in the late nineteenth and early twentieth centuries, consider the following resources:

Budapest 1900: A Historical Portrait of a City and Its Culture by John Lukacs

Scenes of Parisian Modernity: Culture and Consumption in the Nineteenth Century by H. Hazel Hahn

Spectacular Realities: Early Mass Culture in Fin-de-Siècle Paris by Vanessa R. Schwartz

France, Fin de Siècle by Eugen Weber

Mesmerized: Powers of Mind in Victorian Britain by Alison Winter